A STAR THAT WOULD NOT DIM

A STAR THAT WOULD NOT DIM

The Estella Trilogy, Volume III

HUGH SOCKETT

Waterside Productions

Printed in the United States of America

First Printing, 2021

ISBN-13: 978-1-956503-43-2 print edition
ISBN-13: 978-1-956503-44-9 ebook edition

Waterside Productions
2055 Oxford Ave
Cardiff, CA 92007
www.waterside.com

For Ann

TABLE OF CONTENTS

ACKNOWLEDGMENTS

I continue to owe a major debt of gratitude to my friend John O'Connor who has been an invaluable critic, editor, proof-reader and companion as I have been writing these books.

I have also benefitted from the kind comments of friends and the contributors to the Amazon reviews of *Pip and Estella* and *Better Expectations* and I hope that *The Star That Would Not Dim* will prove as worthy as those appraisals.

My sincere thanks are also due to Josh Freel of Waterside for his support in publication, to Catherine Brumwell and Kate Goodwin of Marlborough College, Wiltshire, and to Simon Offen of Christ Church, Oxford who have all been so generous in publicizing these books to the alumni of both institutions.

The cover of this book is a photograph of *magnolia stellata,* the star-shaped flower of one of the species of the magnolia tree, chosen by my dear wife Ann without whom my writing would not be possible.

1874

I

After her visit to Pip's grave in May, Estella took the afternoon train from Charing Cross to the City of Rochester in Kent and from the station was driven in her carriage to Numquam House, her country residence in the village of All Hallows. This beautiful home lay a mile or so up a country lane from the village close to the Medway Estuary, the tidal expanse between the River Thames and the North Sea. The breezy cool weather of April was a feature of nature to which all who lived near that expanse of tidal water were long accustomed.

Her companion servant Nellie came in through the kitchen door early the following morning not expecting Estella to be at home, but on walking into the hall she immediately noticed Estella's outdoor clothes lying on the monk's bench, along with her hat and gloves, so she called out:

"Are you here?"

"Yes, I'm in bed. Come up."

Nellie bounded up the stairs. She was a lithe blonde woman with a figure that would make any woman proud, blue eyes and skin freshened by the sun and the winds of the marshes.

"I arrived late last evening, so I decided to lie in, but what are you doing here?"

"I just came to see all was well and I left the silver last week so that's the little job for today. Let me fetch you some breakfast, and I'll bring a cup of tea for meself."

"That would be a treat."

Nellie went downstairs and was quickly back carrying a mahogany bed-tray, replete with muffins, a boiled egg in a coddler, a silver teapot, two exquisite china teacups and the appropriate cutlery. Estella sat up in bed with the tray on her lap while Nellie arranged the pillows around her.

"How come you're here, love?" as she poured out the tea, a cup for each of them and then took a seat on a nearby chair.

"Charlotte was in Norfolk at her brother Henry's funeral and I went to my husband's grave yesterday, got all teary-eyed and sad so I caught the train up here. Now you are here I can be cheerful again. But first, how are Fletch and the children?"

"Blooming, I'd say. It's been a good year for us so far, plenty of blacksmithing business for Fletch so we feel richer than we's ever bin before."

"I am so pleased for you all, but I have some stories to tell you."

"I loves a good story," said Nellie sipping her tea, "especially about your friends. I never got the whole story about that Honora, was that her name?"

"You mean Honora Brandram, don't you? It is an extraordinary tale, so I will tell you in detail. It must be almost two years or so since she unburdened herself to Charlotte and me."

"That long ago, eh? I think I know bits of it but go on."

"When she was only nineteen she went with some friends from her church on a pilgrimage to Lourdes."

"Where's that?"

"It's a place of pilgrimage in France where a young woman had a vision of Jesus's mother.

"Anyway, she went for a walk one evening and was seized by twin boys who were the sons of the people who owned the pension, that's an inn, where the group was staying, and they raped and violated her. She didn't tell anyone about the rape though she had been viciously assaulted as they were leaving the next morning."

"What bastards, if you'll pardon my language."

"Her parents were strict Catholics so she was sent off to her grandmother as she was pregnant. The baby turned out to be twin boys, and her parents insisted that the boys be adopted."

"Twins, eh? How do women do that?"

"Of childbirth I have no experience whatsoever.

"Anyway, meantime her parents persuaded a bachelor friend of theirs, Frederick Brandram, to marry her just really to look after her. She's never seen her parents since. When we got to know her first, she was as silent as a church mouse. Charlotte and I had to work hard together to get her to tell us her story."

"So how did she cope?"

"She gave birth to her twins while staying with her grandmother in Llanfairfechan."

"Where's that when it's at home?"

"It's a small village on the coast in north Wales. A very sensible childless couple brought them up very well, but both of them died within six months of each other so the boys were placed in an orphanage at ten years old. When Honora told us this extraordinary story, we resolved to find those boys. Charlotte eventually hired a private investigator to track them down in North Wales."

"Those Frenchie twins really were bastards, weren't they? I'd have strung 'em up and put a red-hot poker to their you-know-whats."

"No, they had a far worse punishment than that. They were sent to Devil's Island, a horrendous prison in the tropical heat, but then that war with the Prussians started and they were sent to fight with the French Army: Both were killed."

"Serve 'em bleeding well right. I s'pose an army always wants rapists in its ranks. But you all was lucky, weren't you? To find those boys, I mean. I s'pose I could find my mum that way, though that's the last thing I want."

"You remember when I went to France?

"Yes."

"Honora and I went to the village to confront the twins; we heard that they were sent to prison because they had assaulted numerous young women, even young girls."

"Then they really was bastards, weren't they?"

"I think even I would call them that, but this was the most remarkable thing about recovering the twins.

"Honora would be able to tell the boys were hers, but how could she prove it to the orphanage? She might be just a lunatic woman wanting to steal children.

"The boys knew instantly that she was their mother, even though they were four weeks old when they were parted."

"How was that?"

"It was astounding to me. For almost as long as they lived, these two boys had looked at each other, especially at each other's eyes as one does with close relatives. Because they were identical twins, the four eyes were exactly the same.

"Now when they saw their mother, they both leapt into her arms because her eyes were identical with theirs! They knew she was their mother, instantly."

"Crikey, that is the most wonderful story I have ever heard.

"Cor blimey, I must look again at my kids' eyes. I never really thought about it. I just know they're both blue. I wonder… "

"That made me think too, Nellie, as I now think I recognized my mother all those years ago as much through her eyes as her scarred hands. But that apart, since my husband Pip died I think I have made myself far too busy with other people's affairs, as I did with the Brandrams.

"Perhaps I see it as a duty to help them," she said, smiling at Nellie, and taking a spoonful of egg and then shaking the spoon as she spoke, "but I must now think properly about my life since Pip in terms of new triumphs, things that I am pleased about and which make me feel that my life is worth living."

"Well, you can start with me. I'm a triumph. I tell you; no, listen, seriously you've changed my life completely. I mean; fink about it.

"Five years ago or so, Fletch and me and the kids came to the Cottage starving, not knowing where to turn. Then Mr. Gargery had that Trust save us. Then I worked for you and blimey, I was blown away by your kindness, helping me to read and write so the way I look at the world now is so changed from when Fletch came home from the Crimea and we was wed. I've been reading such a lot. Kids go to school, Fletch works hard. I do my chores and then sit and read often on the bench outside.

"Country life suits you, but it is your triumph, not mine. It's odd, isn't it, why can't others be helped to change and be as happy and contented as you are?

"But perhaps the main thing with you, dearest Nellie, is that with you I feel utterly safe. You may think that odd, for it is the kind of thing you'd say, not me."

"Oh no, I know exactly what you mean."

"I have told you all about my mother, haven't I?"

"Oh yes."

"Somehow I think my sense of safety is that I see you as a mother to me too. I am like a child in your arms."

"Oh, crikey, why have you never said that before? When you're unhappy or summat and I put my arms around you, I gets a feeling that you was my baby, no matter your age or mine."

"You see," said Estella energetically, "we're not just two women who love each other. Nor are we mistress and maid servant. Nor are we wife and husband. We are mother and child. You are my love-mother and I am your love-baby. I know now why I am led to this sense of us together.

"My mother disappeared from my life. I did not really know what it was like to have a mother. Then when I was approaching middle age I found her, only for her to be snatched from me. Then my husband died. Then you and I met. How wonderful that is for me."

"And isn't that a triumph too? Mother and child," said Nellie thoughtfully, as she lifted the tray from the bed and put it on a nearby table.

"You see, Estella," said Nellie gesticulating in her reminiscence, "I grew up being constantly bedded by someone or another. A whore's life. They came and they went, day in day out. Fletch cared for me later, and believe me, I love him dearly. But you showed me, what's the word, tenderness, how loving someone can be so gentle, with no pain, and always expecting it to get better.

"Funny really, when I started whoring, because a man paid me, I'd always ask him whether it was all right. After a while I thought, sod it, I don't care whether he liked it or not."

There was then silence. Nellie climbed up on to the bed, and lay down next to Estella, both of them gazing at the ceiling and then turning to each other, both very contented in their loving friendship.

"Tell me about your other triumphs, Estella."

"I am very pleased now to be the leader in the Trust and leader of a small group of women which we are calling the League of Free Women."

"Oh, can I join?"

"Of course, but we only meet in London so it would be difficult for you. Yet we will have meetings down here sometimes and you shall come. I'd love my friends to hear you speak your mind. You are so like Mary Macdonald in that respect, for she is completely outspoken, married to Hamish the lawyer. You may remember her from Christmas, the woman with baby James and the withered arm."

"Oh, I thought she was just lovely and coping with that little boy with her one arm, she was like a queen, wasn't she?"

"She'll be in company and she'll ask the most daring questions which makes people startled."

"Now that's a real woman. What about them Gargerys, then?"

"Oh dear me, I told him that you'd said they were 'silly buggers,' not a phrase I would normally use, to let their marriage decay just because they had affairs. What was it you said that made me laugh so much? I know — 'it's only sex, you know, not murder!'

"Well, it's true, ain't it?"

"Perhaps, but I told Pip that she could have taken a lover, which made him very anxious. Now, I don't know this, but there was a couple living in their street and I thought, h'mm, James Bollaerts would be the man as he was an artist, rather too fond of women, at any rate, given the way he looked at me. Then he and his wife upped sticks suddenly and left for their country house in Norfolk, leaving their home which was only four doors away from Pip and Susanna."

"Oh, right, he's the one, I'll bet you."

"However, the Gargerys reconciled, probably because Susanna told him she'd had this dalliance with James and he could hardly complain about that, given his own waywardness."

"Who was Mr. Gargery's lover, then? Not one of the crowd, surely?"

"Oh no, that was a lady called Harriet Middleham.

"Pip and she had this four-year relationship when he was a preacher in the North, and before he was married. Charlotte and I met her briefly in Italy and then we had lunch in London, and I talked with Pip who wanted to tell me all about her. Then I asked Susanna whether she'd object to Harriet joining the group I told you about which was probably not a triumph."

"Now that was a mistake. You should have minded your own business."

"I know, I know, but I like Harriet very much, but I just don't see why we can't be friends with Pip and Susanna, and with Harriet."

"If I were Susanna, I'd have told you to go to hell, or somewhere like it. You know, I can see people admiring you so much, they come along and share their woes with you. So that was not a triumph, was it?"

"Not really from my viewpoint, but they are back together again."

Again, a silence of contentment, as they gazed at the ceiling and then looked at each other smiling.

"Since I met you, Nellie, I have been trying from time to time to remember my childhood which I used to want to forget. I did talk with my mother about it, but that was all about my life with her as she didn't want to know about my guardian.

"But what I didn't know has started to come back to me. Of course, I remember the obvious things, the rotting furniture and my guardian in the wedding dress she wore for years, but what was going on inside me? She introduced me to my Pip who was then just a youngster living with a blacksmith, very country ways. I liked him but he was a bit younger, though I did not show it.

"I cannot remember my breasts growing. I cannot remember anything about my body becoming a woman. I don't recall bleeding for the first time but, apart from the day-to-day life with an occasional tutor, meeting my guardian's relatives, I don't know how I felt about my inner being. I drifted along. Is that not very strange? Of course, I was with my mother when I had the change of life, so she talked me through all that."

"I dunno. Maybe you was just so hurt at leaving your mother when you was young that you just sort of forgot everyfink and wandered around in a daze."

"Maybe. Maybe. I am very glad Pip and I married. I'm more than glad we found the energy to help those men and women who have to sell their bodies. I must find ways to move men and women out of the terrible conditions in the city to do the kind of thing Fletch has done, learn a trade, work on building houses, anything to have them employed."

"You's a real darlin', you know, doing that. Blimey, wouldn't the world be different if lots of folks like you did that?"

"But I'm getting old and I often wonder how long I will live. Let me see, I am now seventy-ish. I will try to live another ten, people do you know, but I don't suppose you've known anyone that old, have you?"

"No, if men and women I knew lived to fifty, they was really old. But you don't have a disease like your husband. You must just look after yourself, and I'm sure you should have lots of fings you'll want to do."

"Let me see. I want to spend some months in Paris with Albert and Elizabeth. I want to see the projects the Trust has started grow; that means plenty of discussions, you know, more homes and medical help for those men and women. I'd like to travel around the British Isles too as I have only been to Glasgow for Pip's surgery, and that's it."

"I'd love to do that with Fletch and my babes but they need care. There's talk in the Bargemen of getting a group to go on that paddle-steamer *Princess Alice* all the way up to London Bridge and back. We could go from Sheerness or Gravesend. Fletch thinks Gravesend is better because we'd have to get a boat to Sheerness, though it's nearer. Fletch and Horatio are very excited, me and Victoria not so much. I don't fancy a crowded boat myself."

"Oh, I think you should go, you'd see plenty of sights along the river."

"We'll see. Maybe come to nothing."

"I wouldn't choose it, I must say. I'd prefer to go to Paris with Charlotte, I suppose."

"Why not invite that Harriet to go with you?"

"Well, I like her and I'm sure she'd be a good traveling companion, but I think three would be a crowd. She will come to this League of Free Women I've started and that must become more political as we have to make a nuisance of ourselves in this world controlled by men. There are plenty of avenues there, I am sure.

"Unlike most people these days, I really don't have any regard for religion. You know, when I visit Pip's grave and imagine his body lying there rotting, no one can convince me that he is going to rise again, or that his soul is dancing around in some place called Heaven, or for that matter in Hell. I think I can do good works without those beliefs, yet, getting people involved in such causes is likely to attract religious folks, so I'd have to put up with all that."

"Yeah, Heaven seems a bit far off for me. We went to church that Christmas and Charlotte was really kind and helped us. But when we got home after being with you, Fletch and I sort of understood it, and we felt we would just have to go on living with us killing Whistler. I am now sure we did right by being prepared for him to attack me and by having knives to fight back if he did."

"From what I heard afterwards from the police; the man was a dangerous criminal who would probably have killed you. But religion can help sometimes about what one has done wrong. However, it is all the rest of it that I don't adhere to. I am going to join the National Secular Society since I have read some of their pamphlets."

"A national *sexual* society? Sounds fun, but why would you join that?

Estella started to laugh.

"What? What have I said?" Nellie asked in mock umbrage.

Nellie then started to giggle at Estella weeping with laughter, then her giggles turned into uncontrollable laughter too as she saw how much Estella was laughing; so much they were rolling over on the bed, convulsed.

"No, my dear," she said when they recovered, "secular, not sexual. It is a society founded by Charles Bradlaugh who is a real radical. Secular means non-religious, not believing there is a god. Secular people are indifferent to religion."

"Oh, that is a relief. Ah well, here am I, wasting time talking with you, when I should have been cleaning the silver, but I must be going soon as Fletch and I have to get some groceries and things from Rochester."

After a kiss and a hug, Nellie left. Estella lay back in the bed looking at the sun coming in through the windows. She got up, put on a gown and went downstairs and opened the French windows. It was a little too cold to walk around outside so she shut the windows and sat in her chair overlooking the garden.

Talking with Nellie her love-mother was like getting a blast of fresh air, asking questions and responding, it had enabled her to think more deeply about her life. In terms of social conventions, she thought, there was something immensely strange about their relationship, the mistress and the servant formerly as lovers, now as very close friends in this imaginary mother-child relationship. Whether other women had such a relationship or friendship, indeed, how women treated their maids and servants was mildly puzzling.

Presumably if one had a personal maid, just as if a man had a valet, confidences would inevitably flow between the two. Could they be intimate? Might a gentleman be in love with his valet, which, when all was said and done, was not unlike her own situation? She supposed it must be possible.

At any rate, she could talk and laugh with Nellie with such closeness that it always brought clarity to her life. She was determined to be political, secular and active in pursuit of her philanthropic endeavors. She was going to explore through travel, but to learn more about situations poor people were doomed to inhabit. Her expectations of life could not be better.

Two good men had died: Henry Fitzroy, Charlotte's diplomat brother and Elizabeth's father, and John Wemmick, the Senior Clerk and mainstay of the Courtisone and Jaggers law practice. Estella and Charlotte were each mourning in their distinctive ways, for Estella had not met Henry and Charlotte was not acquainted with John Wemmick.

It was a soggy morning in the middle of May, Estella was back in town, and she was taking tea with her close friend at a small café in Westminster.

"I don't think I am frightened of death," said Charlotte as they discussed these losses.

"Nor am I, it is the preamble that is a worry, fighting a disease or being injured. Nothing worse than a slow death."

"Keats stated my wish perfectly in that gorgeous melancholic phrase, 'to cease upon the midnight with no pain.'"

"I should remember that. Where is it from?"

"We must read it together then, the Ode to a Nightingale."

"My health seems excellent but like every other human being after the age of forty, I think about my own death every day, if only for the briefest of moments."

"That is true of me but with Henry gone," said Charlotte, "I think more of the missed opportunities of being with him. The poor man never had a strong constitution and he had to grapple with life as a senior diplomat at the Embassy in Paris during the Franco-Prussian War.

"Yet after my husband Oliver's bizarre death, I will now get a hold on my life as an independent woman. Apart from my continuing concern about my niece Elizabeth, there is the delight of living here with you."

"Charlotte, is your concern because she is in Paris or because she is living with my step-son Albert? For my part, I am regularly contemplating dire possibilities in that relationship as I think sometimes Albert is not as mature as one might think."

"I don't think the relationship is casual," Charlotte replied, "but it is an object of horror in terms of social convention, condemned roundly by fashionable ladies, envious men, and prelates and pontiffs far and wide who would describe it as living in sin."

"Except in France," said Estella, and they both laughed.

"I must let our friends know of our whereabouts if and when we go to Paris, not least as one or two might wish to visit."

"It will be so interesting to see how those young people are faring. How long is it now?"

"Two years, I think, Estella. At any rate, well after his accident at the end of the war. So, let me see, it is now May 1874, so it must be about three years. I wish they'd marry, though."

"Don't worry my dear. When I am not worrying, I am full of admiration for them, being prepared to flaunt convention. They should be free to live as they wish."

They finished their tea and returned home. After dinner, they resumed their domestic conversation.

"Will you be cut off from Percy if we go to Paris, Charlotte?"

"I don't think so, Percy says he is an assiduous letter-writer and I will send him our address once Albert has found where we are to live. Our meeting is the only good thing that came out of Henry's funeral."

"Is there a future for you with him?"

"Perhaps, but Percy Archibald St. John Vere seems to be a confirmed bachelor. His name sounds as though he is a bachelor, don't you think? Yet we became very good friends at the funeral. He promised me that he would be in touch when he returned from Italy."

"Did you say he is an archaeologist there?"

"Yes, he is in charge of a section of the continuing excavations at Pompeii."

"Oh, I am so thrilled for you, my dear Charlotte, and I hope it comes to pass. Forgive me for enjoying the joke about his name, and it is really quite obvious that Percy Vere would be a man of real determination, resolve and purpose."

"I know, and Percy tries to avoid the jokes by insisting on being St. John Vere, though his name is still a cause for mirth."

"As I grow older, Charlotte, I find my early attachment to convention has gradually crumbled, so I believe that a young couple like Albert and Elizabeth should of course be free to exercise their passion and their intimacy as they wished. My discussions with Harriet have helped me here."

"Is her meeting with Susanna still a possibility?"

"I really don't know, I doubt it. Harriet would not mind, of course, but Susanna is still smoldering and I endeavor to prevent accidental meetings."

"Now Estella, I must retire and write to Elizabeth. She went back to Paris straightaway after the funeral, telling me she needed to be there."

"I would have enjoyed seeing her, but no matter. Yes, time to go, I think. Good night, my dear."

"Good night, Estella."

As she prepared for bed, Estella thought that her expectations of life could not be better: She was mindful of the widowhood of the Queen, who since her husband's death now fifteen years since, had gone into deep and lasting mourning. Estella thought that a laughable excess, almost as if she was following the now illegal Indian rite of *sati* where a widow threw herself on her husband's funeral pyre. As with other conventions, her beliefs in the monarchy as an institution had been mildly shaken by Sir Charles Dilke who advocated its abolition and from which he had still to recover politically.

II

Outside the *Courtisone and Jaggers* law office one Monday morning that June, half a dozen or so young men were clamoring to meet Clarence Fotheringaye-Smythe, but Adam Masterson, the new senior clerk, struggled to prevent them from entering the young lawyer's small office. They were poorly dressed, many with holes in their coats, and the smell they generated encouraged Adam to pull out a large pocket handkerchief until he realized that might be seen as insulting.

"What's the trouble, Adam?"

"This young man says he knows you and he has brought along these others. They seem a rough lot to me."

"Ah, is that Jack Masham?" Said Clarence surveying the group.

"That's me, sir and we need to talk with you," Jack replied amid the hubbub.

"Show them into the main office, Adam."

It was obvious to both Clarence and Adam that Jack's friends were all rent-boys. The Jaggers Trust had already funded a home for female prostitutes and their young children, and Semper House was to about to house young males of similar persuasion. This Soho house had originally been willed to Estella and her late husband by Mr. Jaggers, and the Trust had acquired it thereafter. It would open once renovations were completed.

"What's the problem, Jack?" said Clarence as the men stood in the main office, somewhat cowed by its grandeur relative to any other room they had ever been in, except for a court of law.

"We need your help, sir. In this last three weeks, four of our mates what are rent-boys have been attacked, one murdered."

"Good gracious me! Are the police at work?"

"Nah, first, there was Alfie Miller, like I mentioned him to you before, he was stabbed in his midriff and left to die in that park near Moorfields, though he's in Soho Hospital now and they says he will recover. Then there was young Joey Toombs, we called him Young 'cos he weren't more than fifteen, he were beaten and left naked.

"Harry Hudson, well, he was tied to a tree in that big park up west, Hyde Park, I think it's called, but Mick Evans died soon after his attack, so beaten up around his head and wiv' stab wounds all around his you know what. All he said before he croaked was 'cor' that bloke smelt funny' like he was saying he'd know if he smelt it again, know what I mean?"

"Yes, but what about the police? Are they doing anything?"

"Two of them talked with me," said Sid Murphy, "but they laughed and said they'd see what they could do, but I think they just don't care about us mollies," at which there were murmurs of assent from the group.

"The sooner we get killed off, the better, the bastards."

"But what do you expect me to do?" Asked Clarence, "I'm just a lawyer."

At that point, Adam intervened:

"Young men, Mr. Smythe and I take your concerns very seriously indeed. We will need to investigate further, so let me write down your names and we will contact you through Mr. Masham here, is that name correct?"

"Yes," said Jack.

"We's living in fear and dread it will be us next."

"One piece of advice," said Clarence as they readied to leave.

"Try to stick together at all times. I suspect that all those who have been killed were on their own in some quiet place when they were attacked."

"Yeah, but Harry was just attacked in broad daylight, wasn't he?"

"Yeah," said Big Lefty, "I think he must have had an arrangement if you know what I mean but then we heard he'd got the chop."

"We will see what we can do," said Clarence.

"Thank you," said Jack, "I hopes this don't go on."

As they left Hamish appeared from a short visit to court. Adam and Clarence began to discuss ways they might intervene in what seemed to be a set of savage attacks, almost certainly by one and possibly two men bent on some blood-lust vengeance or other.

"From my uncertain knowledge of practice in the Jaggers days," said Clarence, "I think Wemmick and he acted as police as well as lawyers."

"That is true," said Hamish, "we found Estella's mother killer through John Wemmick's investigations although we would still have handed them over to the police had they still been apprehended and, of course, alive."

"I do not see how we can continue that practice," said Adam.

"But Adam," said Clarence, "surely we must stand up for justice, not let responsibility fall on those who are not interested in it. You just heard the young men telling of police attitudes."

"I don't disagree," said Hamish, "but I wish nowadays that we could stick to our lawyering and avoid policing. Perhaps we should bring in Philip Hardyman from the Courtisone side of the practice. Clarence, might you go over to Cheapside and talk with Philip?"

The problem they had just articulated arose from the merger of the Courtisone and Jaggers practices. Broadly speaking, the Courtisone lawyers were very reluctant to continue the heritage of Mr. Jaggers and John Wemmick. This considerable reluctance was due to theirs being a pre-eminently civil practice but they also believed the Jaggers *modus operandi* to be an anachronism as the police had become much more effective at detection. Nevertheless for the Jaggers lawyers, a strategy for catching the persecutor of the mollies had to be developed, given police indifference.

❧ ❧ ❧

Harriet called on Estella at her London home in New Queen Street for lunch the following week with a young friend of hers, Katherine Bradley.

"How do you two know each other?" asked Estella when they were sitting with a glass of sherry before lunch.

"We don't know each other that well," said Katherine, "as Harriet is much older than me. But our parents were good friends, we both lived in Birmingham, indeed on the same street at one point, and the age difference did not seem to matter as we were both interested in poetry."

"I didn't know that about you, Harriet."

"Yes indeed, I have struggled with writing but I admire the romantics: Lord Byron, of course, Swinburne and Shelley. But Katherine has worked very hard and been encouraged by her tutor to publish. I struggle even with a sonnet."

"Perhaps I will have to live with being precocious," said Katherine with a certain humility, "but I think the publisher Tom Longman is actually going to produce a small book of my poems."

"And the title?"

"At this juncture, it is just *The Minnesinger and Other Poems* which seems unambitious. I may have to think of a *non de plume,* as I am shy of my work."

"Well, well, my congratulations indeed. Tell me, are you not studying at Cambridge? What does that mean? I thought only men could do that."

"No longer. Quite recently Millicent Fawcett enticed Henry Sidgwick a Cambridge don and philosopher to found Newnham College which I attend. The idea was, of course, to ensure women had a higher education, and she is a splendid campaigner for women's votes too."

"How fascinating, but are you chaperoned? What is social life like?"

"The College attracts some radical women like myself and," she said smiling, "I should tell you that I know of your unconventional ways from Harriet."

"Do you mean have I had a woman lover?" Estella asked, looking at Katherine carefully.

"That certainly but also your strange upbringing and the reconciliation with your mother which I can hardly imagine."

"How radical are your colleagues?" Asked Estella, ignoring Katherine's comment.

"All kinds of weird fantasies about us circulate in the University. The dons cannot marry and the students are invariably wealthy young men anxious to spend a fortune in wild oats before what they call settling down. They find little outlet for such expenditure in that dull town so they frequent music-halls and gin-palaces in London.

"They believe that such a collection of women cannot but indulge themselves in what they like to imagine are perverted practices. An alternative view of us is that we are just devoted to our studies and dull as a result which makes us what are called 'blue stockings,' an epithet conjured from the way some of my friends dress."

"Oh, goodness gracious, have we women not a long way to go!" said Harriet.

"Interesting, isn't it?" Katherine continued, "my older sister Emma became an invalid when her second daughter Amy was born, so I care for my darling niece Edith, her other child, now thirteen years old and of whom I am exceptionally fond since I have cared for her virtually since her birth. Motherhood has already passed me by and I do not welcome its tribulations."

"You can see, Estella, why Katherine and I find it so easy to bond together, though the age difference is great."

"But you are not lovers, are you? If so, I might feel a pang of jealousy," said Estella with a smile.

"Good gracious, no," said Harriet, "I am far too fond of men, well one in particular."

"Now then Harriet," replied Estella in a slightly mocking tone, "they do seem to have settled their differences."

"Good, but you never told me how."

"Oh, this is purely speculative, but Charlotte, Nellie and I believe Susanna took a lover, a man who lived up the street and came with us to Italy with his wife: Pure speculation of course, but at the height of what seemed to be a serious rupture in the Gargery's marriage, the man and his wife suddenly packed up and left for Norfolk permanently."

"You live with Charlotte, I understand, but who is Nellie?" asked Katherine.

"Ah, Nellie is my very best friend and companion. We were lovers. I am her child. She was a whore in Chatham when she was young, but she now lives close to my country home where her husband is a blacksmith and he has known of our relationship throughout."

"Goodness me, and I thought I was unconventional. What do you mean about being her child? Surely she is much younger than you."

"Yes, it is simply that her background and perspective makes her so much like my mother; we are not sisters or lovers, but mother and child. Of course, it is a fantasy, but when I lie on her lap, I feel as if she is my mother."

"How tender that is," said Harriet, "but do tell Katherine about your impressive work, Estella."

"I am the Chairman of the Board of the Jaggers Trust for the Relief and Education of the Poor, a very rich endowment, generating some five thousand pounds annually from its investments which are handled by the Board's lawyers. Our first projects have been with prostitutes, female and male.

"We have a building in Clerkenwell where women live who have abandoned that line of work. We can accommodate their children and we try to see the Jaggers Building as somewhere halfway between the street and some kind of occupation for which we will train them. The same is true of the males, or the mollies as they are called. The Trust has acquired my house in Soho as a building to accommodate males and it is at present in the course of rehabilitation.

"I am sure Harriet will have told you too that we have started our League of Free Women with various objects in mind with regard to women's independence, voting among them."

"What an active agenda," said Katherine, "you should go to Cambridge and meet Mrs. Fawcett who is a strong lady in terms of her suffragette ideas. I admire your work, but I cannot imagine myself engaging in it."

As the visitors left the house, Katherine walked ahead into the street.

Harriet put her arms around Estella's shoulders and kissed her on the cheek, whispering,

"There's no need to be jealous, my dear. Come for lunch next week," and she hurried along the street to catch up with Katherine.

John Wemmick's death had left a gaping hole in the practice, but his legacy of contacts was a treasure and it provided a way to discover the mollies' assassin. Clarence and Adam were on their way to meet Philip Hardyman at the Courtisone office to tell him of the situation that Jack and the other rent-boys had revealed. Notwithstanding the tradition of their practice, they were feeling they could do little as lawyers. Yet it was still a travesty of justice that a killer or killers should be on the loose preying on these young men when there was no serious police activity.

"I wonder what Wemmick would have done," Clarence pondered as they turned into Cheapside, "I suspect he would have used his informants."

"Wait one moment, that is interesting," said Adam suddenly, waving his walking-stick, "for before his death he sat me down in his office one day and gave me a list of names and addresses of his informants. What's more, he revealed the strengths and weaknesses of each man, their reliability, their cost and much else. A very important legacy, and, though I say this quietly, criminal cases are so much more interesting.

"Wemmick's list means that we could set five or six informers around the areas where these young men cluster. I think that the broad daylight incident suggests that there are killers and that they have grown over-confident."

"That is excellent," said Clarence, "what a heritage! We will need to use informers to identify the killer or killers but not to have them intervene. In any case they probably would not accept that kind of commission."

They arrived at the Courtisone office and Philip Hardyman welcomed them. After telling him the whole dreadful story, Adam said:

"According to Wemmick's list there is one man, Sidney, who is always eager to intervene if needed. Let us proceed in this way: Deploy our informers and gather as much information as we can about as many men as we can. The killer probably ingratiates himself with a group, becomes known and then finds it easy to seduce a young man prior to killing him."

"Having listened carefully to this," said Philip, "I don't think I am your man for this case. The old Jaggers practice has far greater experience of villains than we have had at Courtisone where our civil side was preferred over the criminal. Please tell Hamish my views."

"I will," said Clarence, "I was not absolutely sure why he wanted to bring you in."

"I have no idea," said Philip with a laugh, remembering how the Gavel Club had provided the opportunity for Hamish and him to agree to disagree on the character of a gay relationship.

Clarence and Adam then returned hurriedly to Little Britain to tell Hamish of Philip's anticipated refusal. As they walked back, they agreed that the newly formed merged practice of Courtisone and Jaggers would have to have lawyers who were focused on either criminal or civil, but rarely both.

Immediately they arrived, Robert, the young clerk said:

"There's this man come to see you Mr. Smythe, name of Masham; been here before as I recall."

"Send him in immediately."

Masham came into the room hurriedly, obviously distraught.

"There's been another one," he said, "Big Lefty was found this morning, bound hand and foot with a notice round his neck saying: 'Death to All Mollies.'"

"Where was he found?"

"By London Bridge near the water, shocking it was. Of course, we're now so frightened, we're staying away. Someone's really got it in for us. But there's some what can't afford to live without being rent-boys, but me, I'm giving it a rest."

"Thank you, Jack. I want you to come to this office every day," said Clarence, "as we are going to try to find out who is doing this."

"Thank you sir, thank you, thank you."

"We are going to hire some men to help us. Please start by coming here tomorrow at five o'clock in the afternoon so you can meet one or two of them and provide them with information."

"I will, I will sir, and thank you again."

As Masham left, Adam asked: "What have we here? Do we have a mad man, or a person with a hatred of sodomites? That could be the same person or is there some kind of financial motive here?"

"A financial motive, what could that be?" Asked Hamish. "I plead ignorance of such arrangements."

"Well, there is clearly money in prostitution. We know that some women, perhaps a much larger group than we think, are managed by men and they pay a fee like a tax to these men in return for some minimal kind of protection."

"But why would young men get killed for financial gain?"

"Put the case, as I am told your Mr. Jaggers used to say, that one man and perhaps a colleague are trying to establish a system for young rent-boys. To encourage them to join, they kill those who refuse. Assuming that is known among that community, my guess is that the men would line up to join."

"How interesting," said Clarence, "do we know of any one country where such practices exist?"

"I am told prostitution in some Italian cities, like Naples, is controlled by groups of what we might call owners who jealously guard their turf and will not tolerate any prostitute trying to work in their area. Often such interlopers are attacked and scarred for life, either on their faces or on their bodies."

"Thus," Hamish suggested, "an Italian or two might realize the opportunity in England and come here to establish such an operation."

"Or, of course, from any other country," Adam concluded.

"With this possibility," said Clarence, "I will question Jack as to whether there are ways in which such individuals might be identified. We need some research as to how such rings operate in European or other countries."

"Of course, I am sure this happens in America and perhaps these Italians are from America, not Naples," said Clarence.

"H'mm, Tom, my second cousin, is a senior policeman at Scotland Yard, though I haven't seen him, oh goodness me, since my wedding. I am sure he would help us and indeed, perhaps we could work together."

When Clarence met Masham next day, the young man was deeply distressed and anxious for his life.

"Tell me, Jack, you know I am sure that some women are controlled by one or more men, who tax the women in exchange for protecting them. Does anything like that happen with mollies?"

"Oh yes, there was a bloke lurking around Moorfields some time ago offering that, but he was really stupid. To get boys in your pay, you have to frighten people."

"Like murdering them."

"Bloody hell, Jesus Christ, of course."

"A man or a couple of men might have started and as a warning just kill the men who refused."

"That's right. I'll have to ask around, won't I?"

"If you would, but this is the good news, we are to open Semper House next week and we will be able to accommodate fifteen men. You can come to live there if you wish. You will be provided for in terms of bed and board and a small income and you will be able to train in a trade without being an apprentice."

"You've saved my life, Mr. Smythe. Of course I'll come. Just let me know when."

Adam Masterson worked for Courtisone for some years and had come to work as Senior Clerk to Hamish. He had settled into the work very well so that Hamish wanted to know more about him. Adam was of medium height, with black hair and a beard that was *de rigeur* for men of his age, an easy winning smile and the burr in his voice associated with Hampshire folk. He was conscientious to a fault, but he was living a disappointment for he had always wanted to become a lawyer for reasons obscure even to him.

"Where are you from, Adam?" said Hamish as they examined a brief together.

"From Hampshire. I joined the *Courtisone* practice at the age of twenty-one as a young man. My father was a sexton at Winchester Cathedral."

"How old are you if it is not impertinent question?"

"Not at all, I am thirty next year and I am married to Ann, whose family keep a small sheep farm at Weyhill near Andover.

"I had particular tuition as I lived with my grandparents in Basingstoke for three years so that I could attend Queen Mary's School. I had two clerical jobs with Winchester lawyers when I was sixteen, but one of the partners thought me promising and urged me to apply for clerkships in the City of London."

"Impressive."

"I'd like to do well as a senior clerk: I'd like to train as a lawyer but I cannot afford it as I have two young children.

"I admire the ethos of the Jaggers practice, Mr. Macdonald, as it is so committed to helping the poor. Take this mollie problem. When confronted with a group of rent-boys wanting help to find the man who was killing their peers, Courtisone would have sniffed and said, 'how interesting, but what can we do?'"

Hamish reflected on this conversation later. Adam clearly liked their stance to the world and it opened up possibilities for him. The three men were roughly the same age, but it might be difficult to develop a social life for Adam and his wife Ann with the lawyers. Rank is the difference, though it should not be and he told himself to mention it to Mary. Pity he cannot qualify as a lawyer as he is such an excellent fellow.

Toward the end of June, Adam was sitting in the small but cozy office that once was John Wemmick's den when the young clerk Robert, knocked at the door.

"Mr. Masterson, sir, there is a lady here to see Mr. Macdonald, but he is in court and Mr. Smythe has gone out. Could you meet her?"

"Certainly, let us use Mr. Macdonald's office."

"Can I help you, ma'am?" said Adam.

It was Angharad Unworthy. She was the daughter of a poor Welsh farmer who had married Ezekiel Unworthy, the bronzed Australian who years before had come to Little Britain trying to find the whereabouts of his father Abel Magwitch. Ezekiel was apparently the love child of the widow whose husband had employed Abel, the convict. Of this Adam knew nothing.

"Oh," she said in an accent mixing Welsh with the occasional Australian intonation, "I come all the way from Australia hoping to see Mr. Pip or Mr. Wemmick."

"Both these gentlemen are dead. Have you been here before then?"

"Oh yes, we was here more than nine years ago March, but to be honest I needed to see a lawyer here in London by myself."

"Are you on your own, then?"

"No, my children are with my Mam and Dad in South Wales, but I'm alone in London to see a lawyer."

"What can we do for you, ma'am, I am afraid both our lawyers are otherwise engaged?"

"Who are you then?"

"I succeeded Mr. Wemmick, whom you perhaps met."

"Oh, yes, he was the cook, I think. Anyway he brought us food."

"No, he was the senior clerk. But what can we do for you?"

"It's been a terrible tragedy, see," she said with tears in her eyes, "my husband Ezekiel was badly wounded a few years ago when there was a war between the Abbos, disgusting they are, and us white people. It was so bad with his head, mentally like."

"Do you mean he has a brain injury?"

"That's right. He's sort of dead in his brain, really. He can't talk or anything, just this empty expression on his face for months now."

"Where is he?"

"I left him in a hospital in Brisbane. I don't like the lawyers in that town and we're not short of money, so I thought I'd bring my kids back for a long holiday.

"Now my mam says I should come and talk to you lawyers. If my husband is not going to recover, I want to keep my family back here in Wales. We're quite well off, I mean, we own a thousand acres and have a wool and a sugar business. Anyway, I come to see these gentlemen to see what can be done. My eldest Gareth, well, he stayed behind as he's twenty years old now and my husband promised him three hundred acres as he's coming to be twenty-one. Now he's running both farms, see, but he can't do that for long."

"But I am still not sure why you're here," said Adam puzzled by this loquacious woman, pretty in her way, but plump probably from having many children, yet still attractive with her blond hair and blue eyes.

"Ezekiel has a will leaving everything to me but I can't run the business, can I, and my eldest is off on his own. So, I want to know whether I should sell it, rent the land or what."

"I see. I believe Queensland has been separated from New South Wales for several years, but English Law still applies unless and until Australia becomes its own country."

"My husband's lawyers, those I don't like as I told you, tell me I can't sell it on my own. They say I have to wait to see if he recovers. But I am fed up with Queensland. If I had control of Ezekiel's money, see, I could pay for him to be looked after here and keep the children in Wales."

Hamish walked into the office and peered at Angharad. She looked at him and smiled.

"I remember you," he said with a grin, "you were here with your husband quite soon after I started with Mr. Pip and Mr. Jaggers. What can we do for you?"

"I've explained it all to this gentleman here. But there was a lady that time we came here, who was very nice to me. Is she still alive?"

"You must mean Estella."

"That's right, that was her name."

"She is very much alive."

"I'd love to see her if I could."

"We can arrange that," said Hamish, anxious to talk with Adam about another matter. "Meantime, I assume you are staying in a hotel, so you may leave us now and I will hear from Mr. Masterson about your problems and we will talk again. Make sure to tell the clerk the name of your hotel on the way out and we will be in contact soon. It may be a week or so which will give you the opportunity to enjoy London and examine the new shops in the West End."

"What a lovely idea. If I tell a cabbie to take me to some new shops, will he know what I mean?"

"I'm sure he will."

The morning of Angharad's appearance, Estella was seated in a comfortable chair in Pip's library. He seemed a little agitated and she asked after Susanna.

"She is looking after Lachlan upstairs, as he came home from school today with a sore throat. But I asked you to come here as I wanted to tell you of the developments I have heard about from Hamish who called last night. Several mollies have been attacked and one, if not two, have been murdered in the last week."

"I beg your pardon: Murdered?" she asked with a gasp of surprise.

"I fear so, and in a rather brutal way."

"But why?"

"That's the question. There must be a motive. Now it could be someone who is mad and hates homosexuals, or it could be someone intent on terrorizing these young men for reasons that can only be guessed at, perhaps to establish some kind of rule, who knows?"

"That is a dreadful situation, but we are ready to have Semper House occupied very soon."

"Clarence and Hamish thought that Jack Masham, the young man who testified against Twaddell, must be offered a place for it is he who has told them of these occurrences. The police do not seem keen to pursue that matter with any speed, though one of Adam's cousins is a senior officer, so there may be some movement there."

"Remind me, who is Adam?"

"Adam Masterson, John Wemmick's successor."

"Ah yes, I think I met him at that Courtisone party," she said standing up.

"Still, I just wanted to let you know of these attacks as they make filling up Semper House quite urgent."

"I agree and I must give it some thought as to how we proceed. Now I must call on Honora while I am in Cheyne Row. Give Susanna my very best wishes and I hope Lachlan recovers. I'll call on her in a day or two. He is not a weak child, is he?"

"Oh, my goodness no, fit as a fiddle usually, which is why she is keen to care for him."

"You know, Pip, you two should have more children. You obviously enjoy those that you have and it will be a blessing for both of you and, if I may say so, for your marriage."

"Do not be concerned, Estella, we have anticipated your advice."

"Oh, goodness me, I am so pleased for you both."

With the usual goodbyes, Estella kissed him affectionately and walked up the street in the summer sunshine to Honora's house.

After she left, Pip went quickly up to Lachlan's bedroom. He had been ill before with the basic illnesses of the young child, measles, rubella and whooping cough which no child could avoid once he was at school. Each time he was laid low he recovered and promptly passed the diseases on to his younger brother.

They shared their delight that Lachlan was recovering. Susanna saw no reason for there to be any threat to her pregnancy from her son's indisposition. Indeed the infection surely could not reach her in part because she learnt from Old Pip's surgery that carbolic had been used to kill infection. She thus insisted on a carbolic being readily available so that her maids washed the floors with it, she washed her hands and face with it and made Pip do the same, though it was painful and smelt dreadfully. Both boys protested violently but got used to it. On some days, the house smelt dreadful.

III

On her way down the Row that June morning, Estella started to feel a deep anger at these unsolved murders, frustrated by the failure to have the villains apprehended. Honora's maid opened the door and showed her into the drawing-room.

"My boys are recovering from a fever which I hope does not affect their singing. I am sure they will be up and about and back to school soon, but how are you, Estella?"

"Very well indeed though I have just come from the Gargerys and Lachlan has a bad cold.

I came to see you to enquire whether you had any thoughts about our League. The other day I met Katherine, a young poet, a friend of Harriet's so we might take up study of our poets, Tennyson, the Brownings, or of course any poet.

"Katherine is completing her studies in one of the new colleges for woman at Cambridge; the founder is Millicent Fawcett who has been advocating for votes for women. We must take part in that as part of the work of the League. Of course, there is also the work of the Trust with which members like to become involved and I am also thinking about how we might engage with women of a lower class, shopkeepers, even house servants in some of our ventures."

"Of all the possible matters for discussion, Estella, I would be most interested in the vote.

"The cause seems to be so obvious. Half the population of any country are excluded from taking part in choosing their government. Of course that is immaterial in countries ruled by monarchs, and I like the idea of 'one man, one vote,' though it should of course be one 'person, one vote.'"

"I have given the matter some thought in discussion with Charlotte, and it seems to me that the challenge lies in getting men of power and influence on our side. Any kind of Chartist type movement with petitions and campaigns won't move the mountains we actually need to scale."

"Perhaps you are right, but the man in the street may be just as influential in denying women their rights as citizens. Of course, the law does not yet cover all a woman's property as it should and I suspect that law is an irrelevance for many households, anyway."

"This is certainly a topic which a League of Free Women cannot ignore."

"No, and it suggests that we need to be politically more active."

"I don't think you were there when we met with that man Dilke at Susanna's: Sir Charles Dilke, a handsome man but, my goodness, overflowing with self-importance which, I suppose, is a requirement for being a politician. I am now less taken with his views about the monarchy than I was."

"What does he believe?"

"He wants to abolish it. What disturbs me about that, Honora, is that once we start dismantling our traditional institutions, where it will end? I mean everyone in this nation has some kind of attachment to the idea of monarchy, if not exactly to the lady herself. Even the Duke of Wellington and Lord Palmerston deferred to her, not because they thought she was a charmer but she was, oh, I don't know, some kind of embodiment of Britain."

"Goodness me, I took you to be a new liberal and here you are sounding like an old-fashioned conservative. I gather some countries have constitutions whereas we rely on traditions and laws. A constitution might insist on women being treated equally. It is complicated of course, especially if you regard marriage as an institution like the monarchy. For then you'd have to wonder about Albert and Elizabeth living together, wouldn't you?"

"Yes, that is true, of course. I suppose that is why men hold women as inferior. Marriage is a traditional institution where women are servants, but of a special status. They are able to sleep with the man of power," at which they both laugh heartily.

"Well, let us cultivate Dilke and he may lead us to others sympathetic to our causes."

"When we meet in a month or so, we must somehow work out what our priorities are, what resources we have, who can work on what, and so on. It is so difficult to get the League going properly, only I suspect if we pursue it single-mindedly without distractions.

"No more of that now, tell me about your boys."

"They are completely settled, I think. Of course, my baby is due in October which will be a great excitement for all of us. I hope it is October 28th for that is the twins' birthday. It is extraordinary how my life has changed, how it now seems perfectly normal and I am so happy.

"Simon and Jude are wonderful and Frederick is too. I had nothing to do when I was alone in his house, but with the advent of the boys he gave me this invaluable book *Mrs. Beeton's Book of Household Management,* and her ideas especially on management of the house; her innumerable recipes are invaluable."

"I believe so. I must confess that Pip gave me a copy when it was published, but I keep it at Numquam and I think Nellie opens it from time to time, mainly to practice her reading."

"However, I can confide in you, Estella, I know. The advent of the boys changed him.

"He looked at me quite differently, seeing me as a subject of deep affection, not as a child he had to look after. We had not been lovers since we were married, and suddenly it was this great source of happiness for us both. He had never been with a woman, and I had only had that one dreadful experience in France. But we enjoyed learning from each other. Then I became pregnant and both of us are overjoyed."

"Has it been easy, being pregnant?"

"I seem to have sailed through it, actually. I hope it is a daughter that we can all cherish. Who knows, it might be only the first of many," and she laughed.

"Really?"

"Why not, if this baby is as wonderful as we all anticipate, I am sure we could make room for at least one more. But I have so much to thank you for, Estella. It was your determination that led my boys back to me and I am forever in your debt."

"Honora, it has been one of the highlights of my life, and now I must go home to hear what Charlotte has been up to."

"Up to? What do you mean?"

"She met a man at her brother's funeral and she has been spending a week with him, as he is back from Italy. She has been staying in the family mansion somewhere in Norfolk, I forget where, and he lives nearby."

"How splendid. She is quite old, if you will forgive me that indiscretion, though with that dreadful husband, she deserves some happiness."

"Oh dear me, the trials of getting old, my dear. I forget to do things, and worse still, I muddle up names. Several times I have referred to the Camerons at the Glencoe Massacre, not the Campbells which, with the Macdonalds as friends is an unfortunate faux-pas each time!

"I will let Charlotte know of your interest in the League, but now I really must be off."

Lachlan had recovered slowly from his cold and had been joyfully back to school for three days for the last two weeks of the summer term. Three months later, in mid-September, Susanna held a dinner party for the new residents of Cheyne Row and her friends. All agreed it was a delightful occasion, with good food, excellent wine, and relatively uncontroversial conversation.

After the guests had all left, Pip and Susanna sat up with a glass of whisky chatting about the newcomers.

"I could tolerate Randolph Culpepper," said Pip, "evidently an established merchant, obviously a person who had made his way in the world selling goods but I can't remember quite what he was a merchant of."

"Nor I," Susanna replied, "and whereas he is tall and gaunt, his wife Eliza was squat and coarse, I thought, dressed well but in poor taste and looking as though she is not used to engagements of this kind."

"I was quite surprised, I must confess, by Aubrey and Antonia Penoyre."

"Aren't they delightful, Pip, obviously very much in love though a little demonstrative for my taste which is not just unconventional, but a major challenge to rules of social decorum?"

"I suspect the wealth comes from her family," said Pip, "as there was something about Aubrey which suggested that he was left to make his own way in the world, although he clearly came from a solid background."

"I really would not guess on that score, but, goodness me, are they not both so good looking?" said Susanna with a smile that was almost a leer.

"Certainly: Then there were the siblings, Clive and Celia Enticott, who seemed a warm-hearted sensible couple, though why neither of them is married is a mystery."

"Yes, that is interesting, my dear. Clive told me he was a banker in a small firm in the City, but what did you make of that Italian?"

"Frankly, I took an immediate dislike to Angelo Bonaccorso or whatever his name was. He said he came from the south of his country and had been on business in America but now wanted a place in London. He must be a merchant of some kind, about which he was very coy, but involved in shady dealings I'd wager."

"I agree, why would he take a house here?"

"That he did not reveal. Time for bed, dear husband.

"I was very pleased that our friends, Estella in particular, shouldered the responsibility of talking with the new neighbors which took some of the burden off us as host and hostess."

"All in all, a very successful evening," concluded Pip. "Pity that Honora and Frederick could not come, but they are cautious about her baby."

They rose from their chairs, both yawning, snuffed out candles, turned down the gas lights and made their way to bed. They looked in on the children as was their habit.

Malcolm was fast asleep in his big bed after he was moved from his cot at Christmas.

Lachlan seemed feverish and sweating.

"Are you all right, darling?" asked his mother.

"I feel very ill," he whispered, hoarsely and then coughing and spluttering.

"Perhaps your cold has come back' said Pip, "you just have a good night's rest and you'll feel better tomorrow,"

"I will sit with you awhile while you go to sleep," Susanna said, as she went to her bedroom to undress and put on a nightgown.

"How long have you felt like this, old chap?"

"Just today, Father. One boy in my class had to go home as he was taken ill," he said slowly with a grating voice, "and my friend Marcus said he didn't feel well."

Lachlan then coughed hoarsely for a few minutes.

"We'll get a doctor in the morning, then," said Pip, surprised by the vehemence of the cough.

Susanna returned to comfort the boy and sat in a chair by the bed. He seemed to sleep a little. Pip went to bed. An hour into the night, the boy moaned and groaned and Susanna fetched a bowl of cool water and mopped his brow to help the fever go down.

"Do you want something to drink or eat, Lachlan dear?"

"My throat is so sore, I don't think I could swallow anything."

It was just before dawn when Susanna called out for Pip. He stumbled out of bed, put on a gown and came into Lachlan's bedroom where Lachlan was coughing noisily.

"Can you fetch Dr. Grant, darling, he is really not well."

"No, I can see."

He dressed hurriedly and rushed to the doctor's house in Oakley Street. Pip had heard that distinctive cough before on several occasions, more like a bark than a cough he recalled as he hurried down the Row. Diphtheria was common among the Salford poor as he knew from visiting many of them when a Primitive Methodist preacher there. The doctor was just coming down to breakfast, but Pip persuaded him to come back to the house with him immediately without mentioning his real concern.

Grant hurried up the stairs to where Susanna was waiting expectantly.

"How is the patient?" said Grant.

"Not well, as you will see," as they all went into the bedroom.

"Ah, yes, Lachlan it is, isn't it? Could you open your mouth for me?"

As Grant moved to look down Lachlan's throat, he recoiled sharply from the foul smell emanating from the boy's mouth. He pulled out his large handkerchief to cover his own mouth and with a small wooden spoon which he got out of his bag, peered into the boy's mouth to see dead respiratory tissue already starting to form the recognizable thick, gray coating building up in the child's throat, about as ugly a sight as there is in nature.

"I think I know what it is," said Pip, "he has diphtheria, hasn't he?"

"What can we do?" Howled Susanna in dismay, "what can we do, Doctor?"

"I am afraid, Mrs. Gargery, there is nothing I can do. We know it is an infection and it is easily passed from one person to another, usually a disease of children. He has not yet developed the bull neck familiar to patients with this disease. But there is this dead tissue in his throat which will certainly grow to cover his tonsils and his voice box and may indeed go up his nose from his mouth. The difficulty then is that he cannot breathe."

"Oh, dear God, this is a punishment on us, Pip. What have we done to our child?"

"It is nothing of the sort, Mrs. Gargery," said Grant. "Tell me, did he mention others in his class who were not at school because they were ill?"

"Yes."

"You see, it has nothing to do with you. The infection is there in the school and I must immediately hurry over there and tell them to isolate any boy who is sick."

"What will happen to him, Grant?" Pip asked.

"If you have seen it before, Gargery, you know very well. There is just a slim chance of recovery, but it is likely he has only two or three days to live, for the strain of the illness will affect his heart. I can give him something to ease the pain, but unless the fever breaks, he will die."

The next two days of agony would be remembered by Pip and Susanna forever. In the early morning on the second day, they watched their lovely child Lachlan quickly becoming unable to talk or breathe, his beautiful young face despoiled with the ravages of the disease, his neck swelling hideously, then as the gray mass choked him, he passed quietly away with scarcely a sigh.

They hardly ever left his side those two days, sitting on the edge of his bed, weeping in each other's arms, then quietly as it grew dark, their arms around each other, leaving him in peaceful silent relief after this appalling encounter with a crippling disease.

Malcolm's nanny had been instructed to keep the boy well away from his brother. Then trying desperately to control themselves, they went to him together to break the news that his big brother was no more which elicited howls of dismay and questions.

None of their friends knew yet of this agony.

Late in the morning on the day following Lachlan's passing, Frederick Brandram stopped at the house on his way back home, shocked by seeing an undertaker's carriage outside the house.

"What's happened?" he asked the maid as he was let in.

"Oh sir, that poor Lachlan," she said, "he's been taken with the diphtheria."

At that moment, Pip came out of his study, his face streaked with tears, looking as bereft as Frederick could imagine. Frederick promptly put his arms around Pip tightly, saying:

"Your only comfort is that you know he is gone to a better place, dear Pip."

"It challenges my faith, Frederick. If I cannot believe that God would take him from us, can I then believe that God watches over and protects us? It all makes no sense."

"How is Susanna?"

"Like me, she is living a nightmare from which she cannot wake up. I cannot describe just how awful it has been," he said, weeping on Frederick's shoulder.

"I believe you. I cannot imagine losing children; indeed I dare not even contemplate it. I will leave you to mourn, as will all your close friends."

Frederick went back up the Row to tell Honora, then made it his responsibility to call on the Macdonalds, and finally he took a cab over to New Queen Street to tell Estella and Charlotte.

The dismay and sorrow was universal, perhaps felt more intensely by those with children. Honora visited all the dinner party guests from the Row to relay the terrible news, though she was unable to contact Angelo, not, she thought, that it mattered. She was frightened too for her boys were now fourteen years old and were still in danger from the disease.

Harriet happened to call on Estella and Charlotte that evening and burst into prolonged weeping when she was told that Lachlan had died.

"Oh, what a terrible, heart-rending blow for them. Years ago, Pip used to tell me how much he had enjoyed playing with Albert when he went to that cottage in the marshes and how it was not possible for us to marry because he wanted children. And now he has lost his first-born; what could be more tragic? I don't think I dare go to the funeral, dare I?"

"Of course not," said Estella, surprised by Harriet's insensitivity about the Gargerys.

"I am not sure I would want anyone there," Estella continued, "I cannot think of any parents with children that I know who are less deserving of this hammer blow than the Gargerys.

"On the other hand, I must also remember that down among the poor in East London, it is a common occurrence: 'There is no armor against Fate,' I fear.

"Death the leveler, indeed. You see," said Harriet, "you are fond of poetry."

"Yes, but I am uninformed about it as I am about much else."

Lachlan was laid to rest privately in Highgate Cemetery in what was to become the Gargery family grave. Malcolm was crying severely so his mother tried in vain to comfort him, for the little brother admired his elder sibling immensely and at five years old, he knew that he would not see him again. The grave was covered with masses of flowers, carnations, roses, lilies, and a large bouquet from the Building to which most of the women had contributed a penny or two. Wreaths arrived sent from Scotland, others being sent by Pip and Susanna's friends. Susanna's Hogarth cousin sent a bunch of rosemary – for remembrance.

As they returned in the carriage to Cheyne Row through Westminster, Pip held Susanna's hands tightly. They looked at each other weeping quietly now, and both knew the look contained an implicit resolve of fidelity and commitment to their marriage and their love. Then, with his left arm protectively around Malcolm, Pip ran his right hand over Susanna's belly, murmuring endearments as she nestled in his arms.

However, it was the birth of Jane Margaret Brandram a month later that provided a cheerful sign, and Frederick and Honora promptly decided that next summer they would host a celebratory outing to Richmond Park and invite all their friends and their children. Pip and Susanna were most pleased for Honora whose travails had been so difficult. Although mourning their dear son, both felt that a new life shone a tiny light into their gloom.

The Semper House Home for Men opened in October 1874. Jack Masham was the first to be accepted and immediately moved in. Each man would have their own small room, a sum of three shillings a week and three meals a day. Mr. and Mrs. Copperstone were appointed, she to cook and to keep the Home clean, and he to superintend the day to day running of the establishment.

There were two maids, Clara Smith and Fanny Filby, both former residents of The Jaggers Building. They had been offered a room with a kitchen and a bathroom with a new water closet at the top of the house which they accepted with delighted astonishment, tinged with disappointment that the young men they served would not show them any interest.

The rules necessary for the running of the home were strict and clear. In particular any man continuing to trade his body would immediately be dismissed from the accommodation.

Although Estella had protested at this rule at an earlier Board meeting, arguing that the purpose of the Building was redemptive rather than punitive, Philip Hardyman pointed out that keeping an active man could lead to a police search and the Home being seen as a male brothel.

Though disappointed, Estella accepted that argument and as a result she invited Philip to join Pip and herself in interviewing the succession of young men anxious to live in the Home. Hamish had already briefed Philip to give him some perspective on these rent-boys whom Philip had always avoided.

Estella's recruitment of Philip was determined by the thought that, as a lawyer, Philip could ask clever questions about men who had used them in order to get some clues to the identity of the murderer or murderers. Neither Estella nor Pip knew that these matters were very sensitive for Philip, a secret sodomite.

Although the married Philip indulged in intimate relations with men when the opportunity arose, he was appalled by this kind of criminal control of young men. Perhaps the killer might be some crazed individual on a religious mission trying to strike out a pestilence, he thought, or a maniac with a mental disturbance of some kind.

Nor was the task easy. Few of the potential guests at the Home were as forthcoming as Jack had been. With lawyer-like skill, Philip was very subtle in leading them to the question he really wanted to ask, namely, did they know of anyone who had tried to draw them into a ring, to offer protection in return for payments, and indeed, whether there had been any suggestion that the young men might work in a brothel rather than on the street. The identity of such a man might lead to the murderer.

Philip really did not want to get involved as he believed that the search for the killer should be left to the police but he saw that the viability of the Semper House Home was at stake, the work of the Trust and, above all, the integrity of the Home for providing protection as well as relief and education was also of vital importance. He had not responded to Estella's invitation with alacrity but saw he could not easily evade the responsibility.

Between the three of them, the interviews passed off well. Twelve men were very delighted to move to the Home, leaving three places available. Four men refused the offer as they wanted to continue as prostitutes and it was this group that caused Philip concern, but it was one young man in particular, Harry Myles, who provided invaluable information.

"Mr. Myles," said Philip, "would you like to reside at the Home?"

"Not likely, sir, I wants my freedom."

"Tell us a bit about yourself."

"Well, I come to meet with you 'cos my rent-boy friends were coming; but I'm not giving up what I do, which you say I'd have to though I likes it, and I can't afford not to anyways, see, as I have to provide for my aged mum and dad, don't I?"

"And for no one else?"

"I have this friend who looks after me and I gives him some money from time to time," said Harry guardedly.

"Who is he?"

"He and I have this arrangement. He uses me occasionally, you know, but he's always around looking after me, makes sure some punter don't beat me up."

"Has anyone else offered to look after you."

"How did you know? There was this geezer a month or so ago who came up to me one night and said he'd look after me but I told him, I was already being protected."

"Do you remember this man?"

"Not really, but he had fancy clothes, you know, a long cloak and big-brimmed hat and spoke with a foreign accent. Phew, did he had a strong smell, scent of some kind, though I don't know about such things."

"You haven't heard from him since?"

"No, but I have seen him about once or twice."

"What does he do?"

"Oh, he sometimes walks around the street where I work but he never seems to pick anyone up and then he leaves."

"Which street is this?"

"Nearby, Shaftesbury Avenue."

Philip looked at Estella and Pip who had to conceal a degree of excitement at Harry's information, so Philip forged ahead believing he had their backing.

"Right, Mr. Myles. We will pay you two pounds for this purpose.

"You will come here to Semper House Home tomorrow at noon and you will meet Sidney. I won't tell you his full name. Once he knows what you look like, he will be around in Shaftesbury Avenue each night and if this man with the foreign accent appears, you should signal to him and then point out the man. Sidney will have you in view all the time, though he will not be close to you and you may not see him."

"Cor, that's great. I'll be here. Two quid? I'd do anything for two quid; Thank you, sir."

❧   ❧   ❧

As Myles left, Estella breathed a sigh of relief, delighted that Philip had been so successful in eliciting the information. Pip was quiet, seemingly somewhere quite different, no doubt thinking about his dead son.

"That is more than satisfactory. It is a real start," she said.

Overnight, however, a young man selling himself on Shaftesbury Avenue was found with his throat cut in a doorway in Wardour Street.

When Myles arrived the following day at Semper House, both Pip and Philip were there to meet him.

"Did you hear about young Johnny?" he asked Philip.

"No, who's Johnny?"

"Johnny North was my friend and he was murdered last night, left to die in a doorway? I tell you, Mr. Hardyman, we's all terrified. And one more thing. I saw him talking to the man with the foreign accent a day or so ago. Do you think they are connected?"

"It could be, I don't know. Come into this room and meet Sidney."

Two days passed with Sidney out on the street watching. On the third day he arrived early at the Cheapside offices. The man with the foreign accent had been identified by Myles. Sidney had then followed him but lost him somewhere in Westminster. He did not think the man knew he was being followed.

"We need to take great care here, Sidney," said Pip. "This man may have accomplices, even young men posing as prostitutes."

"I did see him having a brief conversation with one of the rent-boys whose name I have from Myles. He is Tommy Perkins. I suppose he could be working for this man."

"Right, Pip, Sidney and I will talk to this Perkins this very evening."

⚜ ⚜ ⚜

Lachlan's parents were in an overwhelming struggle with their grief. Susanna had found great consolation in long talks with Honora, and Pip endeavored to concentrate on his responsibilities at the Building which took his mind off Lachlan for a while.

He went to Estella's house to tell her of Sidney's findings. She was eager to take part in meeting with Perkins but he urged her not to appear on the street in the evening.

"I wish we could identify his accent," she said. "It might be of help."

"I know this may offend you, Estella, but this really is no place for a lady. When we go out tonight, it is certainly possible that he might be there. We must not assume he is the killer and a great deal is at stake. If the murderer is not found, it will be a threat to the Home. Who knows? Rings of these young men might be created with such controls by these so-called protectors that they might not be able to come to us. Everything we are working for could be at risk."

"Then all the more important to find out what this man with the foreign accent is doing. I'd like to come with you but I do reluctantly accept your reason for my not being there."

"Thank you, dear Estella, it could well prove violent."

That evening Philip, Pip and Sidney went from Gerrard Street along Wardour Street on to Shaftesbury Avenue. All were dressed in dark clothes with hats well down on their faces. It was some time before Tommy Perkins appeared in the light of a theater doorway.

"Ah, Perkins," said Sidney as they approached, "I wonder if I could have a word?"

"Only a word? My room is nearby, two quid for the night, or ten bob for an hour."

Pip and Philip stayed at a distant from Sidney, but within earshot.

"No, I wanted to know more about the man you meet with the foreign accent."

"Oh, Angelo."

"Do you work for him?" asked Sidney.

"Yes, he protects me from these murderers and I give him part of what I earn of a night."

"That must be useful: I expect he has other rent-boys to protect, doesn't he?"

"Yes. He does not want me to bring my friends to him as he takes care of that his'self."

"He must be very generous."

"Yes, he's Italian. Want to meet him? He's coming soon."

"No need. Good luck."

The three men then walked away from Tommy Perkins and stood quietly in a doorway some distance away. Then a well-dressed man hurried by and crossed the road towards Tommy.

Pip recognized him immediately.

"We must leave urgently," he whispered to Sidney and Philip and he hurried back to the Home with the others trailing behind.

"What on earth is the matter, Pip?" said Philip as they got to the door.

"Angelo is Angelo Bonaccorso. He was a guest at our dinner party recently: He lives only two doors away from me."

"Right," said Philip, "now we must tell the police.

"Get Adam to contact his relative. He is at least extorting money with menaces, if not murdering young men."

Superintendent of Police Jacob Shellhorn, Adam's second cousin, was duly informed and as dawn was breaking the following morning a cohort of police arrived in Cheyne Row to take M. Bonaccorso into custody.

Most of those who had attended Susanna's dinner party were shocked to the core at these events. Pip had messages sent to their friends about this dreadful neighbor which everyone found initially too disgusting to talk about, but then fascination overcame their reservations. Estella and Charlotte were distraught at this shockingly evil man but found some consolation in the fact that the events demonstrated the importance of Semper House.

Courtisone told Hamish that they should refuse to allow anyone in the practice to defend M. Bonaccorso as they had all in different ways been involved in the discovery, advice which was met with great relief by Philip. Hamish was not shocked but delighted that such a criminal had been apprehended, whilst Mary took it all in her stride, pointing out how the vicious laws against sodomy had this kind of consequence.

However, the original charges of extortion against Angelo were soon dropped. Police found incriminating evidence in his Cheyne Row house, including two daggers, and lists of known male prostitutes, not only from London but also from New York. Contact with the New York police established that Angelo was a Sicilian with a criminal record. Some of the young men testified that they had been approached by him and threatened. All this led to his indictment and conviction for the murder of Johnny North.

In the whole period of investigation and trial Angelo refused to answer questions and was silent throughout his trial. After he was given last rites by a priest, Angelo Daniele Bonaccorso was executed by hanging for the murder of Johnny North at Wandsworth Jail at 8 o'clock in the morning of Wednesday, December 6, 1874.

1875

IV

The death of a child and the execution of a neighbor for murder were deplorable and scandalous blows to the tranquility of the Row, but the mood began to improve with the arrival of Spring and the sight of snowdrops and daffodils in the Row gardens, small solace though they were to the grieving Gargerys.

Estella and Charlotte sat in their New Queen Street garden one March afternoon exchanging reports over a whisky. Charlotte said that Percy had sent a letter, writing that he had to stay in Italy another three months, but he proposed to take a very short break of a week quite soon before returning.

"Can you really marry a man who will be away most of time, Charlotte?"

"I don't know, Estella. I think I have a choice. Either I stay here in London and begin to work with your Trust, perhaps on something different from prostitution, something more educational in direction, or I travel with Percy to wherever he is digging. Southern Italy cannot be a bad place to sojourn and I know we would return when the heat makes excavations impossible. Summer in London would not be unappealing."

"An interesting choice, but I suppose the heart of the matter is whether you want to spend time with him, whether his absence makes you morose and unhappy. I don't detect that, but you are a private woman."

"I wish I knew too." The conversation was interrupted by the maid.

"A message for you just come, Ma'am."

"Let me see. Oh Charlotte, how wonderful! Susanna has had a daughter, and Pip says they are both well, and she is to be named Emily Hannah Gargery. We must go to see them later in the week. At least the baby did not arrive on April 1st," she said with a grin.

"Oh, and Hamish wants me to meet this Welsh woman when she is back from her parents and her children in Wales. I suppose you don't want to come."

"No, thank you, I'll leave her to your tender mercies."

Estella was not excited about meeting Mrs. Angharad Unworthy as she thought the woman was a pathetic figure, brought from South Wales to Australia when a young girl to provide children for a thoroughly objectionable man, who happened to be the love child of Abel Magwitch, her own father. Estella had been told that Ezekiel was not with her as he had been seriously injured, a fact that evoked not her sympathy but a sense of rough justice being done.

She arrived in Little Britain early for the meeting. Angharad had been in Wales for several months, prevented from coming up to London earlier by a variety of problems in the Jones family, primarily caused by her own children wanting the freedom and the absence of discipline to which they had been accustomed in Australia. Two of them were constantly chasing the cows to try to milk them.

However, Hamish and Clarence eagerly explained Angharad's situation to Estella and that they needed Mr. Courtisone's advice on her predicament. Eventually Robert showed Angharad into the office, looking distinctly morose not the 'pert young hussy' of Estella's earlier encounter with her.

"How are you, Angharad? asked Estella.

"Well, to be honest," she said with her strong Welsh accent, "I don't really know."

"I gather your husband met with some kind of injury."

"Yes, he was really stupid, as he got those natives very angry and he ganged up with other owners to try to force them to work. But, like I told him, those Abbos were here long before us and he should treat them better, however odd they looked. They were still

God's children. I remembered that from my Chapel days, see," and she giggled.

"But how is he?"

"He's done for, to be honest," she replied as tears came to her eyes, "he got hit in the brain and he can't talk or move his arms or legs. He's, what do you call it, paralyzed, that's what he is."

"Goodness me, how sad. But why did you come to England?"

"I came to Wales with my five youngest, the eldest Gareth is now almost twenty, so he is looking after things down under. He's a clever boy, very strong like his father. But my dad said in the circumstances I should get a lawyer, but, as I told him, the lawyers in Queensland are crooks, crooks they are, right crooks. In that case, my dad said, get your arse to London and see that lawyer you saw with Ezekiel. So here I am again, later than I wanted."

"I see, well, I think you just have to continue to talk to Mr. Macdonald and Mr. Smythe here, as I don't know the law."

"Your problem as we see it is this," said Hamish, "your Queensland lawyers say you cannot do anything with your husband's estate as he is still alive, albeit only just. These lawyers are wrong under English Law which still applics to Queensland."

"Yes, but there's more to it than that, see," said Angharad, "they are worried that I might sell our property to someone who wanted to change things, to respect the heathen Abbos rather than fight them, and to send those slaves back where they came from."

"Ah, I see," said Hamish, "we need a council of war with the other partners, including our senior, Mr. Courtisone. Why don't you just sit here and we'll send a message to Cheapside to see if he is free?"

Courtisone himself appeared a half hour later, with Hardyman and Masterson in tow while Estella took a walk around Old Square. He was quickly apprised of Mrs. Unworthy's problem.

"It is a simple matter, Mrs. Unworthy," said Courtisone.

"We will have a judge here declare that your husband is incompetent by reason of illness to manage his affairs and to give you what is called power of attorney which means that you will have control of all his assets. You can then decide what you wish to do. A judge here can have that jurisdiction although your Queensland lawyers should have decided on this course of action in Australia."

"Well, thank you sir," said Angharad. "I think I understand that.

"I'd like to sell up and for us to come back to Wales. I think I would have enough money from a sale to do that. I don't know whether to bring my husband here or not, especially as the doctors say there is no chance of his ever recovering and he does not know me when I used to visit him."

"Tell me, Mrs. Unworthy, do you have any idea of the value of his property."

"I don't know exactly, but he had a party for his friends last year to celebrate what he called his first million. He was probably bragging, but we do own a lot of sheep and a lot of land."

There were suppressed gasps from all those in attendance.

"Do you know whether he has made a will?"

"Oh yes, soon as we was married, we went to a lawyer's in Cardiff before we set sail. Everything was to come to me. I don't think he would have changed it as he was far too busy, if you know what I mean."

"Who was this lawyer?"

"I think it was Mr. Jones."

"I suspect there may be more than one Jones lawyering in Cardiff."

"Oh yes," replied Angharad, "silly me, he was a Zachary."

"That is most helpful. We will seek him out quickly enough and it is fortunate for you that there is a will made over here.

"You know," said Courtisone, somewhat taken aback that this woman should be so rich, "I think it would make sense for us to send a lawyer and a clerk to Australia with a power of attorney from you and a copy of the will to execute your wishes. We can then help you get your Welsh farm, if you wish.

"Let me see. Mr. Hardyman, Mr. Masterson, would you both fancy a sea voyage to Brisbane? I think we might send a detective with you in case there was any difficulty."

Both men glowed with pleasure and excitement at this opportunity.

"There will then be no need for you to return to Australia, Mrs. Unworthy. If you have no further questions, I will bid you good day."

"Oh, good day, sir, and so many thanks."

Hamish noted that Courtisone was not being generous, as the costs of the voyage for the two lawyers would no doubt appear on Angharad's invoice eventually, not that with her wealth she would notice.

The Spring months passed quickly and the date for the Brandrams party in June at Richmond Park finally arrived. The Culpeppers rode in a carriage with two of their children. Simon and Jude came with their parents in a brougham. Estella and Charlotte picked up Hamish, Mary and the baby on the way. The Penoyres arrived in a cab. Pip and Susanna brought Malcolm and Hannah but they did not stay long as Hannah the baby fretted and these very cautious parents responded immediately. The Enticotts were taking a vacation in northern France, so did not attend.

It was a gorgeous June day and when they had all found a spot under a massive oak tree, lunch was broken out of hampers on to rugs, wine bottles were opened, children were called to eat, and when that was done, groups formed naturally and easily.

Eliza Culpepper and Antonia Penoyre were in Estella's sights as potential members of the League of Free Women. Charlotte began a conversation with Eliza about her children discovering that the eldest son Japheth lived in a world of his own and was very unhappy at his boarding school.

"Why did you him away to school?"

"Randolph wanted us to give them the best future and in the last few years, sending children away from home has become fashionable. Mind you, I find it a terrible pain as I don't know what they are up to, and I have tried to have him come home but Randolph won't hear of it and he has the power, as you know."

"Really, I don't have children but I find these days that more and more women are asserting themselves."

"Oh, I tried that once when we were younger," said Eliza laughing.

"I went out on my own for a day, just to get some fresh air. We were living in the north of London at the time, and I got a cab to Epping Forest for some fresh air while he was running our own store at the time. It wasn't worth it. I had such a row from him when he came home and asked me what I had done."

"What was his concern?" Asked Charlotte.

"Oh, I don't think he'd have bothered if I'd been assaulted or something worse. It was that I had done something without his permission."

"Oh, that must have been a shock."

"Well, not really. You see I was a poor working girl in my father's small shop, and he was this dashing young man already doing well in merchandising material for builders. I was good-looking then, only eighteen and he asked me out. It was a good way to get away from under my dad who was a real male tyrant. But now, all my husband can think about is improving us in society. Moving to Cheyne Row brings us up a rung or two on the social ladder."

"I hope he is right for your sake, but what a sensation that was with the murderer in the Row," said Charlotte, changing the subject abruptly.

"Yes it was. Randolph says the house the man lived in is impossible to let, as the story of the police search and the trial was in the newspapers so there will be a very long delay in finding a tenant, I am sure."

"Continue with your family. What do you want for your daughter Margaret: Look at her, she's a very pretty girl, how old is she?"

"Just fifteen. You have to laugh, don't you," said Eliza, "look at her, those twins buzzing around her like bees."

"Those are Honora's boys."

"They all look gorgeous, don't they?"

It became obvious to Charlotte during this conversation that Eliza was an intelligent, personable woman trying to break out of social conventions: Potentially an excellent recruit to the League.

Meantime, Estella was talking to the young Antonia; they had moved a rug so they could sit on the grass near the party, while Aubrey was deep in conversation with Pip.

"How long have you been married, Antonia?"

"Three months, the best of my life."

"How wonderful, Aubrey is a very lucky man indeed to have such a beautiful woman as his wife."

She could not stop the words coming out of her mouth, aware they might be taken differently from her intention, so she quickly added:

"My husband died five years ago now and I miss him dreadfully."

"Oh, I am sorry. Was he ill?"

"I fear so, but I had known him since I was a child and we only became lovers when we both approaching forty. I still miss his intimacy."

Again, she sensed she was being too frank as such a conversation invites a response in similar vein, but, nevertheless, Antonia astounded her.

"I'm not surprised you miss him; you seem to me to be the sort of woman who craves the intimacy that a man gives. I'll confide in you if I may.

"Aubrey and I met when we were fifteen years old at a very large house party with some thirty people there. The adults ignored us completely, so we went our own way and in a trice were on a bed in a gazebo in the grounds of the mansion, kissing and hugging and then, why not, we thought. So exciting for both of us. My parents would have gone completely mad had they known, and my father would probably have assaulted Aubrey.

"Strange, is it not, adults tell you a lot of mumbo-jumbo about marriage, saving yourself for it and worry you with stories about diseases if you misbehave. Aubrey and I were both virgins, but we knew almost immediately we were introduced, certainly within five minutes, that we desired each other, and neither of us wanted to wait. Making love to each other regularly has heightened our desire for each other; his body is a temple."

"Good gracious," said Estella who would have been open-mouthed if it were not impolite, "that was very precocious of you."

"To tell you the truth, my parents had an odd marriage. They did not tell me, but I guessed, quite rare in these times. Each of them always seemed to have made a 'friend' of the opposite sex. They failed to disguise it from me. Then I found out one night that they were involving servants in their erotic fantasies probably without their consent. I was amazed and upset.

"Oh dear, the stories I could tell about that. I'm sure the maids had no choice but to succumb to them. Terrible, really. I don't have much to do with my parents nowadays."

"Your telling me of Aubrey and you is something of a relief, for my step-son Albert is now twenty years old and lives with his Elizabeth in Paris. I worried whether such a breach of social convention would be a mistake, but they love each other deeply so why should I be concerned? I have a very good friend who believes in free love, much like your parents, perhaps?"

"I don't imagine myself able to encounter another man, as we know each other so very well. Another woman? I don't know. Who knows? We have talked about it a little."

Estella blanched slightly, but then told Antonia of the League of Free Women at which she got very excited and wanted all the details of the group's ambitions.

"You include votes for women, too, don't you?"

"Yes, indeed, and I think we may be able to meet with Millicent Fawcett at some stage."

"Oh, really? I attended Girton the other women's college for two years, while Aubrey was doing a degree at Magdalen, his college. I know of her of course; that would be marvelous."

"Where are you living, then?

"Just down the river at Chiswick. Aubrey's family are wealthy brewers from Hertfordshire. We go up to St. Albans for two nights a week but his father and his brother run the business. It is a very happy arrangement."

"We will see more of each other, I know. I live on the edge of St. James Park and it would be delightful to have you come to lunch."

"I'd be thrilled. I will send you a note as I know Aubrey had to tour some hop fields soon and that does not attract me."

Estella was not surprised by an invitation from Harriet to lunch, but she was also aware that getting older prompted her wish for new experience, as if she was making up for lost time. After all, she had spent almost forty years of her life virtually immune from sexual desire, such was the Havisham curse. As the cab dropped her at Harriet's lodgings in Long Acre, she had a mild fluttering of the heart, but a distinctive wariness deriving from her own nature and a secret about herself that she had never revealed to anyone.

Harriet opened the door looking extraordinarily beautiful as ever in her silk damask gown, her hair down around her shoulders, the russet color so striking, and her smile subtle and ambiguous between charm and desire.

"I am so thrilled to see you, Estella."

"Oh, I am delighted to come, as I have not seen your home before."

They looked at each other, and Harriet reached out and put her arms around Estella's waist, kissing her cheek with affection which was reciprocated politely if not heartily.

"I am sure you know, dear Harriet," as they moved arm in arm into the small living room, "that my experience with Nellie was magical and joyful and above all peaceful and safe. I have thought long and hard about you, after I quipped with your friend Katherine that I could feel a pang of jealousy."

Sitting close to each on a small settee, Estella continued, "to be frank I have often wondered what loving you would be like. That is partly because your attitudes to loving are so radical, at once so threatening and so delightful, quite apart from your spectacular beauty such that I could come to want you with an overwhelming strength."

Turning to look Harriet in the eye, she said, "but I fear it is all too complicated for me to establish a relationship at this juncture, probably never."

"Well, thank you for being so open to talking about these matters," said Harriet, sitting up in her seat and drawing her gown around her.

"I confess this, Estella dear, I have never been with a woman, but as I have come to know you these past months and knowing that you have previously expressed your love for a woman physically, I would like you to teach me about it.

"Does not that seem strange? Let me put it like this. Our friendship is incomplete."

"That may be right," Estella replied, "but I am an old woman, a widow, and I am aware of the wrinkles that hardly make my body a temple of desire for a would-be lover. Yet I must decline, even though I am stunned by your beauty, even jealous of Pip," and they laughed as Estella reached out to hold Harriet's hand.

"Explain your reluctance to me," said Harriet.

"I think I am going to shock you as I am going to tell you things about me no one else knows and I really don't know why I should confide in anyone, let alone you.

"To begin with, I know you cherish your complete independence. I know you feel you must be free to love as and when you desire."

"Indeed," Harriet replied, "I have to be completely independent. I am not expecting that we live together as I will remain committed to free love. I might meet a man, or indeed now a woman, in some context and couple with them, but free love does not mean promiscuity. I mean that I do not go around looking for lovers as some men do.

"I believe quite firmly, Estella, that the most wonderful experience in the world is engaging with a new lover for the first time. The apprehension of discovering a new body is the most tantalizing and exhilarating experience. That apart, I have often thought about whether some kind of permanent relationship for me could even be desirable as I would have to accept that it will restrict my freedom. Pip and I simply wanted different things but retained our love for each other when we parted.

"When we were lovers, however, I did not engage with anyone else because I thought there was something about our relationship that demanded that we would need to ask the other's permission if we wished to be intimate with another person. It never arose of course, but as you see, I am really quite odd," and they laughed again.

"Most interesting, dear Harriet, but I know myself."

"But I interrupted you," said Harriet, "please go on."

"When I realized belong before we married that I was deeply in love with this man I had known for years, also a Pip of course, I entertained the idea of poisoning his wife Beatrice, only partly in fantasy. Not that strange really; after all, my mother Molly had murdered her rival. His wife was, how can I put it? In the way? He and I had long been close in our particular manner. I deserved him, and she was a usurper. "

"Great Heavens, wait," said Harriet deeply shocked, "you actually thought about killing her."

"Yes, have you never felt like killing a person?"

"No, even though my father would like to have had his way with me, his daughter, it never crossed my mind that I might kill him for it."

"I see and I am surprised. I thought that everyone would fantasize about killing someone."

"No, I doubt that is the case."

"I know I can get profoundly jealous, beyond all reason. When I first saw Pip with Beatrice, my mind was immediately filled with visions of them in the throes of passion and I was distraught. I thought of inviting her that day to come upstairs in my house to view the bedrooms and then I would push her down the stairs. Later I thought about how I might hire someone to kill her. Poison was also a possibility. Of course, I managed to control this intense jealousy and no one could have guessed how I felt except perhaps my mother whose jealousy actually did lead to her murdering a rival. Indeed both my parents were killers."

"Goodness me, I am astounded, both crimes of passion?

"My mother yes, my father yes too, if bottomless hatred counts."

"Yours are not mere fantasies, are they, but actual courses of action?"

"Yes, I even acquired a poison, for the garden of course," said she with a grim half-smile.

"But before Beatrice died, I used to wonder what might have been had she been a strong woman with a large healthy family. Fortunately for both of us, Pip confided in me at the outset of their marriage that she was very frail, and indeed she had miscarriages, so the thought of killing her diminished as I knew Nature would do my work for me, so I put my plans aside."

"I hardly know what to say," said Harriet with tears in her eyes, "that this was not mere fantasy leaves me utterly dismayed. Did you ever tell Pip about this?"

"No, but I came very close one night early on after we had ravished each other, but then I stopped, worried about his reaction."

"I should think so too. No one would believe what you have just told me, and I have to say I can only feel tremendous sorrow for you having to contend with such a monster in your mind."

"That is such a good way to put my condition. But now I am telling you that I know I could love you as fiercely as I loved Pip, notwithstanding my affections for my dear Nellie. If you and I began a relationship, it would have to be permanent with total commitment, fidelity and passion.

"I am frightened by my propensity to overpowering jealousy, and I do not refuse you lightly, as my body responds vigorously to you, old as I am. I really do not wish to encounter that monster ever again as it creeps up on me unawares," said Estella, with tears in her eyes.

"I promise to keep secret what you have just told me, yet on your own admission you are far too high a risk to become my lover," said Harriet with a smile.

"I am afraid so, my dear, but I hope we can become close friends."

"We will see," said Harriet.

Over lunch they discussed Pip. Both of them had a real affection for him, but Estella was able to tell Harriet of the underlying difficulty of the difference between Susanna and him in what she called native intelligence.

Harriet's response to this was unsurprising:

"They should have several more children to keep their minds off their personal problems."

"I told him that, and will do so again, though not that you said it."

They kissed affectionately and Estella left Harriet to visit Pip as she had received a message early that morning asking her to call when she was free.

She took a cab out to Chelsea and walked a while along the river before going to his Cheyne Row house. She was satisfied with this encounter with Harriet, as she had confronted her monster at last. She had desperately needed to articulate it to someone and there was Harriet so beautiful, so tempting, that she started to tell of it whilst ignoring the consequences.

She was still not certain that the monster had been slain. Yet once she had got it clear in her head by talking it out, she finally understood that fantasies of killing apart, loving Harriet would never work because of the conflict between Harriet's determined independence and her own prodigious and aberrant jealousy.

But she must now concentrate on her duties, smiling to herself which made an elderly man passing think she was smiling at him.

Estella had listened to the discussions with Angharad and they certainly met with her approval. But it was late in the afternoon, so she invited her to stay with her in New Queen Street more out of a compassion for the poor woman than any particular desire to be her friend. Charlotte would be there to help with the conversation. When all was said and done, this woman's dying husband was her half-brother. She stopped the carriage at Angharad's hotel, asked for a maid pack up her luggage and have it sent to New Queen Street.

It was a beautiful Autumn evening and Charlotte was sitting in the small garden at the rear of the house when they arrived. As it was so mild, so once Estella and Angharad had attended to their respective toilets, they sat on raffia chairs and the maid brought glasses of sherry to them.

"So tell us about your life," Charlotte said after the full introduction had been made.

"Do you want the real story or the story I tell when my husband is present?" she asked with a giggle.

"The real one, of course."

"To be honest, I could not believe how happy I was about going half-way round the world to Australia when I was sixteen, but later how miserable I'd become when we came back from England after meeting you. He'd always worked from dawn to dusk. We had no friends, though he had men he met for business or politics or drinking but I had no friends 'cept my children. I got so lonely I'd sometime go out in the day if he was in a faraway field and beyond where the kiddies could hear, and I'd scream, really scream."

"But do you love him?"

"I thought I did when we met and I think I was still in love with him when we visited England together. But he got very angry with me that night we talked about those slaves of his, you remember that, don't you, Estella?"

"That was a day I will not easily forget."

"When the children were asleep in their rooms that night, he began to beat me. Horribly, but not so anyone would see the bruises. He punched me in my back on the sides after he'd gagged me. He did awful sex things to me. He'd never been like that before, but he said he'd be losing money and I was going to pay for it. Worst night of my life it was."

"Oh, my dear," said Estella, "I hope that was not my doing."

"Well, he said it was. He said if we'd been in Australia he would have had men come round and beat up the whole bleeding lot of them, he said. You see, when he told me of the plan to use slaves, I'd already told him that it was wrong, and he just slapped my face then, but this beating was far worse."

"How terrible, what a brute," said Charlotte.

"Well, when this accident happened and he lost his mind, I thought there was no longer any reason to stay in Australia. I can buy a sheep farm and my Gareth can run it. It would be somewhere in South Wales where we can be near family and near Chapel. Ezekiel won't live long with his injuries. My situation will be different when he dies."

"But do you have money here now?"

"Yes, when he started a bank account, he left instructions that I can draw money. He told me early on he'd do that in case of emergencies. This is an emergency, ain't it, so I was able to draw money from that Coutts Bank when I came. They told me there was over five thousand pounds there should I need it."

"Good, then you have no problems for the present. What are your plans now?"

"I don't want to be a burden to you, but I need to stay in London a few more days and I must meet those lawyers who are going to Queensland very soon."

"You must stay here, relax and enjoy some peace and quiet and I know you have been going to the shops already."

After Angharad had been shown her room and retired for the night, Estella said:

"What a blackguard my half-brother Ezekiel Unworthy is, Charlotte. Not surprising, I suppose, for a child of Abel Magwitch.

"After all," she added, "my father was a killer like my mother."

Charlotte was so shocked by this admission that she got up to go to bed and said good night to her friend with what little compassion she could muster.

Pip and Susanna's life had been completely changed by the thunderbolt of Lachlan's death. Unlike some couples who start to blame each other for a child's death, this pair became much closer, constantly sharing memories of his foibles, his strengths, his inquisitiveness and above all his devotion to both of them. Fortunately, the fracas of their mutual infidelity had passed the child by, so they felt no guilt about that in relation to his passing.

Yet, the loss of a child cannot escape the tyranny of guilt especially when a child is so young. Both knew that young children across the country died in their thousands and that death before the age of five was a commonplace. Yet that provided no solace from the perspectives on which they viewed their tragedy. Was Lachlan's death an act of God, a lottery in which some won and some lost, or somehow their responsibility?

Neither of them could accept it was an act of God, however much they had cried out in their agonized bereavement. One cannot blame God for disease, as Pip put it, and while we believe Lachlan has a place in the hereafter, it is the conditions we have created as human beings that are the cause.

For a time, they inclined to the lottery explanation. Whether a child caught a disease, why or how was just a matter of luck. Pip had witnessed in Salford how disease was common among the poor, so it must have something to do with the conditions of living. But in

Lachlan's school? No explanation was possible. For Pip and Susanna Gargery their child's untimely death was just an unfortunate, ruinous, and unspeakable calamity.

Yet for them, as for many a loving parent, there was always this hidden cry in their breast – what could we have done to prevent it? Indeed, in the weeks following the child's death, such possibilities were constantly turned over in their night-time discussions as they bound themselves closer and closer in their grief.

Yet there was still their son Malcolm and now they had wee Hannah. During the summer, they talked about them both and concluded that they should have more children, though Lachlan's death made them pause and the thought of losing another child would, as Susanna put it, drive both of them to Bedlam. She was awake many a night in terror at Malcolm going to school and contracting a major disease. On Pip's suggestion, they decided that Malcolm should attend school only as compulsorily required but that thereafter he should have a tutor.

Such qualms, worries and fears continued through the summer of 1875 but were partly relieved one night by Pip's proposition.

"Darling, I wonder. A thought has just occurred to me. Why don't we start a small school?"

"A school?"

"Yes, we can educate Malcolm that way. We can use some of your money to start it and charge fees, but also allow poor children to attend free."

"You are a genius in practical matters, are you not, my dear? I remember well how you solved the problem of the Fletchers by having Harry and Biddy move from the Forge and the Cottage where Joe had worked. This is an idea with real promise."

"Let's sleep now and talk more in the morning. I think of the Africa possibility too which we've talked about but never pursued seriously."

Over breakfast the following day, the heavy grief was still on view in the black ribbons decorating pictures on the walls, and in Susanna's somber dress and Pip's black cravat. But the mood was lightened a little as they started to discuss this idea for a school, as it seemed to give their lives purpose.

"We have to take our time to think about what sort of education we will give our scholars," Susanna began, "I would like to think it would be a place where children would find adventure."

"I see us doing different things. I will deal with the administration and the buildings," said Pip, "while you handle the education aspect but we will both hire the teachers when we get going."

"We should start quite small, I think, no more than twenty pupils and then expand."

"I wonder what our neighbors would think if we rented the house along the Row where Rizzio lived. I won't mention his successor. That house is obviously proving difficult to rent but if we changed its purpose, that might banish some of its demons."

"Perhaps we should construct it as a business with a Board, and we can invite some our friends to help; Frederick with the architecture and I am sure Honora would be interested as well as the pair in New Queen Street."

"That would certainly be valuable to have some good minds helping us."

"I remember," said Susanna, "there being quite a furor over the educational writing of Mr. Spencer. I must find some copies of his work and perhaps that will introduce me to others."

"You mean Mr. Herbert Spencer?"

"Indeed. I have certainly heard of him and perhaps we can find someone with knowledge of education to help us. Perhaps we can call it The Lachlan School as a memorial?"

Tears flowed from Pip's eyes as he got up and walked around the table to embrace his wife.

V

Honora arrived that day for lunch to show off Jane Margaret yet again, but she was anxious for advice and it was a matter of some urgency as she believed Estella would be leaving for Paris quite soon.

"Oh, my dear, is she not just perfect? I am sure Frederick is thrilled."

"He is indeed, and the boys are in awe of her. She is six months old now."

"I have here a small silver spoon for her," Estella said, going to a drawer in her small marquetry desk.

"Thank you so much, my dear, but may I share a problem with you?"

"Of course, Honora, what is the problem?"

"You have always had servants and maids in your household, whereas I grew up in a house with just one maid. We could afford little more than that. My devout parents were not wealthy, and my father was very abstemious. I am never quite sure what his employment was.

"He dressed well and went every weekday to a large commercial undertaking although it never occurred to me to ask what he did there. My mother cooked and our one maid helped and cleaned. But I am now in a household with a cook and two maids who clean and serve meals. I go to the kitchen to discuss what we eat, but thereafter do nothing. When I was first married, I was in such a depressed state I went along with this way that Frederick had set up the home.

"I remember you once saying something about teaching Nellie to read and write, but did you do this? I have two nice young women maids, sixteen and seventeen years old who can do neither. They were too late for the schools we now have. Just as I want women to have the vote and to be more independent, I ask myself: Why do my wishes not apply to servants? Or should they? Am I just thinking about my own class when I think of women's independence?"

"I did teach Nellie to read and write," Estella replied, "and she has done wonderful things, renting books to read, like *Emma*, and the last time I saw her, even *Middlemarch*."

"Hmm. You have probably heard that Pip and Susanna might start a school, but that would be a location for us to teach reading and writing on a Saturday afternoon to servants who could walk to the school easily and we would charge them a nominal sum, say a penny a visit."

"That *is* a fascinating idea for a school. I had not heard."

"But there is a different servant problem for me," said Honora, "my boys are now very handsome at fourteen, looking much older than they are, I think."

Estella smiled at this maternal love so gently expressed and at this wonderful woman who had so magnificently survived her tribulations.

"Our two maids live in and are older than the boys. They are housemaids as I won't let a nanny near my gorgeous daughter. Simon or Jude would not respond easily to the maids' flirtations, but I'm sure one of the girls has her eye on either one of them."

"The easy answer is to send her packing, though that does not solve anything. The boys are very polite, I am sure. I don't know whether you should talk to them or not."

"I am completely sure, Estella, that they have not made any advances themselves as yet and the maid concerned Alice is very pretty indeed."

"It has been said that letting any servant go is a sign of weakness, that you have not brought them up properly," pronounced Estella, "but be a stickler for propriety, though not stern or the least bit unfriendly. Taking care of them and being friendly is one's duty."

"The difficulty will be this: If one of the boys' passion starts to be stimulated, then any stance to the girl might seem like a punishment directed at them. Moreover one hears from time-to-time stories about young men misbehaving with servants."

"What does Frederick think?"

"I have not mentioned it; the dear man is so thrilled with a house full of gaiety and laughter, outside his ordinary experience, that anything disturbing will upset him. He has always regarded the servants as my domain."

"You must talk with Alice, I think, and tell her she restricts her behavior or you will tell her she must leave your employment."

Since Elizabeth and Albert settled in Paris together in late 1873, he had regularly attended the *Café Guerbois* where a group of painters gathered on two evenings each week. He sat at a table a little distant from that where the main conversations were held, hoping to gather understanding as he had no accomplishments in painting to his name. Elizabeth took piano lessons from Gilbert Fauré, an organist at the *Eglise Saint-Sulpice*. She found Faure to be a man of excellent musical sense, although it was perhaps a weakness that he was not a professional pianist, but then she had no ambitions to go on the concert stage.

Albert and Elizabeth had been together with a sense of permanence since she returned after her father's funeral. Though the aftermath of the war rumbled on, they started to feel quite Parisian, spending evenings at the Café, such that they became well-known enough for painters and other denizens of the Café scene to chat with them. Elizabeth's sparkling good looks and Albert's handsome demeanor attracted tributes but many an unwanted advance as well.

One evening, Gustave Caillebotte came to their table.

"Albert, mon cher ami, how nice to see you here again, and la belle Elizabeth too."

"Gustave, I am astonished and humbled today to see your new painting *Les Raboteurs de Parquet* (The Floor Strippers). I am stunned by it but I am also in awe of its stark beauty: Those men on their knees, stripping paint off wood floors, now that makes me understand *Impressionisme* properly! I wonder whether I have any talent remotely like yours and other painters."

"It takes time: Work hard, play with ideas, and above all study other painters. Have you seen Berthe Morisot's piece at the Exhibition?"

"No, we hope to attend later in the week," Albert replied.

"You must go as you will be very surprised."

"Surprised, how? Has one of my daubs somehow inserted itself on to the walls?" said Albert laughing.

"No, but la petite fille Elizabeth is there."

"How am I there?" Asked Elizabeth, her curiosity tinged with alarm.

"Do not be alarmed, ma chère Elizabeth, it is a tribute."

"What do you mean?"

"Berthe Morisot submitted her painting *Jeune fille au bal,* a sumptuous painting of a young woman at a ball, her hair in the fashion, her fan and her dress painted with such finesse."

"How lovely," said Elizabeth, "we must see it."

"It is you."

"Me?" said Elizabeth, shocked and surprised.

"I noticed her sketching you a long time ago here in this Café, soon after the War I think. You two were both here, absorbed in each other. She has put your face into this dazzling painting. Of course, you did not pose for her, but she has captured your likeness with brilliance."

The couple rushed to the Exhibition the next day, and there she was. Of course, Elizabeth had never owned such a beautiful dress as Morisot clad her in, but she was immensely flattered as

Morisot had captured the way she held her head and her whole countenance with astounding skill and artistry.

They were both thrilled by the painting and lovers that they were, they enjoyed all that Paris had to offer, not merely café life. They ventured out too, once taking the train to Chartres for a weekend to admire the cathedral, but they enjoyed regular wanderings through the boulevards, parks and gardens of Paris often stopping to watch men restoring buildings damaged in the war.

As time passed, however, Elizabeth became disappointed that such times spent together became less frequent as Albert got more preoccupied with his painting. However, one afternoon they were strolling along the river just opposite the Cathedral of Notre Dame enjoying the late Spring when they met Monty Fortescue and his wife who said:

"Albert, how good to see you. Oh, and Miss Fitzroy, how very good to see you both. This is my wife Felicity. I was alarmed when you struggled into the Embassy wounded and apparently blind on that fateful day now years ago. How are you, Albert?"

"I am well, thank you. My sight is not perfect and I do now have some vision in the eye which, as a struggling artist, I value greatly. My leg is completely healed."

"How about you? Is Lord Lyons still the Ambassador?"

"Yes indeed and as outspoken as ever."

"Miss Fitzroy, I am sorry, I should have expressed my condolences on your father's death, two or three years ago now. He was a very good diplomat and such a nice man."

"Thank you, Mr. Fortescue, that is most kind. We miss him greatly."

"And so do we in the Diplomatic Service. Life is very complicated in the aftermath of the war with the Thiers Government, but in our foreign relations, especially with this new Germany. But forget all that.

"There is to be a great party at the Embassy to celebrate our full restoration in facilities and staff after the War. I have an idea Lyons wants to make it an annual event. I can certainly make sure you are both invited."

"That is most generous, Monty, and might my step-mother, Estella Pirrip, come too?"

"I am sure I can get here an invitation. Is she in Paris?"

"No, but I anticipate her decision to come for the summer shortly. Her address is 29, New Queen Street, St. James, London. She lives with Henry Fitzroy's sister, Mrs. Charlotte Mudge."

"They must both be invited. The gardens could hold a regiment! Let me make a note of the names and addresses, and an ambassadorial invitation will hasten their arrival," he said pulling out a small pocket-book and a tiny pencil which he drew from a small gold case shaped like an owl.

"I am sure they will be thrilled," said Elizabeth, "our profound thanks, Mr. Fortescue."

They parted company and Elizabeth expressed her delight at going to the Embassy again, especially now that it had all been refurbished. Albert too was especially pleased, knowing that the invitation would certainly bring Estella to Paris. He missed her. She had been so solicitous for him that he had come to regard her as his mother, given her devotion to his father and the fact that he could scarcely remember his natural mother.

"You had started to tell me about your visit yesterday to Carolus-Duran's studio before we met the Fortescues," said Elizabeth, "pray go on."

"I don't know whether I will be able to work there, but there are some impressive people there who are not French, mainly English or American. One young man, a bit older than me, is a superb draughtsman from what I was able to see, name of John Sargent.

"The studio is a wonderful setting, a very large room, beset with easels, brushes, scalpel knives and paint, paintings and frames, and various painters at work, all waiting for the great man to comment on their work. I have nothing much yet to show him, though I am thinking of trying to paint from my imagination, such as the whores in the Jaggers Building."

"Can you do that?"

"I'd prefer to sketch it first, but I can imagine it."

"Have Estella describe it to you."

"A good idea. We should invite John and one or two of the others to eat with us, and of course Caillebotte and perhaps our jeweler friend, Nimrod Klein. The painters are going on a sketching expedition soon, but I was not asked, though I would have loved to go."

"Might we invite them for lunch and have a picnic, perhaps in the Bois?"

"Excellent, but we must wait until Estella arrives and the Embassy party is over."

"Will she want to meet all these young men and their lady friends?"

"I am sure she will, especially if the women painters are active; like you they have an interest which they follow, not something their husbands allow them to do."

"How interesting your step-mother is. I do so wish I knew her better. We've met, of course, mainly in Cheyne Row, and once or twice at Semper House, but I have not been to your new home in St. James yet."

"Estella is quite unique.

"I don't think I have ever told you that she had an affair at her country house with a young woman, Nellie Fletcher she is called, who poured out her compassion and sympathy to Estella such that they became lovers."

"That is actually quite lovely, if dreadfully unconventional."

"It is, and at the same time it is a clue to her character. She is very generous, very kind, very loving, not merely to me, but it shines through her philanthropic work. My father told me the detail of her upbringing and when a young woman, she had been brought up to hate men. She was haughty, cold, sarcastic, mean and miserable in her early life.

"While my father was in part an agent of this change, it was her mother who effected it, notwithstanding the fact that her mother had murdered not only a woman who her husband had left her for, but she brought about the death of her younger brother, also out of jealousy."

"Goodness me," cried Elizabeth, stopping their walk and holding Albert's shoulder and looking into his eyes, "Estella's mother was a murderer? What a catastrophe!"

"Not so, as it turned out, for that mother spent five or six years later showering maternal love on Estella which awakened her to life without the dreadful carapace her guardian had thrown over her."

"So her success in life is a triumph over terrible adversity, though she was not poor."

"Exactly. She is an original woman, and I very much hope she will spend some time here in Paris so you can get to know her much better. If all goes well, perhaps we might have an apartment or a house together."

"That would be lovely, and even better if my aunt Charlotte accepts the invitation."

Back in New Queen Street a few days later, two large official envelopes arrived among letters from France. Inside the first to be opened was a gold embossed invitation to The Honorable Charlotte Mudge from Her Britannic Majesty's Ambassador to the Republic of France requesting her presence at a soiree in celebration of the restoration of the Embassy to be held on July 14, 1875. Opening her envelope, Charlotte screamed with delight.

"Estella, how marvelous. Look! An invitation to the Embassy. Let us sit and contemplate, my dear."

"How exciting, Charlotte and here is mine too. There's also a note from Albert," she said quickly scanning the letter, "saying he met a young diplomat he knew from his accident and he was the source of these invitations. Elizabeth is well but is looking for a new piano tutor. They hope we will spend all the summer in Paris and they are planning to have a picnic with young painters and others they know, so we should expect to have a gay time.

"Tomorrow we must get new clothes and I suggest we book our passages as soon as possible. We must be in Paris well before the

Embassy occasion, and I would like to spend the whole summer there, though I will miss Numquam."

"As would I but I am ready to enjoy something quite different to England for a while."

Hamish and Clarence were pondering the fate of the mollies early one morning after another killing near the Semper House Home was reported but this time it was been the result of a fight over territory. Clarence was intrigued, but Hamish was getting sick and tired of talk about these rent-boys whom he viewed with profound disgust. Of course, he understood how some of them were poverty-stricken orphans, or that they had been brutalized like Masham, but for many of them he showed little patience and less interest.

Robert came into the office with a wire from Australia.

"Ah," said Hamish as he opened it, "I expect to hear our brave boys have been tackling the Brisbane lawyers," and he laughed sarcastically.

"It is certainly time we heard something. It's now June and they left in April. Perhaps that wire gives us more than they have arrived," said Clarence.

"More indeed. Ezekiel Unworthy has now died," said Hamish reading the wire.

"More than that it does not say, not even whether Angharad has been informed. At least that should make the position clear for her assuming his will has not been tampered with. I should go to Wales immediately. We have her address, don't we?"

"Yes, I hope you can pronounce it," said Clarence, "I have it here in my bag, but Welsh seems to have no vowels. Look, it is spelt Y-n-y-s-b-w-l Farm, Ogmore Vale. I have no idea how to pronounce it."

"She did say it to me. The Y is like an I or an A; here the Y is pronounced as an A and the W as a U. So it is like Inisabull Farm: Very odd, but I must be on my way directly. I'll find it.

"Robert," he called out, "take this message to Mrs. Macdonald in Walworth in a cab and wait for the bag she gives you and bring it to me at Paddington Station."

It was a long journey. The Severn Tunnel construction had been going on for four years, but trains could only get to South Wales by a railway bridge built further north after which the idea of a tunnel was contemplated. He arrived at Cardiff Station in the late afternoon and had a cab taken him the few miles down to Ogmore Vale. Once there, the cabbie had no difficulty in understanding the name of the farm and within a half hour, Hamish was knocking at the door.

"Who the hell are you?" demanded a large burly man with an enormous white beard and startling blue eyes, obviously Angharad's father, and with an aggression that startled Hamish.

"I am Hamish Macdonald, Mrs. Unworthy's lawyer from London."

"Why didn't you say so, then? Come to the kitchen: Have you got news?"

"Yes, but where is Mrs. Unworthy?"

"Angharad," he shouted with a voice like a trombone, "your lawyer's here."

She came hurriedly into the room drying her hands on her apron, and her mother known to all as Mam Jones followed with a gaggle of small children.

"I have come straight from London, Mrs. Unworthy. We had a wire to say that your husband has died."

"Yes, well, I thought he would, see. Best for him really. To be honest, he had no future, did he? Bless him. I'm glad really for him and for us. I mean I thought it would come..." at which her stoicism snapped and she began to howl a long lament of words and tears which triggered tears from everyone, except Farmer Jones and Hamish.

"Let's leave this bloody cacophony," said the farmer, "come to the parlor and have a drink, boyo. We've got a spare bed somewhere, you won't be going back to London tonight now, will you?"

"That is very kind. I plan to go back to Cardiff to a hotel, but I do need to talk with Mrs. Unworthy tomorrow."

"We're going to sup soon; I am sure Mother has it ready. Let this calm down a bit, first."

"Now, tell me," said the Farmer, lighting his pipe as they sat alone in comfort each with a glass of ale, "is my daughter going to be rich?"

"Why do you ask?"

"Well, she doesn't say much about her money, you know, though I expect she has a bob or two packed away."

"My difficulty, Mr. Jones, is that I am her lawyer and as such I cannot say anything about her affairs to anyone without her express permission. She may not want you to know."

"I don't see why, she's my flesh and blood, you know."

"But the conventions of the law are very precise about such matters. It is a matter of client confidentiality."

"What's that you say, confidentiality? Let me tell you, boyo, it was not bloody confidentiality when I sat up all night feeding her when she was a baby as her mother was sick with her: Nor was it bloody confidentiality when I picked her out of the pond when she was four, I tell you, because her brother pushed her in, now, was it? It wasn't bloody confidentiality when I chased that boy Owen away from her, now was it?"

The crescendo in his voice was such that his wife and Angharad came rushing into the parlor.

"Now, what's going on here, Dai Jones," said Mrs. Jones, "why are you shouting like that?"

"He won't tell me about Angharad's money, says it's about bloody confidentiality, my own daughter, her that I have loved since a baby, her that I have rescued from drowning, her that I gave away to a brute of an Australian. To think, Angharad, that it should have come to this."

"Come to what, Father?"

"Now you look here, my girl. This fancy Scotsman lawyer here, whatever his name is, tells me he cannot tell me, your father, about your money because of some bloody confidentiality."

"Well, he's right," said Angharad, "I don't want you poking your nose into my affairs. God knows I had enough of that before Ezekiel arrived here. You was always wanting to know what I was doing with young Owen up at Ferndale Farm. None of your business then and none of your business, now."

"I knew then, see, what the Preacher at Ebenezer Chapel warned us about: There was an outbreak of fornication and sexual intercourse in Ystradgynlais and it spread down here to the Vale, you know and you caught it. You were a slag, my own daughter."

"You don't know nothing about Owen and me. It was just your dirty mind, like all those deacons up at Chapel. They only have to see a pretty girl and they want her but because they can't have her, they use God and all that to prevent her enjoying herself."

"That's enough," shouted Mr. Jones, "I'll hear no more about it. But I want to know how much money you have."

"Well I am not telling you, and I am telling Mr. Macdonald here not to tell you under any circumstances or you'll be after telling me how to spend it."

"Imagine, Mother," he said, turning to his wife, "that a daughter of mine should be so cruel, so unfriendly, so nasty after all I have done for her."

"Oh, Dai my dear man," said Mrs. Jones, "leave her be, she'll tell you when she wants to. She's a grown woman now with children of her own, and a widow too."

"She's to leave this house with her children as soon as possible."

"No, Dai, she stays."

"She goes or I go," he said, angrily.

"Don't be daft, Dai. Just you go now and show Mr. Macdonald his room."

The following morning, after a Welsh breakfast that would test the strength of twenty men by its volume, Hamish struggled to get a moment with Angharad alone, even though Farmer Jones was long gone out to his sheep. Each time he'd eaten eggs and sausages, numerous rashers of bacon and several potatoes, Mam Jones would urge him to eat more which he declined only to be answered with a typical Welsh challenge: "You didn't like it, then?"

"Well, I loved it, but give me another sausage."

"Only one? Homemade, you know."

Finally with a huge mug of tea, he was able to get Angharad into the parlor, the traditional Welsh room for celebrations like funerals, and sat down with her at the table. The loss of her husband seemed to make her quite tranquil and Hamish thought that she is really quite attractive and won't long be a widow.

"Oh, Mr. Macdonald, I am so grateful you come all this way to tell me," she said, her Welsh accent now not sullied with Australian tones and figures of speech.

"Not at all. What are your general intentions? Do I understand it like this? You want to sell all your husband's property and transfer the results of the sale to you here in Wales?

"Yes."

"Right, I made out this letter of instruction to *Courtisone and Jaggers* for you to sign and for me to take back to London. I will need the name of your bank here, too."

"I don't have a bank here in Wales, just that Coutts place in London which Ezekiel started with."

"Gracious, but you said you had five thousand pounds with you!"

"I do, but it is all in notes and sovereigns."

"Right, you must come with me to Cardiff this morning and put that money in The Bank of Wales, retaining enough for your present needs. When the sales are affected in Australia you will then have an account to receive the money, and whatever money is in Coutts can come to the Bank of Wales too. When you need more cash, you go to the Bank and withdraw it."

"I never had a back account myself so I will have to learn, won't I? Will you teach me?"

Ignoring that invitation, Hamish said, "the second matter is Gareth. I understand he has three hundred acres of his own. I assume that the will is as you said."

"Yes, I have the original here. I took it from his box, see, before I left, in case it got lost."

"Very wise of you. I think you can entrust the will to us. You will have it back once the sales are done. But would you like Gareth to have money, or more land, from your property?"

"I'd really like him to come home."

"Right, so no instructions on Gareth then."

"That is all. Let us prepare to go to the Bank now."

"Right."

They took the Jones' trap to the village where they found a small cab to take them to Cardiff. On the way, Angharad sat close to him, took his left hand and said how grateful she was to him and how nice it was to have such a good man caring for her.

Hamish was relieved the journey was quite short as he thought her friendly smiles might be the beginning of something else she had in mind, especially as she had started to caress his thigh, but her blandishments ceased when they arrived at the Bank, a stone monument of a building in Queen Street.

Honora had been upset by the problem but saw no way out but to confront it. Early one evening she returned home to see Alice coming down the stairs.

"Alice, I need to talk with you."

"Yes, ma'am."

"Do you have a male friend you meet on your afternoon in town?"

"Oh, no, Ma'am, I wouldn't do that."

Honora was slightly shocked by this reply.

"No, I asked whether you had a male friend at all, not what you might do with him."

"Sorry, Ma'am, yes, me and Susie do talk with the young men in the park and we are all very friendly."

"Good, I am glad of that, but I am concerned at some of your flirtatious behavior with my sons. They are at least two years younger than you, though they may not look it. Being young, they may not yet know how to handle advances which they probably do not want."

"No ma'am, I would not dream of trying to get attention from them."

"Then you must stop your goings-on. You must not seek every moment to put yourself in their way. Why were you upstairs just now, while I was out? I assume the boys are studying in their rooms. Did you go into one of them with some excuse?"

At this, Alice began to blush deeply and frown at Honora's implication.

"Yes, ma'am, I remembered that I'd not done a washbasin this morning."

"You mean, you did not complete your work this morning so that you could return when the boy was in there. Which boy was it, by the way?"

"It was Jude, Ma'am."

"Alice, I am not anxious to have this household muddled by inappropriate relationships or for there to be a fog concealing what is going on, so I will give you this one final warning. If I see the slightest hint that you are continuing to put yourself out for either boy, I will have to ask you to leave. If you are not happy to do that, then you can give me your notice and I will give you two weeks' wages now so that you will leave the house this instant."

"I will try, ma'am, but I am very sweet on Jude. He's such a lovely boy."

"Stop there, Alice. That is enough. Pack your things and come down to collect your wages. I can see that any possibility of you restraining your behavior looks impossible. I know a young woman needs to think about a young man, but this is inappropriate and undesirable."

"Oh, please ma'am, I loves working here and I've nowhere to go, Ma'am. I don't know what I'd do."

"All right, perhaps I am being too hasty," said Honora, now quite flustered by going further than she intended: "One more week and we will see how you behave. But just remember, mind, any sign you are flirting with either of my boys and out you go."

Alice left and Honora went upstairs to find her children. They were sprawled out in Jude's bedroom, Simon on the floor reading, and Jude at his desk writing.

"You both look occupied, I can see."

"If the rain would stop, we'd be outside on the river."

"Yes, I am pleased you're rowing, but do be careful, won't you.

"Now I have something important to discuss. What do you think of Alice, the maid?"

"She's very pretty," said Jude.

"She seems to work very hard," said Simon.

"Does she talk to either of you?"

"Not really," said Jude, "though she is always smiling at me which I like."

"I need to say some things to you both. First, you are both my most beautiful boys and I am so proud of you and the miracle that brought you back to me. We want you to grow up over the next few years, perhaps going to a university, getting an excellent position of some kind. Being able to marry someone you love means that you must wait until that someone appears in your life, and you must keep yourself pure and chaste to await that person."

"We have been told about going to university at school," Simon said, "and our tutors think we should do that."

"Excellent, but you have a challenge. In the next few years, there will be all sorts of women, not just like Alice, to whom you feel an attraction, and I do not mean just Alice, but girls you will meet as you grow older. The very important task is not to spoil yourself for the right woman whom you will find. I want you both to protect yourselves against women who will be forward with you."

"Do you mean they will want to kiss you?" Said Jude. "There was a girl in the orphanage who wanted to kiss me all the time, and it was jolly hard not to."

"Oh," said Simon, "do you mean that Susan with the long brown hair?"

"Yes, and I did kiss her once, and I might have gone on meeting her in secret if we hadn't come to Mother, and I suppose we might have gone further."

"Gone further? How do you mean?"

"Oh, Mother," said Jude in a patronizing tone, "you must know what I mean, undressing and linking up your body with hers."

"Goodness me, where did you find out about that?"

"There was this boy, Cyril, a bit older than us, who said he had done it with a girl."

"What?" said Honora, realizing that this was deep water she had not expected to find herself in.

"We didn't believe him, did we, Simon? It seemed quite a disgusting thing to do to a girl, but Cyril said she enjoyed it too."

Honora took a deep breath, and said:

"So you know about how men and women couple to produce a baby."

"Yes, Mother," said Simon, "we learnt all about that at St Deniol's, not from the supervisors, but from the other boys."

"Now look, Jude, Alice is precisely the sort of temptation that you must steel yourself against. As you said, one thing could lead to another, and you'd find yourself in great difficulty. I have told Alice I will let her go if her behavior to you both does not change."

"Don't worry on my account, Mother," said Jude.

She hoped not.

VI

Honora went back downstairs, thinking she must tell Frederick of this encounter and also talk with her friends about it. She sat in her drawing-room gazing out of the window, recalling once again the terrible night that altered her life. There they were as she walked among the plane trees, nice-looking, friendly as they usually were, until.

Even though she was now deliriously happy with her beautiful daughter, her delightful surprise at her conception and her enjoyment of the intimacy with Frederick, her mind could not escape the terrible past where those two men were like devils, with not a morsel of concern for her, just a depraved lust, enhanced by the competition between them.

She got up from her chair, the color draining from her face, and tears coming to her eyes.

They must have competed, each trying to outdo the other in brutality. And when they turned her over, oh God! Yet her beautiful boys were its outcome. Which twins was the father, or could they each have fathered one? Was that possible? Could her boys possibly inherit some of the callous, inhuman, vicious violence that had been perpetrated on her? Might they even be politer versions of it, becoming manipulative, devious, controlling husbands or lovers? Violence in a sympathetic cloak? What to do?

Try as she could, she would never be able to put such thoughts out of her mind. That evening, however, she managed to avoid detailed discussion on the Alice situation with Frederick but instead raised the issue of paternity.

"You were absolutely correct to make certain they knew how things are with women," said Frederick, "but perhaps I should eventually tell them about their father?"

"I think I have to do that, but I want to wait until they are older, perhaps in university."

"I have always urged caution and delay," said Frederick, "and I do really think it is you who should tell them and choose the moment. I am merely offering to tell them."

"I know, darling, but this is such a different matter from telling a child he or she was adopted. I would be telling two fourteen-year-olds that their natural father was a criminal villain, a foreigner who had violated their mother in unspeakable ways."

"You will need to be certain that the time is ripe when you do it. Be sure you are also not wanting just to share your distress at the memory rather than your anxiety about their not knowing their paternity. How would you feel after you have told them, my dear, in contrast to how they might feel?"

"What a dilemma," she replied, "and one I must confront. Would you mind if I went to New Queen Street to talk to Estella?"

"No, my dear, she is the popular fount of wisdom," he said with a wry smile.

With Estella's advice about Alice in her mind, she hurried back the following day to catch Estella before she left for Paris. That lady had a criminal father, though he was a thief and a murderer, not a rapist as far as she knew. New Queen Street was in mild uproar as the packing for Paris was under way.

"I am sorry to share my burdens with you again, Estella, but I wanted so much to do that before you leave. Could you spare a moment?"

"Go ahead, my dear, whether my advice is valuable or not, I know not."

"Oh it is valuable, and my discussions with Alice and the boys cleared the air, and I discover that they know about all matters of the body from other children in the orphanage. But Estella, in talking to the boys about her, should I tell them about their father or fathers."

"But why? Surely that would be catastrophic for them."

"Maybe, but I wanted to talk about it with you because I know you discovered your father's identity when you met your mother. Is that right?"

"Yes it is, but I was a grown woman, a widow, and I was more concerned with my mother at the time, so I never thought deeply about my father Abel Magwitch. Pip told me of his encounters with him and, as he seemed a generous man for all his faults, even fathering that dreadful love-child, my half-brother, he was not an important part of my life. My mother talked to me about him a great deal, but he always seemed to me a figment of my imagination, partly because he lived such an extraordinary life."

"So he was never for you any kind of emotional tie such that, for instance, you were never interested in pursuing more detail about him than you had got from Pip and your mother."

"Indeed, no. Put it like this. Obviously I had a natural father, but I still see myself as father-less from an emotional point of view. Nor did it worry me, ever. When I was a child, Miss Havisham so dominated my life that the very notion of having a father was strange to me."

"I see. You said just now it would be catastrophic to tell the boys: What did you mean?"

"They cannot possibly be mature enough to understand the reality of what happened to you. They obviously have come to love you profoundly and the idea that they are themselves the product of that violence may scar them dreadfully. You have no idea, nor have I, as to how they will react to this revelation. They may feel ashamed by their own existence, don't you think?"

"That is possible certainly and an outcome I had not considered, though Frederick did mention something of the sort, but I am sure my love will be able to combat that."

"I would not be confident of that, yet. Put yourself in a similar context, say, when you were fourteen years old. You are naturally a happy child, whose life has suddenly gone through an extraordinary transformation so that you are now very happy indeed.

"Then the mother you love comes to you and tells you that you arrived in the world as the result of a most brutal attack on her. In your veins runs the blood not only of a rapist, but also a murderer. For you know it won't be enough to tell them about what happened to you, for they will want to know what happened to him – or them."

"Oh dear me, of course that is true: It would become a quagmire."

"The fact is, my dear, that the urge to pursue the truth has to be tempered with the consequences of telling it. My advice to you would be to avoid the topic consistently, to dissemble if they ask questions, which I doubt that they will.

"To be sure, as adults, even fathers themselves, they may want to know more about their father, but even then you may decide to say simply that you had this brief relationship on your visit to Lourdes, and then blame yourself indicating that you had no intention of marrying him anyway."

"So, if asked, I should simply accept a vague responsibility for their conception?"

"Indeed, I'd think some more about putting myself in their shoes. What would it be like to be told, at this stage of one's life, the truth not just about who your father was, itself disputable, but just how terrible was your conception, an act of hatred and lust, so disgusting, so detestable, so abhorrent, that you cannot but take on the guilt and the shame which brought you into the world?

"My dear, telling them will damage severely your relationship with them. Put it on one side for many years.

"And now I must let you go as I have so much to do."

That evening after the family had dinner, the Brandram family retreated to their drawing-room where Jude played the piano and with Simon sang a few popular songs including their favorites, *Bobby Shafto's gone to Sea, Widdecome Fair,* each singing a verse in turn which delighted their parents, Frederick joining in when he knew the words.

As the twins kissed their mother and shook hands with their new father and wished them both good night, Honora felt so proud and so loving that she saw now very clearly that she could not do anything that would in any way risk damaging that love. She told Frederick of her conversation with Estella, at which he remarked on her sensitivity and wisdom.

She had finally realized that the urge to tell was in truth an urge to share her hurt with them. That would yield God knows what.

She resolved never to tell them, ever.

On July 14, 1875, the weather in Paris was delightful. Carriages were lining up in the Rue du Faubourg and elegantly clad men and women were walking on marble floors through the Embassy's carved oak doors into the main entrance hall, with its large portrait of the Royal Family, a single larger portrait of the Queen and a bust of the Duke of Wellington. From the Hall they were guided through the building to the French windows and into the garden, now in full bloom under full sunshine, its two large oak trees that had survived the turbulent years of their growth providing some shade. Liveried servants attended and escorted each group of guests to the Chamberlain who announced their names to Lord and Lady Lyons, the Ambassador and his lady. Standing with them was the Prince of Wales who had come from Windsor to Paris for this occasion and who never missed a chance to get out of England and his royal mother's constant oversight.

Charlotte, Elizabeth and Albert, and Estella moved slowly along the line in this order. Charlotte was introduced to the Prince as The Honorable Charlotte Mudge, and Miss Elizabeth Fitzroy.

"Mrs. Mudge, indeed; Are you not a sister of my shooting chum, Freddie Camberley?

"Yes, I am, sir, and this is my niece, Elizabeth Fitzroy."

The Prince then shook hands with Elizabeth, giving a keen look at such a lovely young woman, but turned back to Charlotte.

"Freddie and I take it in turns. He comes to shoot at Sandringham and then I go to Wymondham. He's a splendid fellow."

"But we are holding up our visitors," he continued, and indeed Lady Lyons appeared a little upset by the delay in the line occasioned by the Prince's brief conversation with Charlotte. Albert bowed, and Estella had only a handshake to which she responded with a curtsey, though none of them was flustered at this royal attention. Monty Fortescue, the diplomat and Albert's acquaintance moved to greet them.

"I say, Albert, you all made a good impression there."

"Not at all Monty, it was Elizabeth and her aunt who are related to one of the Prince's shooting friends in Norfolk."

After introductions, Monty pulled Albert aside.

"Between ourselves, I have been commissioned to look after a Parisian actress of dubious reputation but who is here at the Prince's express wish. Let me take you around to meet her. She is quite *une belle dame*, I tell you."

"Who is she?"

"Mademoiselle Hortense Schneider."

"Great Scot! I saw her in *La Belle Hélène*, immense fun, before the war. Caillebotte took me."

They walked through French windows across the lawn to where Mme. Schneider, now in her forties, was surrounded by men anxious to admire her beautiful broad face, deep brown eyes, and, as befits a singer of operetta, her substantial bosom, with a very fine silk dress that could be mistaken for a peignoir and an elegant hat with an ostrich feather. Both Monty and Albert were in frock coats with colorful cravats. Albert's eye was now free of its patch, still obviously the result of some blow or other but he cut a tall elegant handsome figure.

"Ah, Monty," she called out in her French accent, "who is zis beautiful young man you are bringing to me?"

"This is Albert Pirrip, Mademoiselle."

"Ah, Albert after the Prince's father, I'd believe. A wonderful man. To judge by his numerous children, he must 'ave been a great lover, but his death was *un mort tragique*, I think. But, beautiful young man, do you 'ave a lover?" she asked, much to the amusement of the small group of men clinging to her every word.

Albert blushed very deeply, but found the wit to say:

"*Quand à Paris, faites comme les Parisiens,*" (When in Paris, do what Parisians do) at which Mme. Schneider laughed very loudly and said:

"That is so very funny, and for an Englishman too!

"Monty, you may leave me now as I will have Albert here to care for me."

"Albert," whispered Monty, "do not let her out of your sight."

So Albert felt somewhat commandeered, but this was a woman he had admired on the stage. He soon lost sight of Monty, Elizabeth, Charlotte and Estella as Mme. Schneider walked him across the lawn rather hastily, rarely in conversation together as so many guests came up to her, expressing their delight at her talent in the opera, asking why she had not been invited to sing, and when was Offenbach going to write something new for her.

"Ah," she said to several enquirers, "Jacques now lives in Vienna or London for his work has been regarded as frivolous and not for prudish republican Frenchmen. He was more popular under the Emperor."

As her admirers thinned, it was apparent that she was gradually leading Albert to a more deserted part of the garden. She turned to him resting her arm on his, saying:

"Don't you think that making love is the most wonderful thing in the world? It makes me feel quite new each time, especially some-one new to me. You should take many lovers, Albert."

"Oh, I have my Elizabeth so I am disinclined to find others."

"Nonsense, and she should too. Now, I have not been married, so I do not know of the ties that bind, as they say, but being free is such fun.

"In fact, I am very pleased indeed that you were brought to me as I was then able to stop being looked after by that Monty, who is, how do you say in English, a bore? I can now follow my new secret lover who has come all the way from England to see me. Are you shocked?"

"Oh, no ma'am, *quand a Paris...*"

"Absolument, mon cher Albert," she said which terrified Albert for a moment as he thought that she was about to try to seduce him, especially as they were now in a part of the garden quite sheltered from the main party, walking toward a small summer house which was almost completely invisible from the Embassy building and from the guests. The blood started to course through his veins and his leg began to hurt viciously.

Then an immense surprise.

Giving him a peck on the cheek, she said quietly,

"You can leave me now and I hope you will find lots of lovers."

The door of the summer house was ajar and looking at her with a welcoming smile was the unmistakable figure of the Prince of Wales.

Albert turned around and, without hurrying, walked back to search for Elizabeth. Charlotte and Estella were in a group of women making small talk but searching the crowd he could not see her.

Elizabeth was miffed that Monty had given charge of that actress to Albert and she found herself rather bored with the company around her aunt, all of whom were merely interested in the fact that the Prince had taken an interest in her. She wandered back into the Embassy alone remembering the Music Room from the time she had played duets there with her father.

It was a room intended for small concerts, usually with a string quartet or a soloist, piano or strings, and the piano was indeed a beauty. Lord Lyons, like her father, was an accomplished pianist and he had ordered a sumptuous piano made by Carl Bechstein for the Embassy, delivered only in 1874. It was positioned near the French windows, presumably to give a pianist the natural light, the main body of the grand piano stretching into the room, which was empty apart from some furniture.

So she sat down and began play *Liebestraum* no. 3, a romantic rather than a classical composition, which she was enjoying after the emotional and technical rigors of Beethoven or Schubert sonatas, a gentle piece given the tempestuous nature of some of the composer's work, but the sound drifted along the Embassy corridors. One or two guests looked into the room and stayed, including a tall young man who sat in a corner.

When she finished this *Liebestraum,* as the audience had not grown, she embarked on the much more ambitious *Hungarian Rhapsody no 2.* She wondered whether the composer could play it himself, as parts of it were so difficult, though amusing with its rather military opening and its joyful dance themes connected by scales at a tempo that she found immensely difficult to get right. She persevered.

Shortly after she began this piece, a well-dressed woman came into the room and sat down on a gilded chair at some distance from the piano. When Elizabeth finished, she looked up find the woman smiling and walking towards her. She stopped and stood next to the piano.

"Beautiful, beautiful, Franz would have been delighted to hear your expression."

"Did you know him?"

"Know him? I was an intimate friend for several years in Weimar and we now write to each other regularly. Excuse me, I am Agnes Street-Klindworth and you are?"

"Elizabeth Fitzroy. My father used to be a diplomat here during the War, but he died two years ago on a posting in Athens."

"I am so sorry to hear that. Do you live in Paris now?"

"Yes, with my friend Albert."

"Oh, how modern and how sensible."

At that point Monty entered the room, but he could not see Elizabeth at the keyboard as his view of her was blocked by Agnes.

"Oh, there you are, Agnes," he said, "shall we get down to business?"

Agnes turned toward him so he could now see Elizabeth and his expression drained somewhat.

"I have been listening to this brilliant pianist playing my friend Franz's Rhapsody, and I was beginning to tell her about him."

"Oh, pardon my interruption indeed. Please, Elizabeth, play something for us."

By now the sounds of the piano had obviously attracted other visitors, but Elizabeth scarcely noted them as she started on Liszt's Etudes which, like the Rhapsody, her tutor had her learn by heart. There were perhaps two dozen men and women in the room as she finished. Albert had also been listening and came over to stand near her, and the young man from the corner joined them.

"That was exceptionally beautiful playing," he said.

"Thank you," said Elizabeth, "I am Elizabeth Fitzroy."

"How d'ye do, I am John Sargent."

"Very pleased to meet you, John, though I think I have seen you in the Café Guerbois. You sound almost American," said Elizabeth.

"Ah, yes, my parents are Americans and I suppose I am but I have never lived there, yet my intonations may come from them, I suppose."

"Are you in Paris long?"

"I live here, as do my parents. I am learning to paint at the Carolus-Duran studio."

"We have not been introduced," intervened Albert, "but I saw you recently outside the *Ecole Des Beaux-Arts*, you were talking with a group which included my friend Gustave Caillebotte, but I was too timid to join in."

"That was unwise, we are a great fraternity of young painters here at this moment. I assume you too are a painter, Albert, is that right?"

"Yes, I went to the Kensington School in London and have come here to try to attach myself to a studio."

"That can be a trial, but you should come to *Carolus-Duran*. Auguste is a splendid fellow and I am sure he'd be delighted."

"And what about you, Elizabeth," asked Sargent, "wait, I have seen you before, I know."

"I doubt it, John."

"Wait, I know, I know," he said excitedly, "you are the model for that lovely portrait of Berthe Morisot's, aren't you? Oh, my goodness, how brilliantly she has captured you. I have so much to learn."

"Thank you, thank you indeed. It was not really a portrait. She had sketched my face without my knowing and converted it into that painting. I am most flattered, and not at all put out."

"But your playing! Goodness me. Learning the piano, I suppose, though listening to you it does not seem as though you need much more training."

"I love the piano, but I am not sure I can be rigorous enough in practice to become a concert player."

"You must try, I think. We should find our talents and pursue them to the uttermost."

"Let us walk to the garden, Elizabeth," said Albert, "and take John if he is willing to meet with my step-mother and Elizabeth's aunt."

Introductions were made and Sargent looked admiringly at the two women.

"May I ask you both a question?"

"Of course," said Estella.

"Would you allow me to draw and perhaps paint your portraits? I am still learning how to do that but to be frank you both have very interesting faces which I would like to try to capture."

Estella and Charlotte looked at each other quizzically but Estella spoke first:

"I am an old woman, Mr. Sargent. You need to make portraits of beautiful young women, like Elizabeth, not old hags like me."

"I have to disagree, I'm afraid. I want to paint portraits to earn money at some juncture, but I just need practice. I have had the pleasure of listening to Elizabeth play the piano but being a shy fellow, I cannot dream of asking her until I have mastered further my art. I will ask her sometime in the future and have her seated at the piano as I first saw her today."

"That is once again very flattering, Mr. Sargent," said Elizabeth laughing, "but I must give that some very long-term thought."

"I must be off now," said Sargent.

"I know Albert will be coming to the studio I frequent, so you can think about my invitation and let him bring your answer there when you have considered it further. I have no idea how the portraits will turn out and I'd gladly give them to you when I have finished, though I will not be surprised if you will wish to hide them away in a garret."

With that, Mr. Sargent took his leave.

As he left, Charlotte was waylaid by an old London acquaintance and Estella stayed with her, half-listening and viewing the fashions in the crowd. Albert and Elizabeth walked silently across the lawns around in the direction of a bank of rhododendrons and they sat down quietly on a bench, holding hands.

"I had a very odd experience in the Music Room, Albert," and she told him of Agnes' arrival and Monty's comment as she came in.

"Business? I wonder what business, perhaps they are lovers?"

"Perhaps, but by his tone it sounded more clandestine."

Immediately they sat down they heard voices coming from the other side of the bush, instantly recognizable to Elizabeth as Agnes talking with Monty. She put her fingers to her lips for Albert to be quiet. It was difficult to catch what they said, clearly, except when she raised her voice.

"But I gave the papers to Bismarck personally," she said aggressively, "but he would not give you a single mark. What you sent he knew already, or rather that he had assumed this was the case, that an intervention in Turkey was contemplated and naval plans were being drawn up."

"But, Agnes," said Monty, "I risked my career to give you those papers. Do I not deserve some recompense?"

"Oh, my dear Monty, I would give you a few thousand marks, if I had it, but I don't. He is not giving you anything."

"I thought we had an understanding, and I am very disappointed in you, Agnes. Your reputation as an effective spy is compromised, like your father before you."

"But Monty, you are the spy. I am just the courier."

Albert and Elizabeth looked at each other in astonishment and got up quietly. They walked as silently as they could, but hurriedly and nervously across the lawn towards Estella and Charlotte, murmuring to each other about what seemed to be a very strange conversation.

"We should leave, I think," said Estella as they approached, "it is all winding down. A pity, I so love this garden, such a peaceful spot in Paris."

"An entertaining afternoon, though," said Charlotte, "and we did get royal recognition."

"I will tell you all about the Prince when we get home," said Albert.

Several minutes had passed as they all gathered themselves together to leave when a footman in livery hurriedly caught up with them as they got near to the gates.

"Excuse me, Mr. Pirrip, Miss Fitzroy, the Head of Chancery would value a private word. Please walk this way."

"We will await your return here," said Estella, looking at Charlotte with surprise and moving to the shade of a huge oak tree.

Albert and Elizabeth followed their guide through the marble Hall and into the administrative quarters of the Embassy.

"Come in and please sit down. I am Richard Harvey, Head of Chancery, and I want to ask you both some questions. Let me get straight to the point.

"Miss Fitzroy, you had occasion while you were playing the piano to meet Miss Street-Klindworth, am I right?"

"Yes."

"You will not know this but both she and her father are international spies, quite unconcerned whom they work for. We have watched her while she is in Paris, and though she is formally English, she is out of reach of English Law, even if she had committed any crime."

"Goodness me," said Elizabeth, "she was perfectly pleasant to me and she said she knew Franz Liszt very well."

"Yes, she spent two years in Weimar and we think he was her lover. She had two boys when she was in Weimar, though she was unmarried, but neither of the two have claimed his parentage. We intercept their letters from time to time.

"But Mr. Pirrip, perhaps you will tell me whether you heard their conversation in the garden. Our men were watching them and they saw you the other side of the shrubbery."

"To be frank, Sir Richard, we were rather shocked. Mr. Fortescue was complaining about not being paid for delivery of papers through her to Bismarck."

"Are you absolutely sure of this?"

"Elizabeth," said Albert, "have I got that right?"

"Yes, indeed. She said she was the courier and Bismarck said he knew already about, what was it, some kind of intervention in Turkey."

"I see," said Sir Richard.

"By talking to me you are now sworn to secrecy about this conversation and about your listening to this couple. If you were to spread your knowledge of their conversation, you will both be prosecuted. Mr. Fortescue is clearly an agent while working here, probably for money as we are sure he has gambling debts.

"The law will now take its course though, in cases of this kind, it will not be public but treated as an internal affair for the Foreign Office. You may be required in London to give evidence at some point, though we have built up a large file on Mr. Fortescue. Sadly, I should say.

"But I am most grateful on behalf of Her Majesty's Government for your assistance in this matter. We will not proceed with any indictments on the Street-Klindworth woman, we will just watch her carefully and see where else she might lead."

Albert and Elizabeth walked silently out of the Embassy and joined Charlotte and Estella waiting for their carriage. A carriage passed them bearing the royal coat of arms and there seemed to be two people inside.

"What was that about?" asked Charlotte as they drove away from the Embassy.

"I am afraid, Aunt, we cannot tell you. We have been sworn to secrecy."

"I am sure we can just say this," said Elizabeth, "it was a little matter of treason."

"Great heavens, now you must tell us."

"I am afraid we cannot: We are under an oath, not that we actually swore one, but we gave our word."

"That is certainly enough for both of you," said Estella, "I have only just arrived and all this excitement, royalty and now treason."

"Much more to come, Estella," said Albert. "Let us go to the *Café des Anglais* for an aperitif and dinner."

"Certainly, Estella replied, "and you will be my guests."

"So," said Charlotte as they sat down, "why did Monty palm that big woman off on you, Albert?"

"I thought she was trying to seduce me at first. She is a well-known operetta singer, Offenbach mostly. I did not know where we were headed, but as we approached the summer house, she said goodbye and the door was opened by the Prince of Wales."

"Interesting," said Estella, "what a relief! Now we can believe all the rumors about him!"

VII

Hamish felt rushed off his feet, especially in dealing with the Unworthy woman, but that was all in the process of being settled. She'd sent a message saying how grateful she was and if he could come to Cardiff soon she wanted to make a new will for, as she put it, I am going to be a rich woman. He was not keen to go, but to spend a long day on a train going to and from Cardiff would be something of a relaxation.

In fact, he thought, why don't Mary and James come too?

Mary was thrilled as she rarely went on a train and, indeed with her withered arm she did not go out much except with Hamish, unless it were in a carriage to the home of a friend, for there were always possible incidents or accidents if she went far from their Walworth home. She limited herself to a brief daily walk with James up to the church and back before sitting and playing with him in the garden.

Hamish decided that they would travel first-class as Angharad would be paying for the fares when he sent her the lawyer's bill. It was very comfortable indeed and there was no one else to talk to in their compartment.

"You have been so busy, this is a real treat," said Mary, "I must know everything about this woman."

"Briefly then, she is the widow of an Australian man, Ezekiel Unworthy, whose half-sister is Estella. Their father was this convict of legend, Abel Magwitch, who was Old Pip's benefactor and Estella's father. This Australian came to England to search for his father, and ten years later arrived with his wife and some of his children, anxious to extend his investments in England.

"But Old Pip found out he was using slave labor. I had just arrived in the practice but sat in on this discussion which, when the slavery was revealed, Estella tore him limb from limb. It was an extraordinary display and, as I said at the time, she should really be at the Bar."

"Ah yes, I do remember you telling me part of this when we were in Scotland making up our minds about marrying. It should be interesting to meet this Welsh widow."

"She may be a widow, but she is still quite handsome and a bit of a flirt."

"Oh, that is why you wanted me to come," she said, laughing.

"Well, perhaps partly… to be honest."

"I should hope you're always honest with me, my dear."

"Oh, I am. I was just practicing using the phrase 'to be honest' which seems to appear so regularly in conversation with the Welsh, as you will see."

"Let me be serious for a moment, my dear Hamish," she said as James gurgled on her knee, gripped firmly by her right hand. "I am so happy with our marriage. Are you still attracted by men?"

"I suppose not, though I have not met anyone with whom I really want to have a relationship. I told you, didn't I, about my discussion with Philip Hardyman?"

"You did, yes. I was grateful for your confidence. We are now intimate much more often than I expected and I suspect I will be pregnant again if we continue. I want to know whether that would be an excitement for you or another responsibility you really do not want."

"Oh, Mary, I would love to have another child to enjoy, especially were it to be a daughter."

"You do realize that I will need you much more if we have two children. For several years until they are independent, the three of us will require any spare time you have. With this arm I cannot manage on my own."

"I appreciate that."

"That will mean no dallying around with men friends," she said smiling, "there will simply be no time. We have agreed we don't want nannies; we want to bring up or own children."

"Look, my dearest. I am not sure what has happened to me, but I do feel much less need of a man now that we have such a wonderful marriage. I find our intimacy relaxing and enjoyable and to be honest," he said laughing, "you really are a beautiful woman and a wonderful wife and mother. I always desired a loving and exclusive intimacy and I have found that treasure with you, although I thought in my youth it would be with a man."

Quite unlike her, Mary burst into tears and as he picked up James from her, she put her right arm around him, and they kissed fervently which clearly met with James's approval as the gurgling seemed to change to a giggle. Quite soon, they were hurrying through Wiltshire and Gloucestershire and then rattled across the border and arrived in Cardiff. They walked into the Grand Hotel in time for dinner. There was a message from Angharad to say that she had decided to come and spend the night in the hotel and that she would be glad to meet Hamish for dinner if he arrived early enough.

Hamish showed Mary the message and she laughed.

"I see what you mean," she said, "I can't wait to meet this Welsh witch!"

"Oh, she's not like that."

The following morning Angharad was at her table having breakfast when Hamish walked in with Mary and with James in his arms.

"Good morning, Angharad, meet my wife Mary and our lovely son James."

"Pleased to meet you, Mrs. Macdonald, and what a lovely boy, isn't he? My boys was all lovely too, until they got older when they were little terrors, but we got some sense into them. Oh, look at him now! I could eat him! To be honest, I wish I'd had more girls."

Hamish and Mary smiled at each other at her strange expressions, Welsh no doubt.

"Angharad, we will let you finish your breakfast; we'll have ours, and I will meet with you in the foyer in, say, a half hour."

"Oh," she said, as she left the table, "would you like to come to my room, it will be more private?"

Hamish blanched a little looking at Mary but he agreed, much to his wife's amusement.

When they finished breakfast, Mary took James for a short walk outside the hotel while Hamish went to Angharad's room. She had taken off her morning dress and had a satin gown draped around her.

"I'm going to have a bath when we are done," she said, "you don't mind my preparing for that, do you? I thought you, being a broad-minded lawyer, wouldn't mind."

Hamish blushed and sat down at a small table.

"Perhaps we can discuss your will, Angharad."

"Yes, we must do that," she said as she came over the table, opening the front of her gown slightly as she walked.

"You have no idea," she said, "what it's like not having a husband," and she began to weep slightly, putting her hands to her face, though Hamish noticed her peeping through her fingers at him as she did so, "you see, we had such a lovely life, especially in bed and I miss him so much."

"I am sure," said Hamish stiffly, "but we need to do this will."

"I know your wife is downstairs," she said, "but I could really do with you right now, here, my lawyer lover."

"That is not going to happen, Angharad. I am leaving now and will meet you in the foyer as soon as you are ready."

"You're like all men," she snarled, "you either want my body or my money. In your case, it's the money, so you can get your arse back to London with your maimed wife and ugly baby and I don't want to see you again."

"That," said Hamish, "is entirely satisfactory."

"If I may say so, Angharad, I appreciate both your desires and your loneliness, but don't you think you should find yourself a husband rather than making a spectacle of yourself with your lawyer?"

At that she burst into tears, this time genuinely, increasing to a howl.

"I know, I know, I am sorry, I am so sorry. I do want you to continue as my lawyer. I don't know anyone around here. My parents' friends are all farmers and a dull lot."

"May I make a suggestion?" He said, moving back into the room.

"Perhaps you could find a nice large home in Cardiff with your children, away from your parents, in a fashionable area. Believe me, you will soon make friends with your new-found wealth. Within a year, I am sure, you will have more suitors than you can cope with. You will be spoilt for choice. Just make certain, absolutely certain, that your man has his own money, or in the state of the law, you may have to give most of yours to him."

"See, that's why I want you to be my lawyer. I need advice. I don't know how to do my will."

"Right. Sit down over there and please cover yourself up. Let us assume that we make a will leaving all your money and possessions in trust for your children with me as the trustee, the person who will give out the money as needed. This will just be a temporary will in case you get run over by a carriage in the meantime. Then you must find an agent for big houses in fashionable areas, so that your children can have their own rooms and that you have room for servants.

"You see, Angharad, you are really quite rich and a home of your own will be necessary. As soon as you have found a house, send me a wire and I will complete all the legal requirements. Then you can shop for furniture. You are a very rich woman, you know.

"In the meantime, I have prepared a Trust will which we can use for the moment. Please sign this and I will witness it to make it legal."

"Oh, Hamish, that will be such a relief. I am sorry, I threw myself at you. I just was so excited to be with such a handsome man with that lovely Scottish accent. Oh God, I need a man!

"I know it's not possible, but I am available if ever you need me," she said smiling.

Hamish left, somewhat dazed by this experience. He went downstairs to find Mary and James, and had the concierge find a carriage immediately to take them to the train.

"I don't want to stay here another night, darling. I'll tell you why on the journey but let us stop and find a hotel in Gloucester and spend one, perhaps two nights there and I can tell you all about this Welsh widow."

When they were settled on the train, Hamish told Mary of his encounter with Angharad in detail. She listened carefully, then said:

"I am so proud of you, my husband. Poor woman though, bubbling over with desire and she targets the most sympathetic and devastatingly attractive man she can find who happens to be you. Perhaps," she said teasingly, "you should have comforted her in her distress?"

He laughed, saying " Oh, no, that's a Welsh valley I have no wish to enter."

"Now that really is an odd metaphor, especially from you," she replied smiling and then nestling against him with James on his knee as the train rattled on.

On a bright August morning in Paris, similar envelopes arrived for Albert and Elizabeth, Charlotte and Estella, announcing the engagement of Emma Sophia Victoria Eustace to Clarence Henry Fotheringaye-Smythe. All letters arrived at Albert's address as Estella and Charlotte had their apartment elsewhere. When the four met for lunch that same day at the *Café des Anglais,* they agreed that Albert and Elizabeth would both stay at New Queen Street when the time came for the wedding perhaps as much as a year hence.

Albert then left to follow up John Sargent's invitation to the Carolus-Duran studio where he got into conversation with him while he was idly sketching a portrait of a young woman.

"Did you know that the painter's real name is Charles-Emile Auguste Durand?"

"I did not, but I wondered why you referred to him as Auguste."

"He's had also great success in painting portraits which has always interested me," said John. "He opened this studio in the *Boulevard de Montparnasse* but closed it at the start of the War."

"A sensible move, I am sure," said Albert, "I lived through the Commune and the painters I met spent their days in cafes."

"And their nights in brothels, I would suppose," said John laughing.

"I think I am drawn to painting portraits," said John, his pencil racing across the paper, "as I am enthralled by the idea of trying to capture a piece of life on canvas, what I might call a fragment of time and space. I saw Caillebotte working on a quite simple painting of a woman looking out of a window with a man sitting next to her."

"I love his work. I met him in Paris before the Commune where I got trapped. Did you know it was Courbet who inspired the destruction of the *Colone Vendome*? I heard of several painters who became soldiers under Meissonier's leadership.

"But John, does this make sense as a would-be painter like myself in this era? I am trying to produce invitations on a canvas, almost like saying to my audience, 'come and look at this?'"

"That's an interesting insight, my dear Albert," said John, "you mean the painting is not just something to be admired as if it were an authority and you damn well have to do or believe what it says. H'mm. Could a portrait also be an invitation? I mean, I saw that extravagantly lovely painting of Berthe Morisot's – the *Jeune Fille a Bal,* and we know the subject. It's marvelous, and I suppose it does invite you to look at her delight in dancing, meeting others and so forth.

"I am still a novice in these matters," John continued, "but as I look at a Tintoretto or Titian with stories from the Bible, or a painting of Delilah with Samson's head on a platter I do not feel any invitation to anything. I understand such painters are working on behalf of the Church, like teachers, saying, this is the story, but such works are not invitations to enjoy life, to take pleasure in art. When you look at the painting of Morisot's you want to step right in and ask her to dance, don't you?"

"You do know Berthe's presumption took Elizabeth by surprise, don't you?" Albert asked.

"Yes, I understand. Yet it is Elizabeth. She is so beautiful. No wonder it is such a delightful painting!"

"That is true, on both counts," said Albert, smiling with pleasure at John's compliments on his Elizabeth.

"Then a painter's personality, attitudes, and beliefs about the world," he continued, "appear in one's painting for the invitation has to be issued by somebody, does it not? Yet, that personality is also shaped by individuals, arguing in a café, members of a community in which ideas about color and light, for instance, are constantly being given individual interpretation. I'd guess the next twenty years or so will see an explosion of invitations!"

They laughed heartily together at that.

"Goodness me, we are getting too philosophical," said John, "it's time to head home. Will I see you tomorrow?"

They parted that evening, but at another meeting the following day, the conversations became more personal.

"What did your father do, Albert?"

"He was a lawyer in London, and unfortunately died from cancer."

"Is that wonderful lady your mother, then?"

"You mean Estella?"

"No, she is my step-mother. How do you mean – wonderful? I think so, but why do you?"

"She must have been an extraordinary beauty when she was young, quite exquisite. But now she has this magnificent sheen on her skin, her hair is growing grey, but she has what one might call a presence, with those lovely eyes and quiet expressions.

"She is a very attractive woman even now, assuming her age without asking the question! You know, my dear Albert, you occasionally meet a person who is just an extraordinary example of our species. Estella is one. I do hope she agrees to let me paint her."

"I am sure she will, and when I finish the portrait of my father, she would be thrilled with both. My own mother died in childbirth a year or so after I was born.

"It's an interesting story: Estella and my father knew each other from childhood. She was the ward of a rich mad single woman and he was the son of a country blacksmith. You don't need to know the whole story, but years later, they met and married, though they had been in touch intermittently. How about yours?"

"My parents have become travelers so I have lived for a while in most European capitals and I speak four languages. It's been a great experience, but, you know, I feel rootless at times. I am trying to make Paris my home."

"Paris is lucky, John. We all watched you at work the other day in the studio and your skill is simply out of this world. You will be a very distinguished painter, while I will plod along, doing the odd portrait, painting a few landscapes, maybe getting an exhibit at the Academy."

"That is very kind of you, Albert. Yet you are lucky as I am not. You have captured the heart of a beautiful woman, your Elizabeth. I would give a great deal to play the piano as she does. I tinker and can strum out a few tunes, but, my goodness, her technique is marvelous but secondary to her sensitive interpretations, though I don't know Liszt that well."

"Nor me. Will you be going to Auguste tomorrow?"

"I expect so. Oh, by the way, my parents are now in Paris and planning a small soiree quite soon. I'd love you to come and bring Elizabeth and her aunt, and of course, Estella."

"I'm sure they'd be delighted."

"Please," said Albert as they were at lunch at their usual bistro, "John insists this is not a society occasion, just a collection of twenty or so friends of his parents, so there is no need to go out to shop for new fashionable dresses."

"But these are Americans, my dear, who will flaunt their wealth at us, I know."

"Ah, well, it is your money after all, but I don't think it is necessary."

"We will be shopping all afternoon," said Estella decisively.

The Sargents were staying at the *Hotel le Meurice* on the *Rue Sant-Honore*, a legendary establishment opened shortly after the Battle of Waterloo in 1815. Albert was glad his advice had been ignored by his three women for their new clothes were quite wonderful. As they entered the salon where it was being held, he could see that the American guests had also spent their money extravagantly.

John's parents greeted them very affably, as did John in his somewhat clumsy way. As Charlotte turned around to view the gathering, a woman on the other side of the room fainted, falling back onto a large Louis XIV chair which, fortunately, was sufficiently well built to support her.

Charlotte immediately took Elizabeth's arm.

"My dear, did you notice that woman over there who collapsed?

"No, aunt, I was talking with Albert and John."

"I think it is your mother who passed out when she saw you."

"Goodness me, I must hurry over to her."

"I will follow directly. Estella, Albert," Charlotte called out, "the woman who fainted is Elizabeth's mother."

"Great heavens," said Albert, "no wonder she collapsed."

"What's going on?" said John, "I saw a woman fainted over there but why did Elizabeth go to her?"

"That is her mother. She was married to Elizabeth's father, Henry Fitzroy. He was a diplomat here during the war, but at the first blast of a cannon the mother went first to Monaco, then back to Georgia to her family. She did not return; indeed, she did not even come to see her husband when he was posted to Athens and worse still, she made no effort to see after Elizabeth's future or even attend her husband's funeral. There was ample time for her to have crossed the Atlantic as the body had to be brought from Athens to the family grave in Norfolk."

"Oh dear, that is disgraceful. I doubt whether my parents are well acquainted with her. They simply invited all the American couples staying at the hotel."

"It was a disgrace, as you say. She abandoned her daughter leaving her to care for her husband."

Meantime as Elizabeth approached her mother, a tall man with a flowing mustache was attending to her, fanning her with his hands, and she began to recover as Elizabeth stood over her.

"What are you doing here, Mother?"

"Mother?" Said the man loudly. "Mother? I never knew she had kids."

"Who, pray, are you?" said Elizabeth in the haughtiest manner she could muster.

"I, Mademoiselle, am Count Wassilko von Serecki and this lady, Mary-Lou is my Countess."

"Well, well, well," said Elizabeth slowly, as her mother was struggling to her feet.

"Mother, you remember my aunt Charlotte, I am sure."

There were some other Americans watching this incident unfold and various hushed comments included the suggestion that even at her age she might be pregnant, and another that you would have thought she could hold her drink, and the final query that perhaps she is disguising a wasting disease, most of which Charlotte heard to her quiet amusement. The Count disappeared to find a maid with a tray of champagne.

"Elizabeth, my child," said Mary-Lou, ignoring Charlotte, "what are you doing here?"

"Mother," said Elizabeth in a loud hectoring voice, "you can sail the ocean to Paris with your new husband but when my father needed you most, you stayed away like a coward just because there was a war."

"Don't talk to your mother like that," said Mary-Lou with an exaggerated Georgia twang betraying her anger.

"I can now address you in any way I wish. Tell me, who is this beau you have chosen?"

"He is a Romanian count and I met him in New York and we fell in love. He is related to the present Governor of Bukovina."

"How impressive, Mother, except that he is an impostor; he is speaking English with a London accent, a cockney I shouldn't wonder. He used the word "kids" when he was shocked to hear of my existence."

"It seems to me," said Charlotte, "that you and the supposed Count are deceiving each other. Unsurprising, you always were a somewhat gullible woman. Does he have any money, or are you supporting him?"

"No, he had a tragedy in Romania and was obliged to flee without any money. He is very much in love with me, and I have become quite rich since my father and mother have both died recently."

"Ah, here he comes."

"Count, let me introduce myself," said Charlotte, "I am Mary-Lou's first husband's sister and with my niece Elizabeth here, we are here in Paris for a few months.

"Tell me, in which part of London's East End were you born?"

"What do you mean?" replied the Count angrily.

"Your English is decidedly Cockney, and I suspect your title is an honor bestowed on you by yourself."

"Not at all, madam, I resent such an accusation. When I was young, living in the family castle near *Siblu*, our country's most beautiful city, I was taught English by an itinerant tutor who was born in London. So, I admit that I speak English with a London accent. I am no impostor. That apart, Mary-Lou I wish you'd told me you had kids."

"Children, not kids," said Charlotte, "and she only had Elizabeth, but your explanation seems satisfactory, so my apologies."

"You see," said Mary-Lou, "he is the genuine article and I am a real Countess."

"Except that you disowned me, Mother," interjected Elizabeth.

"I think we can conclude this meeting now. I do not wish to have anything more to do with you, a sentiment which is clearly reciprocated."

"If that is what you really want, then that's that. I know I treated your father very badly. But I am sure Charlotte would agree, we were too young and far too hasty. It was never a good match."

"Yes, I do agree," said Charlotte.

"My father did miss you, you know," said Elizabeth, "we were together most of the time during and after the war in Athens, and while it would be too much to say he pined for you, he really did miss you."

"And I guess I missed him, though when I got back to Charleston, Georgia was in a terrible confusion after the war between the States. We moved to Buffalo near my mother's family, as my daddy lost a lot of money from our plantation. It was such a worrying time."

At that moment, John's mother Mary came over and, without enquiring further on the substance of this conversation, took the Count and Countess Wassilko away to meet another titled couple whom the Sargents had met in Italy, Count Francisco Vitetti and his wife, Countess Magdalena.

Estella crossed the room and Charlotte told her she would tell her of the conversation later, but Estella took no notice.

"Is that lady really your mother, Elizabeth? Well, dear me," she said with heavy sarcasm, "thank goodness you have your father's color and looks."

Albert guffawed and Elizabeth smiled at the complement. Charlotte put her arm around her niece and they moved away, as Elizabeth was starting to weep silently, the emotion of the occasion overcoming her.

"John has been insisting that he paint my portrait, Albert, so he and I are going to discuss some alternatives shortly," said Estella.

"How so?"

"He thinks it could be a formal portrait, or one in the country or indeed in a café. He is very kind about my old looks."

"That will be wonderful, Estella. I must get on with my father's portrait and get some lessons from John on how to do it. I have made so many false starts, I don't know where I am. Perhaps we will return to England after the summer with two portraits to hang in New Queen Street."

They returned in a carriage from the *Le Meurice* and as the carriage trundled along cobbled streets, Estella said to Elizabeth:

"It sounds as though you have completely cut the knot with your mother. I think you know my history with my mother, and though she was a criminal and a murderer, at that time of my life, it was very important to me to be reconciled with her.

"I just wonder, my dear, whether you really need to make the break now. Why not see her on her own while they are in Paris, have lunch with her to try to discover whether you made this decision advisedly."

"To be sure," Elizabeth replied, "I have been feeling guilty about such an abrupt ending. But you know she was such a beast to my father, and she showed no real interest in me as a child."

"Well, this is very easy for me to say, but she is your mother. I would just want for you to be sure, that is all. I am sure she will be gone back to America shortly. In the future, you may miss her at your wedding or when your first baby arrives. What do you think, Charlotte?"

"Your advice seems to be well placed, as ever. I suppose it is a matter of giving her a chance."

"Very well," said Elizabeth with a sigh, "I think the Count said they were staying at that hotel for a week or so. I am not confident that I have much to say to her, but I will try."

"Now, let me be clear, Elizabeth. I am not saying you must restore a relationship with her, merely that you can be certain that the rupture is what you want after meeting her privately.

"Today was too emotional for you," said Charlotte, "and Estella's advice is sensible."

VIII

As the Jaggers Trust's manager, Pip oversaw the activity at the Semper House Home for men and the Jaggers Building for women and it was important for him to ensure that both were well run as they took up a substantial part of the Trust's annual income.

At the Semper House Home Mr. and Mrs. Copperstone, Bert and Alice, had begun well and Fanny and Clara were efficient maids. Bert Copperstone was a burly fellow with arms like tree-trunks, an engaging smile and with a shock of red hair like Pip, while his wife Alice was tough as could be, hair in a bun and with arms to match her husband's. At the Jaggers Building George Holditch was also largely in control alongside Mrs. Pottinger, though the children were proving distinctly difficult not least because their mothers had little idea about their discipline.

Pip decided it was worth the risk to have all the staff employed by the Trust together for a meeting. He had experience of meetings with the Elders in Salford and the Board of the Trust, though these were very different kinds of meetings. He thought of other gatherings he had in Salford where people were invited to speak of their relationship to God or on other more secular matters.

After a long discussion with Susanna, he decided that he would treat this meeting as an opportunity for the staff to give some ideas, report difficulties and contribute to the running of both institutions from their experience. Susanna reminded him that he should make sure the women in the group had their opportunity to speak.

Pip thus arranged for transport to bring the Building staff to Semper House on September 15th, 1876, and Mrs. Copperstone had made up some buns and cakes along with various beverages. Pip began by expressing his intentions for this meeting which he hoped would be a regular event. Everyone nodded.

"Let's start at the bad end of things, where the problems lie. Begin with the Building."

Mrs. Pottinger immediately spoke:

"I don't know, sir, but there's a lot of thieving of food going on. I think it's the little nippers wot have never had no food proper, if you know wot I mean and they can't resist it besides them not thinking thieving is wrong."

"You are sure that it is the children and they that they consume it themselves?"

"Oh, yes, sir, we see them walking around eating and we know it comes from our kitchen."

"How serious is it?"

"Well, not that serious. I mean we can still feed everyone easily."

"All right. Why don't we arrange a meeting with all the children and tell them that we will give them food, but they must come to Mrs. Pottinger and ask for it.

"What other problems do we have?"

'Well, sir," said Mr. Holditch, "I don't think this is serious yet but it could be. You've got men coming in, and I make a list of them when I can, but the worst thing that could happen is that the bobbies see us as a brothel."

"I heard a bloke in the street the other night, telling his mate that he could get a woman in the Building."

"Where did you hear that, Fanny?" asked Mrs. Pottinger.

"Just along the street corner of Shaftesbury."

"Then I think we are going to have rules," said Pip.

"No visitors after 4 o'clock in the afternoon. No visitors before midday. This will protect the women. Everyone who comes in must tell Mr. Holditch who will make a list. Any of our guests using the Building as a base for whoring must leave. Do we have women under suspicion of that?"

"There's a couple of sisters in my estimation," said Mrs. P.

"Right, George, interview them."

"Oh no, you should do that, sir."

"I will. Now, what about Semper House?"

"There's trouble brewing, sir."

"What do you mean?"

"I dunno. It seems to me the young men are forming tight groups, and each man has to be belong to one or the other. The cliques seem to be of two kinds and please forgive me if speak crudely and bluntly in front of the women.

"There's one group that really enjoyed what they did on the streets and, as they are no longer on the streets, they are making up for it by, you know, well enjoying themselves with each other."

At this the two women and the girls gasped in surprised.

Pip had wondered whether that might be an outcome, so he said:

"And the other group are those who want to get out and learn a trade quickly, like Jack Masham?"

"Yes but," Bert continued, "I overheard a couple in the first group talking the other night, indistinctly it is true, but I think they were planning to force a young man in the group that want to stay to submit to them."

"What, do you mean they were planning to rape him?"

"Well, I don't rightly know, but it sounded like that."

"Alright, let us suppose that Bert is indeed correct: We have a group of mollies, rent-boys, if you like, who want to be active queers but as they are at the Home they can use each other within that group or they want to force the would-be reformers to satisfy them.

"What do we do?"

At this Fanny spoke and, as she did so, her voice reminded Pip for all the world of Nellie Fletcher, same words, same intonations, same background he thought.

"The way I see it is this: They takes a place at Semper, you'd think, Mr. Gargery sir, to get out of being mollies. If they don't want that, then they shouldn't be taking up a place of someone who do want out."

"You are right, Fanny."

The others nod in agreement.

"Bert, can you identify those in the first group?"

"Yes sir."

"Gather the second group and then the first group next together tomorrow early in the day and I will speak to them. Thank you all for coming. We will meet again in a month, next time at the Building, and during that time, try to think of anything you think we need to put right. You know, the success of this enterprise does depend on you, all of you. It's like one of Nelson's battle fleet. One weak ship will upset the whole fleet. Thank you again."

Pip appeared the next morning and Bert led him to the dining room where six of the guests in Bert's first group were sitting at tables. He did not remember any of them by name. They appeared in reasonable spirits, and he reminded himself to call upon his religious sentiments about the poor to be able to be civil to them.

"How are you all getting along? Do you like it here? Tell me your name afore you speak."

"Harry Smith, sir. I like it, but there's them that don't."

"That's the pity, sir," said Arthur, "I got attacked and done the other night. Of course, it wasn't as though I'd never had it before, but I didn't expect it and they forced me and then didn't pay me."

"Right, that will do. I will speak with them. But what about other matters?"

"It's wonderful. I never knew I could be so comfortable, a real bed, my own little room and good food. It's a miracle."

Enthusiastic noises from the young men supported these claims.

"We will make it safe for you."

Pip abhorred getting this kind of detailed discussions about what went on between men. He had handled some evil matters when a preacher in Salford but he had to grit his teeth to hear all this which he still regarded at unnatural, animalistic and an affront to God. On these matters in general he had managed to become friendly with Hamish, but he wondered incessantly how on earth Mary could put up with a sodomite husband. Maybe he'd changed.

It took a while for the second group to assemble once the first had left.

"I want to ask you, first, whether you enjoy being in Semper House Home or whether you'd just as soon leave, as I gather from reports that some of you continue to practice your old ways. Tell me your name before you speak."

"Charlie Spence, sir. I'm eighteen, been on the game since I was fourteen. I was able to do wot I liked, but now feel I've lost my freedom," at which several others murmured assent.

"You mean you are not free being here?"

"Yes, you have all these rules and I am not used to that."

"You are free to leave, you know. You were selected for the Home on the basis that you wanted to give up the game and learn a trade. Do you wish to leave, Charlie?"

"I can see what you'se been trying to do for us, sir. I thought it was for me, but it ain't, and I will leave now if that's alright by you."

"Which of you raped Tim recently?" Pip asked scarcely able to get the words out of his mouth.

No replies.

"But he was raped by one or more of you, was he not?"

"It was just a bit of fun, sir," said Charlie.

At that Pip exploded with rage, unable to contain his contempt.

"Fun? You stupid young man! Fun? Not only is your behavior utterly disgusting, but you could get six years hard labor for that and I've a mind to call in the police right now."

"Oh dear, pardon me for living," said Charlie as he got up and left, at which some of the men hung their heads whilst others looked at Pip as if daring him to do what he had just said.

"Alright, we won't report it, but we will be reporting any future rapes. It is clear to me that some of you in this group want to leave the Home. If you do, like Charlie, you should leave this room now, attend to your possessions and be gone in ten minutes."

Two of the six remained in their chairs.

"So you two do not want to leave."

"No, sir," said one of them, " We was like forced to join them and we's really glad they're gone."

Pip went home to Susanna very disenchanted. To clear his head, he walked all the way from Shoreditch to Cheyne Row, thinking deeply about what he had just encountered.

He had also begun to see that Estella was taking the place of his mother Biddy in his life, an older and wiser confidant, so he needed to draw her into a conversation about what was happening. He had tried to confide in her about Harriet but though she would not want to hear the whole story, she made it clear what he should do. Just as now, he felt he must have her advice.

He thought of the contrast between these young men and Estella and Nellie as lovers. Initially he saw the pair as a betrayal of Old Pip, for his religious beliefs and commitments were still strong enough for him to see anything but love between a man and a woman as unnatural and simply wrong. Yet, as he passed along the riverbank near Westminster, he puzzled as to why he found women loving each other as somehow more acceptable than men loving each other.

The latter simply disgusted him, but the former was somehow acceptable. It was more this business of betrayal by Estella that upset him rather than the fact of their loving. Perhaps, he was more likely to forgive women as the weaker sex, who by their nature might the more easily succumb to temptations of the flesh. He dare not share these thoughts with Susanna.

The memory of Lachlan's death still rankled, and they were to visit his grave tomorrow. Malcolm was bereft without his brother over the last couple of years and had started to cling to his parents, especially his mother.

"I am getting more worried about Malcolm, Pip, and I wonder if you can spend more time with him, though I know you are busy with the Trust."

"I am worried too and I really must do more with him. I had thought we might take both of them down to Kent to see where I grew up. Perhaps we can all go, do some walking, perhaps visit Rochester and see the Castle and the Cathedral. But I think I must walk with him every day."

"If we were to go to Kent," said Susanna, "we should go before the winter begins. The Culpeppers are planning a lunch shortly, and it has taken a long time for them to fix a day. That will be fascinating as we don't know them that well, so perhaps after that?"

"I'd enjoy that too, but I must tell you what happened today before I write to Estella."

He then gave her a graphic description of the conditions of the men, the way in which the cliques had developed and the differences in attitude. All the while, she looked at him with love and admiration, especially at his conclusion.

"You were quite right, darling, to cast them out. I think it is important to draw certain lines here. My belief in freedom, in general, is conditional, not absolute. I don't believe, as Mr. Mill wrote, that over his own body a man is sovereign.

"You see, dear Pip, while I am no saint in such matters I do believe that promiscuous use of anything is not right, immoral, if you like. There is a huge difference between Hamish and his desire for a man's love and that Charlie you mentioned who is rotten, whatever his background or upbringing. That kind of wantonness seems despicable to me."

"Thank you for that, Susanna. It has clarified my own mind. I agree wholeheartedly, but how do I explain to the Charlies of this world that what he is doing is wrong, selling his body to anyone who will pay for the experience. He seemed impervious to the very notion of love."

"Probably because he has never received it. Maybe it is first a matter of having him respect himself. Perhaps he just sees himself as an object. Maybe has lost all sense of himself, except as someone wandering around in the darkness of a loss of self-respect. At bottom, he does not like himself, though he would never admit it. Now women in bad marriages can just get to see themselves as the tool of their husbands. They are gradually drained of self-hood which is why asserting a woman's independence is so important."

"Perhaps, but sense of self could come through recognizing Jesus as their savior," said Pip.

"Of course, but are there missionaries to male prostitutes?'

"No, and I suspect that is because clergy find them too obscene to even talk to. On that, I am sure, Jesus would be ashamed."

"You meet these young men fairly regularly, but I suppose you don't try to convert them, do you?"

"I don't. My faith, once so sure and confident, is now more of a tremble between being devout and being uncertain."

"You mean, you don't believe in God?'

"Of course I believe in God, darling. I just don't know what to do about it."

She got up and put her arms around him.

"I love you, darling, for your compassion and your diligent struggle to help others and to challenge yourself. But let's take that excursion to Kent and stay in the Blue Boar. We might even call on Nellie and Fletch."

"I would love that, and I am sure Malcolm would love to see a blacksmith at work."

The following day, they took a cab up to Highgate Cemetery with Malcolm. They bought some flowers from a flower-seller at the gate and walked down the path. The simple unostentatious memorial stone had been installed:

Lachlan Gargery
Born September 15, 1867
Died September 10, 1874
Dearly beloved son and brother
R.I.P

"That is a very nice stone for Lachlan," said Malcolm.

Pip and Susanna held hands with Malcolm between them and Pip prayed for the Lord to deliver them from dangerous diseases.

September was quite balmy in Paris. Estella was stretched out on the grass under a small plane tree in a corner of the *Bois de Boulogne* in her lavender dress with its floral embroideries, resting on her right elbow and turning her head towards the painter who was drawing a quick sketch of her. John Sargent's charcoals and pencils raced over the paper as he wanted urgently to capture her expression first. It was one of a quiet rapture, of a woman content with herself, her age and her passions, indeed of her life. A delight to draw, he thought.

"I am so glad we have chosen this place rather than a café or a studio, Mr. Sargent."

"Please, Estella, call me John."

"I have a country house in Kent which is my real home though my London house has a small garden and, of course, there is St. James Park opposite but there is nothing like sitting in my garden with roses in bloom, birds cackling around and the scents and smiles of the country."

"Why smiles?"

"Oh, I don't know, I always get the feeling that plants and trees and everything around me there has a smile on its face."

"That's a lovely idea. Tell me about the area. I have never been to England, though I do expect to. I want you to talk while I do a few sketches of you, if you please."

"Of course, yet I am sure you will go to England as you will become famous."

"Well, thank you, but we must wait and see in that respect."

"The northern coast of Kent is well-known, mainly because of England's shipping renown and its proximity to the Continent. I live near a very ancient village, All Hallows, itself equidistant from a famous port Chatham, and a Roman town Rochester. Beyond my house about a mile, the land stretches out into marshland, that was where my husband grew up as a child. So did I, living with my eccentric guardian in a large house with a brewery attached nearby."

"Albert has mentioned you and your husband Pip and also Pip Gargery, and that it was what he called a long story."

"Yes, mine is a long story indeed. It can be told from so many viewpoints. Sometimes I think about it from my husband's, or my guardian's, or my mother's or my lawyer's perspectives. Pick one, mine if you wish."

"How intriguing. Let me see," he said looking at her with his pencil resting on his cheek, "let me guess who would find your story most interesting. Why not your mother, please?"

"This is quite interesting to try to put into words what I have thought about a little. Should I begin at the beginning?"

"Oh, I always think that is the best place to start."

"Alright, let me see.

"My name is Molly Magwitch. I was a very jealous child so much so that I brought about the death of my younger brother when I was quite young."

"Good gracious!"

"No, John, you must not interrupt or I will lose my train of thought."

"My father was a prosperous storekeeper but when that happened, my mother found out and died soon after. Losing a son and a wife drove him to drink and he and I ended up in a workhouse where I was raped but had to leave as I bit the face of the man who did it."

At this point, Sargent put down his pencils and looked intently at her.

"I was about fourteen, escaped the workhouse where this happened, went on the road trying to survive and a man, older than me, took pity on me. He was a thief and a criminal but he had a good heart. He took me in, we became lovers and I gave birth to a lovely daughter, Ruth, whom we adored. But Abel was a criminal bounder and he told me one night he was leaving with the wife of a fellow criminal friend of his, and I went completely mad. I lured the wife to a barn and strangled her. I never saw Abel again."

Sargent was almost open-mouthed at this telling. Here was this beautiful elderly lady speaking as if she was her mother, a two-time murderer. It was fascinating, but macabre.

"I was caught, of course. The lawyer who defended me was a Mr. Jaggers, and he argued it was a crime of passion and he offered to install me as his servant and the judge agreed. But there was Ruth my child. Jaggers told me he had a client a rich lady who wanted a ward and he persuaded me to surrender Ruth and I did not have a real choice.

"How are you enjoying this so far, John?"

"It is quite extraordinary your telling it like this; it is like being in a theatre."

"Yes, indeed, I feel to be an actress. But let me go on.

"Years went by and I served Mr. Jaggers in his office and his home. He looked after me completely and I hardly went out. One morning, twenty years or so later, when he was in court, I came out from the pantry into his main office to pick up a glass. There was a very fine lady standing there waiting for him. We glanced at each other and she suddenly screamed 'are you my mother?' Then I could recognize some of her features as my child, and she saw my bruised hands and wrists where I had tried to end it all before I was caught."

"Excuse me. We brought a drink, did we not," said Sargent, "would you like some water?"

"Thank you."

"It was my Ruth, though her guardian had called her Estella. After a loud argument with Mr. Jaggers who came in shortly thereafter, I went away with her and was with her for several good years. She taught me to read and write, to dress properly, indeed gave me manners and we had joyous company. But she, poor girl, had had a dreadful if wealthy upbringing in which her guardian instilled in her a hatred of men.

"Now I, of course, loved men but she seemed not to have any desire for man at all. But I worked on her and she started to have feelings for a man called Pip, and they had known each other since they were children. He was the son of a poor blacksmith and her mad guardian got him to visit, paid for his articles, but only for him to grow up in love with my Estella while she was being taught to hate men. But, of course, by the time she realized she loved him he was married to someone else, and in fact that made her very envious when she saw them together."

Estella stopped, gazed into the sky and tears began to fall from her eyes.

"Oh, Estella," said Sargent, "I am sorry if the telling has made you sad, though mind you," he said picking up a pencil, "you look even more beautiful."

"I am sorry," said Estella, "but my mother had to stop there. She never knew the happiness I found with Pip after his wife died in childbirth. Albert is their living son."

"Why does she have to stop this telling?"

"She was murdered in my garden by the children of the woman she had killed."

"My dear, how terrible, how shocking, how absolutely horrendous. Oh, I am so sorry for you. Her story is like something out of a dark novel."

"Thank you, it feels a long time ago now, but telling you that from her point of view has brought it all back to me so vividly especially her death; calling her in for breakfast and finding her with her head smashed in on a path in the garden she had come to love so powerfully."

"Perhaps it does help to speak of it."

"I suppose so."

Estella gave a tremendous sigh, wiping away her tears, and asked how he was progressing.

"Very well, I think. I am thinking of a medium sized canvas, and I will try to paint all of you, not just head and shoulders as I want to display your elegance."

"How sweet, tell me about yourself if you are not yet done."

"We are speaking about our souls, are we not, not about the peripheral things of life."

"I hope so, I find conversation with you easy, it is though you are Albert's brother, confiding in your mother or a favorite aunt."

"It is strange," said Sargent, "I do feel drawn to you as a person I mean, not just as a subject. But then I think many people feel the same about you. I told Albert it is something about the magnetism of your presence."

"Good heavens, do be careful!" and she laughed.

"Alright, I have never told anyone this, and I trust you. I find myself drawn to both men and women. By that I mean I do befriend people easily and I love both men and women but I am terrified of my sexuality."

"Really? I would thought you have left behind you a series of conquests, women who fell at your feet. You are a good-looking tall man who is as engaging as anyone I have ever met."

"The wish is father to the thought. Let me give an example. I walked into the Embassy music room the other day and there was this beautiful young woman playing Liszt, and it was so wonderful, I wanted to snatch her away to some sunlight palace and make love to her for hours and hours. You know it was Elizabeth, of course."

"I do."

"Yet as these desires and thoughts rattled through my mind, I became terrified, not because of Albert, not because in some earthly paradise I would not know what to do, but because…and this is where I falter. I do not know why. I knew not just that I could not have her, but I could not have her because of something in me, my overwhelming fear."

"We must think about this."

"And it is equally true for men. I find myself looking with immense lust at a man, but almost as I recognize the lust, the fear engulfs me."

He packed up his easel and his pencils, took her by the hand for her to get up, and they walked together across the grass.

"So," she said, "have you ever been with either a man or a woman?"

"No, no, not for want of invitations from both."

There was a small open-air café nearby and they stopped there for a cup of coffee.

"Why should this be, John? Perhaps it is physical, in which case you might engage with a woman or a man, so to speak, for fun."

"Oh, I could never do that."

"Ah, I have a most beautiful woman friend in London, and she invited me into her bed but I had to refuse. I also have a female companion I adore who is married, and her husband knows of our occasional engagements. After my husband died I did not expect to find myself wanting to love women more than men."

"You don't know how fortunate you are."

"But let us return to your fear. Perhaps you are frightened of putting yourself to the test. Perhaps you are thinking of yourself as needing to perform with either a man or a woman, and since you are so successful in life in general, you are frightened of being found wanting."

"That is certainly possible."

"Or perhaps you are frightened of finding out when, let us suppose, you are in bed with a woman, that you would really rather be in bed with a man, or vice versa, perhaps even your imagination might take you there while so engaged."

"That too is possible for I suppose my imagination is wild at times."

"How so?"

"I hope you will not find this embarrassing or insulting but drawing you this afternoon makes me want to make love to you."

"To me?" said Estella with astonishment, "but I am an old woman, though I confess, not without desires."

"I think I am frightened of all the things we have mentioned. But I know that you would help me get over them, that you would handle my lusts with care and discretion. I am serious, Estella, before we get time to think about it further, would you come to my rooms now?'

"Oh, John, I will come to your rooms and we will see whether you want to take your lovely offer further when we get there."

Later, to the surprise of both of them, they briefly embraced in a friendly way and merely lay together on the bed fully dressed talking more about the possibility of their union, neither of them interested in going further.

"I must think about this, John."

"The problem now," John replied, "is that my fears are intensified. I suppose you are right. I am daunted by the prospect of you and really worried I would disappoint you."

"Fiddlesticks," said Estella, "were we to engage in this adventure, we would learn about each other, teach each other and enjoy each other. But I tell you one important matter in this love-making.

"Men cannot help being aggressive, it is part of their nature, somehow. Whereas at any rate in my relationship with a woman, everything is gentle and soft, more passive than active. Peace and softness with ecstasy. But before we decide to take another step, you should go off and find yourself a beautiful young woman to adore, as long it is not Elizabeth. Then I will feel I can teach you what you need to know."

"That is very French. A man becomes engaged, but to ensure he will satisfy his wife to be, he takes a mistress to, so to speak, show him the ropes."

"And what, young John Singer Sargent, would be wrong with that?"

IX

Elizabeth followed Estella's advice, as indeed did everyone else who got advice from her, and arranged to meet her mother, now the Countess Mary-Lou Wassilko. They met for lunch at her hotel, and she had worn well, as it might be said. She was not exactly a beauty, more of a Georgia Peach, with bright cheeks, now pomaded, blue eyes and a clear effort to prevent wrinkles from engulfing her neck, by wearing a high collar. She had that Southern sing-song accent upon which opinion is divided. Some find it charming, others utterly painful.

Her daughter was her radiant self, perhaps more conscious of her looks after the Morisot painting, but nevertheless with an enviable figure. Men's heads turned when she passed and their ladies did not mind as they too were glad to look upon such a beauty.

"You've come on well since we last met," said her mother.

"Thank you, Mother. I hope you have found a happiness with Wassilki that eluded you with my father."

"I think so. Your father was too much bound up in his work, too serious a public servant for me. Wassilki enjoys social life, gadding about from capital to capital, meeting new people and making new friends."

"You probably mean acquaintances, don't you?'

"Well, yes, I suppose so."

"But it was surely rather cowardly for you to leave my father, was it not? I was in London at that time, and I wish I had not been as perhaps you might have stayed."

"Oh no, my dear. I may as well tell you now that he is gone."

"I had a brief romance with an Italian prince and we spent a wonderful four weeks in Monaco. I used the war as an excuse, I'm afraid. And then, well, things got worse, so I fled back home."

"Oh Mother, how shameful. I am so glad my father did not know of your adultery as he would have been very hurt."

"Oh, I made sure he did not know."

"In talking with him about you, Mother, I think he was in two minds about whether he wanted you to return, not for his own sake, he was too generous, but for yours. You clearly feel no guilt or shame about what you did, do you?"

"I used to get some twinges of guilt, that is true..."

"But never about me, of course."

"Right from your birth, you seemed more like your father and more attached to him rather than me."

"But you made so little effort with me. You were usually out; I had a nanny. Father came home from the Embassy, played the piano with me or read to me, but you! You never gave a fig for me, did you?"

"I don't think I was cut out to have children."

"No, Someone as selfish as you should not be allowed to have children whether they felt cut out for it or not."

"Oh, dear Elizabeth, you don't need to be so cruel," she said in her most tremulous singsong voice.

"Why not? Apart from bearing me, what else have you ever done for me truly, from the bottom of your heart?"

"Hmm, not much, perhaps you are right."

"Where do we go from here? If I marry, will you want to attend? Are you remotely interested in grandchildren if you find children so difficult? Do you want to be a part of my life at all?"

"I do, darling. It's just so difficult, me being in America and you being in Europe. I suffer so much when I cross the ocean. It is always such a terrible experience."

"What has that got to do with it? It is just an excuse, isn't it?"

"Well, no, but we can write and you can tell me all about your wedding when it happens."

"I don't think we have anything more to say to each other, Mother. I wish you well, but I don't give a damn if I never hear from you again."

She got up from the table hurriedly but walked out quite slowly, feeling in part of sense of pride but also a sense of wonder that this empty-headed woman was her mother.

She turned to look at her as she reached the door and her mother was chatting eagerly with a handsome waiter.

She rushed over to the studio to share the break-up with Albert.

Estella read Pip's letter about the problems of the Semper House Home and the Building to Charlotte at a small café very near their Paris apartment. A rather official looking letter had also arrived for Albert. They had become quite French in a small way, though they retained the English habit of a cup of tea first before venturing along the street for a croissant and coffee.

"I am not sure that I have ever seen a croissant before coming to France."

"Nor I," said Estella, "but I am going to try to ask the *boulanger* how to do it, get it written down and have the cook make them. Why is Parisian coffee also quite delicious? I disliked it in London, though coffee-houses are a commonplace. Somehow French coffee is coffee without being bitter."

"What should we do about these problems? Should I return to London to address them? Do you think Pip can handle them? After all, I am Chairman of the Trust."

"Yes, but he is the Manager, is he not? You are the person who receives the reports, the listener to the person designated to carry things out."

"That is my problem. Here I am in Paris, enjoying a life of idleness, though not decadence, not yet at least," she said smiling.

"What on earth does that mean?" said Charlotte.

"We have no secrets, do we. I am struggling very hard, and I need your most sober advice."

"Good gracious, am I some kind of Solomon?"

"No, my dear, but let me explain. You know John Sargent is going to paint my portrait – and yours indeed – and that so far I have had one sitting. He is a confused young man, brilliant though he may be, about whether he loves men or women and he is terrified of any sexual engagement. He proposed that I should teach him!"

"Goodness me, at your age? But then better to have a woman of experience first, so I am told," said Charlotte laughing.

"It's not so much funny, as strange, is it not? I said I would think about it."

"Sounds to me like charity work," said Charlotte, laughing again.

"I don't know why you laugh; this is serious."

"Serious? Really? But you do not love him, do you?"

"Of course not. He is attractive in an odd sort of way, tall, a bit bumbling but extraordinarily passionate. I suppose, as one gets older, one should not miss opportunities. On the other hand, one must be very careful not to become an object of ridicule."

"But surely John would be discreet."

"We don't know what this group of painters are like. For all I know, they spend evenings discussing their conquests."

"I don't get that impression," said Charlotte, "from what Elizabeth tells me they spend most of the time arguing about color, light and reality."

"Maybe, but don't tell me that a group of passionate men ignore their lives with women as an object of conversation."

"Then that is a good reason to avoid such an entanglement before it becomes an embarrassment."

"Perhaps, but since I fell properly in love with Pip my husband, I am unable to shake off my desires, whatever you want to call them. I suppose it is partly Harriet's and Nellie's influence, both of whom regard sex as fun on an 'enjoy it if you want it' notion."

"Well, it's not for me. I have decided I am going to give Percy a try. I have written to say that I will come down to his corner of Italy and, without trampling on his findings in the lava of Pompeii, live in a small pension or hotel where we can meet on a daily basis. Then, if marriage beckons, so be it."

"I will miss you dreadfully, of course, my dear companion, but that seems a sensible course of action."

"Thank you, my dear, I am glad of your support. Sometimes I think you are a wise old owl. People come and sit under your tree and you can always comfort people. Not the oracle at Delphi, my dear, prophesying people's fates, but nudging them in a direction which helps them. Quite where this wisdom comes from, I know not."

"Hmm. I have no idea. My conversations with Pip about all manner of things may have helped. Mind you, I am sometimes worried about going too far and being a meddler in the affairs of others."

"But that is what friends are for, is it not? On another tack, I am getting somewhat concerned about Albert and Elizabeth."

"In what way?"

"I am not sure. They seemed more distant than usual from each other when we met. I think she is getting upset by his attention to his painting and to the café round of painters. He does not spend enough time with her, and there is only so much time she can spend at the piano at her tutor's. She has no piano herself and she can hardly treat the Embassy piano as her own."

"Why not? Why don't we ask that man who interviewed her?

"Possible, I suppose."

"You write to him. Say who you are and pop the question. But be precise. Ask, say, for two mornings a week for two hours or whatever is convenient."

"She would love that, would she not?"

"Let's try that. She is satisfied that she did the right thing with her mother. In fact, I believe she was troubled at her because she abandoned Henry, her beloved father, not so much for herself. She thus easily found the strength to end the relationship."

"I must say I'd be wary as burning boats may lead to simmering regrets."

"Of course," said Charlotte, "but she is now an adult and she made that decision not out of petulance or peevishness, and certainly not out of a bad temper. On the contrary, I am sure, she had thought carefully about it after you had given her your counsel on the matter."

"Perhaps. But Albert seems to be immensely happy both in his painting and with her."

"But don't you see, Estella? If I go off to Pompeii, and her relationship with Albert founders on some rock or other, she has absolutely no one, no other friend or relative to be with."

"I would find difficulty in helping her if she broke with Albert, for obvious reasons. All right, let me ask you this. If that were the case, that there were some kind of breakdown, would you delay your visit to Percy to be with her?"

"Absolutely."

"Then, if your surmise is right about there being a crisis in their relationship, you should in all conscience delay your visit."

"I think so, but my alarm about them may be misjudged."

"Why don't you ask her?"

"I will."

The Australian imbroglio was soon settled after the telegraph wires between London and Brisbane burnt with a flurry of messages which led to the clear settlement of the will in favor of Angharad, as, indeed, was only just. It was with a sense of triumph that Philip Hardyman, lawyer, and Adam Masterson, clerk, returned from their long comfortable sea voyage and Philip went the following day to Little Britain, only to be told that Hamish was at Semper House.

Philip had become embarrassed by his non-existent relationship with Hamish, but he wanted to report on the Brisbane work as Hamish was Mrs. Unworthy's lawyer. He was also worried about being on the Board of the Trust which, if he were frank, aroused in him no serious interest and a slight alarm. He was unhappy at having no one else but Hamish to confide in, least of all his wife, and even less happy about any possible regular visits to the Semper House Home given the nature of his secret desires for men.

He had been mildly relieved that the young men he had seen were singularly unattractive to him, looking used and shop-worn. But now he had a useful overview of activity, so that when Courtisone retired and he took up the leadership of the practice, his time would be so busy that he could justify retiring from membership of the Board.

Hamish was not at the Semper House Home, so in a disgruntled mood, he walked down Wardour Street uncertain whether to get back to Little Britain to catch Hamish or not. As he dawdled with indecision, he passed an exceptionally attractive young man standing in a doorway. Surely, he thought, such a man could not be offering himself. He walked on down the street and, against his better judgment, turned round to look at the man from some distance. Was this Adonis really a whore?

Philip had never been tempted by rent-boys, fearing disease and much else. But this man was a serious temptation.

"What's your name?" he asked the young man as he walked back up the street to greet him.

"I'm Michael, but you can call me Mike," he said in a voice that suggested his origins were not working class.

"What do you offer?" asked Philip.

"Anything you want, really. I'm not fussy."

"Do you have a room nearby?"

"Just down Shaftesbury Avenue, I got it this morning."

"Lead me there, please Mike. Shall we say three pounds?"

"That would be generous."

Philip could not believe himself as he followed the young man down the street, the regrets that he had been on that damn boat and in that dreadful outback for too long quickly evaporating. While he had expended his pent-up force on his long-suffering wife, there had been no opportunity to release his desires for a male body. This one was too good to miss.

Once in the room, Mike made no approaches. He simply undressed, throwing his clothes on to a broken-down chair. Philip looked at this beautiful young man who, once unclothed seemed more like a boy-god. Slim, skin the texture of alabaster, eyes a deep blue, and limbs virtually hairless.

Their engagement completed, Mike said: "Philip, you don't do this often, do you? I would be thrilled to be ready for you and you alone, if you'd like that."

The offer went through Philip's mind like a whirlwind. Of course, he had money. He could install Mike in a room and give him enough so that he would not need to be on the street.

"I'd like to continue my studies, you see."

"Have you been studying?"

"Yes, I always wanted to become a lawyer but there have been such a chapter of accidents in my family that I was starving, so I've not been long on the street. I could think of no other way to earn money. I was an only child, my father had a good job but then over a year ago, both my parents died, drowning on a ship returning from Rotterdam where my father had business.

"I was staying with some friends and came home to find this disaster. No insurance of course, so I was destitute. My father had squandered so much in his business. Friends helped a bit, and my aunt and uncle could not help. But that all dried up. So here I am, my first day on the street. I have never thought of women. I have always thought of myself as queer."

"Hmm. I thought you were a virgin, Mike. Well, my dear little one, I must go now and here are the three pounds. Find yourself a permanent room much more salubrious than this and in a better area than Soho. I will meet you outside this building three evenings from now at 6 o'clock when you will have found a lodging and we will go there."

"I will be wholly yours," said Mike with a smile that almost knocked Philip off balance, and he left with a sense of exultation he had rarely felt before, if ever.

They met later as arranged and went in a cab to Bayswater, to a room just off the road out to Edgware in the country.

"This is a delightful spot," said Philip, "you must have put down some money too, didn't you?"

"Yes, a little, but this is ten shillings a week for the room and use of the facilities and the bed is comfortable. How much will you give me each week? If I am to study, I will need four or five pounds and I'll need to buy some books and better furniture."

"That will not be a problem. Here are two five-pound notes which should cover those needs and a month's rent on the room."

The excitement Philip felt as he left to go home was so intense that he almost knocked over an elderly woman on the pavement.

"Mind how you're going, love, you could have killed me then."

"Madam, I am so sorry, are you alright?"

"I am, but look where you're going, don't be in such a hurry."

"I won't, I won't and good evening to you."

Elizabeth and Albert were preparing to meet Estella and Charlotte to visit the museum at the Louvre.

"Darling, before we go, I need to talk with you."

"What about?"

"I am sure you are finding enormous pleasure and excitement with your painting, my dear, but there is only so much I can do with the piano. You are at the studio most of the day, then you are in a café with your friends. You have been getting home here later and later, and I am feeling immensely lonely and getting more and more miserable."

"I am sure that will pass," he said impatiently, "why don't you find something else to do? I am now getting somewhere with my painting under Auguste's direction and I simply need to spend my time there."

"I see. Do I not matter to you, then?"

"Of course, you do, obviously, but this is my one chance to produce something of value after the time in Kensington and now here."

"So I am secondary to your wants and desires?"

"I don't understand you. When we came here you knew that this was immensely important to me and we love each other greatly, but I cannot let this opportunity slip through my fingers."

"Well, I am getting more and more unhappy, and if this is to be how our lives are to be spent in future, I am not at all sure I want to be a part of it."

"We are late for Estella and Charlotte. We'll talk about this some other time."

"Of course, we will. Maybe. If you can find a time in your precious day, that will be a boon."

They left their apartment in silence. She could scarcely contain her anger at his callous disregard for her interests, indeed her life. He was mystified by this outburst of what he saw as her selfishness. How could he stay at home with her, when that portrait of his father was taking shape and his connections with his friends was so exhilarating?

The tension was on full display when they met the others.

"I think we should sit out here for a while," said Charlotte, as they took a table outside the café, thinking that they would not be overheard. Of course they were speaking English but, nevertheless.

Estella spoke first.

"How are you two getting along these days? You've seemed unlike your usual selves when we have met recently and Charlotte and I are concerned. Is it money?"

"No, not money," said Elizabeth.

"I do appreciate Elizabeth's position," said Albert, "I know I am so wrapped up in trying to be a painter and am so attached to the community that she feels neglected."

"Well, my dear," said Estella, "she actually is being neglected, isn't she?"

"I feel so," said Elizabeth, "I have never been lonely before. I know I am not good enough to be a virtuoso pianist, much as I love it. In fact I would not want to be one. Maybe I could teach piano, but that seems rather dull to me."

"Pip and Susanna are opening a school, you know, but that is in London."

"That could well be of interest."

"My difficulty," said Albert, "is that I have set my heart on becoming a painter, here in Paris. I just need four or five years to see what's possible, whether I can succeed. But I know these men, and they are so devoted to their art; they spend every waking moment thinking about it."

"But that hardly leaves room for me, does it?" Asked Elizabeth.

"Well, now, before you make any rash decisions, I am writing to that Head of Chancery you talked to about that treason affair to ask if you can play twice a week in the Embassy music room. After all, your father was there."

"I'd love that as we have no piano and I only play three hours a week at M. Cherniavsky's, my tutor."

"Right, let's have lunch," said Estella, "and see what the Embassy says. I hope neither of you think we are meddling in your affairs, but we both have such regard for you as a couple and as individuals."

"Oh yes, but you must also realize this," said Charlotte.

"If your wishes for your lives are not compatible, then you either compromise which may make both of you unhappy, or, one is the dominant in which case the other is very unhappy. There is no shame, you know, in loving each other, but not be able to construct a life together."

"I don't think, or rather I'd desperately hope that we are not facing that conundrum," said Albert.

"So do I," said Elizabeth "but I feel to be at sea these days."

"Oh, Albert, I have a letter for you which has been forwarded from New Queen Street. It looks rather official."

"Thank you, Estella," and he took the letter and slit it open and read it.

"Oh, good god, oh my goodness, how wonderful, that's exciting."

"What is it?" cried the other three almost in unison.

"My Pocket grandfather died two months ago and has left me five thousand pounds, but, oh dear, there is a condition, namely that I join his timber business. If I decide not, the legacy drops to five hundred pounds. That's a shame. I can't become a timber merchant."

"Why not?" said Elizabeth, "it obviously makes money and you could still paint."

"I'll think about it."

"I think you should think about it very carefully," said Estella, "your father's money will not last forever, and you will need to be very sure your paintings are going to bring you money."

As they went home after lunch, Charlotte mentioned to Estella her profound alarm that Albert made no attempt to comfort Elizabeth. Oh dear, she thought, he thinks he is being hardly done by. Oh, dear, oh dear. Maybe this potential legacy will bring him to his senses.

Estella had noticed Albert's cavalier attitude too, so she gave Elizabeth a specially tight hug on leaving them.

A handwritten note arrived the following day from the Embassy saying that no one was using the piano. Concerts were being planned, but the room was rarely used and Miss Fitzroy would be welcome to play most mornings. The Embassy would notify her if the room were to be required for some other purpose. She should get in touch with Mr. Egerton when she first arrived. The guards at the gate would be notified of her impending visit.

Once she received this message, Elizabeth's mood lightened and she called the Embassy at ten o'clock the following day.

X

Estella had a note from John Sargent asking her to come to the studio at her earliest convenience. He would be there every day for the next month, and please would she wear the floral dress and wear her hair as she had done when they first met for her portrait. She was very excited and over lunch with Charlotte told her that she did not intend to spend any time in bed with Mr. Sargent.

Charlotte was relieved for her friend, because she would undoubtedly be very disappointed and that it was difficult quite to know whether the man was a bounder. Estella thought not, as she remembered the long conversation about his fear of bodily contacts.

"And," said Charlotte, "I had a message delivered from Elizabeth."

"Please read it to me."

'Darling Aunt:

This is to let you know that I met Mr. Egerton at the Embassy and he showed me to the Music Room, which of course I knew. It turns out he is a pianist as well, but as a junior diplomat only in his second year, he feels constrained at asking permission to use this beautiful Bechstein. He did not stay long, though he was very charming, saying he'd linger another day to hear me play. He also mentioned there were one or two string players on the staff and we should play some quartets.

Lord Lyons came in as I was playing the final movement of the Hammerklavier Sonata (very difficult). At the end I introduced *myself and he said how sad he was to learn of my father's death, and what a fine public servant Father was, and how he had hoped to bring him back to Paris as Deputy once his term in Athens was over.*

I thanked him profusely, of course, and he said my playing was so good that he would invite me to play either at a soiree or a formal concert. How wonderful!

Thank you so much for making this possible.

Ever you loving niece,

Elizabeth.' September 15, '75.

"Oh, Charlotte, how thrilling! How clever you were to think of asking the Embassy. And to talk with the Ambassador. How interesting."

"It is really very exciting, isn't it? Perhaps this will refresh her relationships with Albert?"

"But" said Estella, "on the other hand, to look on the matter with a different eye, to be a beautiful and talented pianist in an Embassy replete with handsome young men should make Albert think very carefully.

"But now I really must go to Sargent."

With James' second birthday now on the horizon, Hamish wanted to buy him a special present, though Mary and he would be showering gifts on him. More to the point, he was also keen to buy something wonderful for Mary. To this end, he visited Whiteley's store in Bayswater, although he was not a keen shopper. It was one of these new commodious shops called department stores with masses of eager young salesmen and even some women, though they were confined to areas selling goods for women.

He was at something of a loss, so he went into the store's small café and sat down alone. How about a model omnibus bus with horses, or a wooden train, or another teddy bear? What does one buy for a two-year-old? Another piece of jewelry for Mary? Possibly.

The small number of tables started to fill up as the waitress promised him a pot of tea and a cake but he was in no hurry, taking a newspaper from his pocket. Just as the waitress arrived, a young man he had not noticed sat down next to him, there now being only a few vacant seats. Hamish glanced at the newcomer and looked quickly down at his newspaper, stunned by the young man's Greek-like beauty.

After a few minutes, the young man had been served with a cup of tea and said:

"Good morning, I'm Mike."

"Good morning, I am Hamish."

"Shopping for yourself?"

"No," and here he stumbled as he looked at the young man, "for my wife and my young son."

"Ah, how wonderful to have a wife and family. I don't think that will ever happen to me. I will just grow old alone, I expect."

"I'm sorry to hear that, but one can have lifelong friends even if one is not your wife," making the remark with ambiguity in case his assumption that the young man was queer was mistaken.

"That's what I hope for and, who knows, I may have found him."

"That would be excellent for you, I'm sure," wondering whether the young man thought he was queer.

"I agree with that," said Mike, "but I don't want to be confined. I was saying to Philip the other day, I said, Philip, you know we don't have to just keep to its being us, do we? I don't think he agreed with that, but he is so kind, he has got me all set up in a nice room and is with me as much as he can."

Hamish was now getting thoroughly alarmed. Philip, oh god, it will be Hardyman, I know.

Suddenly, Philip Hardyman was with them, grabbing a chair and sitting down.

"Do you two know each other?" said Philip, as Hamish and he looked at each with an unspoken agreement that they would not reveal themselves as professional partners.

"How d'ye do? I'm Hamish."

"How d'ye do, I'm Philip."

"Ah, you must be the Philip Mike has just been telling me about," said Hamish uneasily and looking Philip directly in the eye said: "Mike came and sat with me as there were no seats and we were just chatting. But I still have not got wee James' present or my gift for my wife Mary, so I must continue shopping. Please excuse me."

"So sorry you have to leave," said Mike, "we were just getting to know each other."

Hamish went to the cash register at the café door to pay his bill.

As the waitress was fiddling around at the cash register, he heard Philip very quietly berating Mike and Hamish wondered whether Philip was revealing their identities.

In the children's department, he bought a small wooden train for James, but his mind was on Philip and Mike. What an extraordinary coincidence, he thought. When Courtisone retires, it will now be extremely difficult for Philip to claim to be senior partner. Mike must be a kept man, and, certainly, he is utterly gorgeous, but how unlucky it is for Philip to be caught out in this way.

James was toddling around their sitting room when he got home, so he picked him up and told him about a hen and a fox, though little James had not yet acquired quite enough vocabulary to follow it and an excited James then unwrapped the train and was off upstairs to play with it, first giving his father a kiss of thanks before doing so. Both Mary and he believed in talking to James as much as possible so he could get used to the idea that words mattered. Mary sat looking proudly at her husband.

"You're looking quite smug this evening," she said.

"I had an extraordinary experience at Whiteley's," and he described what happened.

"What a fool that man must be," she said angrily, "I mean I personally don't care if he gets himself a rent-boy but he is asking for trouble in terms of the court of public opinion, for that cannot be kept secret as his accidental meeting with you illustrates.

"But more than that, he now has to decide the young man's future. Is he going to continue the arrangement and take on even more risk that he will be exposed? If he ends it, how will the young man react? To say nothing of his future at Courtisone and Jaggers."

"Good heavens, Mary, I had not thought that far ahead. The young man struck me as showing off his arrangement with Philip, but also enough of a whore to be prepared to offer himself to me, though I gave no indication that I was even remotely interested. My guess is that he talks to any man on his own as he did with me."

"Probably: Imagine. Suppose that this young man is indeed a rent-boy picked off the street by Philip, a high-risk venture anyway, especially for a lawyer. He is flattered and accepts both the room and presumably money to enable him, well, to go to Whiteleys, for instance, though that must have been just for a rendezvous with Philip."

"But then," said Hamish entering into the scenario, "he is alone most of the day while Philip is working. He has no other interest, so begins to feels constrained by his loneliness and does what he knows best, goes out picking up other men. I am sure I was his target. What's more, Philip has provided him with a room to accommodate his catch."

"How frightful. Are you going to say anything to Philip?"

"I rather think it is his choice as to whether he wants to speak to me about it."

Nathaniel Courtisone, senior partner at the law firm of Courtisone and Jaggers, called a meeting of all the members of the practice to his office at eleven o'clock on Thursday September 30, 1875. Present were Philip Hardyman, Hamish Macdonald, Clarence Smythe, lawyers, Adam Masterson, senior clerk and three junior clerks, one from Little Britain and two from Courtisone's offices.

"I have called you all here today to announce my retirement as from today. I have had many happy years battling for justice, and I plan to retire to Crocketts, the house in Hertfordshire where we held that wonderful party. I am disappointed, as I am sure you are, that O'Grady and Billington, for very different reasons, are no longer with us. I have not attempted to replace them as you must now choose who you want to work with.

"However, I want to tell you that we have a fine team of three young lawyers and I have watched you develop your skills with pride, mixed a little bit with envy at your stage in your career. My daughter tells me this should have happened long ago, though I have not felt any particular loss of faculties, but I do not want to die in harness.

"As to future arrangements of the practice, I do not think it is my right to determine how the practice progresses. I have one word of advice. The lawyers must come together and decide who is to be the senior partner and on that matter, I have nothing to say. The responsibilities of the senior partner, as you know, affect the external and internal work of the practice, and sometimes the allocation of briefs, depending on requests. The practice has so far been predominantly for clients in court as barristers and, as it expands, I would also advise choosing those whose advocacy will be their predominant interest.

"I have not thought it necessary to hold some major event to celebrate my retirement, but I have booked a table at *The Cheshire Cheese* and I hope you will all join me at one o'clock.

"Mr. Hardyman, Mr. Macdonald and Mr. Smythe may now wish to convene to discuss the future. I should add that, while I am personally very much attached to this accommodation, you might find it more appropriate to surrender both sets of premises, here and in Little Britain and rent chambers in one of the Inns of Court."

Courtisone got up from his chair and retired into his inner room. Adam suggested that the clerks should make their way toward the Inn for lunch.

The three lawyers sat in a stunned silence.

"I have no wish to take on the responsibilities of senior partner as I am considering my future as a lawyer," said Philip at which Hamish breathed an inaudible sigh of relief.

"Come, come," said Clarence, "this is impossible, Philip. You have a corpus of knowledge on the clients of the legacy practice and you are much senior to both of us."

"I am grateful for your compliments, Clarence, but I am really not committed to continuing my future in the Law, and it would be unfair of me to accept and then disappear in two years' time."

Clarence continued to try to persuade Philip to change his mind, while Hamish sat not knowing quite what to do. He was not a person for confrontation, unlike his wife Mary. He knew that Philip realized how his relationship with Mike made it impossible for him to assume a leading role. This was not a matter of the public getting to know that Philip kept a rent-boy. Philip was as aware as anyone that it was impossible to keep it secret, given that Mike had told a complete stranger, who happened to be Hamish, of the arrangement. The likelihood of Mike spilling the beans further, as the saying goes, was far too great. Maybe Philip could hide away inside the practice, but a public position was out of the question.

"May I suggest this as a way forward," said Hamish, breaking the deadlock between Philip and Clarence. "I am willing to act as senior partner for a period of say, three years. I may then prefer not to continue. We are clearly going to need to recruit one if not two barristers to our practice very soon and by then they will be established and able to have a view.

"At that point, neither of you may have confidence in my leadership and may wish to change the incumbency of senior partner from me to someone else anyway, assuming Philip does not leave us directly. It is possible, of course, that we could then invite a senior partner from elsewhere to join us. So let us regard this as a temporary measure."

Philip responded:

"I am so grateful for your statesmanlike attitude to this matter, Hamish, and I think Clarence and I should be very grateful to you for this excellent suggestion. You might have three more children, for instance, in three years' time and the burdens of office might be too great. By then, too, Clarence may have enough experience for the position and I may have resolved my personal situation."

"I would add my thanks," said Clarence, "but I do hope Philip will not withdraw."

"Let us see how things develop," said Philip.

"Now let us go to lunch," said Hamish, with the authority of a senior partner.

When he was told of the arrangement over lunch Courtisone was very pleased and he congratulated the lawyers for their wisdom, though he expressed some concern at Philip's reticence.

Philip and Hamish stayed behind as the others left after lunch.

"I am sorry and truly embarrassed by my inadvertent discovery of your arrangement with Mike," said Hamish,

"You can't imagine how shocked I was to see you talking to him."

"How long has this been going on?"

"A month or so now and I find him very possessive."

"That does not surprise me. I thought you had indicated that permanence was the last kind of arrangement you wanted with a man."

"I did and I do, and I have made a terrible mistake which was why I could not risk taking this position. I have been simply overwhelmed by him."

"How did you meet?"

"I saw him on Wardour Street. It was his first afternoon on the street, so he said, as he had just lost his parents and had no money. He does have class of a sort as you can tell by his accent."

"Are you sure it was his first time? He seemed a long-standing practitioner to me."

"Oh, I don't know," said Philip with a sigh.

"At any rate, I have to find a way to break off our relationship and I don't know how. Should I be direct? Should I take it slowly, seeing less and less of him, in the hope that he will find someone else, or go back to the street. I don't know."

"If he really is so possessive, I think an abrupt break could spell disaster. He could turn nasty. On the other hand, if you have him watched to see whether he goes with someone else, then you have a good reason to break with him. To be frank, Philip, you have to put desire aside and regard him as a significant danger."

"You are right. I will not change our arrangements meanwhile and will find someone to watch him."

"You could use Sidney, one of Wemmick's men. If you did, I would suggest this strategy. Tell Mike that you have to be away for a week visiting your sick father or some other excuse. But I think the excuse must be genuine, as he might well come looking for you if you stayed in London and with your luck, he'd find you."

"Excellent proposal. I have a constant invitation to my grandmother's home in Shropshire. I will arrange for us to go as a family and set Sidney to work. I will not tell him the reason of course, but say the individual is mixed up in a complicated case I am dealing with."

"Good. I know we have not been on very good terms recently but I hope we can work together well, especially with the work of the Trust."

"I will be glad to do that, Hamish, and many thanks for your help in this unfortunate and indelicate matter for which I blame myself."

Two young people were regular visitors to the Embassy Music Room. Elizabeth was there to play the piano and Timothy Egerton saw himself in a custodial role for this beautiful young woman, daughter of a well-known former diplomat.

Their conversations was very friendly, and he asked her to have lunch with him in the Embassy refreshment room which pleased her as he was such good company.

"Tell me about yourself, Elizabeth."

"I am in Paris with my partner, Albert. He is an aspiring painter so he slouches around in cafés where they gather and visits the studios of other painters while trying to finish a portrait of his father."

"Oh, I see, you live together then?"

"Yes, we met in London a few years ago, then I went to Versailles and to Athens with my father. At that time, Albert was trapped in the Commune, not unwillingly I should say, and he was injured at the end of it and found his way into the grounds here at the Embassy."

"Well, well, that is a radical domestic arrangement, is it not?"

"I suppose so, and I don't quite know why I am sharing this with you but he has become so obsessed with his paintings that I feel neglected, so it was a great delight to be able to come here and play."

"Goodness me, I cannot imagine you being neglected."

"Why?"

"Well, and I am sure you have been told this before, you are such a beautiful young woman, it inconceivable that you would feel lonely."

"That is so sweet of you, Timothy; oh, excuse me, may I call you Timothy? Please call me Elizabeth."

"Thank you, Elizabeth. I generally answer to Tim, as the diminutive of the Greek origin."

"Enough of me. How about you?"

"I joined the Service after Cambridge now that there are competitive examinations."

"I'm sure you did well."

"Yes, I did get a first and the Greek Prize which eventually gave me choice of Embassy, Paris was an obvious choice, especially as I am bilingual in French and English, though I do speak a little German and Italian."

"My goodness, and what of your family?"

"My name is an ancient one, but we are only very distant relatives of the famous Cheshire family. My father is a Canon at Norwich Cathedral so we now have a splendid house in the Close. It's quite delightful."

"I am an only child, what about you?"

"A younger sister. My mother suffers from aches in her bones. I can't remember the technical term, but I am sure she will be in a wheelchair soon."

"What do you love?

"Apart from listening to you playing the piano?"

"I assumed that," she said with a smile, looking at him almost but not quite seductively.

"I suppose my great delight is reading those classical philosophers who are politicians or who write about politics, Cicero, Aristotle and others. These men were such giants for their time."

"How interesting. I would love to be a scholar."

"You can always learn, you know."

With that, lunch ended. Tim went toward his office, his head swimming with admiration of her, while Elizabeth had to admit to herself that she found him quite charming: So different with his intellect from Albert but she told herself that she must not make such comparisons.

After a hasty visit to see Estella and Charlotte, she arrived back to their fourth-floor apartment in the early evening and Albert was not there. Of course, she thought with some irritation. She sat down and continued to read *The Pallisers.* An hour or so after the sun went down she cooked a croque monsieur for herself, assuming Albert was finding food elsewhere. It was just this sort of loneliness that was an annoyance in her relationship with Albert. No message, just neglect. In fact, she thought, this is happening far too often. Rather angry, she went to bed, and slept.

Waking up well before dawn there was still no sign of Albert. She got up to make herself a cup of tea. She assumed he had drunk too much and slept on the floor of John or Gustave's apartment, but this was the first time he had not been with her at night since they came to Paris. She walked over in the half-light to the tall windows with their lace curtains which looked on to the street.

Under the streetlamp, she was startled to see Albert embracing a girl, kissing her, presumably saying good night, as they clung to each other as if not wanting to part, arms extended, fingers touching, till she turned round and ran down the street, stopping once to wave to him as he slowly climbed the steps to the door of the building.

Elizabeth was incensed. She bolted the entrance door to the apartment and went back to the bedroom, dimming the gas light as she went.

Soon she heard the key in the lock and the door rattling. She crept to the door so that she could hear him.

"*Merde alors*," he said. Then knocking quietly, he said:

"Open the door, Elizabeth, please."

She didn't answer. He continued for ten minutes pleading with her, raising his voice. She ignored him. Finally he went downstairs. She hid behind the curtain, saw him come out on to the street and look up at the darkened apartment.

Seeing no light, he wondered if only for a moment if she was staying with her aunt and the door lock was jammed. But then he realized how stupid an idea that was. She watched him come up the steps again, and a few minutes later, the knocks and the pleading continued.

No answer. She assumed he had sat down with his back to the apartment door.

She went back to bed.

Three hours later, around seven o'clock in the morning, she heard the knocking and the pleading begin again. Her anger had now become a rugged determination.

She opened the door and there he was, dirty and smelling of an expensive perfume.

"Where have you been? Drunk on someone's floor, I suppose?"

"Yes, Gustave and his wife invited a group of us in the studio for a drink and I had rather too much and he kindly offered me a bed. I had slept it off a little and came home as soon as I woke around dawn."

"Really?

"This is the last straw, Albert. I am going round to my aunt's shortly and when I come back, you will have taken all your things and gone. Who knows where? Klein's? Or that girl you were embracing in the street this morning?"

"Oh, Elizabeth darling, I am sorry, I am sorry indeed."

"Stuff and nonsense, Albert. You want to be a painter, and that is your choice. But in the process, you neglect me so that my aunt has to rescue me from dying of boredom by getting permission for me to play the piano at the Embassy. You are developing the morals of an alley cat, like many of your damn painter friends. I am finished with you."

"Oh dear, oh dear, I am sorry, I am sorry."

"But it won't do, Albert. First, you get into bed with some girl or other – – and I wish to know nothing about it — but then you lie about it. The one really common virtue we shared was telling the truth to each other. And you have broken that code. I will now never know in future whether you are or are not being honest with me, and I do not have to put up with you."

"Oh, Elizabeth, please."

"No, I am disgusted with you. You have blown away in a few short months all my feelings for you. Get out of my sight! Begone from this place by noon, or I will have you evicted. I signed the lease remember and I am paying the rent."

Elizabeth stormed out of the apartment, grabbing hat and coat as she went, and ran down the stairs to the street. I should be weeping my heart out, she thought, I am relieved but I must go and tell my aunt. Oh, goodness and there's Estella too. If she take his side in this, so be it.

XI

Charlotte opened the door to Elizabeth who burst into loud and prolonged tears and led her quietly into the room where Estella was having breakfast. She promptly put down her napkin and got up to see what the fuss was about.

"What on earth is the matter?" Asked Estella.

"Now sit down," Charlotte said, "and tell us all about it. What is this sudden explosion of emotion about?"

"I have finished with Albert completely and forever."

"Good gracious," said Estella, "why?"

"He has neglected me for far too long. He did not come home last night. I got up at first light and there he was in the street in the arms of a girl, embracing and kissing before she ran off down the street. How do I know what he has been doing?"

"The stupid fool," said Estella, "What on earth has got into him? You are quite right, my dear. Once a person is an adulterer that itself is difficult to cope with, but I will wager he lied to you about the girl too."

"Yes, he did."

"Then good riddance I say, though he is my step-son of whom I am inordinately fond," she said masking the tears that came to her eyes.

Charlotte then said: "My dear Elizabeth, how hurt you must be, but, you know, Estella and I are not very surprised or shocked. While we adored the thought of you two being together, it was apparent that Albert was going to go off on his own, with or without you."

"Yes," said Estella, "Maybe he will come to his senses and try to make amends but the difficulty will be to restore trust between you.

"I am afraid, my dear, that Albert is becoming so much like so many men. Women are just there as support or objects to admire. He's be as proud as punch with you on his arm, lovely as you are, but he puts his own interests first."

"Oh, Estella, thank you so much. As I was coming to tell you both, I was anxious that I must cause some kind of break between you two, which I could not bear."

"No, dear girl, we have no secrets at all, do we Charlotte?"

"Not that I know of," she replied, and laughter at that remark eased the tension.

"Now, you must go to the bedroom along the corridor and rest. Thank goodness, we chose an apartment with three bedrooms, though, at the time, I could think of no reason why we would need it."

"Thank you so much, aunt. I have had a very disturbed night and need some sleep. I won't go to the Embassy today."

"Go to my bedroom and sleep for a while till Albert is gone," said Charlotte.

"Thank you, Aunt, that will be a godsend."

Estella was very unhappy that Albert had behaved so badly. He had been extremely fortunate to hold on to Elizabeth's affections and she was a loyal soul as she had demonstrated with her caring for her father. What a fool he was not to see her admirable qualities.

Charlotte was disappointed, rather than angry.

"As I think about it, Estella, Albert has got this streak of adventure about him, a sort of devil-may-care attitude to life."

"Yes, indeed. One may admire his determination to stay in Paris during the Commune but Henry described it as foolhardy, so Elizabeth told me once."

"He is a grown man now, but I think he has been seduced by the louche and immoral antics of those painters. Think about it. John Sargent seems a sensible well brought up young man, but he is enough of a bounder to ask you to bed with him. Goodness knows what these French painters get up to."

"To be sure, Charlotte, but I had not realized that there would be young women around them, only aspiring women painters whose names I can't remember but would love to meet."

"Perhaps Albert has not been spending too much time with them but in fact has been chasing young women."

The doorbell rang and the concierge admitted Albert.

Estella looked sternly at Albert and said:

"Wait there, my dear, and we will walk out to the café where we will have lunch."

There was an embarrassed silence as Charlotte read the newspaper while Albert stood waiting for Estella to fetch her hat, coat and gloves. They walked down the street in silence, went into the café, ordered their coffees and sat down.

"What on earth are you up to, Albert?"

"I have been a fool, I know."

"Who was this young woman you were embracing?"

"Oh, I met her at Gustave's house. Actually, I like her a lot."

"But what about Elizabeth?"

"She wants more of me than I can give nowadays. I used to be so committed to her, but now I have my art at which I am improving, I have a group of friends in which she shows no interest."

"So, I suppose this flirtation is really a statement that you no longer wish to be engaged to Elizabeth or to live with her."

"Oh, I don't know. I suppose the kinds of constraints on my life that were there when we live in London are no longer there. I am only twenty-three and I want to enjoy life."

"A common enough complaint. What do you propose to do?"

"Elizabeth insisted I leave our apartment by noon. I have left my belongings with Nimrod Klein and he is thinking about whether he will have me there on a long-term basis. If not, I am sure I could have a bed at Gustave's house until I find my own rooms."

"Are you in any financial difficulties?"

"No, Father left me quite enough to live as I am doing, though I do not have enough resources to marry Elizabeth. We have never talked about money, though she seems to be quite secure in that regard."

"Who, by the way, is this young woman?"

"She is quite lovely, innocent, only seventeen, but seemingly independent. She is dabbling in painting too but she is a young person of many talents."

"Is this just anywhere near being serious?"

"It might be, I don't know."

"It sounds to me as though you gave up on Elizabeth some time ago."

"No, not really, but meeting Simona brought many things into focus."

"That is her name?"

"Yes, Simona."

"Simona who?"

"Oh, Simona Rothschild, She's Jewish and I think her family is quite wealthy."

"Wealthy?" cried Estella, "Only one of the richest families in Europe!"

"Really, I didn't know."

"Well, it is possible she is from a part of the family whose second name is not Croesus, but I doubt it. But do be careful, very careful if you get toward loving her properly, if you know what I mean."

"Oh, that is in the far distance, I think."

"But be aware of the animosity too many people in the country feel towards Jews."

"I am aware of that and we have talked about it briefly."

"But that also means that it is highly unlikely that her family would support any relationship with a Gentile. But enough. You will let me know where you are living. I think Charlotte and I will be heading back to England soon. I need to have John complete my portrait before then. But I wish I had been able to meet some women painters."

"Perhaps I can arrange meetings for you. Some of them used to come each week to the *Café Guerbois,* but they have moved on to meeting at the *Café de La Noveulle-Athenes.* Let me see, there's Berthe Morisot, an American Mary Cassatt, and a rather splendid woman who lives at Fontainebleau, Rosa Bonheur. Auguste meets with them sometimes,."

"That would be very useful. Before you go, my dear Albert, I am deeply sorry that your relationship with Elizabeth is at an end, but, please, do think about what happened and how it will affect you in the future."

"I will, and I am very grateful for your understanding, Estella. Now it has come to a head, I am frankly very relieved."

"I am afraid men behave like that: Deceiving a woman and then putting that treachery behind them. I hope this will be a lesson to you, you nincompoop, just understand that the terms of any new relationship are mutually and openly determined, not assumed."

Philip and Jane actually enjoyed each other's company on their visit to Much Wenlock and walked over the Malvern Hills almost every day. Philip did not reveal what was really on his mind of course, but he could not push it away when he got out of bed in the morning and looked in the mirror where he saw a lawyer in deep trouble.

Philip had briefed Sidney very carefully about watching Mike as he knew the sleuth's formidable reputation, and indeed there was a message from this tireless investigator when he returned to the office requesting an interview. Sidney was thus invited to call shortly after everyone else had left the office for home.

"Ah, Mr. Hardyman, I have some important news for you."

"Thank you, Sidney. I'd like to get this case wrapped up soon. It has been on my mind while I have been in Shropshire."

"It is as you suspected, sir. This individual, Michael Watson by name, is a common male prostitute, a rent-boy as they are called. I have seen him offering himself at a new site for sodomites just near the public conveniences in Hyde Park across the Bayswater Road. That is convenient as his lodging is a mere fifteen minutes from there.

"He has taken home at least ten different men during the week, the last one I saw yesterday being a very posh gentleman in a silk topper, a frock coat, and a cravat. He was a man of military bearing and I know I have seen him before, but I can't for the life of me remember when or where."

"That is excellent, Sidney. That is exactly what I wanted to know. I will charge my clients a hefty sum, so I am glad to give you ten pounds for your services."

"Well thank you sir, but is that all you can spare?

"No, why?'

"I generally expect twenty pounds for a week's work of this kind and as it is not you that's paying, perhaps...?

"Of course, it's a pleasure to work you," said Philip groaning slightly as he gave Sidney another pair of five-pound notes."

Sidney left promptly with his portable property and hurried off to find Mrs. Sidney for a night on the tiles.

Philip sat bemused by his predicament. He decided he must confront Mike simply telling him that their arrangement was finished, as he had gone back on the street. As he rode a cab across London to the road to Edgware Road, he was assessing himself as confoundedly stupid, breaking the irregular pattern of his homosexual life for something more permanent.

Still, Mike was obviously quite able to look after himself, and in ending the relationship he must do so quietly and politely, not in some kind of accusatory tone. He had never seen Mike angry, and Philip thought that if he were to be truculent in any way, he would continue to pay the rent for six months or so.

No, that would be foolish as we would still have to have contact. Determined then to do what was necessary, he asked the cab to put him down a hundred yards from the building where Mike lived and he walked along the road with some stealth.

He was within twenty yards of the door when a very distinguished looking gentleman came out on to the street. Philip recognized him at once. It was Sir Bertram Bloviate, Member of Parliament for London North-East, and a barrister whom Hardyman had seen in court. He seemed to be slightly agitated as he called a cab.

So this must have been the gentleman Sidney told me about. Well, well, well, thought Philip, waiting for several minutes before approaching the building and ensuring Sir Bertram's cab was out of sight on the way to Marble Arch. Quite why he felt he needed to summon up his courage to talk to Mike was a matter he thought about later.

However, he pulled himself together and walked carefully up the stairs which were inadequately lit and, fiddling with his key, he opened the door to the apartment, preparing to tell Mike of his decision. The room had a small kitchen on the left and facilities on the right leading to the room he knew well with its bed and other furniture which he could scarcely make out from the darkness seemed in disarray. It seemed empty. He turned on the gas lamp.

Lying on the floor was Mike. He was clearly dead, his beautiful body had been beaten badly and it looked to Philip as though his head had been hit with a blunt instrument. There was not much blood coming from his head, so whoever did this was probably free of bloodstains. Deeply shocked but sensing that discretion was the better part of valor and that he was now at a terrible risk, he quietly closed the door and went out into the street to walk home to Jane. Not being a person with forensic interests, he did not stop to try to assess the likely time of the murder. He would talk with Hamish, perhaps, tomorrow. As he walked, he shuddered with the shock and stopped at a public house for a large brandy.

There he sat for a while, as one brandy led to another. Far too many questions were tumbling through his mind. Who did this? Why? Was Mike deceiving him and having others enter the same arrangement as his? Was this really Bloviate's work? He didn't seem like someone who had just fought and murdered a young man when he came out of the building? Perhaps he had knocked and getting no reply, simply left?

Perhaps he had even had a key, discovered the body and beaten a hasty retreat ? But there were only two keys, Mike's and his. Was there anything in the room to connect him with Mike? How long would it be before Mike's body was discovered? Did he have men coming to his room without being picked up on the street? What a confounded mess!

What became clear to Philip was that he must at least return to the room to get anything that might link him to Mike. With an air of brandy-fueled confidence, he walked back, went up the stairs and opened the door. The body was, fortunately, head down, so he did not have to look at those lovely blue eyes. All he could find was a notebook which he pocketed. Surveying the rest of the room, he realized there must have been a rent book of some kind and in the bedside drawer it was there, but in Mike's name. He took it at the same time realizing that the police would surely find something to connect him to Mike. Scotland Yard men were not all stupid.

He returned to the pub for two more glasses of brandy and meandered his way home to Jane murmuring "Oh god, oh god, my children."

When he got home, Philip flopped into a chair in the drawing room after emptying the remains of a brandy bottle into a tumbler. Then throwing the liquid down his throat, he slept the turbulent sleep of the serious inebriate. His wife Jane and his children were in bed.

He awoke after an hour, staggered to his feet, and reached into the sideboard for another bottle of brandy. After another four hours with *eau de vie* from Chateau Courvoisier for company, he knocked over the empty bottle on to the Turkish rug, but in a noisy attempt to find another one containing the famous liquid, he disturbed his wife in their bedroom upstairs and after a while she came downstairs in her nightgown to find him sprawled across a sofa in their living room.

"What is the matter with you, Philip?" she asked almost as if she thought he was sober. "You have been acting strangely since we got back from Shropshire and now you come home very late and are obviously as drunk as a lord. What on earth can be bothering you?"

"Come and sit with me, my dear Jane, for a moment," he said with a pronounced slur in his voice punctuated by the occasional hiccough.

"Can I ask you something?"

"Of course, Philip, anything."

"Tell me truly, truly now, I won't take anything else for an answer, do you love me?"

"Of course I do."

"No, not of course, woman, that's the formal response. I mean, deep down, deep in the recesses of your heart, do you love me?'

"Yes, I do."

"Are you sure, absolutely and without the shade of a lie that you love me?" he asked again with the impertinent insistence of the drunkard.

"I find you very trying at times and I wish you were at home more with the children, and I wish we spent more time together as we have just done and as we did when we first married. I know your work is a trial and will be more so with Courtisone retiring."

"H'mm."

He hesitated and got uneasily to his feet and turned away from her with a loud belch. He then tried, as drunks do, to look directly at her, but his focus was gone and he could only gaze in her general direction.

"But do you really, Jane, really love me for better, for worse, for richer, for poorer?"

"That was my oath before God, but there is obviously some terrible problem you have. You can tell me about it, you know. It is for better, for worse."

"Steel yourself then, Jane," he said dropping back on to the couch next to her and grasping her hand to which she reacted given the foul smell of alcohol on his breath.

"Have you been gambling or something?"

"No, far worse, I'm afraid. Let me explain," he said, managing to become more coherent.

"Before I married you, as you know," he said, gazing now at bottle on the rug, "I had two loving relationships with women which failed. Then I met you and we fell in love.

"What I did not tell you then was that I had also been with men."

"Oh, dear God, with men? That is so unnatural."

"No, Jane, quite natural. But, but, but, let me continue while the brandy is still enabling me to confess. Since we married I have from time to time had very brief liaisons with men, but never with women, so I did not regard myself as being unfaithful, merely enjoying myself," he said now giggling to himself slightly, as if he were proud of it.

"Oh heavens, I wondered why our intimacy had become so very abrupt and now I know why I was always left unsatisfied."

"But it gets worse," he said, now beginning to achieve something like sobriety.

"I recently found a desirable young man and I rented a room where he could live, so that our relationship would be exclusive. I went to see him to end the relationship tonight which I had planned to do immediately we got back from Shropshire.

"Where's the brandy?"

Staggering to the sideboard, he opened the cupboard and exclaimed:

"Dammit, that was the last bottle."

By now Jane was weeping copiously into a kerchief, getting up and walking round the room, saying silently to herself; "no, no, no, oh my children, my children."

"But this is the shock, Jane, this is the shock," as he wandered around the room, "when I got to his room and opened the door, I saw that he was dead, brutally murdered," he said beginning to weep, "the poor child was dead, his lovely body cold and still"

At that, Jane howled with deepening dismay such that both children appeared at the top of the stairs at which Philip staggered out into the hall and called out:

"Go back to bed now, children, your Mother is very distressed but she will be fine," and he went back into the drawing room and closed the door.

"I didn't know what to do, Jane. I went back to rescue his pocketbook in case it had my name in it. I don't know whether to report it anonymously. I can't go to the police, can I, and admit the relationship, can I, or I will be sent to prison?"

Jane had got up and was pacing the room, still weeping silently.

"I suppose you had no alternative but to bring me into your sordid life by telling me all this as if I would somehow be able to forgive you. You have tested my loyalty and my solemn oath to its limit, for this is the most dreadful, fearsome thing to have happened to me.

"While you were cavorting with male whores, you were also destroying my life. I do not know what to do. I need advice. Who was that older woman we met at the Courtisone's, she seemed a woman of the world?"

"That must have been Estella Pirrip, but she is in Paris."

"I can trust her advice, I think. I will go there tomorrow and you will give me the money I need. I expect Hamish Macdonald will have her address at the office. Perhaps I could talk with Mary Macdonald too."

Jane then fled upstairs, weeping at her marriage collapsing in ruins around her with the speed and impact of an avalanche.

Philip fell onto the couch and slept, his snores resounding through the house.

The following morning Hamish arrived at the office and was surprised to find Philip there waiting for him, looking somewhat disheveled and obviously recovering from too much drink.

"Hamish, we must talk. Let's us walk."

They walked down to the river near London Bridge and sat on a bench.

"The most terrible thing has happened. I went to break it off with Mike and I found his body brutally assaulted lying on the floor with blood around his head which was smashed. I retrieved his pocketbook and then went home and confessed everything to Jane."

"My dear fellow, how terrible, but was that not extremely foolhardy?"

"When I left Mike's room, I stopped in a couple of bars and when I got home I thought this is all going to come out and I may as well get it off my chest which I did after a bottle of brandy. Indeed it was a relief. Jane was utterly dismayed."

"Good god, man, what did you expect? Forgiveness? I am not surprised she is dismayed, as you put it. I would think she is apoplectic. Why did you not come to us?"

"I never thought I'd be welcome late at night."

"No, that's true and I think Mary is best left in the dark."

"Hamish, what do I do? How can I just wait until someone, for some reason, finds the body? I must alert someone, surely."

"Let us work out a strategy. Perhaps you should go immediately to the police, tell them you had rented this room for the son of an old friend who had died, that he was behind with his rent, you turned up this morning to collect and there he was – murdered? You know nothing of his profession or habits."

"Apart from the fact that is almost entirely untrue, it sounds excellent. Except that he paid the rent to someone I don't know."

"Tell me, honestly, have you ever paid a rent-boy before Mike?"

"Never, the Gavel Club has supplied my needs."

"Good, for that means that when the police start to make enquiries about Mike, none of them will know you or name you. You are not well known at Semper House, I assume, and in any case, you said it was Mike's first day."

"But while I was away, according to Sidney, Mike had several men, including the distinguished gentleman whom I saw leaving the building as I approached."

"Who was he?"

"A Member of Parliament, but I think he may had the same experience as I had. That is, he had an appointment, went to Mike's room, saw the chaos and promptly left."

"But how did he get into the room to see? Did he have a key?"

"Oh dear, I don't know. I thought earlier Mike could have made him a key."

"Your problem is this: if you do not go this very minute to the police, then this strategy is dead, and you will have to say you went there early this morning, say, catching him before he went to work. Apart from me, does anyone else know of your connection with Mike?"

"Not to my knowledge, but who knows whom he might have told, as he told you in Whiteley's?"

"This all seems contrary somehow. By that, I mean you are not the murderer.

"Your legal jeopardy hangs on the laws on sodomy first, and then failure to report a crime. Think about it now from the viewpoint of a lawyer. How would you advise a lawyer who came to you in this predicament?"

"I'd tell him to report the murder to the police."

"Right, do you think Adam Masterson knows you are queer, though married?"

"I don't know, why?

"His cousin is a senior police officer, you know."

"Oh, no, I don't want to involve Adam at all."

"All right, now, can your conscience stand not doing anything at all, just wait until someone discovers the body, somehow? The longer the delay, the more difficult an investigation will be to determine the time of death and then you can say you were not back from Shropshire, if asked."

"I think that's right and now I have to handle Jane. She will be coming round this morning to ask for Estella's address. She has some half-witted idea that Estella will give good advice and she plans to go to Paris to meet her. As I have damaged her so fearfully, I can but comply. If you think of any advice, let me know. Meantime, I must leave before Jane gets to the office."

Philip immediately left to walk hurriedly to the old Courtisone offices confident that leaving Mike where he was seemed the only sensible strategy. As he walked, he realized that he was very selfish indeed, and that, in truth, if he were to disappear, he would not miss bringing up his children and nor would he miss Jane, nor would he face any consequences of the murder.

One alternative that sprang into his mind was to leave immediately for Australia. He had been to Brisbane and it was a bit of a pioneer town, but it was expanding, the lawyers were terrible and he could set up a practice there. He would write to Jane a short note saying he need to get away for a few days, not telling her where he was headed, take a large proportion of his liquid assets from the bank, but leaving enough for Jane and the children to survive.

He could stand the situation no longer. He had to get out.

He knew himself well. He was a coward, and a rotten one too.

On the way to his office, he stopped at the agent's booking office, saying that the case he had earlier in Australia had not been resolved and he needed to return there promptly.

He left the agent's office with a booked passage from Southampton two days hence on Friday, for Melbourne, not Brisbane as there was no boat for that destination for a month. He could make his way to Brisbane from Melbourne by sea if not by land. As he knew his children would be at school and Jane was headed to see Estella, he took a cab to his house, packed a variety of personal things including clothes suitable for Australia and hurried to the station, rather than waiting in London two days for the boat train.

He got to Southampton Wednesday evening, and booked into the Railway Hotel. From there on Friday morning, he posted longer letters to Hamish and to Jane. To Hamish he explained that he could no longer face the situation and described where he was going, saying that he could trust him to keep his destination secret. He asked Hamish also to negotiate with Jane on a divorce and that he would mail him from Brisbane when he was settled. To Jane, he said only that he was going away for a long while.

He included a separate letter to Hamish resigning from his position at Courtisone and Jaggers.

In the early afternoon, he walked into his small cabin and berth on the SS *Endeavour* bound for Melbourne.

Meantime Jane visited Hamish for Estella's address and returned home to pack things to go to Paris, leaving Hamish to send a wire to Estella saying she would arrive the following day needing essential advice. When Jane got home, she found the short note from Philip. She saw that Philip had filled a suitcase with some of his things. The little painting of her by his bedside was still there.

Her assumption from his note was that he would hide out somewhere for a few days and that he would return. She called her children together with Florence, her elderly maid, and told them that their father had gone away for a few days and that she had to go to Paris on family business, but they were to go to school as usual, Florence would look after them, and she would be back quite quickly.

Throughout their marriage, she had been able to draw money from his bank, so she was not concerned about her financial position. She was still in a turbulent state of mind now being without a husband and without her children from whom she had never before been parted. She was convinced that Estella could help her, help she needed immediately.

She bought a newspaper as she boarded the boat train for Folkestone at Victoria, and quickly noted a small column telling of the murder of a young male prostitute and would anyone with knowledge of the young man contact the Bayswater police station. Of course, she thought, police are not going to waste their time on such an undesirable member of society.

XII

At last Estella had arranged to meet John Sargent for the completion of her portrait. The trouble with Albert and Elizabeth had occupied too much of her time. It was not that she was not most distressed at Albert's behavior, but this emotion coincided with a devout wish that he would mature into something like a respectable human being like his father and thereby be free from her oversight.

John hailed her as she walked to the small knoll in the Bois where she had lain for his sketches, the speed of his pencils across the paper earlier were a matter of astonishment for her. She was curious as to why he wanted her to be there not the studio, especially as it was November and while it was not a wintry day, it was not clement either. She wore the floral dress as he had asked but was wrapped in a mink coat.

"Ah, Estella," he said, "how are you?"

"I am well in myself, but not with the world at large, so I hope this will not last long."

"Albert, I suppose."

"Yes."

"I did not think he could be that foolish, I must confess."

"Has he told you what happened?"

"Yes, I think he told everyone who could listen that now he was in love with Simona Rothschild, who is rather a silly little thing, attractive no doubt, but a little empty-headed even for a Jew."

"That is harsh."

"Yes, probably an indication of my affection and admiration for Elizabeth."

"So, how about the portrait?"

"It is completed and I want to show it to you this afternoon but I want to meet here because I wanted you just to recline as you were in the dress as I want the hem of the dress to be accurate as it leads the eye into the picture and along your arm. I think I have it right, but I wanted to make sure."

She threw off her mink and sat shivering for a few minutes while he made some jottings in his book. Then he asked:

"On a more serious note, do you think it is too early for me to ask Elizabeth to spend some time with me? I have a view of her and me spending a long and happy life together."

"Oh my dear John, I have no idea. I know she is very angry indeed with Albert as she feels he has lead her a dance."

"Hmm, shall we walk to the studio or would you prefer a cab?"

"Let us walk."

There were several painters there, and in particular a woman talking with Auguste who was introduced as Rosa Bonheur.

"Mme. Bonheur," said Estella in French, "I have heard about you from my step-son Albert Pirrip whom I don't see here at the moment."

"Oh, Albert," said Mme. Bonheur, replying in English, "such a pretty boy and a promising painter, I think, but no flair."

Ignoring that comment, Estella said, "I have founded a League for Free Women in London and I would love to meet other women painters in Paris, as I think of them as inspirations to all of us. I wonder if we might meet some time when I return to Paris?"

"Of course, ma cherie, but you have come to see John's portrait of you. Let us go and look."

John was hovering during that conversation, getting the more anxious by the minute as to whether the portrait was successful. He approached the easel, drew off the cover, and Estella gasped in amazement, reached for a chair and sat down. It was utterly splendid, rich in color, capturing her most beautifully. Other painters came to admire it, Gustave especially approving the textures and tints he had worked into the painting. It was also so fresh and light.

"Excellent, Mr. Sargent, excellent. I wish to own it. How much do I owe you?"

"Oh, Estella, I would like to present it to you."

"Fiddlesticks, I will write a note for two hundred pounds."

The painters around the easel gasped, especially when Sargent told them how much that was in francs.

"I am leaving Paris for London shortly and would like to take it with me. Can you see to its being packed properly? Come here, young man," and she reached up and kissed him fervently on the lips, at which he staggered back in surprise while everyone cheered.

Crashing through the studio door came Albert. He had seen the painting in construction but not finished. He stopped, looking at it and gasped at its beauty and its composition.

"Now, Estella, I assume you have bought it, so that you are now the proud possessor of an early Sargent portrait of which I am sure there will be many."

"That is so, my friend. I have two commissions up my sleeve. I wish I could persuade Estella to allow me to put the portrait up for the next exhibition."

"Of course John, but not too often. I'll install it either in my London house or my country house dining room. I cannot decide presently where it will look more enticing. Oh my goodness, my mother would have loved to see this, and I am sure Nellie will too."

Jane did not speak French but she managed the Gare du Nord well, and at four o'clock in the afternoon, got into a cab and handed the driver a note with Estella's address. Estella had returned from the studio after seeing the heart-stopping portrait and was rehearsing the occasion to Charlotte when they heard a cab stopping and looked out of the window. Standing there, looking up at the house was a woman Estella said she thought she had met briefly once, at Crocketts, the Courtisone's place in Hertfordshire.

Once introductions were made and after Jane's hat and coat had been taken away, a maid took Jane's bag to the guest room assuming she would be staying.

"Now," said Estella, "what is all this?" at which Jane burst into tears.

"When I heard you at Crocketts talking with others, I was mightily impressed by your gentle wisdom. I remember thinking that if I ever had a serious problem, I would consult you. Now my problem is so wrenching that I had to come and meet with you."

"You are welcome, of course, but forgive me, I don't remember you clearly."

"My husband is Philip Hardyman."

"Oh, I know Philip. He has helped the Trust in the selection of male prostitutes for our Semper House Home which gives them accommodation and is now providing training in skills to enable them to get off the streets."

"He rarely talks about his work, so I did not know that. He says he wants to forget about it when he comes home."

"So what is the cause of your distress?"

"I will be brief.

"Philip came home very drunk indeed in the early hours of one morning last week. He then told me that he had been having casual affairs with men during our marriage, and that he had recently installed a young man in rooms in the Edgware Road. We spent a week in Shropshire with his mother recently and on his return and he went there, he said, to terminate the arrangemenr and found the young man brutally murdered."

Both Estella and Charlotte gasped in astonishment, stunned into silence by this appalling story.

"That is certainly brief," said Estella quietly.

"I don't know what to do, nor does he. He is a lawyer, remember. To begin with, he has not told the police about the body when legally he was bound to do so, but he has been living this secret life which will ruin him completely if it is revealed."

"Where is he?"

"Before I left, he had packed a bag and said he needed to be away for a few days."

"I am not surprised about that," said Estella, moved beyond measure by this poor woman's plight. She looked closely at Jane, a nice-looking, slim woman, with dark eyes and a slightly sallow complexion, pretty in a formal English sort of way, but not a traditional English rose.

"Let us think carefully about this.

"I should say, you are welcome to stay with us, but we will be returning soon to England after our sojourn here."

"Oh, I have my children to care for, so must return in a day or two."

"Frankly, Jane, I cannot imagine being in your shocking predicament. The major question is whether you wish to continue to be married to your husband. Once that is clear, either way, then different paths of action can be examined."

"I cannot be married to him and I want a divorce if I can afford it. He is someone I no longer know. He behaves in one way with me and my children, but then has this secret life which I find disgusting and unnatural.

"I used to enjoy his intimacy, although that has become increasingly a rare occurrence. Now I have to face that his body I loved was being used on other bodies which is so awful, so repellent, so revolting, so nauseating that it make me sick both in my heart and in my stomach."

"Yes, indeed," said Estella, "one of the understandings of a good marriage, I think, is that the other's body is a common possession. Of course, many people do not see their lives that way, of whom Philip is clearly one."

She was uneasy with that remark, calling to mind her love with the married Nellie.

"Jane," said Charlotte, "there is also the deceit, is there not? The lies and fabrications he must have constructed for you which are so demeaning."

"Of course," said Estella, "and there are also the legal implications of his behavior. I assume that there would be only circumstantial evidence of his sodomy, but once the police start, who knows what witnesses might come forward?"

"That could leave me destitute if his assets were to be confiscated."

"Let me ask you this. Do you want revenge? He has quite obviously shattered your life leaving you with an unforeseeable future. Do you wish to damage his future, perhaps conclusively?"

"This is where I need your advice. As I was travelling here, I felt I wanted to hurt him in any possible way I could, as he has hurt me. Then I thought, no, for my children's sake, I want to never see him again ever and not extend to him any rights over my children."

Her voice rose in anger, as she continued:

"I certainly want to clear my house of everything personal that belonged to him, his law books, his clothes, his tennis rackets, his cricket bats, everything, everything that would remind me of him. I hope he dies in agony of some terrible disease," she cried loudly bursting into tears.

When she had settled a little, Estella asked if she had any close relations.

"My parents are dead. My sister is married to a corn merchant in the West Country and we communicate little. My brother is something of an adventurer and he emigrated to America, thinking he would find the streets paved with gold."

"My question was really whether you have anyone to stay with for a while."

"Not really."

"And you have no money of your own, not that it matters in the current state of the law."

"Philip was very secure financially from his profession and from his inheritance after his father died, he was very generous. He made arrangements with his bank that I could draw money from it whenever I needed it."

"That is unusual, perhaps a decoy."

"How do you mean?"

"Well, he felt quite guilty about his behavior, so giving you plenty of money assuaged that guilt somewhat."

"This is such a terrible nightmare. Why did he marry me if he really wanted men? Was our marriage just a cover such that no one would suspect him?"

"We don't know, do we?" asked Charlotte.

"Tell me," she continued, "was he not the lawyer who went to Australia last year, or am I mistaken? I remember Hamish telling me something about that, or was it Angharad saying Hardyman and Masterson had gone to investigate that half-brother of yours, Estella?"

"Goodness me," said Jane, "if he has deserted me, a divorce would be straightforward. I must ask Hamish about that possibility."

"Think about it," said Estella, "he knows publicly he will be disgraced one way or the other. He is legal jeopardy from his sodomy and from not telling the police he had found the body. His marriage is in ruins. What would we expect a man to do in such a situation? Flee to the ends of the earth, I should say."

"If that has happened, I must get a divorce. I knew you would have the wisdom to help me. Now I must get the first possible train back to London. I won't stay, thank you so much again. I am sure there will be an overnight train. Let me see. Your clock says it is about seven. I will take a cab to the Gare du Nord and get back to London forthwith."

Sidney had had a busy day tracking a woman across Chelsea to what he assumed was her lover's house in Westminster. So he was glad to be sitting with his feet propped up on a small stool, his shirt open to the waist, a glass of mild ale in his hand as his wife was in the kitchen making his supper. He was leafing through the *Daily Telegraph* for the day as he liked to be kept informed of events in the capital.

"Goodness me," he said putting down his ale and the paper and rising from his chair to go to the kitchen.

"Betty, my treasure, there's a notice in the paper here about a young man found murdered in the Bayswater area. I wonder if that's the young man Hardyman asked me to follow. Who knows, there might be a reward of some kind?"

"Wasn't that the place you saw men coming and going and that posh geezer too?"

"Quite right, my poppet. I must gather together my wits and my memory to describe all those punters."

"Then Sidney, my love, you must get your arse over there tomorrow and claim the reward. We could do with a trip to the seaside."

"I will, I will, my poppet. You won't see me for dust when dawn breaks."

"That's my little Sidney."

The following morning found Sidney in the foyer of the Bayswater police station.

"I think I might have information about that young man that was murdered near here," he said to a constable at a desk.

"Oh really? Well, there's no reward, so unless it is useful, you can bugger off."

"Don't be like that, constable. Just tell me the young man's address and if it isn't him, I will do as you say."

"All right, I'll ask Detective Johnstone. He should know," at which he disappeared down a hallway, returning with a portly middle-aged man, who introduced himself as Detective Johnstone."

"What can I do for you, my friend?" he asked.

"I think I may have information about the young man who was murdered."

"You mean, the mollie his neighbor called us about?'

"Yes, he was a mollie, certainly, but where did he live?"

"Oh, you can't go there, my friend, we are still working to find out what was going on."

"No, I want to be sure it is the young man I was tracking."

"P'raps it is, we don't have many rent-boys on the Edgware Road, but yes, it was Sharlington Buildings."

"Right," said Sidney, "then that's the man I was tracking for a week not a month ago."

"You'd best come with me and talk to the Super."

In the conversation that followed, Sidney told of Philip Hardyman's interest in the young man as he was a party to a case that lawyer was working on. He gave descriptions of all the men the young man had taken back to his room, including the rich gent.

Superintendent Charles Etherington was very interested in getting a precise description of the gent, but Sidney was not very helpful, except to say that he had a moustache, a beard, was wearing a frock coat, a colored cravat and a silk top hat and his walking stick had a silver top, like every other rich gent in the metropolis.

"Is that all you can remember about him, because we think he may have been the last to have seen him, and we found a silver cufflink under the bed which had a coat of arms engraved on it. We will send an officer to the College of Arms and we may be able to get a surname."

"Now that's clever," said Sidney, "who would have thought of that?"

"I did, it's my job."

"Well done, Super," said Sidney with sincere admiration.

"But we will need to speak with this Mr. Hardyman. Where is he?"

Sidney gave the Super the address of Courtisone and Jaggers at which the Super exclaimed:

"Is this the real Mr. Jaggers? Oh I remember him. Must be dead now, but when I was a young man I saw him twist a witness and then a jury round his little finger and they returned a not guilty verdict. Amazing he was."

Clarence was ever cheerful and excited these days, whistling his way across the Square as he made his way to Little Britain that morning.

He was more than ever in love with his Emma and their marriage was now not six months away.

"Good morning, Hamish, my dear chap," he said cheerfully as he came in, but then looked at Hamish more closely and said:

"Oh dear, what is the matter? You look as though you have been stuck by a thunderbolt."

"Clarence," replied Hamish, "we have a mountain of problems to face and we will need all our energy and wisdom to confront them."

"What on earth has happened?"

"Philip is in a dreadful legal mess and he has resigned from the practice. There was a note here this morning from him, saying he was leaving for Australia. I am checking the list of passengers on a ship that left for Melbourne from Southampton on Friday and I am sure he will be on it."

"But why?"

"Although he swore me to secrecy, I must tell you so that you realize the gravity of his situation, but also that we have confidence in each other as we try to rebuild this practice. O'Grady, Billington, Courtisone and now Hardyman. Gone. We are two lawyers where six are needed."

Hamish then took Clarence through what had happened, leaving him dazed and shocked at the revelations.

"What about his wife, his children? He has compounded his vices with abandoning them. What an appalling character! I am speechless at this wretched behavior. Oh dear, I am quite knocked off balance. Can we walk outside a little?"

They reached the door but were stopped by a couple of men, one in police uniform.

"I am Superintendent Charles Etherington and I wish to meet with Mr. Philip Hardyman."

No point in lying, thought Hamish, though almost shivering with dread, but he said without quaver in his voice:

"I am afraid, much to our disappointment and anger, Mr. Hardyman left for Australia last Friday and he has resigned from the practice, leaving us in great turmoil as our former senior partner, Mr. Courtisone retired only last month. So I am not sure how we can help you."

"I'm afraid I have little knowledge of Philip Hardyman," interrupted Clarence.

"I know he was married to Jane, has two children and seems to have had a very happy life. He has been active in the work of the Jaggers Trust for the Relief and Education of the Poor which we administer. He was a Board member bringing great wisdom and energy to the role. He distinguished himself at the Bar and we have no idea why he has suddenly taken off for the Antipodes."

Hamish was sighing with relief as Clarence took the lead.

"Mind you, I can tell you this and it may explain his sudden departure. This practice had a long-standing client from Brisbane in Queensland, Australia, who died recently after being badly injured in a fight with some natives. His wife returned here before his unhappy demise, and we have constructed a will for her as she has become very wealthy.

"Hardyman and our senior clerk Adam Masterson had to go to Brisbane as the lawyers there were thought to be corrupt. Journeys to Australia are long and arduous, but they accomplished their task with great elegance. Perhaps he formed a relationship, professional or personal, while he was there and decided he wished to develop it."

"That is very interesting indeed and we will pursue that line of enquiry as we do need to speak to him."

"Why is that?"

"We understand from a man who has come forward in regard to the murder of a young man at a building in the Edgware Road. He states that Mr. Hardyman employed him to watch this young man, a rent-boy with numerous callers to his room in one week, the last one being a very distinguished looking gentleman.

"Our interest is whether Mr. Hardyman could shed any light on the young man and why he wished him to be followed."

"Well," said Hamish, his confidence now rising, "I think Mr. Hardyman's brief was quite new and he did mention that he needed to get some information, and he may well have employed this man who has come forward but I am afraid that any information about that client is in strictest confidence, so we cannot reveal his name.

"I doubt you have any reason to pursue that side of the case, however, as I understand it."

"His name wouldn't be Bloviate, would it?" asked the Superintendent with a trace of a smile.

"I can assure you that it certainly is not and my statement breaches no confidence. I hope you are not fishing, Superintendent. Our lips are sealed, but the client certainly did not have that name."

"Might you be able to give me the name of the woman who returned from Australia and who might be able to help with Hardyman's whereabouts?"

"Again, Superintendent, we have a reputation to preserve. If you knew your lawyer was going to tell someone that you had recently made your will with him, I suspect that the bond of trust between him and you would be undermined.

"Now this woman's name might be revealed as we could ask her permission, but I think we would deserve rather more justification for approaching her than is presently apparent. She is, after all, recently widowed. With Hardyman's client, it would require the permission of both, with Hardyman making the request to that client."

"That's fine, I do understand. We do have other lines of enquiry to pursue, so we won't take up any more of your time, but if anything comes to mind whereby we might track down this young man's assailant, please do let us know."

"Absolutely, Superintendent, we lawyers are keen to track down villainy wherever it is to be found."

"Hmm," said the Superintendent, "good day to you both."

Pulling his cigar case from his pocket outside on the pavement, the Superintendent walked slowly down Little Britain and then back again towards his police cab. He lit his cigar and puffed for a while.

"They're hiding something, Johnstone, and I don't mean the names of clients. There is something else I can't put my finger on.

Meantime, we must pursue this Bloviate gentleman. I am sure he was honest about that.

"What I do not understand is why Hardyman rushes off to Australia. Maybe he met the love of his life, but who knows? Perhaps we should talk to this wife, though that contains lots of risks.

"The thing is I can't see a lawyer being a murderer. They just don't do that sort of thing, even paying someone to do it. He has a fine reputation as an advocate, so I am told, too."

Hamish got on a chair to look out of the window on to the street and saw the policemen in conference. When they rode away, he turned to Clarence:

"Clarence, we are sworn to secrecy. Philip has bolted, unable to face his troubles. I do not believe he murdered the boy, and I was so grateful for your sending the police down another track. Very ingenious, and I expect Angharad would love the attention of two swarthy policemen.

"But our main problem now is not Hardyman. He has sent a formal letter of resignation by the way. We have to find two if not three lawyers to start with us, as soon as possible. I suppose I am by default the senior partner. We no longer have any justification for running two premises, so we should make enquiries about taking chambers in one of the Inns of Court."

"This is a real challenge, Hamish, but not a bad moment for me as my wedding will now be in May next year and I will then be away for a three-week honeymoon."

"Then we must have lawyers before then. Let us talk with Adam about the briefs coming in."

"Should we bring him into our confidence, Hamish?"

"We have to tell him Philip is gone, for reasons unknown, but more than that, I see no reason to inform him of the details. I do want to bring him in on the selection of lawyers."

"Hamish, there are a number of options here, I think.

"We could find another small practice and merge with them. We could go to Courtisone out in the country and ask for his help, once again, in finding promising lawyers. We could take it stealthily, just getting one person to join us and take our time to find a second and a third."

"I have an idea, Clarence. Call Adam in."

Adam came in and Hamish said:

"Adam, as you know we are in need of lawyers. Have you ever thought of becoming one?"

"Well, yes, it has always been my aspiration."

"Oh, goodness me, and I am in court today. Thank God I remembered, being transfixed with all this Philip stuff. Think about it as a possibility, Adam, and we'll talk again."

"What's the case?

"I'm defending Mrs. Pennyfeather once again. This time she will lose and be locked up. I will be as enthusiastic as I can, but the jury will see through her, I am sure."

"Let me walk with you, Hamish," said Clarence as they went out into the street, "would you mind if I shared our predicament with Lord Eustace, my father-in-law to be? He wants to see me at lunchtime, I think, to tell about his daughter's dowry. But I could ask his advice then?"

"Of course, the more sensible advice, the better," and he hurried away.

This exchange with Hamish left Adam bewildered and uncertain whether there was any likelihood of his getting help to become a lawyer. 'Wait and see' was inevitable as Hamish clearly had many things on his mind.

Indeed, as he rode to the Court, he was thinking more about Philip than Mrs. Pennyfeather. The damage to his family was the worst of his moral problems, followed by his breaking the law when a lawyer. Beside those two overwhelming matters, the actual business of employing someone to satisfy his sexual desire was relatively trivial. Proximate cause indeed, but of no consequence in the day of judgement when all sins would be revealed.

XIII

It was almost a week since Philip had departed and Jane had rushed to Paris and back. Hamish was confounded by the outcome in terms of its problems and called Adam to join him in his office.

"This practice is in crisis," said Hamish, "no two ways about it. Incidentally I am sorry to have rushed off the other day."

"No matter. We are certainly getting short of lawyers."

"But the briefs are coming in, right?"

"Indeed, at the usual steady pace to keep six lawyers at work, and we are now only half that number."

"No, only two now. I am afraid Clarence and I are the only ones left. Philip has resigned amidst a sea of troubles, as the poet put it. Truth to tell, if his behavior was made public, he would be struck off and totally disgraced. As it is, he has left home and taken the boat to Australia."

"Good heavens, how extraordinary. I thought from our visit there he hated the whole place. He made no attempt to cultivate the locals."

"He didn't cavort with a woman while you were there?"

"Good heavens, no. He hated the heat and spent most of the time in his room reading."

"Then he has definitely gone there to escape."

"Mr. Macdonald," said Adam, using the formal mode of address, "I think if we are to make progress, you must take me into your confidence about Mr. Hardyman. Clearly the three of us are going to have to be a very close-knit team if we are to re-build."

"You are right, but if ever asked, you must deny knowledge of this."

"Briefly, and I fear this is very sordid, Philip kept a rent-boy in a room on the Edgware Road and he arrived one night to find the boy had been murdered. He wanted to end the relationship, believing it had been a terrible mistake, so he hired Sidney to track the young man while he was in Shropshire, telling Sidney the observation was on behalf of a client. Sidney obviously read the newspapers about the murder, and volunteered information to the police, anticipating a large reward no doubt."

"What on earth was he thinking?"

"As you know, the police came here wanting to interview Philip and asked us for the name of the client. But, of course, there was no client, so we fell back on confidentiality. We did not raise the question whether there was a client, and, had they asked, we would have had to reveal there was none. All very messy for us, but disastrous for Philip.

"I am afraid he showed his true mettle. He got very drunk and told all this to his wife which was heinous. She then took off to Paris to consult Estella whose advice she values."

"I am stunned, Hamish, absolutely stunned. I have known Philip since I joined the Courtisone practice. This seems so totally and completely out of character. It's as if he were two completely different people.

"That is a possibility, but I'd prefer to see him as a devious blackguard. We must put it all behind us, though I do anticipate the police wanting to examine Philip's office as he must be under suspicion. So you might take a close look there and destroy anything that might interest the police."

"Are you sure we should get rid of any evidence?"

"No, how stupid of me: You see how Philip has thrown me into a basket of quandaries. However, they did seem more interested in another gentleman whom Sidney saw at the premises. If Philip were to be identified and then billed by the newspapers as the murderer, we are finished, absolutely finished."

"I appreciate your taking me into your confidence as we must have a completely open channel of communication between senior partner and senior clerk, don't you agree?"

"I agree completely, Masterson," said Hamish with inappropriate formality.

For two days after her return from Paris Jane Hardyman postponed telling the children about their father. She had arrived home very early the following morning, having travelled on the boat overnight and come from Folkestone on an early train, much calmer than she had been when she left London. She went directly to her bed deciding to wait to prepare herself to see the lawyer.

She was on edge as she sat at the breakfast table with her children on the third day and she called Florence so that she might listen too.

"Children, I am very sorry to say that your father has gone to Australia to live. He got himself into a lot of trouble here. I don't know why, but we are going to have to get used to his not being here with us, though I think we may hear from him from time to time."

The children started to snivel and, while she was usually a gentle caring mother, she suddenly displayed an unfamiliar hardness, snapping at them.

"Stop that nonsense at once. It is enough to bear his loss without you both making it worse. I have to go to the city this morning," and she got up and swept out of the room, leaving her children sobbing and distressed while Florence tried to comfort them.

Jane arrived later that morning at Hamish's office.

"Good afternoon, Mrs. Hardyman, I thought you were in Paris."

"Yes I was, Mr. Macdonald, and I am here to demand you file for divorce from my husband."

"I have not argued a divorce case before, but my senior clerk will know how this can be done. I should add that it has become easier as your husband has also instructed me to accept any claim for a divorce you might make."

"Thank God for that, the swine. I suppose you know what he did and how he told me of his bestiality, his lusts, his..." and she burst into tears..

"Yes, Mrs. Hardyman, he did tell me and I cannot say how grieved I am at all aspects of his behavior. But let me explain the process. First, divorce is no longer a matter for the ecclesiastical courts. Second, responsibility was transferred four years ago from the Court for Divorce and Matrimonial Causes to a division of the new Supreme Court.

"There will be some expenses connected with this petition, but Courtisone and Jaggers will be pleased to offer their services *pro bono.* Your husband is offering no defense, as indicated in his letter to me which I will present to the Court. The most sensible path is to petition on grounds of desertion."

"Thank you, Mr. Macdonald. I need to ask: Were you aware of his behavior?"

"Not until he confided in me just before you went to Shropshire that he had this disgraceful arrangement and that he wanted to break it off," said Hamish, embarrassed by his dissembling.

"I suppose men share secrets as women do."

"How are your finances? Has he taken assets with him?"

"I still have to find that out. That is one side of his character that is fortunate for me. I have access to our resources and I would be surprised and even more distressed if I find that he had emptied our accounts. On the other hand, who knows the man? I don't."

"May I ask? How were Estella and her friend Mrs. Mudge?

"Most helpful. It was they who convinced me to sue for divorce, not that I took much persuading and they are returning to England shortly. I gathered that their young people, Albert and Elizabeth have parted."

"Really? Now that is a surprise and will disappoint my wife who admired them both greatly. Now if we are finished for the moment,

I must get over to our offices in Cheapside. I am senior partner now and in six months we have slid from having six lawyers to two."

"Thank you, Mr. Macdonald. I don't think I am ever going to understand this betrayal."

"Nor I and you have my profound sympathy."

She left slowly. Robert called her a cab and then one for Hamish.

When he arrived, he could see that there were several police vehicles down the street outside the Gavel Club, so he hurried into the Courtisone offices.

There but for the grace of God, he thought.

The following evening, Hamish and Mary were sitting out in their small conservatory with James as the November rain came down, admiring their greenhouse flowers in that relaxed sort of way that people who are happy with each other, a peace which, while not quite passing all understanding, was nevertheless brim with quiet love and mutual confidence.

"Do you think we should try to be friendly with Jane Hardyman after this terrible experience? Sometimes people stay away from those who have disasters as if somehow the tragedies might pass to them. On the other hand, we have not met her and she may well have other friends and relations we don't know about. I am sure Estella will provide her with some comfort."

"Hmm," mused Hamish, "it is quite odd, isn't it, how Estella has become such a fount of wisdom for people. Her running of the Trust and her ideas perhaps stimulate the idea that she must have superior knowledge if she is running that organization."

"I am not sure it's that. Of course I did not know her before she married, but I think it is to do with her demeanor. She carries herself like a battleship, a friendly one I should add, moving grandly across the seas. I mean, have you ever seen her in distress? I will always remember the way she told us about her lover which took my breath away as she revealed her sense of herself and especially that she was proud of it."

"Yes, I will remember that, too. It will be very interesting to watch her growing older. How old is she now? Fifty-five?"

"Oh, no, I think she is in her late sixties, extraordinarily well-preserved. Maybe even older. I hope I grow old like that."

"You, my dear Mary, will always be beautiful. I want to just tell you that I believe our marriage has been a thundering success. I love you dearly, my darling, and I will not in any way trespass on your goodwill. In fact, my sexual desire for men has gone to sleep. Perhaps it was just my lack of experience with women which brought out that desire for men which I hope now to be in full abeyance as a feature of my life."

"That is quite wonderful, darling, but we married with a certain understanding. I will be glad if you do not form any relationships with another man, but I am prepared for it. Perhaps we all have a bit of desire for a man or a woman built into us by nature, but the nurture we have fosters our love one way or the other.

"You know," Mary continued, "I am more than ever convinced that the woman who seeks love as a basis for marriage loses her independence."

"So much for the romantic," said Hamish with a smile.

"No, seriously, perhaps she is confused by the whole notion, in her heart just seeking love which gives her marriage as a status which she also believes will allow some freedom. That is most often a mistake as marriage and love become muddled up together in her head.

"Unlike us, my dear, we did not start with love for each other, but we have grown into it. Very confusing. I must say, however, that I am shocked to the core with Philip's behavior."

"Me too," replied Hamish, "though I did my best to help him. I think he is supremely selfish and a coward. He clearly thought only of himself, not of his wife or his children throughout the whole wicked episode. I know he did not have the understanding with his wife which we have. But I am very glad he is no longer in the practice, though I am now very anxious indeed as we are down to two lawyers, and Clarence will be marrying in May."

"I am sure that will settle itself under your direction. We might host a dinner and invite Jane to attend."

"I would particularly like to ask Adam Masterson and his wife as I am thinking of helping him become a lawyer."

"That is a splendid idea. Now, you started to tell me last evening about this club which the police visited, but we were distracted."

"Oh, my goodness, yes. I learnt all this today. Evidently the police have started a quiet war on sodomites. The gossip is that, in questioning men about this murder, someone revealed the club's existence and all hell broke loose. The police arrived like a swarm of bees, rushing into every room, demanding the membership list, and catching two couples engaged in illegal practices in the small rooms available for that purpose.

"It is now shuttered and goodness knows where it may lead with prosecutions. I am sure the community will know about Philip as he was a member. I hope against hope that individuals will not come to us to act for them in court."

"Will you not do that?"

"My impulse is to steer clear of it. Oh, dear me, I don't know. I would consult with Clarence, but maybe I am jumping too far ahead of myself. If one of the men in the Club was well connected, I doubt whether leading barristers will be lining up to defend them for fear of being tarred with the same brush."

"My reaction is to say that you should pick up the cudgels, to use a different metaphor, if asked."

"I have to work out plans for the practice first."

They walked into their dining room hand in hand, Hamish carrying his son on his right arm, so that Mary could hold his left with her right, as her withered left arm drooped beside her, swinging slightly on its own as she walked almost as if it was disconnected from her.

"By the way," she said, "I am going to look tomorrow at that house in Cheyne Row, unoccupied since that murderer lived there."

"That will be interesting," said Hamish, completely perplexed as to what to say to that.

Clarence came into the office beaming with delight the following Monday morning.

"Hamish, I have wonderful news. Lord Eustace has given Emma a large dowry which will enable us to live very comfortably in London and I can then rescue the decaying house in Sussex where my mother lives and which I have owned since my father died."

"That is splendid, but did you talk to him about our loss of lawyers?"

"Yes, and he mentioned a couple of options for us, one of which is to give up and join his chambers. He would welcome that, but he thought it would be an unnecessary surrender. He also thought we might attract a more senior person and offer him the lead position. But, he argued that would be very risky. So much depends on intimate knowledge of others in a practice, he said, and one would have no idea whether that would work.

"So, we are left with recruiting lawyers, either novices or young people, as was my situation. However, he did give us permission to ask Sam, one of his younger sons, whom he thinks needs a new challenge."

"I don't like any of the alternatives to recruiting new lawyers. But tell me, didn't Emma think that Sam might be queer? I am the last person to be concerned on that score, but with the Hardyman debacle, I am a little uneasy."

"I have met him frequently and I think Emma's discussion of him reflected a nervousness on her father's part. Of course, by suggesting him, he may just want to be rid of him. It must be a challenge to have four sons in the same chambers."

"Four indeed? I've not met them," said Hamish.

"We have no option. As you know him, Clarence, get a message to Sam Eustace as soon as you can and invite him to meet with us."

"I am dining there tonight so will approach him then."

"Excellent. Now, how about Adam? Would you value him as a lawyer?'

"Indeed, but can he afford the training and the dinners in the Temple?"

"I thought we might pay for his membership and dinners. He would have to study for the examinations and we can help him."

"That's most generous and I concur. Ask him. I'm sure he will jump at the chance. That means a new clerk, of course.

"Hamish, I hope I was not jumping the gun, but while I was in the Temple seeing Lord Eustace I scouted around for chambers. Nothing available. But I was advised to try Lincolns Inn, so I walked over there and found an empty set at Old Square, number eleven. I saw the appropriate officials and said we were anxious to move. The reply was that the set was available but it was in poor condition, as it had been the chambers of two very eccentric elderly lawyers and their even more eccentric clerk."

"That's very good news. Let's walk there now, no time like the present. Both Courtisone and Jaggers owned their properties, so we should generate good capital from the sale of both buildings, enabling us to afford the rent in the Chambers and have some capital besides."

After taking lunch on the way they arrived at Number 11 Old Square with the pleasant gardens of Lincolns Inn and the Hall close by. They were asked whether they want to be shown around the chambers, but they agreed just to take the key.

To say that it was in poor condition was an understatement. Mold and decay were everywhere. The furniture looked as if it had been made to celebrate the coronation of Queen Anne. They coughed their way around the building, the dust flowing freely as they moved from room to room. However, there would enough room for seven for eight lawyers as the building had a basement and three floors.

"We will take it," said Hamish with a determination that signified his status as the senior partner.

"It is wonderful," agreed Clarence.

"I am sure it can be transformed in three weeks. We can borrow money from Coutts, the bank that handles Courtisone and Jaggers affairs against the collateral of Little Britain and Cheapside. Emma and you can then look at those lovely homes in Russell or Tavistock Square."

"Very sensible. Merely walking distance. Maybe Mary and you should rent a property in that area too, though you like living south of the river, I know."

"No, Mary is investigating a move to Cheyne Row."

"Really?"

"She has her eye on the house previously occupied by that murderer of young men. It has been vacant for some time, the stigma not attracting worthy people to live there. But you know my wife, not a woman to endure superstition, and with my knowledge she went to view the place and liked it. I visited the other day and have hummed and hawed since."

"You'd be close to the Brandrams and the Gargerys then."

"Yes, that is a major part of its attraction, certainly."

They went their separate ways after Hamish had signed the lease in the Lincolns Inn office, and he rushed home to tell Mary all the good news. There were still many problems ahead, but they had made a start.

"Now we are moving home and office which makes for an exciting time."

"I am more than excited by the possibility of our new home," said Mary, "and I have arranged to meet decorators to find out costs."

"Most sensible, we need not decide quite yet. You know, Mary, Clarence is a real joy to work with. He is never ruffled, always keen with new ideas, but I suspect he will not stay very long."

"Why not?"

"I think he plans to enter politics as an MP. Of course he could still practice, but his time would be very limited. On the other hand, having an MP in chambers could be an asset."

❧ ❧ ❧

It was a calm crossing for December 1875 on the SS Dover Castle, so much so that Estella and Charlotte stood on the deck watching the cliffs get closer as the boat approached Folkestone, while Elizabeth walked around the boat. They thought about how they had helped Honora and wondered whether Jane Handyman might be open to support too.

"One strange fact about her," Estella remarked, "is that she always talked about 'the children,' never mentioned them by name. Indeed we do not know their names. What could be the implications of that?"

"Perhaps," said Charlotte, "she doesn't like them much. In fact to rush over to Paris and leave them with an elderly nanny, what was her name, Florence I think, does show a certain distance from them."

"Not only by their names, my dear, by their ages. I have no idea how old they are. I suppose Philip must be well into his thirties and she too, so we might assume 'the children' are older than ten but younger than fifteen."

"It is odd, isn't it? Moreover we have no idea whether they are boys or girls or a mix of the two. I have also no idea where they live."

"But, oh dear me," said Estella, "what a plight to be in. Never doubting your husband's fidelity and then hit with this terrible admission, almost worse than saying he had murdered someone, I think, because of the betrayal."

"I agree. Yet, even after that meeting, I don't know who she is."

"Nor I."

"We will find out and perhaps an entry into the League of Free Women would help her."

They stood on the quay watching porters unloading their baggage and, of course, the Estella portrait boxed up very carefully by the Duran studio. They then walked slowly on to the train platform while the baggage and the portraits were loaded in the van at the back of the train where the guard operated.

"Overall, did you enjoy Paris?" Asked Charlotte when they were sitting comfortably in their first-class carriage.

"Oh, yes, I think so. We had that adventure at the Embassy, my little flirtation with young John Sargent and, of course, the terrible disappointment of Albert's neglect of Elizabeth about which I am very sad indeed. I will try to return next year as I would like to expand my knowledge of the painters, especially the women."

"I am not sure whether I will join you, but what of Percy Vere," said Estella with a gay laugh, "How is that relationship?"

"You know, I am at a loss. He has said that, with winter, he can't do much in Pompeii, so will be in touch with me when we get to London as he expects to be there then. We have corresponded but not with nay, how shall I say close affection or commitment. So I really do not know."

"Let us hope fervently that you spend some time with him and make up your mind – and of course that he make up his."

"I will rely on you for advice, as indeed does everyone else, when you have met him."

"I do look forward to that.

Christmas beckoned.

Estella decided not to go to Wymondham with Charlotte, though she had an invitation from the Earl of Camberley. In part this was because she thought Percy might well turn up there and Charlotte could more easily meet with him without having to consider her presence.

She had sent Nellie a note of her arrival, so one morning in mid-December there was Nellie cheerful as ever. They kissed and hugged and Estella wanted to survey her garden, so they walked arm in arm across the lawn, stopping for a moment at Molly's memorial stone.

"How are you, my dearest?'

"I don't rightly know," said Nellie, "but first you shall come to the Cottage for Christmas, we can't have you here all alone."

"That will be wonderful. I have never been inside your home even though its walls hold some many memories of my husband growing up. So, thank you, my dear, but what's wrong?"

"What's right is the question."

"Come and sit down and talk about it."

"Fletch's business is low, not just because its winter. He's shoeing horses, of course, but he's got no orders for repairing farm machinery. For a start, we've had these terrible harvest for a couple of years. The weather has been somefink awful in the growing season."

"How remiss of me. I had not noticed, being in London and then in Paris."

"No, you wouldn't have done.

"We was in the Bargemen last week and, do you know, half the men there wot had been used to work on the farms growing barley were no longer employed. It was a sad sight I can tell you. We've got these friends, Jack and Maggie Friendly. I think Jack's dad knew your Pip. Anyway, they've got four little ones to feed and no money coming in."

"Oh, how terrible. The Trust must do something about that."

"Fletch says that them Americans are sending over crops wot we used to grow and selling them cheaper than wot farmers would get for their crops. So, the year before last, the barley just rotted in the field, because of the weather too, and no one bought it."

"So, of course, that affects Fletch's business, doesn't it?"

"It certainly does. There's the hops for the beer here in Kent and there'll always be a good market for them, but hops is difficult to grow, he says, and bad weather really hurts 'em. So, I don't know what will happen.

"We are just keeping up, able to get food wot we aren't growing. I started on chickens last year, and me and Fletch dug a big patch then for all kinds of vegetables. Victoria wants to keep rabbits, but I don't think she would like to see her dad shooting them for us to eat!"

"Let us go into the house Nellie, have a cup of tea and think about this. I am so selfish, you know. I read about the depression in agriculture in the newspaper and I completely failed to connect it to you and to this area.

"How foolish. I just saw it as an abstract problem, of no particular interest, when of course I should have been thinking about the poor men and women so affected by it. You know that is the trouble when you are comfortable financially and not involved in politics. Every problem is someone else's problem."

They returned to the house through the orchard. Estella told Nellie to bring her children and pick as much fruit as they wanted and Nellie thought that would help some of those poor laborers too.

"You know," said Nellie, "while people want food where they can get it, they'd much prefer money for them to choose."

"Right," said Estella, "I will go back to London for two nights and call a meeting of the Trust and perhaps of the League of Free Women and put the position to both groups. I do plan to have the League meet here soon, though I am not sure that we can have them all staying in the house."

"Who have you got now?"

"There's the originals; myself, Charlotte, Harriet, and I must try to get Susanna to come."

'You'll be lucky."

"Maybe, but you'll remember her son Lachlan died of diphtheria?"

"Oh, yes. Crikey, poor them. He was such a nice little boy, but then kids die of that all the time," said Nellie, reflecting on her youth.

"Let me continue. Then there is Honora and Mary, but I also hope that Antonia Penoyre will come. You'll like her, she is very free with descriptions of her husband and their loving."

"That'll be fun."

"And maybe Emma who is about to marry Clarence in the Spring.

"Then there's Eliza Culpepper whose family have moved near Pip and Susanna, so it could be quite a crowd really, eight probably and you makes nine. But there's a couple of others I might talk to. There is a woman called Jane Hardyman who has just had the most terrible shock. Her husband set up a mollie in a room, intending for him to be his little man. Then he wanted to stop the arrangement, but when he went to tell him, the man had been murdered."

"Blimey, you don't half know some people."

"Then he got drunk and told his wife everything. She came over to Paris to see me to ask advice. I told her to divorce him."

"All very well, but can she afford it?"

"Well, he skedaddled to Australia."

"What do you mean?"

"He bolted."

"What was that word again, 'skedaddle?'"

"Yes, it seems to be a new word I heard recently."

"Anyway there she was in our living room in Paris telling Charlotte and me all this, but once I told her she should divorce him, she skedaddled too – back to London," and they both laughed heartily.

"Now, I have to ask, don't I? What about Harriet?"

There was a pause.

"I'se never seen you blush before, Estella! Well?

"H'mm. I was surprised at myself for refusing. It's complicated and we'll talk about it sometime," said Estella not wanting to reveal to Nellie her murderous fantasies, "but I think you could help with a more urgent matter on behalf of the Trust."

"What's that?"

"Start with All Hallows and try to make a list of all those families where the man is out of work and make a mark against the list of them if they work on farms. If the Trust agrees, then we can move to other neighboring villages or even towns, perhaps as far as Whitstable. They have to be farming villages, though. We can give them money to relieve their distress."

"I can do that. I'll start with Harry Shoreham. He's still alive, you know. Lucky you taught me to write."

"Oh, of course, Biddy's second husband."

"He will know everyone. I won't go to the Church as I think the pub will have better information."

"Now I know I give my gardener five shillings a week, but he lives in the shed. How much would a working farm laborer get in this county?"

"I don't rightly know but I would say anything from thirteen shillings and maybe up to one pound a week. Of course, like us, he'll save some for a funeral, and he'll put something by for difficult times, like now or for sickness. We're different, of course. Fletch can earn up to five pound a week in a good week and we have put away almost thirty pounds now for any emergency."

"You're both very thrifty."

"Once you've known the poverty we've known, you try to make sure you never get like that again, I can tell you. We've been so lucky and it's all down to the Trust."

"But darling, if I asked the Trust to provide for one pound a week for a man with two or more children, would that be sufficient: And then fifteen shillings a week for a man with fewer children."

"Blimey, they'll think they've died and gone to heaven. Of course, when they work, they do ten hours a day, six days a week, don't they?"

"Really? That seems hard work."

"It is."

"The Trust does have a great deal of money to spend and we must spend more. You know we now have two homes for whores, one for men in our old home, Semper House, and the Jaggers Building for women. They are quite difficult to run, but I can see we should devote more of our income to housing the poor but helping them with money before that."

"That would be good. Some of the cottages here are just terrible, and I've heard tell of a village which has what they called alms-houses, though these was mainly for the elderly, but the money came from some rich geezer or other."

"Now that is a real possibility, too. But now I must prepare letters calling those meetings for next week. As usual, my darling, you have been so helpful. Before you go, wait."

Estella went to her desk and took out five sovereigns.

"This is to help you and your family. Don't ever hesitate to ask if you're in trouble. I will always look after you."

1876

XIV

Elizabeth was still very upset indeed at the end of her relationship with Albert, even after six months apart. She had loved him deeply, but she knew she wanted a husband who was close as possible to her. He never really talked to her seriously about his painting, indeed she was coming around to the view that it was the social life with this group that was more important to him than actually producing work. Sargent and others seemed to be able to produce good paintings quickly as far as she could tell, but his portrait of Pip's father remained unfinished.

Sitting at the Bechstein piano in the Music Room at the Embassy, she played some of the melancholic movements from the Beethoven sonatas that she could remember and then cheered herself up with the first of Haydn's 48th. As she was finishing, Tim revealed himself: He had been sitting just outside the room enraptured.

"Good morning, Elizabeth."

"Oh what a surprise, good morning, Tim."

"You seemed rather sad this morning in the early pieces you played."

"Yes, I fear so. I did not tell you earlier, but Albert and I are now completely finished."

"Really? Oh I am sorry. Do you wish to tell me?"

"It doesn't matter. I saw him in the street embracing a young girl a few months ago. He was coming home in the early hours of the morning, and I happened to be looking out for him. He lied about it as he had not seen me. So I refused to let him in and told him to be out of my apartment by noon. If I am honest, I think both of us are relieved. We were not headed in the same direction."

"I am sure that is wise for both of you then, so I need not be sorry. In fact I am pleased as it gives me the opportunity to court you and seek to be your friend, if not more."

"That is very sweet of you, Tim, but I have decided to return to England later this month."

"How wonderful! I have just received a posting to London and I will have to attend the wedding of a dear friend in London."

"I'll wager it is Clarence Smythe."

"How did you know? I know only the bride, Emma Eustace, whom I used to play with as a child."

"I have not met Clarence but he is in a practice with a friend of my aunt."

"We will meet there, then if not elsewhere. I am bidden to the Foreign Office on the Balkans desk, not on the French desk as I had hoped. I think Lyons recommended me."

'What do you mean by desk?"

"Oh that's just a term for the group of diplomats working on an area of the world."

"Well, that is such a nice surprise, and it alters my perspective. I will need to have a friend in London as I have none since I have lived the life of a diplomat's daughter. I will be coming here to play only two or three more times, but you may take me to lunch now, if you wish."

"I would like nothing better. I do admire you greatly, you know."

"I know, Tim, but I am coming out from under a sunken vessel, my anticipated marriage to Albert. It will take me time to decide my future, especially with regard to a relationship."

"Then we can be friends, I am sure. I will invite you to the theatre, to concerts and for walks in Hyde Park if I may when we are in London."

"My aunt lives in New Queen Street near St James Park."

"But that is a stone's throw from my future offices."

'How convenient. I am thinking of becoming a student of those classics you mentioned. I do not particularly want to go to Cambridge, so I am going to enquire at the University of London."

"That would be admirable, for many reasons."

"What will you be doing at your desk?"

"I am not sure, yet, but there is a huge diplomatic challenge following the end of this war to make sure the French are our friends. There is a strong sense that this increasingly powerful Germany which Bismarck has created may well become rather tiresome in the years ahead, so I think I may also be engaged in building links with the French civil service, given what we have been doing here. There is also what has come to be called the Eastern Question, but do you want to know about that?

"Of course, I am a diplomat's daughter, but I am unfamiliar with the Eastern Question."

"The Ottoman Empire, ruled by the Sultan, is based in Turkey and it extends into the Balkans to the north and down into Arabia in the south. It has been called the sick man of Europe. It contains a number of small provinces, each of which seems to favor a different religion, two sorts of Christianity for example. The Ottoman Emperors do not have a reputation for benign rule and they can be especially vicious if a province rebels.

The Tsars are interested, of course, because they are Slavs as are the Christian Serbs who are very restless under this Ottoman domination so there are frequent outbreaks of violence. Last year, one province revolted. The European Emperors wanted the Sultan to reform and he agreed. We were not a party this, and it is in the process of breaking down because the Sultan failed to implement those reforms. However, there are well confirmed reports of terrible atrocities on a very large scale. So here we are in 1876, anticipating Russia will invade the Ottoman Empire to protect the Slavs and as a result, get their ships into the Black Sea, to which they as yet have no access.

So I expect to be engaged on that, and goodness knows where it will go. Whatever happens, Disraeli, presently Prime Minister, will need all his formidable skill though Gladstone has stirred up the British public about the atrocities which Dizzy does not seem to appreciate."

"It sounds enormously interesting, if lives were not at stake."

"How do you mean?"

"You and I are sitting here comfortably in Paris while in those areas you mentioned women are scared stiff for their children, young women are expecting be raped, probably many times, old men are scratching their beard and expecting to be killed, and young men are being forced into conflict they neither understand nor care about. The old women, I am sure, are saying their rosaries or whatever is the equivalent in the different religions."

"I appreciate that reminder. We do tend to think of diplomacy as a game of chess and if there is a war here or a war there we hope to move the pawns around, box in the King and mate, taking a few knights and castles on the way. We back the victors and are usually totally unconcerned with loss of life, poverty and disease."

"I wonder sometimes when those European empires will collapse, as Rome did."

"That took hundreds of years. I don't see the British Empire collapsing."

"Be careful, Tim. What is the Greek word? Hubris."

"Of course that is right. All will be well with our Empire if we don't get bogged down in Europe."

"Most interesting. What an intelligent man you are. I look forward to continuing our conversations in London. Where will you live?

"I will try to find myself a lodging in Westminster when I get back. The Foreign Office does own some accommodation and I will apply for that, but I don't think I am senior enough."

"How old are you then?"

"I'm twenty-five and you?"

"Twenty-four."

"Just right. I very much hope we can explore a friendship, my dear Elizabeth."

"I think that's possible: Especially in London when we are on home territory."

Clarence decided not to sit in on the interview as Sam was his future brother-in-law but Hamish invited Adam. Sam was the next to youngest son of Lord and Lady Eustace, tall, elegantly dressed, with the bearing of a military man like his father and his brothers, though that profession has been far from his aspirations. He had not had much experience with the criminal law, which suited Hamish well, as specialists in civil law were urgently needed.

"We have a client, Mr. Eustace," said Hamish after introductions and as the interview began, "whose husband was involved in illegal practices which we need not detail. He has left us with a note saying he consents to a divorce from his wife. She was told of his nefarious activities in one dramatic and disastrous conversation. The following day he left for Australia, leaving her with some money, their house and two children. For reasons not germane to the case at the moment, we are to act *pro bono* for her and construct her petition to file before the Supreme Count.

"I take it," concluded Hamish, "that you are familiar enough with divorce law to handle this case if you join us."

"Indeed I am," said Sam, playing with his signet ring which Hamish found very distracting, but he continued: "I am sure that you read of the divorce of that notorious Irish peer, Lord Binding, whose wife decided she had had enough of being beaten incessantly. Unfortunately he was almost bankrupt so, though we appeared for Lady Binding, we have yet to receive our fees."

"I believe Mr. Jaggers opposed him once in an assault case."

"Oh, indeed, that was the major cause of his lack of funds. He became so exasperated losing to Jaggers again and again that he appealed twice if not three times leaving himself with astronomical lawyers' fees: Somewhat like the famous Jarndyce case.

"However, in the case you mention, the process should be simple. The lady will have to appear and, with this letter from the husband and your affidavit that it is genuine, the Court should be able to grant a decree nisi with a probable period of three months before it becomes absolute. Of course judges can be cantankerous, so there might be difficulties.

"For instance, the Court might want to know reasons why the husband absconded. Was he of sound mind? Without reasons for the desertion, the Court might not be of a mind to hand down a decree, so to speak, willy-nilly."

"At this moment, this husband is a member of our profession, as of course will be clear from his letter, and he failed to report a serious crime, namely the murder of a man with whom he was illicitly involved?"

"Was he a suspect?"

"We think not, as it would be entirely out of character."

"Again, these circumstances could invite an inquisitive judge to go down this track, irrelevant though it is.

"But alternatively, the judges might just look with great sympathy on the poor distressed lady and bring the proceedings to an abrupt end. One never knows with judges.

"I would of course be appearing on behalf of the petitioner, *mutatis mutandis.*(other things being equal) She might well have to give evidence too, but as it is not contested we hope that will not be necessary."

"Thank you, Mr. Eustace, what other aspects of the civil law interest you?"

"Wills and conveyancing."

"Excellent, we have a very wealthy Welsh widow who will require both of these services. You will find her quite friendly, indeed she can be over-friendly in my experience.

"Now, what would you like to discuss with us."

"I am sure that your remuneration will be satisfactory and no doubt your senior clerk will let me know about that. I understand your situation in terms of lawyers in my brief discussion with

Clarence yesterday. I should add my father is enthusiastic for me to join you, though he would benefit from my leaving," and he smiled quietly to himself.

"I do hope to aspire to be a full partner, of course, and given that there are no elderly lawyers clinging to your practice, I would hope that will be sooner rather than later. As you know, Clarence is about to marry my sister, but as I have worked in a family firm for almost ten years I do not foresee problems on that account."

"I urgently hope you will join us, Mr. Eustace.

"On the partnership front, I intend that Clarence and you become partners immediately. We need to recover from the body blow of losing two-thirds of our legal expertise. I am anxious to bring those numbers back to six, so a major part of your partnership would be searching out good material, people who will fit with us, not merely those who are lawyers anxious for wealth."

"Are you offering me a partnership then?"

"Och, I think so indeed. I am delighted that a member of such an august legal family should even consider joining us, bereft as we are."

"I gladly accept and will start forthwith."

"That will be here in Little Britain. We have acquired chambers in Lincolns Inn and will be selling both this building and the Courtisone premises. Indeed I am proposing to close down the Courtisone office forthwith to sell it, bring our staff over here and if need be, we can share offices until our Old Square building is ready."

"Most propitious. I will begin my work here on Monday if you wish and we can sign an agreement then."

"Capital. Our Senior Clerk Adam Masterson here will have prepared it."

"Indeed," said Adam.

Sam got up, retrieved his hat and coat, they all shook hands enthusiastically and with a broad smile he said goodbye and left.

Hamish then asked Robert to ask Clarence to come to the office.

"Two decisions, Clarence. I am offering both you and Sam full partnerships with me. I am closing the Courtisone office today to sell the building although we may have to share offices before moving to Old Square."

"Good for you, Hamish. Many thanks indeed, I am delighted and now I can get married knowing that Sam will be here."

"Yes, and he will run Mrs. Hardyman's petition for divorce, a weight off both our shoulders, and there's Mrs. Unworthy is waiting in the wings, claws at the ready, but I think Sam will be up to it.

"So, congratulations are in order and a quick retreat to a bar is called for: A wee dram never did anyone any harm."

Adam was thrilled at the prospect of these additional partners, but another discussion about his future with Hamish had hardly begun when it was interrupted by Robert announcing Superintendent Etherington.

"Good morning, Superintendent, what can I do for you?" said Hamish

"Nothing as it turns out. I thought you should know that in November we tracked Mr. Hardyman's ship and were able to get messages there and back with a Captain Rogerstone, asking if Hardyman was indeed on board as the records in the steamship company indicated. I had it in mind to have people we know there to question him when he arrived, but we missed him.

"However, we got an urgent message this morning to say that Mr. Hardyman had hanged himself in Brisbane, so questions that I had prepared for you are no longer in need of an answer."

"Goodness me, that is a shock, poor man. Why would he do that after six months in Brisbane?"

"I neither know nor care. In a suicide note, he asked that a substantial amount of currency in sterling in a bank be sent home to his wife which is more than suitable as he had virtually emptied their account before he left. I am glad that his small Brisbane bank has ensured that the money will be returned promptly to Mrs. Hardyman."

"Indeed, so Mrs. Hardyman need not pursue her divorce case, which has been in the wings for some time."

"Excuse me, but I thought you were sticklers for client confidentiality," said Etherington with a smile.

"Reproof accepted, though the divorce plea would have been public within a day or two when our new lawyer, Mr. Sam Eustace joins us."

The sun shone brightly though it was a crisp day for May as carriages were arriving in the court of Middle Temple after negotiating Temple Bar. They put down men and women who needed to hold on to their hats as they walked to Temple Church. The church was awash in white flowers, lilies, carnations and roses. A very distinguished covered carriage with the Eustace coat-of-arms emblazoned on its doors, drew up, its two white horses decorated with white plumes and flowers. A footman sprang down and opened the door for Emma's father to get down and holding out his hand he steadied his daughter as she put her right foot down, encased in a bejeweled shoe.

The walk to Temple Church began. Two bridesmaids were in attendance, Clarence's young sister, Hermione, and Emma's cousin, Anna Pemberton.

"I want to say to you, my dear," said Lord Eustace as they walked slowly on the cobbles down to the Church, "I am both overjoyed but immensely saddened. You are such a splendid woman and my heart aches with pride as I attend you now to give you to a very good man."

"Oh, Father, you have always been such an object of my admiration, not because of your success at the Bar, but because you and Mamma have been so wise in bringing us all up. I really cannot remember any single thing when I have felt aggrieved by anything either of you have said or done. My brothers," she said smiling, "are another matter."

"Just remember, darling, while I live, I am always available for counsel, though I doubt whether you will need it."

"Here we are, Father, on a day I will cherish all my life. I don't intend to go away, you know. I want to come to see Mamma and you very often."

As the organ began, the bride in stunning white and with a bouquet of white lilies on her left arm walked up the aisle with her beloved father. There stood her Clarence, what a handsome lovely man, she mused, with whom I am about to spend the rest of my life. Smiling lightly at the assembled company, she reached the chancel steps, turning to hand Hermione the bouquet before committing herself to love, honor and obey.

Later, Lord and Lady Eustace received their guests at the main door of Middle Temple Hall, a grand medieval structure which had seen most of the country's great lawyers regularly dine in collegial grandeur, an institution of great traditions, with its huge silver loving cup always passed round the tables at celebration dinners. The line passed quite slowly, Estella, Charlotte and Elizabeth together. Albert had decided to stay in Paris, happily now in love with Simona who ran around him like the young puppy of seventeen that she was.

Champagne flowed freely. A selection of sensible speeches were made, and Estella remarked on how they could be listened to as rather solemn. Marriage was not merely the celebration of romantic love in this sector of British society, but a contract of a different sort in which families of class and distinction came together as a means of preserving their heritage and wealth.

After the speeches had been completed, Charlotte saw Percy Vere across the Hall. He was tall and short-sighted and had clearly been late for the service, but he seemed to be looking around and once he caught her eye, he hurried over to her.

"Oh, my dear Charlotte, how wonderful to see you. I got back from Italy only last night having received the invitation to this wedding only a week ago. Italian post is notoriously eccentric, but here you are and I was hoping against hope that you had an invitation to this high society do and that I would meet you here. I am sorry to have missed Christmas, but, don't you know, I had the devil of a cold. But enough of me, how are you? You look quite radiant if I may say so."

"Well, thank you Percy, I am quite well after our sojourn in Paris."

"Can we take a walk outside? It is getting a little hot in here."

They walked out into the courtyard and down toward Temple Gardens overlooking the Thames River.

"I want to ask you something, Charlotte."

"Yes, Percy?"

"I know I have not been a good correspondent and that we are both getting on a bit, but I wondered if you would consent to become my wife? Don't answer immediately, as I would want you to come back to Pompeii with me as I must finish this dig which, oh I don't know, will last another three years at least."

"Percy, dear, that is as nice a proposal as I have ever had. I would be delighted to be with you in Italy and to marry you. I am sure we can get a house to rent nearby, preferably overlooking the sea and I can brush up on my Pliny. I know you will be very busy, but we will make good company."

"That is marvelous. Now, there is one catch. I do have to return next week, and I am not sure whether you can be ready by then."

"Of course I can, and I am sure we can get a license to marry immediately rather than waiting three weeks for the banns to be called."

"Indeed, the husband of one of my sisters is a bishop of some kind," said Percy, "and I am sure he will oblige with a license."

"But where will we marry?"

"Does it matter?"

"I suppose not, Percy, but where are you staying here?"

"I have a house in Norfolk which is rather large and unkempt. My aunt lives there, looked after by a nurse. She handed it over to me when she was sprightly, but I don't intend to take it from her."

"I have another house in Windsor by the river, but that is let. Oh, I am forgetting my what do they call it in French, I know, a pied-a-terre in Kensington. Now you are in New Queen Street, so we could find its parish, which may be St. Margaret's Westminster, a nice little church. Oh my goodness me, my excitement is running away with me."

"Your accommodation seems extensive, my dear."

"It is indeed. Elderly female relations all seem to think I need a house. Each of these has been willed to me, which is all very well but I am mostly out of England. Let us walk back to the Hall to say goodbye to the bride and groom."

They arrived back to find quite a crowd waiting for Clarence and Emma who, it had been determined, were off to Nice for three weeks. Charlotte took notice of a young man she assumed to be Tim Egerton in close conversation with Elizabeth as he lifted his hand and gently replaced a hair which had slipped down on to her cheek. She took his hand after he had done so and gave him a smile that would have lit up the English Channel enabling ships to steer by it if she were not where she was, in the court of Middle Temple Hall.

Charlotte had not seen that smile for ages and she would keep the memory of it with her in Italy.

The gathering swallows had departed long since when the Trust met in October for the third time in a year to review its work. First, Pip formally announced the suicide of Philip Hardyman which created a vacancy on the Board, and Estella agreed to meet Jane regularly to see if the family needed help, a matter she had neglected. The members of the Board expressed conventional opinions on his death, and truth to tell, no one liked the man whom most regarded as a queer fish, a use of the phrase that Clarence found diverting.

The Board had thus lost John Wemmick and Philip Hardyman but had added Sam Eustace and Adam Masterson as full members. Albert had resigned because it made no sense for him to continue

as he was living in Paris, though it was agreed that his membership would be abeyance. From the Chair, Estella recommended
that Adam Masterson be the Board's secretary and that he should
become a full member. So with Pip and Susanna Gargery, Clarence
Smythe, Hamish and Mary Macdonald, the Board was complete
with Estella Pirrip in the Chair.

Estella was concerned that only Susanna and she were the
women on the Board and she had sounded out all the members
before raising the matter. It was agreed that one additional woman
member should be invited to join. Sam suggested that his mother,
Lady Eustace, might be interested. Estella privately wanted Harriet
to join, but with Pip and Susanna on the Board that was impossible.
Charlotte was now in Pompeii with Percy. Discussion of a nominee
was then abandoned as the Trust reviewed its work.

First, Pip reported on the two homes for prostitutes. They were
run well, but, as with earlier problems, there were rivalries and
cliques, and some fisticuffs, especially among some of the women,
though that was stable. Training in trades for the men had proceeded well, primarily as carpenters and bricklayers.

This was a difficult matter as the apprenticeship system that had
existed for centuries was still only being phased out. Nevertheless,
as he told the Board, Jack Masham had learnt enough carpentry
for Frederick Brandram, the architect, to recommend him to a firm
he worked with. Jack was now in lodgings in Ealing and properly
employed. Jack's growth became a model for other young men,
Pip said, such that the Trust now had a waiting list for the Semper
House Home and it was agreed that Pip should search for another
building to cope with the demand.

Estella reported on the developments in Kent. In All Hallows
there were forty-five families headed by men who had worked on
the farms but were now out of work due to the agricultural depression. The Trust agreed to distribute £1 weekly to each of these families which, in a full year, would amount to £2,340.

Pip then reported on The Trust's investments which had been
brilliantly managed by Mr. Courtisone, facilitating an investment

income that had risen from the anticipated £5,000 to £10,000 annually and the basic endowment had risen to over £100,000. The cost of the homes was £4,500 each year. The result was that, in terms of income for a year, the Trust could spend another £2,000 to £3,000 annually beyond its present commitments and Estella felt the Board was duty bound to try.

"That presents us with a choice," said Estella.

"We can pursue the idea of another home for male prostitutes which will involve capital expenditure and an estimated £1,500 running expenses; or we can expand our support for agricultural laborers. A third possibility is to build houses or cottages in those depressed agricultural areas. The work of other Trusts in London, such as that led by Miss Hill, are already well endowed, so that does not need replication here in the city."

"Or, of course, other ideas. What do members think?"

"I wonder," said Clarence, "whether we might focus on children. I met one of Emma's cousins who is one of these new Inspectors of Schools and he said that every day he was seeing filthy and ragged children in the schools, some with disease, not physically developed, starving, clothes falling of their bodies and much neglected by their parents. Many of them have no home and no hope."

"That is very interesting," said Susanna, "after Lachlan died, Pip and I thought of opening a school but we have not got much further with it. I'd be very pleased to work with a school for very poor children if the Trust were able to finance it."

"My own sentiment," said Hamish, "is to choose an activity which will have lasting rather than ephemeral impact. Support for agricultural laborers is all very well, but we can hardly continue that forever."

"But that does have lasting impact," replied Sam, "for presumably the children in those families do not then grow up starving and badly clothed but go to their schools confident there will be food on the table."

"I like the idea of a school," said Pip, "as I agree we could have an impact. But I am also keen on buildings. I know from growing up there that village cottages are often little more than shacks. Even to build half a dozen would be valuable."

"For my part," said Adam, "I think we should have a balance between different sorts of investments. Of course, it's a choice, but all of these seem such splendid ideas, we should find ways to do all of them, perhaps in partnership with other Trusts. At this moment in time, though we know the Government has made provision for schooling for all young children up to age 11, perhaps the school should be for children from say eleven to fourteen and should focus on equipping them for a trade."

"Perhaps Pip," said Estella, "you would draw up costs for all these possibilities so that we can make some decisions on these four at our next meeting: Another home for prostitutes, cottages for affordable long-lease, help for children so far unspecified, and a trade school. Once we know costs, we can allocate responsibility for each to one or two members of the Board.

"Of course," said Clarence, "we are all getting to know that trade is starting to slow down so that some are saying we could be in for very hard times. That could affect our endowment in the longer run. This agricultural depression is very serious. On the other hand, when goods become cheaper by 40% which is a figure I have seen quoted, then a £1 laborer can do more with his money in terms of goods he can buy. I'd like that support to continue."

As was customary for the Board, they retired to *The Cheshire Cheese* for lunch and further discussion, and it seemed to be now customary also to have jugged hare and claret.

XV

Estella was in fact thrilled by the work of the Trust after that meeting and she was taking great pride in guiding it, though she sometimes wished the Board was a full-time organization which would make its presence felt much more widely. Charlotte was off to Pompeii to be with Percy and his dig, and Elizabeth was no longer there as she had set herself up in her own small apartment in the Victoria area of London. She was meeting Tim Egerton regularly, but she did not neglect Estella, calling frequently at New Queen Street. Albert was still on his painting adventure in Paris. She was alone.

Sitting in her living room that evening, she tried to embrace Browning's new volume but she was distracted by her wandering mind. Concentration did not come easily these days. Why did Susanna still find it difficult to handle her dislike for Harriet, this adulterous woman with her husband? Had nothing changed with Lachlan's death in this respect? Certainly Susanna's marriage seemed to have gained strength thereafter, although Estella had always thought it would be somewhat brittle, but then, as she constantly had to remind herself, how much can one know about another couple's marriage?

She was sure that Harriet, beautiful desirable Harriet, would be accommodating and friendly if Susanna were to put the past finally behind her. That took her mind back to that meeting eighteen months ago when she had told Harriet about the monster in her mind, and then further thoughts tumbled out from her imagination with Harriet and herself as committed lovers in New Queen Street. Why, oh, why was she so fascinated with that woman?

Perhaps I am reverting to the form of a woman Miss Havisham wanted me to be but without that contempt for men. Men were simply now of little interest. I flirted with the idea of John Sargent, but then thought it ridiculous. I would probably refuse an engagement even with a suitable man, but not since Nellie would I refuse a woman on principle. Might this have been true of Miss Havisham? There's a thought, a Sapphic Miss Havisham.

Since Pip's death, I have truly not desired any man. Nellie smashed through all my inhibitions to make me see my real self as a Sapphic lover. Indeed, I often look at women these days as potential bedfellows; Emma, a virgin at her wedding, the enticing Antonia Penoyre at the picnic, both completely out of my reach of course. What would they want with this old body? I do fancy them, as Nellie would say, and, oh dear, I dare not allow myself to think of the beautiful Elizabeth.

When in this mood, she simply could not put Miss Havisham behind her. She had once told Nellie that her memories of becoming a woman were non-existent, and Miss Havisham was no help in her weathering that particular storm. Miss Havisham's pernicious influence was still there in some deep dark corner of her mind.

Did my guardian turn me away from men with such force that women became my natural love objects, though I did admire Pip when he was a mere boy? Perhaps what I got from her was her raw passion and her untrammeled determination as with my mother. My killing fantasies are as full of passion as my mother and father's stark passions were. Instead of calming that inheritance, Miss Havisham enhanced them, in her eccentric way. Oh dear, what a confused and troubled woman I am beneath the skin.

It was a monumental struggle to put such evil and erotic thoughts behind her. Nevertheless, her mind ranged over less unlikely possibilities more carefully.

Suppose Pip had lost interest in her by the time he returned from his travels and not called that day. After all, the day he came to see her she was marooned in a small country lodge with her maid.

Suppose he had merely been helpful on the matter of finding a house.

Suppose she had not been reconciled to Molly with the earthquake of relationships that followed.

Pip would have married Beatrice anyway and she would have remained trapped within her conventions, growing old as an embittered virgin, unable to unlock her sexuality while Beatrice survived in a very happy marriage with Pip. Much like her guardian, perhaps, except that she would have sounded like an elderly vengeful predator to anyone who had the temerity to listen.

She raised herself out of her chair and walked across the small cupboard to pour herself a glass of whisky and shake off all these imaginings.

Once down to earth, what was she doing founding this League? As she had told Hamish at the Courtisone party, she was caught between leisure and philanthropic action. With men, it was not that she did not want their company, but that she only really came alive in the company of women where there was openness, tenderness, laughter and gaiety at these strange unfathomable beings called men.

Not that she was unhappy with that.

All a mystery, really.

Now, she thought, what *am* I to about Susanna and Harriet?

She sent a note through the post, inviting herself or offering Susanna the opportunity to call at New Queen Street. As a result, Susanna called one morning, intrigued by being invited as she knew the street, but not the house.

"What a beautiful home, Estella," said Susanna as she stood in the hallway which looked into the living room and the dining room."

"Indeed, I am very pleased indeed with it. Of course, now Charlotte is in Italy, Albert is in Paris, and Elizabeth has moved to a place in Victoria. I feel it is far too big for me, but its advantages are so great I am not considering surrendering them, and of course, I have been in France for some time."

The maid brought some tea and various small pastries as the two chatted about inconsequential things.

"I think I can guess why you have invited me here, Estella."

"I would be very pleased indeed if your guess is correct. I am sure we will need at some point soon to talk about the school we discussed at the Trust meeting."

"No, I am assuming this is about my membership of The League of Free Women and whether I am prepared to come if Harriet is a member."

"You are right, my dear Susanna. Let me explain.

"I am hoping that as the months have gone by and my mistaken interference has become more of a dim memory, I do hope you will join. I think the League will grow. I anticipate being nine in number and inviting each woman to invite an other person. We are, I think, going to get into major matters which are evolving presently in the public consciousness, like voting, but across the whole range of women's freedom.

"Frankly you have such a keen mind, indeed, such a brilliant mind that the League could benefit enormously from your perspective and what I suspect would be our determination. So, I think you have a great contribution to make."

"You are nothing if not persistent, Estella. Without being arrogant, Estella, I think that I do have a good mind and I am also a wealthy woman, thanks to my father, which might ease some of the burdens for the League, were I to commit. Tell me more about Harriet, first, without any reference to Pip."

"She is very charming, easy to get to know, very self-confident, intellectually very strong, very well read and as I see her, very beautiful. She has a number of diverse interests, including writing poetry. I lunched with her sometime last year and she brought a young woman friend of hers who is already a published poet."

"She sounds splendid.

"Alright. As you know my whole life was shattered by Lachlan's death, much more so than anything I have ever encountered or expect to encounter. Everything before that is something of a haze as it so dominates my thinking and my life. I am frightened of life, Estella.

"Could this happen to my other children? Why Lachlan? I have come to think of my husband's brief dalliance with Harriet as so trivial, compared to the loss of Lachlan, that I do not want it to cut me off from engagements that I know I can contribute to. What was it Pip said to me you have told him? Its only sex, not murder?"

"Ah, yes, that originated elsewhere, but your point there is such an excellent example of your wisdom, Susanna dear," worried that Susanna would think she had spread the news of their marriage difficulties far and wide in Kent.

"Thank you, but I want to tell you also that in all that chaos of learning about Pip and Harriet, I become so vengeful that I took James Bollaerts as my lover."

"What?" said Estella feigning surprise.

"It was physically very exciting, but when I realized what a cad he was, I felt so dirty, so soiled, so disgusted with myself that I had to clean all that out of my life and my marriage by telling Pip I had had a lover, though I did not tell him it was James and he did not want to know. As the Bollaerts left almost to the day after I told Pip, I am sure he had his suspicions. All a long time ago now."

"I confess that I thought you might have taken a lover and now I am certainly surprised, though perhaps someone more attractive than that fellow," and they laughed.

"Is it not odd the way jealousy works? My mother quite simply murdered her husband's lover. I don't know what I would have done, had Pip taken a lover; probably followed my mother's actions.

"All that apart, I cannot tell you how delighted your friends are that you have righted the ship. Pip is a wonderful man who commands love and respect. He has many excellent qualities and yours is a complementary marriage."

"I hope so. So, I will come to your meeting with Harriet then. I anticipate it will take me some time to accommodate myself to it, and, of course, Pip is going to have to do the same, for I am sure there will be events where husbands come to League meetings to be told what to do!"

They both laughed again.

"Oh, I am sure Pip will take it in his stride. I must tell you that Harriet was terribly upset when I told her about Lachlan."

"Why?"

"She said that their relationship ended in Salford after Pip spent a week at the Cottage playing with young Albert. He told her when he got back to Salford that he definitely wanted children, which Harriet did not want. Lachlan's death upset her so much because she realized what a tragedy it must have been for you both, but especially for Pip as she had known him."

"That is very nice of her: Perhaps I might get to like her after all."

"Knowing both your characters, I think you would make excellent friends."

Fanny and Clara shared a room at Semper House in what used to be the attic before Brandram's conversion of the property. They loved the room, each with a bed under the sloping roof but with a small dormer window from which they could see Westminster Abbey and the newly constructed Houses of Parliament with its big clock. They slept well and enjoyed their work. The Copperstones ran the Home efficiently, though these young men were rather rough and never did any of them show any interest whatsoever in these young servant women, much to their chagrin.

The Copperstones had a couple of rooms just beneath them and Brandram had placed the office from which the Home was run on this third floor. The young men occupied rooms on the first and second floors, and the ground floor housed the dining room and the living room. The kitchen was in the basement, and Fanny and Clara brought the food up the stairs, often with help from the young men, and they all would have chafed at the absence of a dumb waiter, had they known what it was.

Every night there was the occasional merchant's cart running down Gerrard Street, either on its way to Covent Garden or back for greengroceries from the Garden. Gareth Prothero lived in Acton where he was a small but prosperous greengrocer. His parents had come to London from Carmathenshire the year the Queen married her Prince, and in the fullness of time he inherited his father's business.

The sun was up that July morning and he was on his way back from the Garden in the early hours. He did not take the direct route that day. He'd always enjoyed exploring other parts of London, frequently taking his cart into highways and byways to get to know the city, an ideal time to make such journeys as the streets were quite empty. He found himself in Soho with his cart now laden with boxes containing the customary vegetables, potatoes, apples and pears, cabbages, cauliflowers, parsnips, carrots and leeks, and even some runner beans even though that season was almost over.

He turned into Gerrard Street, ambling along with his horse Dolly clipping her shoes on the pavement.

"Whoa, Dolly, what's going on there?"

He dismounted and moved over to take a look at the basement windows of Semper House. They seemed to be black and the faint smell of smoke indicated that something in the house was on fire. He banged on the main door, but there was no answer. He picked up a stone and hurled it at an upstairs window which smashed. Mr. Copperstone got out of bed and went to the window.

"You've got a fire," shouted Gareth, "you're on fire."

Copperstone then realized that he could smell smoke.

"Wake up, Mrs. C., we're on fire."

He rushed to the hand bell he kept in the room precisely for emergencies and he did as Mr. Gargery had told him, going out of the room, shouting "Fire, Fire," and ringing the handbell as hard as he could. He helped Mrs. C into the chute and then descended himself, going urgently to the main tap for the gas which was in the street under a cover. That was a struggle, but he got it open and turned off the gas which was clearly fueling flames from the kitchen below.

In his anxiety to help and being unable to get through the locked front door, Gareth had smashed a basement window so he could get at some water to douse whatever fire was there.

That was a mistake.

Once the air got into the basement through the smashed window, the fire in the kitchen went up like an inferno. It blew up through the staircase with intensifying heat. By now, everyone was awake. Fanny and Clara came down to the Copperstone's floor and realized they should use those chutes by the window which they had seen demonstrated by the men who installed them two or three years earlier, an inspiration of Frederick Brandram's. Every resident had been instructed how to use them.

Windows opened, chutes were thrown out and one by one the Home was almost emptied of young men as Gareth watched. Fanny was a thin young woman and she did not master the need to slow one's descent by holding arms against the canvas, so she broke her foot on landing on the pavement. Clara was terrified when she saw Fanny go down so fast, though she had seen the Copperstones descend. She stood paralyzed with fear and the home was now almost fully ablaze.

"Get in the chute," roared Copperstone, and the young men huddling on the pavement joined in: "Get in the bleeding chute, Clara."

But by now the smoke and flames had rendered her almost unconscious. The bells of a fire engine could be heard coming down the street. It would be impossible for a fireman to go through the hallway and attempt a rescue. The stairs were ablaze, timbers were crashing around, the wall decorations William Morris had installed were peeling off with the heat, and flames now began to assault the roof.

With a terrific effort of will, and holding her nightdress against her mouth, the semi-conscious Clara got into the chute and came down as fast as Fanny had done, crashed on to the pavement, broke both legs and badly injured her hands. Mrs. Copperstone rushed to cover up Clara's naked broken body as she lost her nightdress in the descent. Shelter was needed for the poor girl from the astonished gaze of the assembled young men.

Several hours later, the house was a complete ruin, smoldering in the cool of the morning. Gareth was trying to explain to anyone who would listen that he had been trying to help. The firemen looked at him with sorrow, though they thought the house would have been a goner anyway, so no need to pile on the blame. Obviously something in the kitchen had started the blaze but neither the Copperstones nor Fanny or Clara could shed any light on the matter.

As they always did, every fireman nevertheless wondered if it could have been started deliberately, and their chief said that it was a matter for the police. A constable who had earlier been on patrol but was in fact having forty winks in a doorway on Shaftesbury Avenue arrived on the scene just as Clara dropped down the chute. After consultation with the firemen, he hurried to the Leicester Square Police Station to report to his superiors.

Like all of her species faced with fire, Dolly had cantered off down Gerrard Street, showering the road with baskets of vegetables as she went, and Gareth found her later, grazing on the banks of the river near the bottom of Northumberland Avenue, but with only half his morning's purchases intact. He rode home, mortification dripping from the reins, but that soon turned to pride that he had called the alarm and he spent at least three days retelling the harrowing course of events to his enthralled customers. His wife Gladys did not let on to nosy customers, though she had the whole story. He was a good man without an ounce of malice in his body and she loved him for it.

Copperstone did not know what to do. All the shivering inhabitants of Semper House Home were now gathered on the other side of the road, gazing at the smoldering remains of the august home of Nathaniel Jaggers, some in tears, some comforting each other, all shocked but grateful to be alive. First and foremost, Copperstone realized, he had to get a message to Mr. Gargery and, he thought, to Mrs. Pirrip as well.

Estella was reading after her breakfast when she noticed a cab arriving at her door and Pip leapt out. He darted to the front door, ringing the bell furiously and the maid hurried to answer.

He burst into her living room and said:

"Semper House has burnt down."

"Goodness gracious," she said, bolting out of her chair, "is everyone alright?"

"Thanks to the installation of those chutes at Frederick's insistence, we only have two accidents. Fanny broke one leg and Clara broke both as they were terrified of the chute and came down far too fast. Both survived and are in the Dean Street hospital."

"How did you hear about it?"

"Copperstone sent a message. I think we should go there as quickly as possible. How on earth are we going to house the men and the staff? This is such an infernal tragedy."

"It certainly sounds to have been infernal, but stay calm, Pip, and we will take ourselves there immediately. Read the newspaper while I prepare myself."

An hour later, they arrived to see the still smoldering wreck of Semper House. The former inhabitants were all gathered still on the pavement, and the proprietor of a café in Wardour Street had kindly supplied some food and some coffee at Mr. Copperstone's request assuring the man that the Trust would reimburse him for it.

"First things first, Mr. Copperstone," said Estella, "we must find accommodation for everyone. Please find as many lodging rooms as can be obtained, preferably near Gerrard Street."

"Yes, Ma'am, Mrs. C. and I will begin that immediately."

"Here," she said ruffling in her bag, "take my Trust card and ask them to send me their account at that address."

"Ma'am," said Copperstone, "I think it is urgent that you talk to the police."

"I will, but meantime, as that café proprietor has been so helpful, perhaps we could rent it for the day. Pip, could you negotiate a price for us to use it and by this afternoon I am sure we will have rooms. Now, the police."

"Oh, Pip, I do beg your pardon. It is you who manages these homes, not me. I apologize, I am so anxious."

"That is quite acceptable, Estella dear. You just took charge by instinct, but I am glad to take over and we can both talk to the police."

On the other side of the road, gazing at Semper House was the former Superintendent Etherington, now Detective Inspector, a type of position newly created at Scotland Yard. Etherington stubbed out his cigar and introduced himself, as he had not met either Pip or Estella before.

"Tell me," said Estella with as much charm as she could muster in the face of this catastrophe, "why is it called Scotland Yard?"

"I don't rightly know, but I was told once there was a palace there where Scottish kings used to stay."

"Ah, quite obvious, now I think about it. Now what do you make of this fire, Inspector?"

"I have called in some specialists from the Yard and they are working inside to try to determine the cause and whether it was arson or not."

"Arson, really?"

"Think about it," interjected Pip, "we have had contact with some shady customers. We have had to turn away some, and then there may be people like that Italian."

"Angelo?"

"That is the way we are thinking, Ma'am. Mr. Copperstone can vouch for everyone who came down the chutes. Great invention, those. No one would set fire to a building, go to sleep and then escape from it, now, would they? So it's not one of the guests."

"I'd like a list of any young man who has either left or been thrown out or who might have a grudge against someone inside."

"That will take some time to recall, as the office upstairs was completely destroyed, unless the safe has survived. It was sold to me as fireproof, but the blaze was most intense, apparently. We needed to keep documents under tight lock and key."

"Very wise, I am sure. If it a heavy safe, I would wager it will be found in the basement. But is there anyone you can think of who might wish to see the building destroyed, or an individual within it harmed."

"I don't know of anyone: I could ask Hamish."

"Do you mean Hamish Macdonald the lawyer?

"Indeed, why?"

"I was in charge of the case of Mike Watson, the young man who was murdered and his lover was a Philip Hardyman who whose rent-boy he was. Hardyman disappeared, but we discovered it was an MP, name of Bloviate, but by the time we got to him, he had vamoosed to America, I was told."

"Vamoosed or skedaddled?"

"Vamoosed, I'd say. Unsurprising," said the Detective Inspector in that ruminative way senior policemen have which conveys to members of the public that beneath their hats they carry brains capable of immense deductive and inductive ability, but then turning to Estella said suddenly, "you know Hardyman killed himself in Australia."

"Indeed I do: I suppose there is a point at which shame overwhelms a man, haunting and even taunting them, daring them to end their existence. That would not happen with guilt."

"Very wise, Mrs. Pirrip, I had not thought of it like that."

"However, enough philosophy, Inspector, you should talk to Mr. Macdonald about this arson possibility.

"It must be two years ago, there was a disgruntled Scotsman, Twaddell, that's right, Twaddell was his name. I was in court when he was sentenced to two years hard labor. He had earlier been refused employment with Mr. Macdonald. He might have tried to get his own back, as Macdonald is the lawyer for the Trust which owned this building of which I am the Chairman and my friend Pip Gargery is the Manager."

"Oh, I remember the case, Mrs. Pirrip, only too well. He was the man who called a lawyer down from the gallery. He told the judge he would be a hostile witness but then, as the saying goes, collapse of stout party!

"Thank you very much for this discussion, sir and madam, it gives us plenty to go on, but we will await the findings of our specialists before jumping to any conclusions. I think the notion that this unemployed lawyer would arrange for the fire a little far-fetched, but we will check his present whereabouts. More likely, in my estimation, it was just a typical kitchen fire which caught everyone by surprise."

"I hope so."

"And presumably you were insured."

"Yes, indeed, Inspector."

1877

XVI

The fire at Semper House Home threw the Trust into a major reconsideration of policy. If, the argument ran, the Trust was paying out weekly sums to agricultural laborers, why not to the rent-boys? That would not work, however, as if they went back to the streets they would be in effect being subsidized by the Trust. On the other hand, not having to keep up the building, and perhaps including the Jaggers Building, might it not be more sensible to make the allowances and to train the men at least for a trade? For the women, the existence of sweat shops in East London made consideration of work for women complicated.

A brief meeting of the Trust in the New Year 1877 was held as an emergency since one of its major assets had been destroyed. Pip had not yet finished preparing costs of the list of possibilities discussed, which included another home for males, cottages or allowances for agricultural laborers, and a trade school for very poor children after their compulsory education.

Susanna took the lead.

"I suspect that our idea of homes for men and women prostitutes has run its course. We can find other ways to help such men and women pay rent and learn a trade without having the burden of buildings. We can sell the land at Semper House and phase out the Jaggers Building which we then sell, adding to the capital we have."

"I don't dissent from that," said Estella, "but I think we must find work for these poor souls, and that does mean their having a trade. Perhaps we could employ them rebuilding Semper House, learning a trade from the bricklayers and carpenters and even plumbers or gas workers. By the way I learned that Mr. Copperstone had the presence of mind to turn the gas off once he got into the street. I have given them five pounds for their work with the fire, by the way."

"It sounds to me as though we are at a turning point," said Hamish, "the baw is up on the slates, as they say in Scotland."

"What on earth does that mean?" asked Pip.

"Aye," said Susanna joining in the Scottish brogue, "it means the game is over as the ball is on someone's roof, hence the baw is on the slates."

"Aye," repeated Hamish, to everyone's laughter, "I think we have made the young men and the women we are helping too dependent on us. They have to make their own way, get out and find jobs. I agree certainly that allowances with rent and food are a base, and maybe helping them to learn a trade is sensible, but I suspect we are realizing we have done too much molly-coddling," at which there was loud laughter around the room.

Hamish was surprised by the laughter but then looked rather sheepish, saying, "that's gee-in me the boak."

"I know what you mean," said Susanna laughing loudly, "you are sick at your mistake, my Scottish friend, but a better choice of words, such as spoiling, indulging, even cosseting might have been more appropriate."

"I agree, and I apologize for my slowness of wit, wee dour Scot that I am."

"Not at all," said Pip, "It gave us some relief from our dire position."

"It's not dire," said Estella, "but we are at Hamish's turning point, are we not? Let us meet in a month when Pip has worked out costs and we have all had time to think."

"I'd like everyone to know that Trust offices will, as from two weeks next Monday be at 11, Old Square in Lincolns Inn," Hamish announced.

"We have had workmen slaving away day and night to refurbish these neglected chambers; we are in the process of selling the old

Courtisone premises and will sell off this Little Britain office as soon as the move is complete. I should add there will be a large room devoted to the work of the Trust, and the meeting room on the ground floor can host meetings such as this. It is further to the Cheshire Cheese of course, but a good walk will make us healthy."

"Many congratulations are in order, Hamish," said Estella. "I gather you have appointed a new partner too."

"Yes, he is The Honorable Sam Eustace, fourth son of the Lord Justice Eustace of the court of Appeals: A Fine man, and we are delighted to have him working with us. We are searching for three additional lawyers and would be glad to receive nominations."

"Mrs. Hardyman is a source of concern," said Susanna, "she is a private and immensely distressed woman."

"I will meet her as I promised," said Estella, "she came to Paris for advice you know."

With that, the emergency meeting of the Trust broke up.

Estella took a cab to New Queen Street to send out letters to a meeting of the League of Free Women to be held at her home to try to establish a convenient date.

⚜ ⚜ ⚜

She opened her front door and noticed a man's coat hanging on the stand in the hall.

"Who is there?" she called and from the living room came a young man she immediately recognized as Albert.

"Darling Albert, what are you doing here? You look quite different with your long beard and mustache and what is this cap you are wearing. It looks like a beret, take it off," and she gave him a big embrace.

"Oh, dear, we must have the maid fill a bath for you. You stink of tobacco. It's in all your clothes."

"Estella, *ma cherie*, how are you? Yes, yes, I know I need to clean up but I arrived at Dover early this morning."

"So have you come for a break?"

"No, I am finished with painting."

"Ah, I can see this will be a long story. Call the maid to fill a bath, you will find your room as you left it, and have the maid burn everything you are wearing."

An hour later, Albert came down the stairs looking presentable to Estella's eyes. Lunch had been prepared so they sat in the dining room to enjoy some pickled ham, poached eggs, breads and various fruits.

"Start at the beginning from when we left," said Estella.

"I am sorry not to have written more recently. I was very upset with losing Elizabeth but I think we got so close because we were too young."

"Perhaps, but what of the Rothschild girl?"

"Simona? Or that was long ago finished when she tentatively hinted to her mother that she was in love with a Gentile, following which she was promptly dispatched to the family home in Tuscany and not allowed back for a year."

"I am not surprised, but go on."

"I have had several female acquaintances since. I thought I might try to make it up with Elizabeth, but it is probably too late."

"I am afraid it is. She is very much attached now to Tim Egerton, the diplomat."

"I do not blame her, you know. The more I went to the studio and the more I met these painters socially, the more I realized I simply did not have their talent, their imagination, or, for that matter, their devotion to what they were doing, their incessant discussions and mutual criticisms. I looked at the work compared to my pettyfogging little pieces and for the last three months I have not picked up a brush or looked at a canvas."

"Did you finish you father's portrait?"

"Finally, yes, and it is on its way here. Yet I was inspired to complete it with help from John Sargent who assisted me with technique. It is nothing like as good as yours which I see hanging over the mantelshelf.

"In fact, it was one very drunken night that he said to me that he thought I was not a painter really, just a dauber. He was being kind, of course, though I resented it at the time, but it stopped me posing as a painter and from that night onwards, I knew I had to do something else."

"Perhaps this is not really a disappointment," said Estella, "but what will you do?"

"You'll no doubt have forgotten that my grandfather Algernon Pocket left me money in his will. At the time, I thought, I'll just go for the five hundred instead of the five thousand available if I worked in the business. I wrote to them originally and said I would consider it, but I dithered, because five thousand is a lot of money to dangle before an incompetent painter. Then I got a second letter a month or so ago, asking me whether I'd received their letter as the opportunity was still open."

"Good heavens, my dear Albert, you, a businessman?"

"Why not?"

"Forgive me, pray continue."

"So I wrote back saying that I had considered carefully the opportunity my grandfather offered and that I would like to follow it up. They replied almost immediately, saying that the business was in limbo since his death and that a manager was badly needed, though there was no danger of its imminent collapse as a temporary manager was in place. Grandfather Pocket has in effect left me the business."

"Oh my goodness, don't tell me, you are going to try to run it?"

"Yes. In some abstract way, I think of it as a family inheritance, as indeed it is, and that I had a duty to try it."

"Ah yes, I had not thought about it that way, but you are right and I can see the sense of obligation."

"Now I only know about it vaguely and the lawyers sent me some papers when I said to them I would accept so I am to go there the day after tomorrow. They have found me some temporary lodging."

"Well, well," said Estella, "I am sure your mother would be very pleased and I know your father would have supported you in any venture you cared to take up. For my part, you are an intelligent man and can be hard-working to boot. I think you might call on Frederick Brandram tomorrow as he is an architect and he knows the building business very well. I'll send a note to him today."

"I have met him, have I not? Is he the step-father of those twins?"

"That's right."

"Oh, I liked him a lot, from a distance, of course."

"Now, why don't you do something enlightening this afternoon as I must send out letters for a meeting of the League of Free Women which I have founded."

"I noticed in the cab on the way that there was some large buildings being constructed just outside Victoria. I'll take a cab and go look at them if I am to be in the timber business."

Estella sat back at her desk, slightly stunned by this development. Yet she had been attracted by his painting, but not his dilettantism and louche life, so she was thrilled he had given all that up. However, she put Albert aside and started a letter to Frederick and then to Harriet, telling her of the meeting with Susanna saying that she was quite reconciled to attending and that she thought any animosities were now resolved.

Then to Eliza Culpepper, Emma now Fotheringaye-Smythe, formerly Eustace, and Antonia Penoyre she wrote a different invitation, explaining more about the intentions of the League and hoping they would find time to join. She added the names of those she was inviting.

She also wrote a special letter to Jane Hardyman, hoping she might find comfort within a group of women, but explaining that Charlotte whom she had met was now married and living in Italy. So, then it was merely a matter of notifying Susanna Gargery, Honora Brandram and Mary Macdonald. That made a possible eight at the meeting, but nine if Charlotte were in England.

That voluminous correspondence completed, she sat down with the afternoon paper and was shocked to read that one of the

Queen's daughters, Princess Alice, had died of diphtheria. That really is the most terrible disease and the news would have certainly brought the grim memories of Lachlan into the Gargery household.

Following the meeting of the Trust, Pip sent a message to Estella saying that he wanted to visit the Building so that he could monitor progress, hoping she would care to come with him. Truth to tell, her interest in prostitution had begun to flag, in part because conversations with Nellie had awakened her to the need for a working wage for the rural poor.

After all, these were very worthy folk who deserved support certainly in preference to the decadent young men who had occupied Semper House. The women prostitutes were differently placed in terms of their needs for their children, often violent husbands and much else. Yet here too, she wondered whether support for rent and for a weekly support wage would not really be a better solution than the Building as the Trust had discussed.

Pip and Estella went across London in a cab the following day to the Building where Mr. Holditch said he was quite surprised that they had a few months of peace and quiet. True, some of the young children misbehaved, but then they 'was just kids' as he put it.

Estella's experience told her, if Nellie had not, that the views of those closest to the situation were often the most valuable, rather than outsiders doing inspections.

"Do you think this solution works for these women, Mr. Holditch?" she asked.

"Definitely," he replied, "but, you know, I wish they'd move on. Most of the women have been here more than two years. They have got into a rut. They don't have to cook, though we encourage those that are interested to take part. I mean, are they going to be here for years? Till they're old? It's a comfortable life compared with what they came from."

"Do you think they lose their independence, then?"

"Most definitely, and some of them have not been out of the building for months. That's not because they're frightened of anyone, they've become frightened of the street with its noise and bustle."

"Let me take you into our confidence," said Pip.

"The situation is different for the young male rent-boys than for women who have families. You've probably heard that Semper House burnt down, and we don't know yet whether it was arson or not. But we are thinking that the Trust should support them through rent and an allowance, we hope in a context where they can learn a trade, rather than restoring a building."

"Oh, I definitely think that would be good for the men."

"Now, Mr. Holditch," said Estella, "you have been a wonderful manager and caretaker of this building and if we decided to close it we would support you and your wife to the same extent as we have so far until you find yourself another employment. So you can be free with your advice about what we should do."

"Well, thank you, that is very generous of you, and I was worried about the direction of this conversation. But if it were my responsibility, I would gradually close the Building, finding the right situation for each woman in terms of a home and rent.

"In some ways, you know, the Building has become a kind of very fancy prison, for like some old lags, they hate leaving prison where they get food, not like it used to be with workhouses, mind, and a bed at night. I think some of the women really think about their life like that."

"Right, now, can we call a meeting as I'd like to talk to them," said Pip.

"Are you sure you can handle this? asked Estella.

"Oh, yes."

Some of the women were instantly recognizable to both Estella and Pip and they were both quietly satisfied with the obvious friendships that had developed and, in fact the women looked much better in term of their health than heretofore.

Pip began by saying that the Trust was reviewing its work, promoted by the terrible fire at Semper House. The Trust was of a mind not to rebuild the Home as such, but to give allowances for rent and upkeep to the men and to find ways in which they could learn a trade. He then asked whether any of the women there would like to think about that possibility.

"Let me get this straight," said Emily Collins, a relative newcomer, "you'll give us money for rent and an allowance instead of us living 'ere."

"That's right. Of course we'd want you to swear you wouldn't go back on the game, as, if you did, the Police would close us down arguing that we were aiding prostitution."

"Oh, well, I'd have a word with the old man about that, I tell you."

"Your husband?" Asked Estella.

"No, Ma'am, he's what the Prime Minister, you know, old Gladstone."

Everyone laughed uproariously at the idea that she'd ask Gladstone.

"No, I'm serious. On my life, there I was, on the game around Victoria, and this old geezer comes up and starts talking to me, and I say 'it's one quid' and he says, 'no', with a funny accent, and then he says 'I am not in need of your services,' so I says "well you can bugger off then,' and he then gets dead serious and says 'what makes you do this?' 'do what?' says I, 'well,' says he, 'sell your body on the street, of course,' real fancy like he was, and I says, 'how else am I going to support my kiddies?' And then he did bugger off."

The raucous laughter in the room while Emily was telling her story was intense and Estella, Pip and Mr. Holditch could not avoid joining in. The very thought of the Prime Minister himself talking with a whore was a sensation, and Estella laughed particularly at the quick-fire description of the conversation which reminded her of Nellie.

"No, that weren't the end of it," Emily continued, "there he was the next night, it was very late, and he says, 'Good evening' in his la-de-da way, and I says, 'I know you from somewhere,' and he says, 'have you heard me speak?" and I says, "Of course, I'm not deaf,' and he says, 'no, I mean in public.'" Everyone laughed again.

"I thought and thought, and then I remembered, I had seen him before on those hustings when I was walking up West once.

"'Who are you then?" I said, and he said, 'I'm Mr. Gladstone, the Prime Minister,' and I said, 'pleased to meet you, I'm Queen Victoria,' at which the laughter and cackles of the women once again made the rafters ring.

"Anyway, he'd come round and chat from time to time, always on about what I liked about being a tart. I offered it to him once or twice as he looked as though he could do with a good one, relax him, slow him down, you know, satisfy him before he went before all those big knobs in Parliament. But he never did. I expect he went straight home and did you know what, 'cos I'm sure he weren't doing it with his missus.

"Pity I'm not on the street no longer, I could have asked him to stop us being closed down."

"Well, a lovely story," said Estella.

"It's not a story, ma'am, it's God honest truth, I tell you."

"I believe you, Emily, but no commitment now, put your hands up if you like the idea of getting money for rent and an allowance rather than being here."

Half the women raised their hands very quickly.

"Now what about the rest of you, why do you not want that?"

Answers varied from being frightened of the street, of being beaten up, all the kinds of reasons they could expect.

'Thank you anyway," said Pip, "we know now who you feel about it and we will take that into consideration when the Trust meets."

Albert was now seriously intrigued by the idea of becoming a timber merchant. He could not help wondering why there was no one closer to his grandfather in the family to take over the business, and, as he said to Estella that night, that would surely have been the natural course of events. He decided to start formally as soon as possible, to which Algernon's lawyers had no objection; he would take time to meet with staff beforehand and do some reading about business in general before his position became legal and public.

"It has suddenly occurred to me, Estella. I wonder if Herbert Pocket is still alive. He was a good friend of Father's and he would know all about the weird and wonderful Pocket family. Was it really like that?"

"Oh indeed, the family was like some oak tree, sprouting branches everywhere. They were relatives of my guardian, Miss Havisham, you know. As I think about it, one or two of the cousins had the same kind of frailty that your mother had."

"Really, I did not know that."

"How foolish of me: Of course, in my desk I have your father's book in which he kept addresses. Let me get it and you can try to track down old Herbert."

"That sounds to me more important than talking with Brandram tomorrow."

Estella disappeared upstairs and then returned with the book:

"Here you are. There are two addresses, one in the City which I take to be lodgings but one out on the northern fringes near Hackney. A house called Bell's Meadow in Walthamstow. That will be a country village in or near the Epping Forest, I would say."

"I must find a map. The merchant premises are on the River Lea just north of Hackney Village."

"Oh, my goodness, of course. I went with my mother to your father and mother's wedding. That was in St. John's Hackney and we then went about two miles north to a very nice house on that river which, I believe, adjoined the merchant premises. How strange, all that seems to have been in another life."

"I have taken a lodging in Hackney and propose to present myself later in the week. But I will see Herbert and his wife first."

Albert set off for Walthamstow early the next morning and the carriage rumbled into the village about ten o'clock on a bright if windy March morning.

He knocked on the door of *The Three Tuns* public house and asked the landlord for a house called Bell's Meadow.

"Oh yes, that's where Mr. and Mrs. Pocket live. Been here as long as I have, I'd swear. Go up through the village and it's an old house back from the road on the right. You can't miss it."

A few minutes later, the carriage drew up on the road, but then Albert decided to have the carriage drive through the entrance along a short drive to the very pretty house. He dismounted and knocked quietly at the door. A maid answered:

"It's Mr. Pirrip to see Mr. and Mrs. Pocket, if you please," said Albert.

There was the sound of elderly feet scraping along a tile floor.

"Who is this?" a man asked the maid in a loud voice.

'It's a Mr. Pirrip," she shouted in his ear.

"Can't be, he's been dead all these years."

"No it's a young Mr. Pirrip."

"Great heavens," he exclaimed opening the door, "Celia, come here my dear, as fast as you can."

Herbert was now bent with age, his hair grey in wisps common to old men, spectacles slipping off his nose, his whiskers all awry, but getting to the front door, he cried:

"You must be Albert," as the tears flooded down his face.

"Come here, my dear, dear boy. Oh, what larks eh? Celia, come and meet Albert, my dear," and an old lady with a stick also in tears but with a beautiful smile, said:

"Oh my, Oh my, how much he looks like Pip, doesn't he, Herbert?"

"Come in, come in, dear Albert. Come and sit down and have some breakfast with us."

"Now what brings you here, my dear?" asked Celia, twisting her hands pocked with liver spots around her apron.

"I don't know whether you know this. My grandfather Algernon left me five thousand pounds if I were to join his firm and only five hundred if not. I have decided to join the firm and I am visiting there tomorrow to establish the connection and what I assume will be to assist with the management. It carries with it ownership of the business."

"Great heavens, no, we did not know this. We went to his funeral, of course, as I am a distant relative, but we had no idea about his will. Algernon had no sons, you know. Your mother Beatrice died so tragically and there was another sister whose whereabouts we do not know, but she married an adventurer and went to America, we believe. She was devastated when Beatrice died."

"How did you meet Algernon?" Asked Herbert.

"It was a coincidence. Estella and I were at the cemetery, she to mourn my father, and me too, and in the next grave but one was my mother and her daughter who died at birth, you know. This elderly man asked who I was. I liked him, and as he was my grandfather he explained my grandmother's hostility to my father and her wish for no contact.

"Shortly after that meeting I went to Paris to study painting and to become a painter, but working with the cream of painters in Paris, I realized I had neither real talent nor mastery of technique or indeed the imagination. I thought some more about the offer from the lawyers and here I am."

"This is wonderful to meet you," said Herbert, "we must be second, third or fourth cousins but related however distant and I suppose you will need to come and live on this side of London."

"Yes, I have taken a temporary lodging in Hackney, but with my legacy I intend to find a comfortable house nearby in the country. I have had my fill of living in big cities."

"And how is Estella?"

"She is blooming as ever, extraordinarily active in good causes. Did you know Jaggers left eighty-thousand pounds for a Trust for the Relief and Education of the Poor? "

"Goodness gracious, how did he become so rich?"

"Inheritance and remaining unmarried, I expect. Estella is Chairman of the Board of the Trust. Now, let me think, you met Abel Magwitch, did you not?"

"Oh, indeed I did, several weeks with your father and me hiding him in London before he was captured."

"Well, a man came from Australia to my father's office looking for him, claiming to be his love-child."

That began a full day's set of reminiscences: twelve-year old Pip knocking Herbert down in the yard at Miss Havisham's; Jaggers having Herbert teach Pip to be a gentleman; Pip's gift of five hundred pounds when he was rich to get Herbert into Clarrickers agency; Herbert reciprocating; Herbert and Celia overseas and losing touch with Pip; Beatrice's wedding, her funeral; Albert's father funeral, and much more.

"Oh my," said Herbert suddenly, "what larks, eh?"

"Now I have not heard that expression for years, though I think it was Joe Gargery's favorite. I lived with them at the Cottage, you know, when I was a young child."

"How did that come about?"

"When my mother died, my father had just started to work to become a lawyer with Mr. Jaggers, and he wanted me to be with family not with a nanny. Oh, it was a lovely time down there on the Kentish marshes with such nice people as Joe and Biddy."

"Salt of the earth they were," said Celia.

"Then my father married Estella and I came down to London to be with them, but that was after Joe died and when Biddy remarried.

"However, this has been wonderful," said Albert, "but I must get back to St. James and return here tomorrow to my temporary lodging. I'll come to see you both regularly, and I will tell Estella all about you, I am sure she will be very pleased to know."

"You know," said Herbert, "I never thought Pip and she would come together. She was such a haughty, frigid sort of woman. I used to meet her as Miss Havisham was some sort of cousin, I forget which. What on earth happened to Estella? I saw her at your mother's wedding with an older woman but for reason we weren't introduced."

"Don't you know?"

"No, should we?"

"Oh, my father urged her to see Jaggers about buying a house and while waiting for him, Jaggers' servant walked into the room to fetch a glass. It was her mother, of course. As I understand the story, there was uproar as they recognized each other and Estella and her mother went off to live together. The older woman you saw was Estella's mother. She became a changed woman, for her mother undid all of what Estella now calls 'the Havisham curse.' After my mother died, Estella found herself in love with my father and, to be frank, I think there was a part of him that was always in love with her, or so he told me once."

"I am glad he told you that, Albert. He must have been a wonderful father."

"Yes indeed, but I really must go, and we have so many more family stories to catch up on. What shall I call you both?"

"Herbert and Celia will do," she said, "oh, it is like having dear Pip in the house once again. Keep yourself warm against this cold wind, dear Albert."

The three of them embraced, and Albert went to his carriage realizing that this old couple were real family, blood relatives through his mother.

He knew no others.

XVII

Estella was quite thrilled that all those she had invited to the meeting of the League answered affirmatively and all came to New Queen Street for lunch on the first Thursday in September which she hoped could be a quarterly meeting time. The first hurdle, even before talking about its interests, was the meeting of Harriet and Susanna.

Susanna arrived early, quite composed and exceptionally well-dressed, almost as if this was a royal garden party. Harriet arrived later, after all the others had come, which made Estella wonder how far that was planned. Introductions were made; some of the women had met before, some knew of others, but perhaps only one pair with any intimate acquaintance. When Harriet arrived, Estella took her by the arm to meet Susanna while conversation flowed among the women.

"Susanna, this is Harriet Middleham," said Estella, and the two women exchanged polite how d'ye do's and Estella moved away.

"It is a pleasure to meet you, Susanna," said Harriet, "can I first say how deeply sorry I am for your loss of Lachlan. Frankly I can imagine nothing worse."

"No," said Susanna, "losing Lachlan made me feel as wretched as it is possible for a human being to feel. But then, it has changed my life and I am resolved to see it differently, to judge what is important and what is not.

"You see, Harriet, I have always known of my husband's deep affection for you. After all, had you wished it, I am sure you two would have married. So, your renewal of that acquaintance is different from, say, his taking a whore from time to time, or hiding someone away like that dreadful Philip Hardyman."

"Yes, I think we could well have married, had I not been so obstinate."

"I certainly thought that when he met you again he no longer loved me, so I took a lover out of revenge, as I felt so hurt, but that was a mistake. Yet you were, after all, very old friends. What would one expect?"

"Yes, but immediately after that meeting, I realized I might be on a path to being responsible for the break-up of your marriage which I did not want, so we ended it as quickly as we started it again."

"Oh, I am sure it was you, rather than he, who ended it."

"Perhaps, but I do hope you and I can get to know each other."

"I think we may."

Estella could see that conversation going on without rancor, so she delayed starting the meeting, but when some kind of reconciliation seemed to have been made between Susanna and Harriet, she asked everyone to sit down. She had chosen the living room, rather than the more formal dining room, not least because they would adjourn there for lunch later.

"I have become increasingly aware through my life that women do not have the status as human beings that we deserve," she began.

"I do not here think of all the different particular matters, such as property in marriage, or the vote, or access to types of employment, but to a fundamental flaw in our social arrangements which we might call the absence of equality with men.

"Notice I am not saying we should be like men, far from it, but have equal respect and equal opportunity. I am not saying anything new. If you have read various writers, John Mill and Harriet Taylor or Mary Wollstencraft, you will know where this notion of equality comes from.

"But I am very fortunate. I am financially independent, a widow without children, but a person more determined as I get older to seek to improve the lot of women, if you like, to make women free. To this end, I thought we might re-form this group to promote that equality. I thought we might have a period of two to three months trying to formulate a direction and to choose activities in which we might engage.

"Let me raise two other matters close to my heart. The first is that we seek to create a group across the classes. I see little point in being a philanthropic group dispensing largesse to women in distress. Then I want us to be friends, not just co-workers. I want us to be able to share our lives, to be confident that we can call on each other for help, for love, for sustenance in times of joy and of distress."

Mary Macdonald spoke first.

"That's very encouraging indeed, Estella, especially in your last comment about class. Surely class is so much a part of our social life that we don't realize how it is a major obstacle to any sort of equality."

Eliza Culpepper was forthright, too: "I think we all need to know who we are first. I am Eliza Culpepper, and I am married to a good man, Randolph, who is a real stick-in-the-mud when it comes to women's equality. Marriage will be an important topic for us. I come from a lower class than many of you, I expect, as my parents were shopkeepers, and I know I don't have the airs and graces a society woman is expected to have."

Then it was Honora's turn.

"Some of you know my history, but I am Honora Brandram so you won't be surprised if I say how important sexual relations are."

"Excuse me," said Emma Smythe, the youngest in the group, recently married to Clarence, "I am Emma Smythe, but can we know your history or would you rather keep it to yourself?"

"It's quite simple. I was brutally raped in France when I was almost twenty by twins who were later imprisoned for other rapes. I gave birth to identical twin boys as a result and with Estella and Charlotte's help, we found them three years ago in an orphanage, so they now live with us."

Emma was so shocked that she blushed deeply and did not reply.

"I am Antonia Penoyre. Can there be rape within marriage, I mean actually, not legally?" she asked.

"Of course," said Jane Hardyman, "Of course, oh, and I am Jane Hardyman."

"You see," said Honora, "how significant issues of sexual relationships are, and on an appropriate occasion soon I will share with you the delights of having two young men in the house and two young maids," at which everyone laughed.

"I think getting women the vote is vital," said Susanna, "for it seems to be the key to influence on politics and the law, and, oh, I am Susanna Gargery."

With that, the group moved into lunch, chattering and talking at a substantial volume.

Estella sidled up to Harriet, slipping her arm around her waist, "Do you think you've slain the dragon?"

"Oh indeed, she is quite delightful, but it will take time: Did you invite Katherine?"

"No, I forgot about her completely: Next time?

Over lunch Estella enjoyed the compliments showered by members of the League on her portrait. She said what she knew about John Sargent, the artist, but it was luck that Pip's portrait had arrived and was hanging opposite hers in the dining room in New Queen Street. Of course, Albert had only his own immature sketches from which to work, and clearly he was a follower of John Sargent. Its execution was not flawed but one could tell at a glance why the portrait of her was superior.

Antonia was the most perceptive critic of the artist's work but Emma was quite trenchant in her analysis of character from the painting which was almost entirely accurate.

"He was in great pain and the artist seems to be remembering it."

"How clever of you. Albert sat with him for two days as he was dying and I am sure that image of pain is there; I had not noticed that."

When Emma she started to examine Estella's portrait, she was equally interesting.

"He's portrayed you as a sexual object, I think, not as a proud woman of quality. Do you notice the suggestions he makes about your body in the way your dress is hanging. I am sure it hung something like that when he drew you but then he exaggerated the way it lies on your flesh."

Mary was listening to this and exclaimed:

"My goodness, Emma, what insight! It makes one wonder whether the artist and the sitter have not been lovers, doesn't it? He also gives the sitter that somewhat dreamy look, almost the look of a young woman."

"Oh, my goodness," exclaimed Estella, "I had not seen any of this. I shall have to have it taken down, I think," she said laughing, "and Mary my dear, I love your outspokenness, and you are somewhat close to the situation I faced with him. He did invite me to his bed after a tortuous discussion about his terror at the idea, but I declined. In the end, I should say," she concluded with a laugh.

Emma, the young bride, looked at the two of them slightly startled and said:

"I can see I am going to have to get used to very frank exchanges in this League, something I have not been accustomed to."

"Now that," exclaimed Antonia, "is precisely what freedom for women is about. Not being trapped by any kind of convention. I'd be very happy to discuss my relationships with my husband if that arose."

"Oh, no," said Emma, "absolutely not for me, far too precious secrets, I'm afraid."

"Now," said Estella, "those matters will only be one minor topic arising from our friendship, not our main purpose. After our next meeting, I plan to go back to Paris as I want to meet the women painters again, in particular Rosa Bonheur now living in Fontainebleau which is not too distant from Paris."

"How about an outing for the League?" asked Mary, "Springtime in Paris is wonderful, so they say."

"We should consider that, certainly."

"I'd love to do that," said Antonia.

"Let us see whether there is interest among the others."

"I know Paris fairly well," said Harriet, joining the conversation.

"And there are our Embassy contacts," said Estella.

"My apologies now, but I must go to another meeting. Please do stay here and get to know each other."

"Are you taking your carriage to the City, Estella? May I join you?"

"Harriet, my dear, you will be most welcome."

Estella looked at Harriet carefully as her carriage rumbled toward Long Acre:

"I have something of importance to ask you. I would like you come and share my house. I am alone now and I think we might find living together an opportunity to explore our friendship further. What do you say?"

"Estella, let me be clear once again and I hope I am not just repeating what I said when we met at my home. I want and need my total independence. If I was living with anyone in a house that you were responsible for, through rent or ownership, my life would be constrained in all manner of ways."

"But you would be free to pay half the rent, and to come and go as you wished, of course."

"I doubt that. Say I wanted to have a man in my bed for three or four nights, would that be acceptable?"

"It would depend who he was."

"You see, that is a perfectly sensible thing to say when it is your house, but you can surely see that is a constraint on what I might wish. I don't want to have you vetting anyone I might chose to bring to my bed. It is impossible to live separately under the same roof."

"Well, that is a disappointment, especially as I grow older."

"Now then, Estella, it is unlike you to put pressure on me. I know you value your independence as much as I value mine."

"Yes, yes, I am sorry. You are right. Perhaps I will spend more time in Kent."

"No, Estella, don't do that. Please, my dear, just accept that I wish to live an independent life, coming and going as I please without being beholden to anyone whose wishes or wants I have to respect. While I might have got some joy out of having children, I know I would have felt as though I was living in a prison."

"Might you not reconsider at all?"

"Never, my dear," said Harriet. "There is another aspect to this that needs to be said.

"I enjoy your company, I care about you, but I do not love you in any sense that establishes some kind of mutual obligation. Were you or I sick, for instance, I would not want you to feel obliged to care for me, and I would not feel the same about you."

"Do you mean you never want that kind of obligation?"

"No, I am not saying that I would never want that; to rule it out of my life would be foolish. At this moment, in time, however, I am not going to surrender one iota of total control of my life."

"All right, I think I understand. I have told you how much I might come to care for you."

"I know, but we will still be friends."

"Perhaps."

The carriage stopped outside Harriet's lodgings. They embraced a little stiffly as Harriet descended waving her hand at Estella who smiled wanly as the carriage started off for Little Britain.

The journey was a mere fifteen minutes, as the traffic was lighter than usual, but Estella seethed with indignation. But her indignation was not righteous, and she knew it. For the first time since she could remember she had been rebuffed, and as she was in two minds beforehand whether to invite her or not, she now felt she had made a ghastly mistake.

What she needed was companionship, which Charlotte had provided so comfortably. She had to face it. She was lonely, very lonely. No Charlotte. Albert starting at Hackney. Only Nellie and she was in Kent.

Since Pip's death she had managed the unattainable; to have total independence within a framework of companionship, people who depended on her to some degree. She knew too that this signaled a breach with Harriet and they might never heal it.

Nevertheless, she sent a letter to those who attended the League meeting, inviting them all to meet the following months for a business meeting. She said she would also enjoy having the meeting at her country house in Kent and perhaps then a suitable date could be found. She wanted that date fixed as she hoped to return to Paris on her own to develop her acquaintance with the women painters she had met.

The invitation to see the new offices was too much difficult to resist, but when Estella arrived at Little Britain after the month in Kent, everything was in chaos as the move to Old Square was in progress. Carts outside were being filled with crates of law books, voluminous records which represented Mr. Jaggers' view that no piece of paper, however unimportant, should ever be discarded, and, of course furniture of all shapes and sizes. Neither Hamish nor Pip were there and Robert suggested she go to Old Square.

"This is most impressive, Hamish," she said as she walked into the freshly painted, bright hallway.

"Pip came with me to meet you, but Adam and I are deciding how rooms are to be used, given that we know that records will be in the basement."

"Records, of course. I suppose the correspondence with Miss Havisham about me will be there somewhere."

"Would you like to see it? I'll have Robert dig it out."

"Yes, I think so, but you must have all this move settled before that is undertaken."

She saw what was to become the meeting room on the left and the Senior Clerk's office behind that. On the right of the main door was to be the senior partner's office which, as the building was at the end of a long set of buildings in use for the same purpose, had windows on two sides, one looking on to the street, the other on to the square with its formal gardens. Altogether a sensible move and splendid premises made affordable by that fact that both Courtisone and Jaggers were owners of their respective buildings.

After Hamish and Estella had returned from a light lunch, the correspondence relating to her guardian had been retrieved and she was welcome to view it. She felt giddy with anticipation and it was Adam who introduced her to it.

"The correspondence with Miss Havisham is extensive, and it is divided into a file relation to her property, her investments and her will, and a file containing all the letters about you. Mr. Jaggers' letters were of course, copied by the clerk. I suggest you come and sit in the rear office where I have put both sets of correspondence. I have not read any of them."

"Thank you, Adam. I am rather nervous about this."

"I understand, and although the letters must be about you, it was a long time ago."

"I know. My profound thanks."

She walked along the hallway past a rather gloomy portrait of Mr. Courtisone and on the opposite wall a smaller, livelier portrait of Mr. Jaggers which she had not seen but she was far too preoccupied to examine it at length.

On the table was a large box of papers relating to Miss Havisham' property, but there was a much smaller lawyer's folder bearing the legend 'Havisham: Guardianship.'" She opened the folder with both excitement and foreboding.

'Dear Mr. Jaggers,

As you are aware, I find myself lonely and bereft.

It occurred to me that I might have a ward, a little girl, that I could bring up and cherish. I could not countenance being responsible for a male child, so I look forward to hearing from you with regard to finding a girl to be my ward.

Have you thoughts on the matter?

—E. Havisham. September 25th, 1810'

'Dear Miss Havisham,

I sincerely hope on behalf of my sex that the particular bad apple you encountered was plucked from a barrel replete with more perfect specimens. I refer of course to Compeyson's treachery which, I am assured, is not a common feature of manhood. Not tempted to marry myself, I can, however, extend to you my most sincere sympathies on your distress. Your dear father and mother would, I know, be shocked to the core.

I am always rather busy these days. Old Father Crime, forgive the pun, seems unrelenting in the spread of his villainy here in the Great Wen. I will, however, give your question my earnest and unremitting attention in due course,

Ever your obedient servant, etc.

—Nathaniel Jaggers, October 4, 1810.'

'Dear Mr. Jaggers:

Thank you for your recent note of comfort, but I find nothing in the world can minister to my tribulation which, I fear, is turning into a profound hatred of Compeyson in particular and of the male sex in general. I care not about matters of class as I will imbue a female child with the best that I can conjure up in these times of great distress.

—E.H. October 6, 1810'

'Dear Miss Havisham,

May I say again how sorry I am for the betrayal you experienced with Mr. Compeyson. I know of no other case where such a wicked act has occurred. I earnestly hope you will find someone else with whom to find happiness.

As I am constantly in touch with the criminal classes, I know of several little girls that might be appropriate wards. If this suits, I will bring two of them to Satis House next week. We will journey overnight, meet in the morning and then return in my carriage in the afternoon.

Ever your obedient servant, etc.
Nathaniel Jaggers, October 13, 1810'

'Dear Jaggers:
Next Tuesday would be an admirable date.
E.H.'

'Dear Miss Havisham:
I am indeed sad that neither of the two girls were satisfactory for you.

I understand your reluctance to take Elsie, whose cleft palette might prove a hindrance in introducing her to society in future years.

I was surprised that you found Emily unacceptable. She has fair hair, a very English look about her, and, I agree, it was unfortunate that she could not help urinating in your hallway, no doubt because she was unaccustomed to being in a residence so well endowed, notwithstanding its decoration for the event which did not take place. Her attempt to eat the cake on the table was also the kind of mistake young children not well brought up tend to make.

Your reaction to her suggests you are not looking for a child who is, how shall I put it, not yet house-trained?

I will therefore continue my search. Yet it will convey responsibilities which might be a detriment to your resuming a social life in which old friendships may be renewed.

Ever your obedient servant etc.
Nathaniel Jaggers, October 19th, 1810.'

'Dear Mr. Jaggers,
Your letter implies that I am of a mind to rejoin society after this crippling blow. I intend nothing of the sort but simply to eke out my existence surrounded by the bric-a-brac

of a not-to-have-been wedding which will keep the memory of my despair ever with me.

As for those two waifs you imposed on me, I am looking for a child who will undoubtedly become a great beauty, so please take care about your selection.
E.H. October 20, 1810.'

'Dear Miss Havisham,

I now have two very pretty little things to bring to you for inspection. They may, however, be younger than you wish, being only between two and three years old. Let me know.

Ever your obedient servant, etc.
Nathaniel Jaggers, October 27th, 1810.'

'Dear Jaggers:

What are you thinking about? Such children can hardly walk at that age! I am not anxious to take on the responsibilities of a nursemaid, though I grant you that the younger the child would be, the easier to make a strong impression on her upbringing. But I am getting tired of this to-ing and fro-ing. One more only, or I will give up the whole idea.
E.H. October 31, 1810'

'Dear Miss Havisham:

I have found a small girl, not yet five years old, whose mother I have recently defended in court. If you believe in inherited characteristics, then I must let you know her background before making introductions. I should add that the mother is coming to realize with some reluctance that her daughter would best live a life without her care and protection.

Please let me know whether you wish to be apprised of the mother's background before we proceed further.

Ever your obedient servant, etc.
Nathaniel Jaggers, November 4th, 1810.'

'Dear Jaggers,

I told you – no to-ing and froing. I do not wish to seem impatient, but I care neither a jot nor a tittle as to the child's background as I am confident in the power of my own influence. Let us hope that this child proves acceptable.

I assume you will be charging me your usual exorbitant fee for a commission which cannot have taken much of your valuable time.

I expect to see you on Saturday this week.

E.H. November 6th, 1810'

'Dear Miss Havisham,

The child is Ruth Magwitch. Her father is Abel Magwitch, a convict on a prison hulk now serving time for burglary, larceny and most other felonies barring murder. Her mother is Molly Magwitch who has recently been convicted of the murder of Abel's lover. The motive was jealousy and I was able to argue for merciful treatment on grounds of *crime passionelle* which, though not a statute, does provide grounds for a judge to respond to suggestions as to an accused's future.

I have taken the mother Molly as my servant and have undertaken to protect and shield her from the world as she will have duties in my home and in my office here in Little Britain.

The child, Ruth, is a pleasant enough little thing, quite pretty in some ways with dark hair and blue eyes. The child is here since yesterday and I will be happy to bring her to you in Kent on any convenient day for you when you may decide whether you wish to act as her guardian. If you accept her, the mother will not be told of her destination.

My fee will be fifty guineas.

Ever your obedient servant, etc.

Nathaniel Jaggers, November 10, 1810'

'Dear Mr. Jaggers:

I am always available. When you bring this child, I wish you to examine my financial position once again. With the inheritance of the brewery, I believe I am quite wealthy and, subject to my satisfaction with this female child, it will be my intention to leave all my possessions and wealth to her. With that understanding I will call her Estella, not Ruth a name I urgently dislike.

Your proposed fee is exactly as exorbitant as I anticipated. E.H. November 12, 1810.'

'Dear Miss Havisham:

Ruth's mother has finally agreed that she will surrender all rights over her and agree not to try to discover here whereabouts if you decide to proceed. The child understands what is in process, though she is obviously not eager to leave her mother. I am sure, however, that with your tender ministrations, she would soon adapt to her new circumstances.

I plan to bring her next Wednesday with the same arrangements for the journey. I respect your decision to rename the child, though you will no doubt appreciate the difficulty the child might have in becoming reconciled to such a change.

Ever your obedient servant, etc.

Nathaniel Jaggers, November 15th, 1810.'

Here the correspondence about the guardianship ended, but Jaggers made voluminous notes about his client and the acquisition of her ward. Estella was amused by the correspondence and was surprised that she was not the first choice, so to speak, though it seemed as if her guardian was looking for a prize hunting dog or a horse, not a child.

Glancing through them she finds such phrases as:

'Better for that child to be brought up by that damn woman than by her cursed mother;'

and

'Not sure I can stand going down to Kent again, but the child seems to have settled, seeming content and pretty,' and

'Miss H again resisting my fee when I know she has at least thirty thousand pounds in investments and money.'

'Visit to Satis. Estella now quite lovely at 14. Very stern. Won't talk to me. Miss H. getting a village boy to amuse her; talk of her paying for his articles.

'Miss H is going quite mad, madder even than the child's real mother.'

Estella had spent an hour looking at these documents but realized that there was nothing to be discovered which she had not assumed or been told. However, it brought back some very sad memories, and she wept a little as she closed the file. She did remember leaving her mother and the journey to Satis House, and her difficulty in having to respond to a different name. She was not interested in the financial dealings, not least because she had inherited it all. She came out of the room and thanked Hamish profusely before getting to her carriage. At some juncture, she thought, I will ask to see Jaggers' files on my father. They will be very interesting, what with Pip and his great expectations.

On her visit a week later to talk with Mary about the League, she found Hamish in the drawing room and Mary upstairs attending to James.

"Estella, I heard from Pip that you had been to The Building to talk with women about their living elsewhere."

"Well, not quite, but we are wondering whether we should not seek to put them back in the world, albeit with our protection."

"I see. I know we were also considering activity with younger children, boys only I think.

"Now, I do not know how the Gargerys will react to this suggestion but might not The Building accommodate the school they were thinking of, though maybe their initial thought was for something that would attract a higher class of parent."

"That is pure dead brilliant, Estella, with my apologies for the Scottish expression. No, they mentioned poor children at the Board meeting. You and I need a strategy to persuade them that their ideas for a school could well be realized through this arrangement. Not that I think it will be much trouble."

"Two obvious things. First, the school should be called the Lachlan School."

"Absolutely, and the second?"

"This should be their school. That is, it should not be a matter of the Trust's oversight. It would be theirs and theirs alone with a large initial grant or endowment from the Trust. They should inform the Trust but preferably set up their own Trust so that they can easily obtain money from other philanthropic sources."

"You are the lawyer. Do you think that can work in practice?"

"I'll make it legally water-tight, Estella. I somehow think that they need to get their teeth into something. Susanna is fairly wealthy, and if she provides some of her own money too, then an independent Trust is essential."

"That sound sensible to me. I think it would be helpful to have a Jaggers Board member on their Trust more to link the two bodies with a little formality. But tell me, Hamish, is your enthusiasm for the Project connected in any way to the status of their marriage?"

"Are they troubled, then?"

"Hmm. I am sure that Mary knows of it, but perhaps she decided it was not her concern. I did mention that we were wondering about the use of The Building and she did ask whether it would make a school?"

"I tell you, my dear Hamish, your wife is one of the most brilliant women I have ever met with a mind like a razor, and I am sure that her confidence arises from the happiness of her marriage."

"That is nice of you to say so, Estella. I have already told Mary how much I adore her and I am not going to put my marriage in any sort of jeopardy."

"As one gets older, it seems absolutely unavoidable that men and women see other men or women who they find desirable. That could happen to you, you know."

"What could happen?" asked Mary entering the room holding James hand as he walked.

"Oh, just that we can meet people whom we desire," said Hamish, "and I was about to tell Estella about Angharad.

"I went down to Cardiff to meet Angharad, Estella, taking Mary and James with me. We met in a hotel about her will. With Mary there, she asked me to come to her room to sign the documents as it would be more private than the hotel foyer, which seemed reasonable to us both. I made some arrangements with Mary and then followed Angharad up to her room where to my complete astonishment she attempted to lure me into her bed."

"Good gracious me. I am not in one sense surprised as I suspect her dead husband, my half-brother, was a lusty fellow."

They all laughed greatly, but then Estella resumed:

"I was simply going to say that there is nothing special about having desires which makes them more demanding than those of every other person in the world."

"You protest too much, Estella, if I understand where you are going with that comment. I have just said that is behind me. What do we really know what goes one within a marriage? Yet after many years of observing people through the prism of sexual desire, it can become quite obvious.

"You are such a wise old owl, Estella, if I may use that expression but you do not need to be so persistent with me, you know."

"We have crossed the bridge together, have we not, darling?" Said Mary.

"Wonderful, I must go," said Estella, "will you broach this school idea with Pip and Susanna, or shall I?"

"I leave it to you."

After she left Hamish wondered whether Estella in her old age was now beginning to lose her judgment in dispensing her advice and wisdom, but Mary had whispered to her that she was a bright star not about to dim.

When she got home, she read a letter from Albert, saying he had had a wonderful meeting with Herbert and Celia who sent their warm regards. He had spent the week walking round the premises trying to acquaint himself with the business. There were no managers. One had left when there was a meeting held by Algernon's lawyers to say that a young Mr. Pirrip, Mr. Pocket's grandson would be coming to manage the business, as expressed in Mr. Pocket's will.

However, Estella was delighted to learn that there was a trusted senior foreman, an older man, with the strange name of Basil Woolhandler, who was helping him. She was also pleased that he admitted he knew nothing at all about running a business. He hoped that all the employees, fifty in number, knew what they have to do, and do it, because he didn't.

XVIII

A rmed with Hamish's idea that Pip and Susanna open the
School with Jaggers Trust support, Estella sent a note to Pip
and Susanna saying she would like to call on them both to suggest
that they use The Building once all the prostitutes had left. An invitation to lunch followed. She was apprehensive, not because of the
ructions caused some months back by what was seen by the couple
as interference in their marriage, but for reasons that eluded her.
Unusual for her, therefore, she was quite nervous when she rang
the bell in Cheyne Row.

She was greeted very warmly and offered a glass of sherry. The
baby Hannah was on Susanna's knee, and as they began to talk they
were interrupted by a rather morose Malcolm with a nanny tailing
in his wake, saying:

"I want a boy to play with. Nanny is no good at football."

"Alright, Malcolm, we will see what we can do," said his father,
"meantime, have your meal with Nanny and I will go to the park
with you this afternoon."

Estella quietly admired Pip's willingness to occupy his son.
Tenderness, she thought, was a perquisite for a bereaved child.

"I have come to see you both with an idea which Hamish
and I have developed. In fact, it was Hamish's idea and I am the
messenger."

"That sounds most interesting," said Susanna, "tell us more."

"We love the idea of a school which you both had thought about
creating. But we wonder about two aspects of its possible development: First, whether the Jaggers Building might not become the

school as it is about to clear of women, as you both know. It is in a very poor neighborhood and very well equipped from the viewpoint of the structure and the internal layout.

"That is an interesting idea," said Susanna. "And the second part?"

"That the school be run by both of you independently of the Trust, though the Trust would make money available, and you can be free to seek other support. You would not have to report to the Board or seek it approval for any of the way in which you spent the grant, which would be, therefore, unencumbered."

"That sounds an excellent suggestion which we will have to consider carefully. But Pip, my dear, why don't you share with Estella what we have been thinking?"

"Are you sure?"

"Yes, I think we can now begin to share our ideas with our friends."

"This makes me very curious," said Estella.

"Very well," said Susanna, "but on second thoughts I would rather you did not share this with anyone until we have completed investigations and our minds have finally been made up."

"Of course, you have my word."

"As you know, Pip was a Primitive Methodist preacher before Jaggers died and I attended his congregation, though I am formally a Presbyterian. We have been lax since our marriage in our religious practices and, indeed, that may have in part occasioned our marital difficulties. Our determination to open a school remains, but we think of it in two ways.

"First, that it should have a strongly religious ethos, as would befit a Christian school.

"Second, that it should be located in as deprived an environment we can think of, for example, in Africa."

"Goodness me, Africa? Why Africa?"

"Well," said Pip, "we would seek to open a school in a religious mission. I should stress that we have not yet made any decisions as we are still researching the possible colonies where such a venture would be acceptable. Of course, we would want it to be within British jurisdiction so that we will be working in a familiar legal environment."

"It is not only our religious derelictions, or our marriage," said Susanna, "but the loss of our son has been so awful that we also feel we need to get away from all these places where memories flood in every moment of every day, not just occasionally. Lachlan was our simply our pride and joy, the child of our intense love, and we need to achieve some balance not by living this life of luxury that we feel is somehow an insult to his memory."

"To put it even more simply," said Pip, "we do not want to live here anymore. We want to make a drastic change which will give both of us an immense challenge to revive our religious instincts not merely in belief but in practice."

"Why can you not move out to Reigate, as you suggested once, or indeed to Kent, and still come to London to run, well at least oversee a school for very poor children? You've seen poverty in Salford, haven't you, Pip? Why not here?"

"There is more to it than that," said Susanna, "as I think about it.

"I actually do not enjoy this kind of life anymore. I find it trivial in its interests, boring in its rhythms, and immoral in its structure of the way wealth is distributed. I have read this radical writer Karl Marx and I see what he is portraying, though I abhor his idea of revolution and especially his total rejection of religion. Yet in terms of the power that the wealthy – usually men, of course – exercise over people, and I include myself, that is intolerable. So my wealth should be directed at the very poor."

"And, of course," added Pip, "our colonies exploit the people, as Marx tells us."

"So Africa seems to us to be the place where we can do our best with our religious principles, our money, and as a living memorial to our dear dead son. Of course, it might be elsewhere, but Africa is our focus for the moment, and we feel, it is also an attempt to give back to Africa because of the evils of slavery."

"I am nothing but moved by your sentiments and your proposals. I would still like the Trust to be able to support your work, even if it is in the colonies. Interesting, isn't it, I don't suppose either Jaggers or Courtisone ever considered the possibility that Trust funds might be used outside of England, nay, even out of London, but the lawyers will help us there."

"We are anticipating meeting with the Church Missionary Society that supports a small mission in the center of Africa, an area called Barotseland which I had not heard of. More hopeful is working with the United Presbyterian Church's Foreign Mission Board which is a Scottish church organization. They have mentioned a woman, Mary Slessor, a Scot from Aberdeen, who had gone to work in Africa two years ago. So there are precedents.

"We will certainly have to consider the alternatives you have suggested," said Susanna, "but we are very excited about missionary work. Of course, we are not leaving next week! There is an immense amount of preparation, learning about diseases there, what we have to do to survive, including how to travel there. A major expense would be the building of a chapel, and we will not know what tools we can use or what materials there are in the area in which we settle. So we have months of preparation."

Estella left shortly thereafter and she needed to talk to someone so badly that she went across the river to Walworth to find Mary who had decided against the house of Angelo the murderer of rent-boys after three visits to the house and reading the relevant newspapers which described how the murderer had used the rooms.

"Tell me, Mary, why do the Gargerys want to go to Africa? What goes on in Africa?"

"I know little of it. We all know it was a continent from which slaves were captured and that, there are settlers at what I think of as the bottom end of the continent. What happens in the middle, I fear I know nothing of?"

"Do you think the Gargerys are being brave or foolhardy?"

"I don't know. I admire their religious convictions though I do not share them."

"Nor me, said Estella, "but I can scarcely imagine what life will be like for their children, even though it seemed as though what they were really doing had nothing to do with religion or being tired of London life. It feels to me just an expression of profound grief. No more. No less."

'But perhaps," Mary suggested, "it was also a matter of shame and guilt about their marriage. Somehow they became very muddled, linking in their minds Lachlan's death and their infidelities, perhaps seeing themselves as bringing about their son's death through their different liaisons."

"That also seems right to me. Moreover, it could be that in the process of reconciliation they had put each other in the position of being unable to refuse such a grand selfless notion as a school in Africa, which at the bottom of each of their hearts, each individually really did not want."

"I doubt that, Estella, or of course they were simply choosing to become Christian missionaries and your speculations are simply a response by you, an agnostic if not a full-blown atheist, and perhaps well off the mark."

Ridiculous, Estella said to herself, quite ridiculous.

But I like them both and I must try to persuade them not to be so foolhardy.

Albert came to the offices and warehouses of *Pocket, Timber Merchant* and went to his grandfather's office which had been left untouched since his short illness and death from what Albert understood to be a condition of the heart. His first visit which, as he had told Estella, was exploratory, but now the inheritance was his.

He came through substantial wooden gates, obviously shut and bolted each evening into a large yard, perhaps an acre in total. Around the site were stacks of various woods, some like the oak, mahogany and walnut, lying in large piles of planks for seasoning. The bulk of the wood was the softer woods, such as poplar and spruce, also in piles extending well over twelve feet high. It seemed to Albert an impressive sight.

He was due to meet with Mr. Woolhandler at noon, so he decided to explore the office of the company's founder. Orienting himself to this new situation would require a degree of familiarization with his work setting first. The office was located in a small totally unpretentious wooden building, with a room on the ground floor which looked like a tiny simple restaurant which, he assumed, would provide lunch and beverages to the employees.

He went up the staircase and at the other end of a short corridor was a door with his grandfather's name on it. It was unlocked. The office had a very low ceiling and was completely without charm. In a pile to right of the desk were copies of two newspapers, both prophesying the fall of Disraeli's government. The desk itself was a magnificent oak construction with a leather top, engraved on the edges in a gold leaf which looked as though it might have been made especially for him. The chair was old and somewhat worn, looking as though it was mourning the body that had sat there for so long.

On the desk itself was a stack of financial reports going back to the week of his death. Albert sat down and began to look at the most recent report, signed by a Mr. Simplick, obviously the financial clerk in the company. He learnt that Algernon had decided to split orders for softwoods which was the most significant for the building trade, between Osterlings, a Canadian timber company, and two or three Scandanavian companies. He was not sure how to read them, except to note that the bottom line on the right in each folder showed a declining monthly profit which worried Albert even though he knew economic conditions generally had worsened.

The bookcases contained old ledgers and many catalogues from forest-base companies at home and abroad. The mahogany catalogue caught his eye, the company being based in Kingston, Jamaica where presumably the trees grew. However, it was obvious from the yard that the bulk of the business was selling to the developers and builders and he made a mental note to talk with Brandram about it.

Searching the desk drawers, he found several statements from a bank, all of which indicated the company was profitable. He walked out of what was now his office and there were two other such rooms, one for Mr. Simplick and one which seemed to house three clerks sitting at high desks. He knocked on Mr. Simplick's door.

"Good morning, Mr. Simplick. I am Mr. Pocket's successor, Albert Pirrip. Perhaps you would be good enough to come to my office to inform me of the company's financial state."

"Indeed, Mr. Pirrip, and I am very pleased to meet you and I know we are all very grateful indeed that you have decided to keep up the family tradition. If I may say so, your grandfather was not just a solid man of business but a great pleasure to work with, so kind to everyone who worked with him, though he did not suffer fools gladly."

Once back in his office, Albert sat at his desk while Simplick made himself comfortable in an armchair.

"Let me have your overall impression before we go into detail."

"As you will see from the reports I compose, the company continues to make solid profits on a monthly basis, though these have been declining since 1873."

"Why is that?"

"Well, Mr. Albert, I try to understand national prosperity, its rise and fall. I have few acquaintances, if any, in the City of London where all the financial people gather and trade, so I rely on *Lloyd's Weekly*. There is some commentary each month on the state of the nation though the main sections of the journal refer to politics or news stories. Yet from these perusals, I have the impression that our trade, import and export, has been declining.

"Now, we in the domestic timber trade have not seen a serious decline that would affect us because most of our trade is with builders and construction people, or with manufactories making doors, windows or roofing. London has expanded so much in this century and construction with it. Of course we must be careful with credit as there are many small companies – one can hardly call them companies – which build a house or two here or there."

"I have much to learn and will profit from your instruction, Mr. Simplick."

"Thank you, but I have served your grandfather, man and boy, for long enough to have acquired much knowledge and, I hope, wisdom."

"Certainly."

"Your grandfather had total control of these profits as it is a private firm. He was very generous, however, raising salaries and wages on a regular annual basis which meant that men who got a job here stayed. Last year, when a young man was injured moving wood, Mr. Pocket paid for his doctor and made sure that, when he recovered after three weeks, he came back to work. Moreover, Mr. Pocket continued to pay his wages because, as he said to me, I don't want those children on short commons."

"That is precisely how I would like to run this business. It is obvious that a generous employer creates a sense of trust, vital to any undertaking. I think we should celebrate my grandfather, not so much my arrival, by giving each employee a lump sum. What do you think?"

"That would be excellent and it would make a very good start to your tenure. I will work out ratios and costs and bring them to you."

"Thank you. Now on the business side. I assume we have employees responsible buying and others for selling the material."

"Mr. Pocket himself did all the buying. He had a nose for a good product and the woods here have been in high demand, hence the profit."

"Tell me how that works. He surely does not travel to Canada or to Scandinavia."

"No, the representatives of companies come to him, and he has got to know them well over the years. But so stable are our relationships with those companies, and so stable are the demands from builders, that we continue what I call repeat orders. I am responsible for writing orders each month to ensure that our stocks in the yard are kept at the level of demand."

"Hmm… that must be a fine balance; enough stock but not too much."

"Provided a boat from Norway does not founder, as it did twenty years ago now, we can maintain that balance."

"Did you lose everything?"

"The company did not lose anything, as Mr. Algernon was always doubly insured. A prudent and careful man your grandfather, Mr. Albert."

Albert continued his discovery of the management side of the business before meeting with Mr. Woolhandler at noon. Walking around the premises, he learnt about the different kinds of jobs the men did, cutting, stacking, preparing orders, a group of eighteen men in all. Inside a large shed there were mechanical saws where the smell of spruce was enchanting. He made sure to shake hands with all the men, asking their names and about their families as he knew instinctively that getting to know the men personally would be good business, quite apart from the fact that he was very interested.

Late in the afternoon, he walked home to his lodgings feeling both daunted and excited. Above all, he felt very fortunate that his grandfather had two such reliable men in the central positions in his business. One immediate challenge was to find capable younger men who could be trained as their successors.

Honora herself felt herself on the horns of a dilemma and talked to her husband Frederick about it.

"Darling," she said as they finished breakfast one July Sunday, "can we take a walk in the garden as I want to talk about the boys outside their hearing?"

"What is the problem?" he asked once they had gathered their hats and coats and walked down the steps into the garden at the back of the house.

"The boys have been together since birth, and I am as proud as could be of them. They are very good looking, much more handsome indeed than their French father(s). They are both clearly very musical, engendered no doubt by their lives in North Wales and our house seems always to be full of their singing."

"Indeed," said Frederick, "they are doing so well at school such that a university such as Oxford or London is a possibility. The financial future is a little uncertain for me as the country is beginning to feel the effects of an economic depression which will influence building. They are such good souls, however, enjoying playing with our Jane Margaret which delights me."

"Frederick, I am still concerned about their paternity. Perhaps blood will out, after all their father was a rapist and a murderer, creating despair and anger among the young women of that village. I have not followed the arguments of Mr. Darwin, but if indeed the key to understanding how we came to be how we are was a matter of our evolutionary progress in which the phrase 'survival of the fittest' implied inherited characteristics, then our boys must have some of their father or fathers in them."

"Perhaps, my dear, but you worry too much. They are splendid young men."

"I get very irritated that I cannot identify which twin was the father or whether our twins had different fathers between those twin young men. I have completely forgotten their names, but I know that they were inseparable, always in each other's company, companionship which led to vice not virtue.

"So, I want to share with you my resolve that Simon and Jude should go to separate universities and begin to build their own lives independently of the other, though with the obvious closeness that being a twin implies. Does that all make sense?

"That is such an important and interesting idea, Honora. My goodness what a wonderful, thoughtful mamma you are."

"Thank you. I feel that because of their closeness they might want to study the same subjects or pursue the same profession which one or the other of them might be totally unsuited. That could only lead to difficulties for them."

"Important, I think, is this. If they really do have the same pursuits and professions in mind, then we should support them, but let us open the discussion with them tonight and see what they think. After all, they are approaching seventeen and will soon have to make life choices."

As they sat down to dinner that evening, Honora decided to raise the topic.

"Simon, Jude, we have been thinking about your future. We would very much like you to go to a good university and eventually become professional men in whatever line you choose."

"Simon says he'd like to be a politician someday and probably study law at Oxford. I don't want to be a lawyer, but I don't know what I want."

"There is plenty of time to think about that, Jude, but we were thinking that as you both have different ideas about your futures at this early stage, maybe you should think of going to different universities. Would you mind that?'

"I can think of nothing better," laughed Simon.

"I love my brother as much as anyone but if we think about the future, at the very least we are going to have separate lives when we get married. We will have different houses, different wives, different children."

"That is true," said Jude, "obviously we spend all our waking lives together, one way or another, but I think we have to go our separate ways for our futures."

"Let me be clear," said Honora, "none of that would imply a breakdown in your love for each other, merely the adjustments that we all make as we grow older."

"That is an excellent discussion, my dear boys," said Frederick. "Now comes the easy part. Who would like to study where? No need to answer that now but talk with your teachers as I am sure we will need to make decisions within twelve months or so."

Eliza Culpepper had her sights on a lunch party for some months, and even her children were enthusiastic. Timothy was the elder of three and a university student in London with some ideas about becoming a lawyer, though his father wanted him in business. Japheth and Margaret were slightly older than Honora's twins. Eliza wondered whether Honora was either snobbish, not wanting to be friendly with anyone in trade, or whether she had become even more protective of her twins as they grew older.

When the Culpepper lunch party was eventually held, it was hardly satisfactory for any of those who attended. To begin with, even though it was August, it had rained heavily for twenty-four hours and was continuing to do so as guests began to arrive, shedding coats, gloves and hats which were sopping wet, so that there was a procession of maids carrying clothes into the downstairs kitchen to dry and early conversation was dominated by the weather.

The rain put Eliza's cook in an abominable mood too, and as she was Eliza's third cook in as many months, it was a question whether this was the result of an interfering mistress, a hard task overseer, or just an incompetent wife managing a household. Both mistress and cook failed to pay attention to the central nostrums of Mrs. Beeton's *Book of Household Management,* which represented all that was good and true in middle class life in mid-century and beyond.

Eliza had convinced herself long since that she was naturally endowed as a mistress, especially as she had been a virtual servant in her youth. This particular cook, Mrs. Nancy Bird was long past her best to put it mildly, and she was certainly too stuck in her ways to have any truck with the likes of Mrs. Beeton. After a week in Eliza's employ, it dawned on this mistress that the excellence of her cook's references simply reflected the desire of her previous employers to part with her.

Now it was perfectly true that within Mrs. Bird's repertoire there were a few meals, which though traditional, would pass muster in any dining room, steak and kidney pie, roast beef with root vegetables. At boiled mutton she was a dab hand, but when she was asked to cook fish, of almost any size or description, the result stayed remorselessly with the bounds of the tragic. The same was true of any vegetable that required delicate handling, such as a tomato. With desserts, she could handle a plum pudding quite well, but any kind of souffle or even a lemon barley cake tested her skills and she was invariably found wanting. Yet even with those areas in which she was reasonably competent, there was always a sense of impending disaster.

Lunch was conventionally a relatively light meal but Eliza wanted to show off with a grand menu for such a large company, so oysters were served first. Master of the household Randolph was served with a plate of one of the species of the Ostreidae, a serving which unfortunately still contained small parts of the creature's shell creating severe discomfort for his teeth, his rapid departure from the table and the sounds of a severe reprimand billowing up from the kitchen.

After a soup unsuccessfully incorporating elements of previous repastes, the main meal was marked by the fact that each dish manifestly required a little more time in the oven or on the range, such that, for example, the florets of the cauliflower created a crackled unison around the table as each guest sought to master his or her portion. Mrs. Bird also had underestimated the time needed to roast a leg of lamb large enough for such a party so that each guest had to endure, only in two cases to enjoy, blood red cool meat. The gravy was cold, and the desert ice cream was warm.

The only successful part of the lunch was the wine which, in the absence of good food, provided such an excellent replacement that it was liberally consumed, particularly by Randolph, though it served to increase his bad temper after the oyster incident rather than mollify it.

The vagaries of Mrs. Bird's cooking soon became apparent round the table, plates with large portions of food not tackled and an unspoken sense of disappointment when maids arrived to clear the table. Estella and Charlotte were too polite to say anything but to complement Eliza. Hamish was holding Mary's knee firmly under the table as he was afraid her natural candor would break out. Eliza's face had a look of an approaching storm, and this time her children were silent in the presence of guests, though Timothy did murmur at one point that this lunch had showed what Mrs. Bird could do, at which Margaret got a fit of the giggles and had to leave the table whilst Japheth struggled to control himself. Pip and Susanna looked with condescension at the table, their half-smiles concealing their astonishment.

Conversation was enervated, apart from Aubrey and Antonia who brought to Eliza's table the kind of behavior that those with some imagination would have thought more appropriate to their bedroom which amused Estella, baffled Charlotte and aggravated Eliza. Hamish and Frederick were silent observers regularly charging their glasses with claret from the decanters. Simon and Jude were more interested in Margaret, but as they had been accustomed to orphanage food in their recent memory, they thought the meal was really good.

Now that might have been that.

Polite conversation would have drifted on, perhaps Eliza might have suggested a walk in the garden, and the lunch party might have dissolved into small groups, though it was probable that Aubrey and Antonia would have left in order to resume their conversation elsewhere, as they in fact did.

Yet Randolph, poor man, recovered from his mishap with the oyster shell and valiantly tried to imbue the conversation with some jollity, spiced with several glasses of wine which dulled the pain in the tooth molested by the shell. He was not to know, of course, that Pip and Susanna were considering life as missionaries in the dark continent. Yet, notwithstanding the body blow that Mrs. Bird had already dealt to the occasion, he suddenly embarked on an inebriated tirade against the Irish as being like African savages which was not the finest introduction to an after-lunch conversation of friendly exchange and universal gaiety. Indeed, he had committed a colossal *faux pas.*

Pip immediately took up the cudgels.

"My dear Randolph, you really are talking poppycock. I doubt whether you know anything about Africa, and less still about the Irish. You are just following along with the prejudices of the ignorant in our country who do not realize how much the Irish have been damaged for so long by the rich English taking over their land."

Annoyed by this dismissal and very much on a high horse fueled by red wine, Randolph found this brutal set of insinuations to his knowledge and his character quite unacceptable. Rather than relaxing the mood and changing the subject, he upped the ante, as his card-playing acquaintances at his club would have described his next remarks.

"You, my dear sir, are one of those religious types who thinks that just because God loves us, we should follow suit and love each other. I have no qualms at all about saying that I hate the Irish and I suspect most Africans are cannibals or worse."

"I have not been to Ireland or to Africa," interjected Susanna, "but are not your sentiments conducive to yet more misery in both places you mentioned?"

"What do you mean?" he asked, his eyes glazing slightly but with a look of thunder at this woman who dared question him.

"I mean, sir, that if your disgraceful sentiments are shared by those whose responsibility it is to bring the Irish Question to some sort of resolution, that will lead to chaos not to a solution."

"My dear young lady, you should not trouble yourself with matters of state, for which women are temperamentally unsuited."

Now the fat was really in the fire.

"I agree with Pip," said Estella, "I thought your earlier remark was poppycock but you have now complemented that with idiotic codswallop in your assumption that Susanna, who is probably the cleverest woman around this table, and if I may so, far more intelligent than you, sir, is somehow incapable of having an intelligent view about the most important question of our time."

"Oh, he talks rubbish all the time," said Eliza loudly to anyone listening, "You see what I have to put up with."

"Now," said Pip, determined not to let this oaf off the hook, "I return to your prejudicial remarks about Africans. Because they happen not to have yet encountered the teachings of the Lord Jesus Christ does not make them savages, any more than the poor women and children living from day to day in hideous circumstances in this country are savages."

"But the very color of their skin," said Randolph, "makes them savages. Enslaving them for the purposes the white man holds dear was a justified use of the labor that God, in his wisdom, put upon the earth. I've read the Bible too, you know. Slavery is part of the human condition."

"Wait," said Estella.

"I find your attitudes so reprehensible that I do not wish to continue to endure your hospitality any longer. Moreover, I do not wish to be in your company any longer than it takes me to collect my coat and leave. I can only say how much I pity you for your ignorance, and I am sorry for your children. You truly are an unspeakable human being."

At that, Randolph took a large swig from his wine glass and left the table, stumbling as he reached the door and cursing loudly.

The guests around that table were stunned into silence by Estella's virulent response to Randolph's humbug. Susanna looked at her with immense admiration. Pip marveled about Estella's ability to be so forthright.

That woman, Susanna thought, really is like a shining star, a stellar person. She is a beacon of intelligence, moral probity and good faith. It is a star I wish to follow, and I hope that her age does not dim it. I know she is warning us about Africa, and we must talk again with her.

Estella got up from her chair and walked out of the dining room. Eliza followed with tears in her eyes, apologizing for her husband profusely.

"It is always worse when he has drunk red wine," she said, "whisky does not do that to him."

"I don't think that was the drink, Eliza," said Estella, "that merely revealed who he is."

As other guests left, Honora said quietly to Estella:

"What are we going to do to help poor Eliza?"

"Make sure she comes to meetings of the League for a start."

XIX

Frederick and Honora were their quiet selves at the lunch, observers and spectators rather than active participants. They shared Susanna's sentiments about Estella's criticism of Randolph, but much more important to Honora was the apparent close friendship that now seemed to be developing between the two younger Culpeppers and her boys. Japheth was nineteen, and Margaret, Simon and Jude were each seventeen, the twins being three months older.

Honora knew they recently had started to all walk out together and Japheth had even taken them out on a small boat rowing on the river. They had once played tennis and she overheard talk of interchanging books. Not that she felt any particular qualms about the Culpepper children, though their parents were another matter, for reasons they had demonstrated at the lunch.

One afternoon in late October, when Honora was out walking Jane Margaret in her perambulator, Margaret went quickly down Cheyne Row without Japheth to visit the twins. It was a lovely autumn afternoon in London, one of those rare treats Mother Nature provided and the three of them were on the rear lawn of the Brandram home after a game of croquet. Simon was in a chair and Margaret and Jude were lounging on a large rug next to him. It was clear to those who knew them that there was plenty of immature sexual attraction between these seventeen-year-olds but all three were demure and well brought up.

"Can I ask you something private?" asked Margaret.

"Of course," said Jude.

"Have either of you ever kissed a girl?'

"What a question," said Simon, "why do you want to know?"

"Oh, I just wondered if you'd tell me what it was like. You see, I don't have any sisters to ask and as we are now such good friends I did not think it impertinent or forward to ask you both. I mean did you kiss a girl in the orphanage?"

"Good gracious, we were only twelve," said Simon, "though there was a girl who gave me a peck like a bird on my cheek, but I did not kiss her lips."

"I did," said Jude, "I stayed behind after you left her and we had a good kiss. It was really nice."

"How nice?" asked Margaret.

"Well, it feels nice and it makes your body tremble a bit. Come here, and I'll show you."

"No, let me see you kiss Simon first."

"Oh, we stopped doing that a long time ago well before we came to my mother's, but I don't suppose Simon will mind, will you, brother?"

"Not at all. You see, Margaret, when you have a twin it is like having two of yourself if you can understand that. Like we have the same eyes, and while I have a slight birthmark, apart from that we are identical."

He got up from his chair and sat down on the rug next to Margaret, leaning across her to kiss Jude on the lips, albeit briefly.

"Oh, that was lovely," said Margaret, "You two are so close."

"Shall we show you how identical we are even in kissing, Margaret?" Asked Jude.

"I don't know: Will I be alright?"

"Of course, it's only a kiss."

Jude lent over to Margaret and pushed her ever so gently on to her back that she hardly realized what she was enjoying. For Jude kissed her with immense tenderness and she was soon caught up in the kiss, opening her mouth a little. Simon on the other side of her was watching closely when Jude said:

"Now you can see if we are identical, Margaret," said Simon, at which he lent down and began kissing her more fervently than his brother.

"You are not quite the same," Margaret said when Simon pulled back.

"No," said Jude, "one of us has to be the better kisser. You have to be the judge," and he promptly then began to kiss her again but this time, putting his arms around her and pulling her on top of him, as they kissed with abandon.

"But you have not judged my kissing," said Simon, now lying next to them, at which Margaret moved on top of Simon, now completely taken over by kissing these two beautiful boys.

She sat up suddenly, sitting on Simon, and said:

"I really can't judge now. I will have to try again another day," at which they both shouted "No, No," and began to wrestle her over each other in what, in less constrained contexts, would be called horseplay.

Meantime Honora had returned from her shopping and had brought Jane Margaret upstairs to the nursery which overlooked the rear garden. She was transfixed with horror at seeing her boys tumbling around with a girl, such that it triggered her most unhappy memories.

She threw up the sash window and shouted:

"Stop that this instant. All of you come into the house immediately."

The three youngsters had enjoyed themselves without any malice or persuasion involved, but Honora could only see her rapists.

The three sat down in the living room, and Honora was steaming with anger.

"Please explain to me what was going on," she said in a voice that crackled with emotion.

No one spoke.

"I am waiting."

"It was my fault," said Margaret, "I wanted to know what it was like to be kissed and then there was a sort of competition as to which of Simon and Jude was the best kisser, and then we were just romping around. No harm was done, though I have not decided who wins," she said with a giggle.

"Margaret, would you like me to tell your mother about this?"

"Oh, no, please don't."

"Now look young woman, pretty as you are, you are not a trollop, offering yourself to any man who happens to be available. A kiss is a mark of love and respect and should not be a matter of competitive fun, ever."

"But I do like the boys. We are great friends, and the kissing did not mean anything other than a bit of fun."

"I think you should leave now," she said, aware that she would not value a conversation with the young woman's mother about the incident, "I am sure Simon and Jude value your friendship, but please no more competitions."

"I am sorry, Mrs. Brandram, we meant no harm," said Margaret as Honora showed her to the door and hurried back, deciding that the moment had come.

"I think you are both now old enough to know what I am now going to tell you which will explain why I am so upset. There is no good time in your lives to explain this to you, but your frolicking with that young lady suggests to me that is the time."

"What for?" asked Simon.

"Wait, wait," said Honora, as tears came to her eyes such that the boys looked at her with some alarm as she was clearly distressed.

"Since you came to me I have been very confounded about when I should tell you this."

"What is it you want to tell us?" said Jude.

"It is about your father," she said, at which the silence could be cut with a knife. It persisted for almost a minute with the three of them looking anxiously at each other.

Drawing herself together, Honora began:

"When I was nineteen, I went to France on a pilgrimage with some friends. We stayed in a small guest-house near Lourdes where Saint Bernadette had seen a vision of the Virgin Mary. The owners were obliging in providing single rooms for all six of us. They had two sons who were twins. We guests went to the church and the grotto and we prayed each day.

"The night before we left, I wanted to see more of the village, so I walked alone in the twilight into the village square where the twin sons of the owners of the Pension were standing talking. They came up to me, said they wanted to show me something interesting, and they hustled me towards a shed.

"I could not get away, and I thought they were playing some kind of game with me.

"But," and here her voice faltered slightly, "they stripped my clothes from me, raped me and assaulted me terribly, and I assume you know what rape is. They then took me back to the Pension and said they had found me in this state and they said it looked as though I'd been raped. The village policeman was the owner's son and he shrugged his shoulder about what should be done. We were leaving the next day and I was too ashamed to tell anyone."

Both boys had got up from their chairs and come over hurriedly to hug their mother, one or each side of her as she sat on the settee. Dreadful cries soon came pouring out of the boys as if they were emptying their souls and Honora's tears flooded down her cheeks.

"Oh, Mamma," said Simon, "how unspeakable, how terrible."

"And I suppose one of these villains is our natural father," said Jude through his tears.

"Yes, it was the most terrifying night of my short life but let me tell you this. It has all been almost obliterated by having you both with me, as whether I was raped or not, when I had you both at my breast, I was overjoyed."

"You said our father was killed in the war?"

"They were both in a prison on Devils Island for raping many village girls after me, one of whom was only twelve. It will never be possible to know your exact parentage, that is, which one fathered you. You understand, don't you?

"But let me explain why I am telling you this now. When I came to the window and saw you both rolling over with Margaret, the vision of what happened to me flashed before my eyes and I was horrified. I suddenly thought you might be like them, though I see nothing of either of them in you, no glance, no facial expression, nothing, but I wonder whether you may have inherited something from him or them."

"Oh, dearest Mother," said Jude, "neither of us could ever dream of doing to anyone what those blackguards did to you, father or no father."

"But now you have warned us," said Simon, "we will have to think much more carefully about how we behave as boys and as men with women."

"I love you both so much that I would give my life or any of my limbs for you. I am so proud of you. When I first realized I was pregnant, I was terrified of my parents. They behaved very badly and sent me to my grandmother. But as the months wore on and you were both growing inside me – of course I did not know there would be two of you – I became very pleased to be having a child. I could feel you moving inside me, and when you were both born and I had both of you at my breast, I was so happy I could have burst.

"But," through more tears, "I knew I had to give you up."

"What happened when we were given away, Mother, how did you feel?"

"As if my life was not worth living. My parents said I had disgraced them, but my father introduced me to Frederick and we were married, though it was very one-sided, not at all as it now is. He looked after me, of course, but I grew to be ashamed and silent. I never talked to anyone, until Estella and Charlotte took me up and I found you."

"He is such a nice man," said Jude, "if I could have chosen a father, I would have picked him. But Simon and I have talked about it from time to time. Neither of us really believed your story about our father. We knew there was more to it and I am so grateful now that I know my parentage completely."

"Yes," concluded Simon, "we have Papa and you as people to follow and our natural father as a warning. I suppose that is the kind of experience that growing up is."

"But dearest Mother," said Jude, "you found us and we have found you and it has been the most wondrous change in our lives."

"And for me, too, my darlings."

Estella had felt some degree of satisfaction that she was able to tell that boor Randolph what she felt. It had given her great pleasure to assault his views on human beings and natural slavery, something close to her heart because she felt that many English women, like Africans, were treated as slaves and that the whole business of dowries came close to a market. She saw that the suffering of any group of human beings for any reason should be attacked through providing support.

She was also aware that not many people shared her view. Indeed, the predominant view of Africa, let alone Ireland was much more akin to the nonsense that came out of Randolph's mouth, that Africans were cannibals and that the Irish were poor because they were lazy and an inferior race with a religion that was primarily superstition. Such a view of other people had simply never occurred to her as the topic never arose with Miss Havisham in the cocoon of Satis House. She had been surprised to see men with different colored skin when she saw them in her excursion to Chatham with Nellie, or with Pip in the slums around Clerkenwell, but while she felt a tinge of disgust, her mind was dominated by the desire to help, and feeling sorrowful at these pitiful creatures, she could never despise them.

She had received a note from Susanna and Pip that they would like to call and they appeared one morning a few days after the disastrous lunch party.

After the usual greetings, Pip said:

"We are lost in wonder, love and praise at your trouncing of Culpepper. In the coming months I am sure that he will squirm with shame when he thinks about it."

"That may be a little exaggerated because he is so self-righteous and smug that I suspect he has never felt ashamed. I am getting to imitate Mary Macdonald, and every time I see her I expect a cannon of forthrightness! She just says what she thinks. You remember the occasion when she asked me about Nellie, don't you?"

"Oh indeed," said Susanna, "but I think the silence around the table after she asked you that was very different from the silence that followed your assault on poor Randolph."

"Fiddlesticks, 'poor' Randolph? He is just a coarse ignorant oaf as well as a pompous and self-satisfied buffoon. I mean what nonsense that man talked. I am not sorry and I won't apologize, and you were a powerful cannon yourself, Susanna."

"He may demand an apology from a mere woman, but on the other hand he may also think we women are far too emotional to concern himself with."

"Well, let us put Culpepper to one side," said Pip, "as we wanted to discuss Africa again with you. Darling, why don't you take the lead?"

"Estella, you know enough about our lives, its ups and downs and our tragedy. We have decided finally that we want to become Christian missionaries in Africa. We talked about it with you a little while ago, but we need your wisdom and support."

"Of course you have my support and I will endeavor to ensure that the Trust can support you, though I must clarify the legal situation with Hamish and Clarence.

"There are two matters I think about in my concern for you both.

"The first is disease. I really don't know much about this, but I suspect there are diseases in Africa which we don't have here to which you will be susceptible. You have seen how disease can suddenly envelope you, as with Lachlan. I don't suppose you will have a doctor, so you must take with you the latest in medical books, and some of the things we now have, like carbolic."

"We have done some thinking about how we cope with illness," said Pip, "although we don't yet know where we will be going. It is likely to be rural, certainly. What was your second matter?'

"I am sure you have given this much thought. It is about Malcolm and your daughter Hannah. Will you be able to spend the time to teach them? You are both likely to be very busy, I would think. When Malcolm grows up, how will he cope with England coming back, having been away for so long? Of course he might follow you into missionary work, but you cannot assume that, can you?

"No, but we think they will both see it as an adventure. We are minded not to have more children to complicate matters, especially since what I thought was my most recent pregnancy turned out to be a false alarm, not a miscarriage, thank the Lord."

"Yet, an adventure without end?"

"Perhaps."

"Of course there are now some very good boarding schools, as you know. You see, I wonder whether you are sacrificing your children's futures to your mission. Sacrifice is too strong a word, but it is clear that your children's future is not a priority, is it?"

"Thank you," said Susanna slightly disconcerted at this point of view, "I don't think we have thought deeply enough about that. I think we have always assumed it would be easy for them. Perhaps we could take them with us on the understanding that we would send them or bring them back in two years for their schooling here. I must also try to consult Mary Slessor, though I don't know how."

"Well, my dears, I admire your plans, as I have said before. My next task is to talk with the lawyers, if you will allow me, to ascertain whether the Trust can support you. For example, you will need your independent transport and be able easily to buy mules or other pack-animals and, of course, horses and carts. I have no idea about currency, though I am sure the British sovereign will work wonders."

They then retired to Estella's dining room where lunch had been prepared.

Some days later, Estella arrived at Old Square for a light lunch and a glass of wine which was some indication of how the practice was beginning to prosper. The hunt for additional lawyers had ceased. With consultation, Hamish as senior partner decided to fund Adam's legal training and to find a new senior clerk to replace him. He also decided that they would be careful about accepting briefs and be able to charge more to set the practice on a sound financial footing. The sale of the other two buildings was completed. His first-year strategy would be reviewed at the end of the second year by his colleagues.

He was delighted to see Estella again as he admired her management of the Trust, although he did not know yet of Pip and Susanna's plans which would affect the composition of the Board. Estella admired his office and noted the small portrait of Mary on his desk which, as she told him, was quite delightful.

"Tell me," he said, "it is a pleasure to see you again, but, pray, is this visit more than a social call?"

"More than social," she said with a smile.

"Do you know whether the terms of the Trust's endowment allow it to fund projects outside Great Britain?

"Good heavens, I don't know. Let me see if Clarence and Sam are here."

He rang the bell on his desk and Robert received instructions which led almost immediately to both Clarence and Sam appearing, with the usual volume of greetings and encomiums.

"Estella has come to inquire whether the terms of the Jaggers Trust would permit the funding of activity outside Great Britain. I have not yet inquired as to why she is asking the question and do not propose to do so. She will no doubt tell us all in good time."

"I read the will some years ago when I joined the Board," said Clarence, "as I thought I ought to know what my fiduciary responsibility covered. It is one of those interesting questions in law. Does the absence of a specific prohibition imply that it is not intended?"

"Or," Sam chimed in, "does the absence of a prohibition leave everything that is not specified to the discretion of the Board?

"If we take the American Constitution as an interesting case, it says, roughly, that any power which is not specifically given to the Federal Government is the responsibility of the individual states.

"So," said Hamish, "we could take that as our guide and say, given that there are stipulations specifying 'the relief and education of the poor,' then, where such poor are located is not ruled out, and indeed need not be confined to the territory within which the will was probated."

"Indeed," said Sam, "but as with the American excitement about the so-called Founding Fathers do we not have to consider the donor's intentions?"

"We can assume little from that," said Clarence, "for we cannot know what the donor might have said had he been asked about the relief and education of the poor outside the country. I think it reasonable to assume that he gave no thought at all to the possibility that the Trust funds might be used in the colonies, or in India for example."

"But that brings us back to square one. If it is not expressly prohibited, is it allowed, and what are the criteria to be used in determining that?"

"We need to be careful," said Hamish, "we clearly do not want to go to Court to ask a judge to decide. A judge, any judge will be in the same position as we are."

"Hmm," said Sam, "I hesitate to suggest this but we are with my parents this weekend, aren't we, Clarence?"

"We are indeed. He is retired, of course, but we could ask Lord Eustace as a hypothetical. We do not have to accept his argument of course."

"That would be useful."

"Your discussion is fascinating, gentlemen," said Estella. Like many a man who has gone to a lawyer for advice and regretted it, I am probably mistaken in asking for permission. Would the Trust be in jeopardy if we simply treated such a request for Trust support as a matter of Trust policy not of law?

"From your discussions, I perceive no certain legal solution emerging, and even if you were to spend your valuable hours searching through cases, I do not see how different cases in different contexts, though relevant perhaps, can yield a conclusion.

"I yearn for the day when I will meet a one-handed lawyer."

"Why on earth is that?" asked Sam in a mildly hostile tone.

"Then I would not have to listen to lawyers saying, 'on the one hand' and 'on the other hand,'" at which everyone laughed at Estella's neat wit, though Hamish pointed out that if they were all one handed, they would soon be out of business.

"I suggest that we lawyers on the Board take our own counsel and at the next meeting make a decision on policy unless we see supervenient objections."

That much was agreed. Clarence and Sam returned to their offices, and Hamish was curious to know why she has asked the question at which he was told that he would know all in good time.

Through the United Presbyterian Church pamphlets, Susanna had got to know of the work of Mary Slessor, a missionary in Calabar, so she was both grieved and elated when she read in a pamphlet of the United Presbyterian Church that Mary had contracted malaria and was recovering at her home in Dundee.

It was not difficult to contact her, and in November Susanna took the train on her own to Edinburgh, and then on to Dundee where she stayed at the Queens Hotel which had been open only a few months and was the pride of the city. There was a note from Mary Slessor welcoming her to Dundee and suggesting she come and visit Susanna there rather than Susanna venturing out to find her house.

Susanna was sitting demurely in the foyer when a young woman with red hair and blue eyes, a small bonnet and a pallor which indicated illness walked slowly into the hotel, looking around. Susanna got up and walked over to her,

"Mary Slessor?"

"Aye," replied Mary in a Scottish accent much broader than Susanna's, "you sound Scottish."

"Och, yes, my father was a banker in Edinburgh, but my parents died in freak weather in Sicily some years ago. I am now married with two children to Philip Gargery who was a Primitive Methodist preacher at the time I met him."

"Oh, how interesting, and you wanted to talk to me about my work in Calabar?"

"If you have the time."

"Of course."

"Let us go into the dining room and we can eat or drink or both."

They walked slowly into the dining room and were assigned a small table looking out on the street. Tea was ordered as it was mid-morning, and Susanna began:

"My husband and I want to create a Christian mission in Africa. This is occasioned largely by the death of our dear ten-year-old son, Lachlan, of diphtheria. We have come to feel that our lives in London, though good in their way, do not do justice to his memory. To be frank, I am wealthy enough to finance our work, though my husband Pip also manages the well-endowed Jaggers Trust for the Relief and Education of the Poor.

"We also anticipate there being support from the Trust though the lawyers are considering whether supporting such work outside Great Britain is permitted under the terms of the will. We have two young children who would accompany us. I am looking for your assessment of whether our project is a sensible one, and if so, what advice can you give us."

"My goodness, I admire your courage and even more that you propose to devote your personal wealth to it and," she said with a smile, "if the Trust agrees, perhaps I will follow with a request for support too."

"Oh, you definitely should as it is such a wealthy organization. However, my husband and I have been shocked to the core of our religious beliefs by Lachlan's death."

"I offer you my most sincere condolences. Every death of a child is an insult to God and our country is riddled with it. In Calabar there is twin infanticide, a fearful practice I am determined to stop."

"Good gracious, why kill twins?"

"One is believed to be a devil-child, or that that mother has misbehaved. Twins are put out in the bush to die."

"Oh, good Lord, how awful."

"You see the kind of problem you may encounter."

"Indeed."

"Now, I am suffering from malaria which I caught in Calabar and I have come home to recover. It is endemic there and there are precious few medicines to alleviate its effect, though quinine seems to do some good, but let me address some of the problems you will face.

"There is the simple matter of personal comfort for those who have regularly slept in a bed with sheets and pillows and an ability to somewhat regulate the temperature of the room. That is impossible. Sleeping is very rough, a straw mat on the floor will suffice.

"Standards of hygiene that we know well are unknown and the individuals in the tribe I work with have bodies which over centuries have accustomed themselves to those conditions. So white people are prone to infections of many kinds.

"What people eat differs hugely from our diets here in Scotland. My stomach took several weeks, even months, to get used to it and, of course, you must cook yourself.

"Social relationships differ, too. Don't think you can get there, build a church, and people will flock to listen. They won't, especially as you won't speak their language which you must learn.

"There will be leaders in any place you establish yourselves, and your presence may be seen as an attempt to lead or as has happened to some missionaries, you may be seen as slavers or just a malign influence and be killed.

"Do not therefore assume any good will. It takes months even years to build trust.

"These are all matters I have had to encounter as an individual, but Susanna you are proposing to take your children and I have not heard of missionaries who have done this, though there may well one or two."

"Oh dear," said Susanna, "you make it sound impossible and make us sound so unprepared."

"I don't think you can be prepared, however much you feel the Lord God is calling you to this work. It involves a colossal leap of faith, not in God's willingness to protect and help you, but in your own ability to endure privations, suffer indignities and relish suffering."

"Mary, I hope I am not an obstinate woman who cannot listen. Is there some path or other we could take which would lead us gently into our mission? I am reluctant indeed to surrender before we have started."

"You should not take me as an example. I have only myself to think of, and I grew up in the slums of this city, one of seven children. My father took to drink. He and my two brothers died of pneumonia. I started work half time when I was eleven and worked full-time in a factory when I was fourteen. I knew from birth what poverty is like, a place where disease, early death and hunger are the staples of life. What about your lives and upbringing?"

"I am the daughter of an Edinburgh banker, as I have said, so I have always lived very comfortably, really without privation of any kind. My husband was the son of a blacksmith in the country in Kent, a simple life but without hazard. My husband did spend several years as a preacher in the slums of Manchester, but he did not face unknown disease or hunger."

"I admire your spirit and your dedication, but I think you could do much good by supporting missions financially than you ever could by following your present plans. But, if you decide to go ahead, then I do suggest a gentle immersion.

"Why not go to live in a city like Tunis in the north for a while to explore the rhythms of Africa and perhaps start a church there? Alternatively go to the south of the Continent, to Capetown. The Dutch Calvinists are strong there. From either city, you could examine alternatives, make contacts, find out how to develop resources. As long as God wills it, I will be in Calabar and you might perhaps be able to make the difficult journey to see me on your way south."

"You have been so kind, Mary. May you continue with God's work. I have brought you a note with some money to assist your endeavors."

"Oh, my dear Susanna," she said with surprise looking at the note, "you have no idea how far two hundred guineas will go for my work. My sincere thanks and God's blessing be upon you."

As the train brought Susanna back to London, she was divided between enjoying the challenge and thinking it was complete folly to even think of such an upheaval. She wondered what Pip would make of such strictures.

1878

XX

The New Year 1878 came and went. Estella spent some time with Mary and Honora wondering how it was possible to thwart the Gargerys' intentions for a mission in Africa which they all thought was a mistake. The work of the Board continued, with several new ideas circulating. Estella felt lonely throughout that Spring which she spent predominantly in New Queen Street with only one or two short visits to Numquam, not a destination she relished in the winter, apart from Christmas celebrations.

As Charlotte was still in Pompeii at Percy's dig, she invited Harriet to come to Numquam for a week in April. This was not without its risk, given their recent meetings, but she still wanted to sustain a friendship with her notwithstanding the difficulties of their past which she saw were all engendered by her.

She met Harriet at Charing Cross Station which since 1864 had become the South-Eastern Railway's main station for northern Kent. They greeted each other warmly and sat next to each other as the train cantered on toward Rochester, where Estella's carriage met them. Harriet was, of course, delighted by Numquam House, its gardens, the field of daffodils, and its privacy.

Nellie arrived in her cart the next day with her daughter Victoria, about to be nineteen. Estella saw them coming and went to the front of the house to welcome them, leading them inside.. She had met Nellie's daughter several times when she was growing up, but now the girl had become a very attractive young woman, so much as her mother would have been without her harrowing upbringing and early life.

"You look so well, Estella," said Nellie, with a hug and a kiss, "and this is Victoria, my daughter."

"Oh, my goodness," said Estella, "you are like sisters. This is my friend, Harriet, who has come to stay with me for a week."

"How d'ye do, Miss," said Nellie, "I've heard a lot about you. You're even more beautiful than I'd been told."

"Well, thank you, Nellie. A book would not be enough to hold what I've been told about you."

"Nah, well, we've been good for each other, haven't we darling," she said, putting her arm around Estella's waist. "Now, Victoria has come specially to ask you somefink."

"Go ahead, Victoria."

"Well, if you please miss,"

"Don't be shy."

"I'm almost nineteen and I've been growing up here in the marshes with my mum and dad, and my bruvver is appreniced to my dad. I helps my mum, of course, and we have larks together, don't we, mum. But I wondered whether I could get a position in London. I mean, I know it is easy to get into service and be a maid, but my mum and dad and me, we don't really want that, but somefink better, but we don't know how to go about it."

"I had no idea that this might be what you wanted, Victoria. Of course, I will help. Now I know you have been to school, but just till you were fourteen, right?"

"Yes, ma'am, I can read and write easily and my mum has been giving me books to read."

"Yes," interjected Nellie, "I've given her all those books you gave me."

Estella looked at Nellie carefully while still engaged with Victoria and she saw how proud she was, positively glowing at this lovely sensible young woman, her daughter.

"How about this," said Estella, "you come and live in my house in London as my guest, not my servant, though I hope you will do one or two chores, looking after your bedroom for instance. But you will not live below stairs. I will teach you as I taught your mother. I know your mother dislikes London, but we might persuade her to come and visit us and bring your father. We will look around and see what you might do, perhaps work in a department store."

"What's that?" asked Nellie.

"Of course, you've been here in the country for years, so you would not have seen how these large shops have now become quite common, sometimes on three or four levels. Astonishing. Young women assist ladies with buying clothes or jewelry or other things, but we would see what might suit you. I will give you an allowance too."

"No money please," said Nellie, "staying in your house would be lovely, but we have done well, you know, and we will send her money regular.

"What's that work like?"

"To begin with," said Harriet, "you have to be very presentable. Nice clothes, well-kept hands and hair, as you are constantly meeting women who have money to spend and you have to be polite and sometimes, take no notice of those women who are nasty to you. What's the expression, Estella?"

"I don't know anything about it, I'm afraid."

"Oh, I remember, the customer is always right: So you never argue with a customer. But I am getting ahead of myself. You may do something quite different."

"Come to London as soon as you like and we'll work something out, and you will come to visit us, won't you dear Nellie?"

"Wild horses would not keep me away if my lovely Victoria is there."

"Harriet and I are going back next Thursday, but I think Victoria should be ready to come in a month or so, let us say the end of May."

"Oh yes, she'll be ready then."

"Now what about your son, Horatio isn't it?"

"Oh, he's doing splendid, twenty-one years old, working very hard for his dad. And he's courting!"

"So he won't be coming to London, then?"

"Oh, no, he's a son of the marshes, fishing, walking, drinking in the Bargemen. He's here for good, I'm sure. We think, he'll marry his Susie, don't we Victoria?"

"Well, let's hope there's no war to carry him off like his father," Estella said, "but would you all like to come to lunch on Saturday? I'd like to see Fletch while I am down here and Albert said he might come up from Hackney for the weekend."

"Oh, we'd love too, I know."

Hugs and kisses all round included Harriet which surprised her and after the pair left, she and Estella wandered around the garden, arm in arm.

"That was a quite astonishing introduction to Nellie, dear Estella. It is strange, isn't it, how we tend to think that people from a lower class are somehow unintelligent, or morally inferior. We must do things in the League which will cross the barrier. I am sure we can all learn from it."

"Yes, it is surprising, isn't it," Estella replied, "I may be deceiving myself but I don't think I have ever quite assumed that lofty sentiment. I was brought up by my guardian to regard men as not merely inferior but as revolting creatures to be avoided, or where necessary, treated with contempt. I hope now I take people as they are, whatever their background. Of course, I am not friends with my staff here or in London, but I do try to treat them properly."

"Well, I must say, Estella, you are going to have to keep a careful eye on that Victoria. That's how Nellie must have looked when she was nineteen, blond hair, round blue eyes, splendid figures with breasts neither too large nor too small, a target for many a young blood."

"I suppose so, but I suspect I am going to have a lot to teach her. In fact I invited them to lunch to see whether she knows her table manners, though I am sure she does. Anyway, as an old woman, I will do what I can,."

❧ ❧ ❧

On Friday evening, a trap drove up to the house and Albert got out, carrying a hold-all, capacious enough to indicate that he was intending to stay a night or two.

Estella rushed out to see him and threw her arms around him.

"Oh my dear Albert, you look more like your father every day. Forgive the ebullience of my welcome."

"Oh, no," said Albert teasingly, "being embraced by a lovely woman is a pleasure I have not had for months. I have just been too engaged with my business."

"Come in, go to your room and come down for a glass of whisky. But just let me introduce you to Harriet first."

After the introduction, he vaulted up the stairs two at a time, an expression of his joy at being at home, for he still felt that home was where Estella lived.

"I'll be down in a jiffy."

"My goodness," said Harriet, "first the Fletchers, now Albert. Where do you get these beautiful people!"

"Nothing to do with my loins, I can tell you with the utmost confidence," and they laughed with gusto as Albert appeared.

"To let you know before you talk to us about your business, the Fletchers are coming to lunch tomorrow, son Horatio and daughter Victoria as well."

"Good, I have not met them. They must be quite grown-up by now."

"Indeed, but tell us about *Pocket, Timber Merchants.*"

"First, I have changed the name to *Pocket and Pirrip* which accurately reflects the situation. Although the building trade has not suffered as much from the economic depression as they call it, the business was run very well indeed by my grandfather and he has a splendid loyal workforce.

"Profits are such that I am becoming quite wealthy, quite apart from the five thousand pounds my grandfather left me. Yet I know from growing up here in the marshes that working people are often on short commons, so I gave them all a sum of money in recognition of my grandfather and I have twice increased their wages since. My finance clerk is excellent and I have rewarded the foreman and him."

"But what exactly is the business?" asked Harriet.

"In brief, we buy soft wood from Canada and Scandinavia, stock it, and sell it on to builders for doors, windows and the framework of a roof, anywhere wood is needed. Of course wood is also needed for all manner of erections in the docks, gangways on ships and so on. We turn the wood on machines into all kinds of sizes, from large beams to very small sizes, for instance, to go round a door. We keep a small stock of hardwoods, oak, mahogany and so on, but we don't have a large enough market for those. Oak is scarce in England and very expensive. We import mahogany from our colonies in the Caribbean."

"How does it arrive with you?"

"By small barges up the River Lea after being unloaded at the docks. That is a mark of Algernon's genius, placing his business there. A place away from the river would mean horses and carts.

"He built up excellent contacts with buyers, based primarily on a sense of confidence and trust, so we have not yet had to send men around selling our wares. Of course we are constantly on the lookout for sellers who might undercut our prices, and there are many different mechanical inventions we can use. Saws these days are extraordinary.

"So, I am very content with my work where I spend twelve hours a day except Sundays. My lodgings are excellent. I have seen Herbert and Celia a couple of times. They hope you might visit them sometime."

"I will see. I am dithering about my next excursion to Paris as I want John to introduce me to those women painters. I met Berthe Morisot, of course but there are others too."

"Indeed. You know, I am very glad indeed I gave up trying to be a painter. I also now do not regret so much my break up with

Elizabeth who, I hear, is getting close to Timothy Egerton and there is talk of their engagement soon."

"Then Harriet and I will find you a wife," and they laughed.

The following day Numquam House was bathed in the pale November sun but it was finally determined that lunch should not be served outside under the elderly elm tree, as was sometimes the custom.

The Fletchers arrived in their trap. Fletch and his son were big men with arms like tree-trunks, created at the anvil. Nellie and her daughter were a picture of beauty and good health. Harriet could see Albert being quite taken aback by Victoria's looks and, sure enough, he made a beeline for her immediately. He was, after all, very well experienced in relationships with women.

"I am very glad to meet you, Victoria," he said. "I spent about seven years as a child in your Cottage."

"Did you really, how was that?"

"My mother died when I was scarcely one and my father, who later married Estella, was just starting as a lawyer, so he asked his very old friend Joe and Biddy Gargery to care for me and I came to live with them."

"My goodness, I never knew much about them who lived there before us, except Mrs. Shoreham of course."

Conversation between the two became rapidly animated by Albert's memories of the Cottage and all that had happened there. Victoria seemed to take the conversation in her stride, and when Albert asked her whether she was going to work in the neighborhood, nothing could have satisfied him more than her reply.

"I am to going to live with Miss Estella in London soon. She is going to teach me like she taught my mother and then I will be able to find a position which is not in service."

"How wonderful," said Albert, "then we will be seeing more of each other. At least I hope so."

While chatting with Estella, Nellie had been watching this pair with a mild amusement but, also with some hope if she was honest.

Perhaps, perhaps, would it not be strange, she thought, if Estella's stepson were to marry her daughter.

Meantime, Fletcher had been asked to show Harriet the gates to Numquam House that he had made for Estella, and Horatio went too as he remembered the times they had driven around Kent looking at gates. By this time, Albert and Victoria were walking round the rose garden.

As they left to walk down the drive, Nellie put her arm in Estella's and suggested a walk on the lawn before lunch.

"This is so kind of you, darling Estella. I don't know. It's always the same with you. Such generosity, such friendship, such love, and I tell you what. Look at those two, your son and my daughter. What about that, eh?"

"You mean Albert and Victoria."

"Yes, the queen and her husband," she said laughing.

"I have a very good feeling about this, darling," said Estella. "I woke in the middle of the night and thought how marvelous it would be if Albert and Victoria fell in love. I expect I will see a great deal of him in my house in the coming months."

"It would be strange, though, wouldn't it?

"Why?" asked Estella.

"Well, you know, you being rich and us being poor and me being a whore..."

"And my mother being a criminal murderer? See? You and me are of the same class, you know. It's just I was brought up out of my class. This class business is dreadful, causing all manner of problems among which is that it often prevents people from loving whom they desire. Or if they do, men and women get cut off without money. Nothing, absolutely nothing, would give me greater pleasure than for our children to marry and for us to share grandchildren. If, of course, I live that long."

"Don't say that, lovey."

"I know, but I am old, you know. Let's call everyone for lunch."

Conversation was intense and varied, with much laughter and fun. Harriet asked Nellie whether she had seen Estella's portrait.

"No, she said she'll have it brought to Numquam some time, but I suppose I will just have to come to London to see it."

"You know, I think you should all come when Victoria is living with me. It is easy by train nowadays and you can see all the sights in a few days. Then you'll see the portrait."

"Are you still hanging the portrait of my father?" Asked Albert. "If so, I think you should take it down, it really is terrible."

"Not at all, Albert dear, I think you capture your father very well."

"Did you paint his portrait, then?" Asked Victoria with great interest.

"Yes, I was in Paris and it took me ages. The trouble was I was in a group of really outstanding painters, one of whom did Estella's portrait."

"I expect it is very good, if you put your heart into it and he was your dad."

"How kind is that?" said Estella. "Thank you, Victoria, you are right. His heart really is in it."

Lunch proceeded with great joy, friendship and love and as desert was cleared away, Estella said: "Now we are done, how about a song, Fletch. Whenever you come here, we always finish with a song."

"We do a lot of singing in our family, don't we, Nell?" said Fletch. "It expresses our good fortune, I suppose. Oh, I've been putting Horatio and Victoria up to singing."

"Yes, I have often heard Nellie singing in this house."

"Do you have a preference," asked Fletch.

"Some jolly country songs."

"Right, come on Fletcher family. *The Lincolnshire Poacher!*"

Fletch sounded the note and then they were off:

'When I was bound apprentice in famous Lincolnshire....'
right through to
"And it's my delight on a shiny night in the season of the year."

Albert was clearly transfixed watching Victoria sing so sweetly. Harriet was entranced in seeing such a close-knit family, and with their backgrounds too, but when Fletch was persuaded to sing 'Drink to me only', the tears came to her eyes and, perhaps for the very first time in her life, she saw properly what she was missing in being a single woman, with no family, no children, and age creeping up on her.

She left Numquam with Estella quietly determined to find herself a husband. At forty-one years of age, she was on the verge of that hectic period in a woman's life in which her ability to have children is diminished by nature. Dammit, she thought, if I can't find a husband, I can at least find someone who will give me children. Soon, she knew, she would have to share that ambition with Estella.

On the morning of a meeting of the Trust directors at the end of April 1878, a letter from Australia awaited Hamish as he arrived at his office. It was from a Brisbane law office *Whereabout and Gottlieb*, stating that they had heard recently of Mr. Hardyman's sad death, and saying he had made a will there on his original visit to Brisbane to discover the Unworthy situation, apparently frightened that he might suffer at the hands of Brisbane brigands. It established a Trust in favor of his children with the Trustees as Hamish and Mary.

As he read the letter, Hamish thanked the gods for Sam Eustace, because much of the Hardyman wealth had already come back to her which surely would make the will moot, quite apart from the question of whether a will made in Australia would be valid under English Law. But that confusion was for Sam to sort out.

At ten o'clock, Pip and Susanna, Estella and Clarence convened in the meeting room at Old Square. Adam Masterson and Sam Eustace were also in attendance.

"Before we start, might Albert be invited to rejoin the Board as he is now permanently back in England as owner and managing-director of *Pocket and Pirrip, Timber Merchants*?" asked Estella.

That proposal was accepted *nem con,* and Pip then spoke.

"It will be of great value to have Albert as the son of my older namesake back on the Board. However, I have to give formal notice that Susanna and I will be resigning as from the end of this year and that will also create a vacancy in the day-to-day management of the Prostitution Project."

Most of the Board members were open-mouthed at this declaration.

"Have you come to a decision, then?" Asked Estella.

"Yes. As Estella knows, my friends, we have been considering moving to Africa to become missionaries."

"Great Scot," said Hamish, "that really is courageous."

"Susanna has been in Dundee recently talking with Mary Slessor, a young woman who is on health leave from her work in Calabar. She presented Susanna with a catalogue of the difficulties of trying to go directly to a mission or, in our case, to try and create one, and we are taking her advice and approaching our mission gradually.

"We will leave next month on a ship that travels to Capetown but calls at Tunis. We propose to disembark at Tunis, where there is a large Muslim population but a small Christian entity and make decisions from there."

"I admire your sense of mission," said Clarence, and others murmured their assent.

"We will miss you both, your counsel and your energy very much indeed."

"However, let us begin with Pip's report," said Estella.

"Indeed. First, the Semper House is being rebuilt with insurance money but will not be finished for at least another year. The Building in Clerkenwell still houses four young women, but we are arranging for them to live elsewhere and be supported by grants. I suggest we examine that whole policy later when I complete my report.

"Our support for agricultural workers in Kent has been a great success and it has been expensive, costing nearly two thousand five hundred pounds each year. This economic depression is now said to be over, and it has been something of a tragedy for the working poor, but there is now hope that these laborers will find work and the need for our support thereby diminished.

"The final question affects me personally in terms of our intent to be missionaries. The lawyers around the table will know that it has been discussed as to whether the terms of Mr. Jaggers' endowment allow funds to be used for projects outside Great Britain. I will say no more at the moment but suggest that we discuss each of these three activities in turn."

"May I contribute?" asked Clarence.

"Please proceed," said Estella.

"The three matters are obviously related, given the Gargerys departure for sunnier climes. I propose that we now focus our attention on two geographic areas – Clerkenwell and Northern Kent. Put all our resources into these two areas where we have experience rather than taking a social problem, like prostitution, and creating various bases for it across London. We can sell the Soho buildings and buy another in Clerkenwell, both as our bases, but also for training young men and women in trades and whatever else occurs as necessary for poor relief and education.

"In other words," said Hamish, "you are proposing that we shift our attention to two specific areas of the country and the metropolis and work at whatever needs there happen to be there."

"Thank you – that puts it very clearly."

Discussion followed for at least one hour and all thought a firmer focus would be a sensible strategy.

Concluding the discussion, Estella said: "That seems admirable to me. Perhaps, that Clarence, you would look after the Clerkenwell activity. Sam, perhaps you would oversee the North Kent project. Both of you could assess needs and management arrangements for our next meeting.

"Now I would like to discuss the matter of the Gargery mission further to see whether we are on common ground here. Might Pip and Susanna wait in Hamish's office while we consider this? I am sure it will not be long but as a matter of decorum, that seems to me to be wise."

Once the Gargerys had left, Estella asked if we could assume that any contribution would not be outside the terms of the endowment. She mused that perhaps we could use a medium to get Mr. Jaggers' approval.

Hamish promptly proposed that an annual grant of one thousand pounds be given to the Gargery mission but not before it had begun and they were settled on a location. At this juncture, he said, there was no mission to support. That was agreed, though it was clear that Adam had reservations, but felt it infelicitous to raise them, especially as he was not yet a qualified lawyer.

Then, as was their custom, the Board retreated to *The Cheshire Cheese* for lunch.

XXI

"Shall we take lunch, Harriet?"

"Yes, indeed."

Estella had finally written a note suggesting they meet at a small restaurant in the Strand as they had not seen much of each other since April and it was now the end of August.

"I have some special news for you, Estella," said Harriet as they sat down.

"I am intrigued."

"I am two months pregnant."

"Good gracious me! How....wonderful: Or is it? Are you sure? At your age?"

"It is four months now since we were at Numquam. I found the presence of the young people so fascinating that, a day later, I decided on a whim to go to Paris, and I returned last week, not that you would have noticed," she said acidly.

"Oh my dear, I am so sorry. I got caught up with all manner of problems with the Trust, trying to find a suitable replacement for Pip as manager. None of the lawyers wanted to do it. It prevented my own plans to go to Paris."

"No matter. I went there to find myself a husband, or at least a lover from among those painters you talked about so volubly a year or so ago. Now that Pip is really out of my life forever, my major ambition was to have a baby and I was uncertain whether I could, and if a husband came with it, so be it."

"How did it all happen?"

"It was much easier than I expected. Once there, I was sure I did not want a husband as making such a permanent relationship would take time and thought, and time was running out for me. I knew the area you had spoken of, so I found the Duran studio and asked for John Sargent."

"Good heavens, he's the father?"

"No, no, no. Be patient!

"I told him you were my great friend and I wanted to study the group of painters you had told me about, not to paint. Actually, I would like to have taken him as my lover, but he was very busy being about to leave Paris for Spain.

"He introduced me to several men in the studio, and we met several times in the *Café Guerbois* and the *Café de la Novelle-Athenes,* where one night a young man named Aristide Bruant got up to sing. Perhaps fifteen years younger than me. I don't know as I didn't ask him. Beautiful romantic melodies I had not heard before. He is such a beautiful man, my dear, with marvelous ambitions to open a café or somewhere he can sing to customers, as I later found out."

"So he is the father of your child?"

"Yes. We struck up an instant interest in each other. For three weeks we were together every night at his small apartment, magical, somewhat exotic, but what I wanted. I knew I would be pregnant, if indeed my body allowed it at my age. I told Aristide our first night that I would be returning to England shortly to which, like a typical Frenchman, he replied that we had no time to lose."

"Will you marry him?"

"I don't know. I like him very much, and he seemed to like the idea but was a little alarmed by the possibility, give the differences in our ages. I would need to decide whether to raise my child in Paris. He certainly would not come to London."

"Harriet, dear, you may well find difficulty in a pregnancy, so why don't you come and live with me in New Queen Street?"

"That is sweet of you, Estella, and as I get nearer my confinement I will, if I don't go to Paris. I am now properly independent financially. My father died many years ago and my mother died within a week of my return, and her estate leaves me very comfortable as far as money is concerned. In any case, given our history together, let us just remain friends. If I need serious care, and perhaps just before the birth and after, I may well accept your invitation."

"I understand. Did you tell your mother?"

"Good gracious, no, but I was with her when she died, poor thing. Her mind had gone and she scarcely knew me."

"Did you know Pip and Susanna are considering becoming missionaries in Africa?"

"What? Oh my god, then I really do have to get him out of my mind. Seriously? How stupid can one be? I can think of nothing more dangerous and foolish than such a venture. How naïve, how ridiculous."

"It is a reaction to Lachlan's death, as I understand it."

"It's daft. Have they considered what it could do to their children? Being raised in some appallingly primitive environment, a village no doubt where they will be distrusted from the outset. It is perfectly appropriate for a single man or woman to engage in such nonsense, but a family? Neither of them are doctors. She's a pampered girl and he's a preacher. That makes me very angry."

"Goodness me, any more invective?"

"That's the sort of idealism that is so misplaced. They could so easily do the same thing in Manchester or Birmingham."

"I do happen to agree, but I have not tried to stop them. I expect they'll be back within six months."

"That I doubt: They are far too proud, and foolish with it."

The delight in the Brandram household was unconfined when Simon's application was accepted at New College in Oxford, and Jude's at Trinity College in Cambridge. Jude had applied to two colleges for a choral scholarship but was unsuccessful. Frederick felt they were a little young as they would be eighteen during their first term. Jane Margaret was now the most spoilt child that could be imagined with her two big brothers doting on her, though that would cease once the brothers were gone.

Honora's words of advice to the twins and the story she told them about their father brought an aura of solemnity to them both. It was as if the knowledge propelled them overnight from youth to adulthood. They were somehow more serious, both worked immensely hard for their entrance examinations and pleased that they were going to different universities. Honora sent a brief note to Estella telling her what had happened.

Frederick had been working very hard too. He had met with Albert several times too, and his advice was not merely welcome, but essential to this young man starting out in business at the top level. Honora began to be worried about her husband's health. He came home, dog-tired, spent little time at the dinner table and went to bed early.

"Darling," she said one night, "would you do something for me?"

"What is that?"

"Would you take me on a vacation to Switzerland? I have never seen mountains and lakes. I have lived almost entirely in my life on flat land. I don't want to climb Mont Blanc," she said laughing, "but I read in a magazine that a funicular railway was to be built in Switzerland."

"I would love to, my dear, but I cannot leave my work."

"You will kill yourself if you continue to work as hard as this. I want to go and I want you to come with me. We will leave Jane Margaret with the nanny and the boys will look after her, I am sure. Please say yes and let us go immediately."

"You know, my dear, perhaps that is exactly what I need."

Within two days, the Brandrams were crossing the channel for the train to take them via Paris to Zurich and within another two days were lodging at a small inn at Lauterbrunnen. Frederick had talked with a travel agent who had himself completed a walking tour in the Jungfrau region a few years before and recommended the village for its marvelous valley, guided walks and within short distances of such famous mountains as the Eiger and such falls as the Staubbach.

Honora watched Frederick gradually relax in the fresh air. They went on an excursion every other day and walked on the mountains regularly, not merely sleeping well but enjoying comfortable intimacy.

After a few days, Honora felt able to discuss what was on her mind.

At one of their evening meals, she asked:

"My dear, we celebrated your sixtieth birthday last year. Don't you think it is near the time for you to retire? I worry so much about you working so hard, you know. You seem to be very strong, but I don't recall you ever taking advice from a doctor."

"I did not tell you for fear of upsetting you. A few weeks ago I had a stabbing pain in my chest, and I did see a doctor and he too advised me to slow down and take life more easily. But I am within a few short months of achieving my goal. I want to have forty-thousand pounds in the bank. We have to pay for the boys to go to university, of course, but with that money we can safely retire and perhaps move out of London to a congenial town like Bath or Brighton."

"But I do not like the thought that you are getting these unexplained pains. Have you had them while we have been here?"

"I have had one bout, when I asked you to sit down with me on that bench when we walking toward the Eiger mountain the other day."

"You see how much you need the rest."

"I know, I know. I really will try. But I must reach that money target, my dear."

Their last day, they took the most exciting excursion available with a guide up to Wengen from Lauterbrunnen which was a steep climb slowly zig-zagging up the mountain in the cart. The views across this part of Switzerland were stupendous, the mountains in all their glory visible in the brilliant August sun. They walked around on the high plateau breathing in the pure air, holding hands.

"This is so delightful," said Frederick, "you know, my dear, we have had a very exciting life since your boys came to us. The past years have been made even more wonderful with the arrival of Jane Margaret."

"But this is why you must retire, my dear, if you are to see her grow up. Don't concern yourself with the goal. Consider what you have achieved already."

"No, my dear, the last mile is essential."

"Alright, but at any rate, you are now rested and this has been the most exciting experience, one I won't forget."

Travelling back was very tiring, but they arrived in Cheyne Row in time for Jane Margaret's bedtime and an emotional welcome from the twins.

It was a lively party that set out from the Three Jolly Bargemen mid-morning on September 3, 1878, for the *Princess Alice* excursion. Josiah, the landlord and his wife Jezzy were up front on high seats, with the reins in his hands. Like his brother down the road at the *Blue Boar*, he ran a joyful public house, a center for fraternity in the small village of All Hallows and had done so for many a year.

There were the Friendly and the Butterworths too, both elderly couples, none of whom had ever seen London. They had decided that before they got too old, they would join the excursion. There was some raucous debate about whether to join the steamer at Gravesend or Sheerness, but Gravesend was selected, about fifteen miles by road. Fletch and his son Horatio made up the party as neither Nellie nor Victoria fancied a trip on water.

The cart rattled along with its eight passengers, and the singing was so loud that the tremor in the axle was hardly noticeable. Fletch noticed it, but he was not going to upset this particular apple cart by calling a halt. He was in two minds about it as it seemed to be getting worse, thinking he would look at it when they got to

Gravesend if there was time before the steamer left or when they returned from London.

The old people were amazed by the town of Gravesend, since neither the Friendlys nor the Butterworths had even been more than ten miles from All Hallows in their lives. All four of them went once on a village outing to Rochester, but, apart from that, like country folk the world over, they were profoundly conservative in their outlook. As Mrs. Butterworth had said when discussing a change:

"If we've never done it before, why should we do it now?"

The cart turned into the High Street where there was a large sign pointing to the Pier where the steamers docked. They had timed the run from All Hallows well, as there was just half an hour till the steamer was to leave. All they needed was a place for the cart, but just as Josiah was thinking out where that might be, there was a loud crack from the rear cartwheels.

"What's the matter here?" asked Jezzy.

"Let me see," said Fletch, "get down carefully, everyone, as we have only half an hour till the steamer sails." The party stood by the cart while Fletch examined it.

"Now," he said, "this is a blow. The rear axle shaft looks almost broke to me."

"What's to do?" said Josiah urgently, "We need to catch yon boat."

"I don't really want to miss the boat, but we have to make a decision. We must mend the cart or it will be days waiting here when we come back. Tell you what: Horatio and I will stay behind and get the cart mended. I'll find a smithy tomorrow and work on it. Then it will be as right as rain when you all come back."

"But we can't leave you here, you're part of the party," said Jezzy.

"Now, see here," said Fletch, "you are all much older than me. You have set your heart on seeing London and you may not be able to go again. For me and Horatio, we'll go another time. We will find some lodgings and be ready to take you all home in the cart when you come back. I think I have a cousin lives here too, so we may stay with him."

"That's so kind of you, Fletch. We'll bring you something from the Tower of London."

"Off you all go now or the steamer will be off without you."

So the six of them hurried up the street to the Pier. They were never to return.

The damage to the cart was not too bad. Fletch was up at the crack of dawn and while he noticed there seemed to be more people about than he would have expected, Horatio and he rode the damaged cart carefully just out of town to a smithy he had seen on the roadside as they approached the town the previous day. The blacksmith, Tom Jennings, was only too pleased to help a fellow smithy and by early afternoon the cart was mended. So, they thanked Tom and especially his wife Martha who had given them a pie each and a warm beverage.

As they rode back into town, they saw a commotion of people at the pier.

Fletch called out to a passer-by, "What's going on?"

"Haven't you heard, the steamer was hit by a collier last night and everyone has drowned."

"Which steamer?"

"The Princess Alice."

Father and son threw their arms around each other, both in tears.

"Oh, dear God," said Fletch, "what about my Nellie? What will she do if she's found out? She'll think we're dead."

"But how will she find out, Dad, out there in the cottage?"

"Someone might stop by to tell her, if all the folk from the Bargemen are drowned.

"Right," continued Fletch, "I'm going to take the horse, though it's going to take a while, and ride back to tell her we are alright. No, wait, I think you should go, son. One of us has to stay here just in case there are survivors. I'll go to the Pier and get a newspaper and find out what's what."

They took the cart back to the smithy and explained to Tom what was happening. Horatio then borrowed a saddle and was off on the road to All Hallows. By now it was into the afternoon but he could expect to get there before dusk, even though the horse was not used to anything but the cart.

Estella came down to breakfast on Wednesday morning early feeling refreshed. She had come back in a hurry from Kent for a wedding and she had felt that she was getting too old for all this rushing about the country, even though the train journey to Kent made it straightforward enough. But travelling, she thought, is a tiring business. Charlotte was not yet down, but she helped herself from the buffet and sat down to eat.

Charlotte then came into the room, just as the maid brought in copies of *the Daily Telegraph* which Estella ignored. As most English gentlewomen do, Charlotte took a cup of tea from the maid before eating and sat down next to Estella.

"Oh, how awful," she exclaimed.

"What is awful, my dear?"

"This steamer: Sunk with much loss of life, and in the Thames too."

At that, Estella hurriedly took her paper and read.

"Oh, goodness gracious me, that's the paddle-steamer Fletch and his son were to go on. I must go to Kent immediately to comfort Nellie. How awful!"

Reading the details, Charlotte started to weep.

"Oh, my dear, there were almost seven hundred men and women on board and she sank in fifteen minutes."

"I can see, and, oh, how terrible, how frightful, she was hit by another ship carrying coal, and did you read that, she sank at just the point where the human sewage had been let into the river."

As the two women read of this dreadful accident, they reacted in horror.

"Think of the children, Estella, suddenly thrown into such a river full of sewage."

"What about those who were trapped underneath?"

"Were there no survivors?"

"It seems not."

"Why were they on a steamer in the Thames in the dark of an evening?"

"I understood from Nellie that the pub had arranged an outing. Eight were planning to go. They would go up the river, see the sights, stay in lodgings for the night, and then come back in the morning later."

"Where from?"

"I think she said Sheerness, but it may have been Gravesend. But I must get to her immediately."

With that she rushed from the room and within half an hour was calling for a cab to take her to Victoria Station, making sure to take the newspaper with her. She knew Nellie would not know of the accident. By mid-afternoon, she was urging the horse leading her trap to hurry down the track to the Cottage.

It was a windy day and as the trap stopped at the door, Nellie appeared:

"Estella, lovey, what are you doing here?"

"Let me come inside and sit with you," and they walked into the cottage.

"My dearest, there's been a terrible accident; The *Princess Alice,* that paddle-steamer was hit by another ship and sank in the Thames and it seems as though everyone is dead."

"What? My Fletch? My Horatio? I don't believe it."

"I'm afraid it's true."

The birds on the trees fell silent, and the wind dropped as Nellie fled the house running around the yard shrieking and howling as her cries rang out over the marshes. It was as if a pack of several dozen wolves were in song together. It was not just scream-ing, but ear-shattering wails dissolving into tears. Estella got up and went outside and took her arm as they walked in a circle as this avalanche of sadness streamed out from Nellie.

"O, my poor darling Fletch, and him surviving that war too, only to get this. And my lovely boy, pride of my heart."

The afternoon wore on. Nellie was inconsolable, though Estella did her best to provide comfort where it was impossible but the distress paralyzed the three of them until, as it began to get dark, they heard a horse running down to the track. They had hardly got up from their chairs when Horatio burst in.

"Dad and me didn't go on the boat," he shouted: "The cart broke down in Gravesend and we let the others go as we had to mend the cart for when they came back. Though I suppose they won't be coming back now."

Nellie was transfixed looking at her son, but then shrieked with joy and relief as she threw herself into his arms, dragging Victoria with her.

"Dad has stayed to try to find out about the other six. I'll ride back in the morning and see, and we'll bring the cart back or wait for the others."

"Miracles, miracles, miracles," said Nellie, now weeping with sorrow and joy, as Estella quietly left the family to their relief and rode her trap slowly to Numquam House.

Estella now intended to stay a week or so on her own to absorb the shock but hoping Nellie would come to see her soon, and two days later she heard her beloved friend approach in the Fletcher's cart singing her heart out. Estella opened the door and went out to greet her, and they embraced closely and kissed as was their wont.

"Come, darling, let me get my trug and scissors, and let's wan-der around the garden."

"I have to pinch myself of a morning when I think what might have happened if my two men had gone on the boat. You hurried off when Horatio came home, didn't you lovey? I wanted to share it all wiv' you."

"That is so kind, but that miracle was something to be shared only between the three of you."

"I suppose so. When everything died down, I said to Horatio 'what happened to Estella?' and he said: 'I dunno, was she here?' Of course, he didn't know till he got home whether I knew about the accident or not, but, though he saw your carriage, he was so excited he had forgotten completely you was there."

"I can't tell you what those few hours with you in your distress meant to me, darling. I had all sorts of wild imaginings about them and how awful such a death must have been. I was at a total loss to know how to comfort you."

"Well, I was so frightened about losing them, wondering what I was to do. Crikey, it's still so real."

"I would have looked after you and Victoria, you know."

"No, it wasn't just the living, the money and all that, but the kind of feeling I had been emptied out like a milk churn, and all my life was spilling out on the ground."

"I can believe that and share it."

"Of course, when he got home yesterday, Fletch was so sad that the six of 'em in the party are lost, and so was I, but truth now, I was so relieved my two was back."

"Of course, oh dear, I had put the others out of my mind."

"They was all the older members of the families. I told you about the younger Friendly's before, how these was with four kids and a shack of a cottage and out of work. Well, it was his mother and father. It was Tom Friendly that came with Josiah to help after we'd killed Whistler in your dining room. They saved my life," and she began to weep.

"It is the most terrible circumstance and the guilty people must be brought to justice."

"Then there was the Butterworths and the Steppings wot was the landlord of the Bargemen, Josiah and his wife Jezzy. His brother what kept the Blue Boar, he's been at the Bargemen since. We had a big wake at the pub last night, and I still don't know whether their bodies have been discovered. They've put up a board as a memorial, too"

"I can't imagine that kind of distress, I'm afraid."

"Nor can we. Fletch read to me all about the boat after it happened and what it was like, noisy, very crowded, so that you had to push through people to see the sights along the river as they went up to London. But then, he talked about what it must have been like when the boat got hit. He dreamed about it last night, waking up shouting for our son. I s'pose he'll gradually get over it. Sometimes I think he feels guilty he wasn't on the boat."

"Now that is very sad but I would say he does not need to feel that although miraculously not being on the boat maybe worse than being there and surviving."

"P'raps, but I tell you, lovey, it's made us both feel how much we matter to each other and how much the kids mean to us."

"I am sure. Yet, think what might have happened if Victoria and you had gone with them. I know you. You would have had them all on the boat a good half hour before it left. You'd have told them to leave the cart, wouldn't you if there was all four of you. And then what?"

"Lorks-a-mussy, you'se right, ain't you? Can't think about it anymore.

"I meant to ask. When are you going to have those women here? I'd love to meet them."

"I must do that soon. I'll write the letters today and post them when I get back to town."

XXII

Estella lay in bed one night as the autumn sun went quickly down. She was thinking about Victoria who had been with her now for almost a month, coming to London two weeks after the Princess Alice Disaster.

Victoria was becoming like a step-daughter of a sort. And what a daughter! So extraordinarily beautiful, a real English rose, the sort any Viking would have carried home in his long-boat. She had so much of Nellie in her looks, but this young woman was quite self-confident, self-possessed, charming and yet completely unsophisticated, and certainly no flibbertigibbet. Estella had not had a deep personal conversation with Victoria yet, allowing her to settle into the rhythm of life in New Queen Street. Her mother was coming to London for a few days too which would be a joy.

They had taken a stroll in St. James Park on a couple of summer evenings, chatting rather aimlessly about the grass, the flowers, the view of Buckingham Palace through the trees. The following day, however, Estella decided to realize her promise.

"Today we will go to shop for clothes. The garments you have are charming, but not really in fashion."

"Oh, Mam insisted I wear the two dresses you bought for her in Chatham as they still look nice and she now does not wear them that often. I remember her coming home with 'em and you couldn't get them off her. She would dance around in them for hours, and my dad thought she was so funny."

"Oh, yes, I remember. Today we'll take a cab up into Bond Street which is very fashionable and has been for years, maybe a century, and Oxford Street where the newer shops are. I want you to have the dresses, hats and every piece of attire that suits you."

"Oh, miss, you are so kind and generous," she replied in such an intonation that if Estella had not been looking at Victoria, she would have assumed it was Nellie.

The following day they walked again in St. James Park and Victoria's wardrobe was now in the height of fashion making her fully equipped to appear in London at any gathering,

"It seems to me, Victoria, that you and I should spend about six months together. You can accompany me most everywhere and you can learn all sorts of things about life from being with me, how to talk to people, when to speak your mind, how to dress and so on."

"That would be lovely."

"Did you know that my husband, now dead of course, grew up in the Cottage? His brother-in-law, Joe Gargery, was the blacksmith."

"All we knew was that Mrs. Shoreham lived there and that her husband had been the smithy and Albert has told me about his years there as a child."

"Yes, that was Joe Gargery, and Biddy – Mrs. Shoreham – was his second wife and he was her first."

"Sounds very complicated."

"I suppose so. You see I lived quite near the cottage with my guardian in Satis House, now knocked down."

"So you are a child of the marshes, too?"

"Well, not exactly."

"Oh yes, my mum told me about you and your mother."

"Did she just?"

"Albert's not your son, right?"

"No, he is my step-son. His mother died when he was very young and I married his father."

"You know, Miss, apart from my bruvver, I've never really talked to another man before. I mean I left school five years ago now and my Mum and me, we are great friends, always doing things together but I don't go out on my own, ever."

"Please call me Estella. So now you have met Albert, is he nice to you?"

"Oh, yes, though he is much older than me, I mean he says he is twenty-five, practically an old man and with a business to run."

Estella laughed at the idea of Albert being an old man but said: "I think he admires you greatly."

"But there, see, you must help me. He is so grown-up I feel like a baby talking to him."

"Ah, I tell you what we will do. I will have him come to see us twice a week and then you can tell whether you like him more, or not. I am sure he will want to tell you about his life before he went into the business."

"He's said something about wanting to be a painter."

Over dinner, Estella was curious to know what Nellie had told her as she was due from Kent the following day.

"Your mother has been coming to my house for several years now, hasn't she?"

"Oh, she wouldn't miss it for the world. She told me how much she loved you."

"That's very sweet of her, and I love her too."

"She is such a treasure, my mum. She's told me all about her days whoring in Chatham and about the murder of that soldier, everything really. She says if there are no secrets, there won't be any lies."

"Very wise."

"She's told me all about you and her, too."

"Has she indeed?"

"Oh, miss, you don't mind, do you?"

"Not at all, I once told a group of friends that loving your mother made me proud."

"Well, I'm not sure she intended to, but we was sitting in the garden of an afternoon and she started to tell me all about herself as a way of telling me about men. I knew how babies were born already, and I think it all just came out as she was talking about life and herself."

"Your parents are wonderful people, how they have constructed their lives is a miracle."

"Yes, but not without help from that Trust or whatever it is. Oh, I love my parents so. I am so lucky."

The next afternoon Estella went in her carriage to pick up Nellie at Charing Cross.

"Cor, I'd never been on a train before; it's fun isn't it to see the fields and the houses rushing by. But how's my daughter?"

"Like a rose in summer. Sometimes I look at her and think she's my dream of you."

"Nah, she's the real thing, not me. Well, here it is, old London. Mind you I was never up West before," then imitating Estella's accent she said, "looks really quite charming," and they both laughed.

They chatted about nothing of consequence and arrived at New Queen Street. Victoria rushed out to greet her mother and they all walked arm in arm into the house. Nellie gave her coat and hat to the maid and they went into the living room.

"I have something to show you, dear," said Estella and took her into the dining room.

"Cor blimey, darling, isn't that amazing! You look wonderful, really sexy."

"Oh, no that surely."

"No, p'raps not, but you do look very beautiful and how he gets your dress like that with flowers baffles me."

"The painter will be a very famous painter one day. The one of Pip, my husband, was painted by Albert."

"Crikey, he did that?"

"Yes, but if you look at them both carefully, you can see the difference in the quality."

After they had a cup of tea, the three of them went out for a walk in the Park.

As they turned the corner to go back home, Estella said:

"Victoria, you have a lovely voice, you know, You Fletchers really know how to sing."

"Oh, yes, miss, we are always singing."

"But would you like to play the piano? I have this nice piano, but I really don't play and I would love to have you playing and singing."

"Oh, that would be a big challenge, but I'd love it."

"I will write then to Elizabeth, the niece of a friend of mine who was taught by a Mr. Pauer, as I recall. She is an accomplished pianist, but I am sure he would take on a novice. Maybe she would teach you herself?"

They returned to the house and Albert was in the living room.

"Hallo, stranger," said Estella, embracing him closely, "Victoria is just up to her room to put her hat and coat away and you know Nellie, don't you?"

"It's all right, I haven't come to check up on you, Albert, but I must just go and powder my nose, as women say when they want to pee," and she quickly left.

"I want to say one important thing to you, Albert, as they are both out of the room. I treat Victoria as my daughter and you will answer to me if anything untoward is instigated with her by you. You are courting her already and this will not for some time be a courtship of equals. If you make her fall in love with you and then break it off, I will be beyond anger."

"My dear Estella, I feel an affinity with Victoria, after all we grew up in the same cottage. It is not my intention to rush anything and certainly not to treat her except with the utmost respect."

"Very good, but I am watching you."

At which moment, Victoria came into the room and with an enormous smile of welcome to Albert sat down on the settee. He joined her but was careful not to sit too close.

"Albert, Miss Estella says you painted that portrait of your father. It is a marvel to me how anyone can do that."

"Oh, no, it is not that good. You can see the difference if you compare the portrait of Estella with it. That is far finer, far more texture, subtle colors, life in every corner of the painting. Do you see the detail in the flowers on her dress? I could never paint eyes with John's brilliance.

"I see the differences, but I still like the one of your father. Funny, isn't it, to think we was all children in the Cottage?"

"That is the strangest thing, ain't it," said Nellie returning.

"The biggest commotion there," said Estella, "was when my husband's older sister was attacked and dreadfully wounded. I was a young girl with Miss Havisham at the time. It was some part-time laborer or other who beat her brutally in the kitchen."

"In the cottage kitchen?" cried Victoria.

"I fear so. She was Joe Gargery's first wife as well as Pip's sister, but she treated Pip badly, as I recall. She later died of her injuries."

"Oh dear, oh dear, that cottage is now such a happy place," said Nellie.

Yes," said Albert, "and then didn't Pip, the young one, come home from the Crimean War badly wounded and they all nursed him back to health?"

"That's right," said Estella, "and do you want to tell Victoria of the other sadness in the Cottage?'

"Victoria, which room do you use as your bedroom?"

"The one at the back on the right of the stairs."

"That is the room where my mother died."

Victoria burst into tears, crying out:

"Oh, no, please, no. How come she died there? Tell me, tell me."

Albert moved across and put his arm around her, saying:

"There, my dear, it was long ago, over twenty years. Very few houses have not witnessed a death, you know."

"But how come she died there?" said Victoria weeping, while both Estella and Nellie watched the pair carefully, wondering what Albert would say, for Pip had never told him all the details.

"She was a frail woman, my mother. She had lost two or three babies. So when I was born, everyone was thrilled, but then she was pregnant again quite soon. My father arranged for her to live with the Gargerys at the Cottage, rather than in London's filthy air, and they made sure a midwife was on hand for her to give birth there."

"Oh dear, oh dear," said Victoria, continuing to weep at this tragedy.

"Shall I go on?"

"Oh yes, oh yes, now you have begun."

"You know all this don't you, Nellie? "said Estella.

"Oh yes, that Biddy, she told me about every little nook and cranny in the cottage and every event."

"My father and mother were returning to the Cottage after seeing Estella at Numquam House," Albert continued, "and the horse leading the trap reared when a fox ran across the road and she immediately started to have the baby. I was downstairs being looked after by Joe and then my father too, as she was helped up into that room. This is the saddest part now. The midwife told her the baby was fine, after she listened to her stomach, but my baby sister died being born."

"Oh dear, oh dear, no more, no more, please," and the three women were all in tears as Albert concluded:

"All I remember is asking my father where my mother had gone and he said he didn't know."

"Your father never told me that detail," said Estella, "I suppose because I did not ask, but also because he was so shocked at your mother's passing."

"We talked about it, usually when we went to her grave, and his voice always had this deep sadness about it. I know your history with him, of course, but I do think he loved my mother."

"But of course he did, Albert, and he told me so. He was such a generous man."

Victoria's tears had dried up and they each looked at each smiling.

"I suppose I should not be upset at your mother dying in my room all those years ago."

"Oh, no," said Estella, "of course you should, but only because it is such a sad story, not because it is your room."

"Yes, I see."

"Now let us go and have dinner."

Albert left shortly afterwards, and the three women sat and talked. The next few days were a hilarity of shopping, walking, sitting, strumming at the piano and even, one night, going to a performance of *HMS Pinafore at* the Savoy.

"Funny, isn't it," said Nellie on the way home from the theater, "I mean that was marvelous, but women always get laughed at, don't they, or made out to be stupid.

After the Gargerys declaration that they were bound for Africa, the next few months before they left cast a shadow over all the friendships and intimacies that their friends shared. No one wanted them to go; some thought it was sheer madness. Attempts to persuade them otherwise faltered.

However, on a brisk morning in April 1879, these close friends were on the quay at Tilbury, waving goodbye to the Gargerys on the SS *Ethiopia* bound first for Tunis, then Lagos and finally Capetown, though the Gargerys planned to leave the boat at the first port of call. As Estella thought about it afterwards, it was a joyful occasion, but odd for being that. The Gargerys were so committed to this next phase of their lives, however much their friends were distressed. Malcolm the youngster and his sister Hannah seemed excited by the journey, neither able to comprehend exactly what was happening.

"Come back before I die," Estella whispered to Pip, "I don't suppose there will be much chance of letter-writing wherever it is you are destined for."

"We will do our best to write," said Susanna.

Estella was suddenly shocked as she watched Susanna go up the gangplank, looking for all the world like a frail little schoolgirl being sent away from those she loved.

Hamish and Mary were there, as were Harriet, Clarence and Emma. Estella was still amazed at the vehemence with which Harriet had condemned their mission. She was not obviously with child, so there was no comment from the others, but Estella could see that it was the loss of Pip, her former lover, that was at the heart of her distress. She put her arms around Harriet, as she began to weep silently as the boat was pulled away from the dock.

"I still love him, you know," she said between tears.

"I know, my dear Harriet. You must see that this is another chapter in his work as a preacher and he has been shocked back into that religious commitment after the death of his son."

"Maybe, but I should have married him in Salford, dammit. I was so stupid not to realize what a treasure he is, how we could have had several wonderful children. When I was thinking I would get pregnant, I very nearly went to their house to ask him in front of Susanna whether he would father my child."

"Now that would have been a mistake."

"But then I thought I could ask him without Susanna knowing."

"That would have been a worse mistake."

"Yet I am convinced," she said, as they stood away from the others on the dock, "that had I asked him, he would have agreed. I just know that deep in his heart, he longed for me all right, and not just for my body. When we met after everything died down, I could read his struggle, the struggle to overcome his desire for me. I could see it in his eyes. And me for him."

"Well, I am pleased for you that you are to have a baby."

"So am I, though I wish it was his. What a world, eh, Estella? Let me tell you something now, as I am opening up my soul, if anything were to happen to Susanna in the god-forsaken places they intend to live, I would go there immediately and beg him to marry me. Moreover, I know he would say yes."

"Put that out of your mind this instant," said Estella firmly.

Tugs began their work. Horns blasted out the imminence of the ship's departure. Tears were shed on ship and on shore, and those left behind gradually stopped waving handkerchiefs and retreated to Estella's carriage. A murmured conversation between them all was the overriding question: Would they ever meet again?

Finally, the meeting of the League of Free Women took place at Numquam House.

It was held on a lovely summery weekend in April 1879 and began with an evening of general chatter and getting reacquainted, and Estella had managed to find a way for each woman to have her own room, apart from Honora and Mary who agreed to share. The women who lived in Cheyne Row, Honora Brandram and Mary Macdonald chattered to each other about their famous neighbor, Thomas Carlyle.

The political sisterhood, Antonia Penoyre, Emma Smythe and Estella were discussing the death of Disraeli and the somewhat astonishing occurrence of Gladstone's ministry. A new member of the group was Ann Masterson who tagged along with Nellie and Eliza Culpepper who were exchanging stories about their husbands, and, as Nellie said afterward to Estella, she had no idea how they had got to that topic. Susanna was in Tunis.

Saturday morning also promised good weather and Estella had had a small marquee erected on the grass which proved an immensely welcome arrangement. Two tables were joined together such that everyone could see everyone else. Estella had thought long and hard about how they might proceed and she wished Charlotte or Susanna were there to give advice, though in talking to Harriet beforehand, her plans seemed sensible.

"We have had a preliminary meeting, but there are some new faces here. I would like to begin by asking us to create a wish list, and list of topics, activities, projects that would be good for the League to pursue. No discussion on the topics, just a list first. I'll make the list as you call out ideas.

"Voting," said Mary,

"Property rights," said Eliza,

"Divorce laws," said Honora,

"Public Education and Professions opened to women," said Emma,

"Laws on Prostitution," said Nellie,

"Birth Control Rights," said Antonia,

"Membership of this League," said Ann.

"My oh my," said Estella, what an agenda! You, my dear friends, are of exceptional intellectual quality!

"Ann, you suggested membership of this League, so begin."

"I think that we need to make sure we have women from all walks of life here. I am so pleased to see Nellie, the wife of a blacksmith, unlike most of us who are professional wives. It is a matter of getting all points of view."

"It is also a matter of success. We stand no chance at all of effecting changes in voting, for instance, without women across the land coming together."

"I don't think any of us would dissent from broadening our membership. Important to me," said Antonia, "is that we do not suddenly have a large group which would be too large for us to make our voices clear and coherent. How about we began by each inviting one woman to our meeting who is not a professional's wife?"

"Can I bring Estella?" Asked Nellie at which there was loud and prolonged laughter.

"No, seriously," she continued, "I like that idea very much, but it would be best if women came from different situations, if you all know what I mean, a bunch of house servants all of the same age won't get the variety."

"I don't think we can lay down rules," said Ann, "my suggestion implies that, as we go along, we are constantly aware of the need."

"I take it, then," said Estella, "that we all think of ways we can expand or membership.

"We have seven other topics. We are nine. What shall we discuss first?

"May I make a suggestion? We must think deeply about all of these questions, not just think in clichés about the topics. We need to practice talking to each other. So I suggest we start with a topic that is relatively uncomplicated, and I suggest birth control rights as a place to begin."

"I agree with that, Estella," said Eliza, "as it affects every young woman, like my Margaret for example. For some of us here it doesn't matter much."

"I suppose I am an innocent about this," said Emma, "it has never occurred to me to think that whether I get pregnant or not could be controlled."

"Oh yes, love," said Nellie, "when I was young and whoring, it was the most important thing to do. I had a sort of tube I'd insert and flush it all out, if you know what I mean. Still do."

Emma almost fainted at this frank account and Honora looked very uncomfortable.

"I use olive oil," said Antonia, and Aubrey often helps me, "it cleans you out, you know.

I have had heard that the man can use a kind of covering over himself, but I don't know of what sort."

"This all sounds quite disgusting to me," said Honora.

"But the point is this," said Estella, "thousands upon thousands of women have children they do not want and cannot bring up which increases the poverty in this country. It's all very well for those who are rich enough not to worry about how many children they have."

"Brought up as a Catholic," said Honora, "I think the Church would be violently opposed to any thing that interfered with natural processes."

"That's because they are all men," said Antonia with a grin.

Mary intervened quickly: "That's true, but this is not a matter of just shutting the door after the horse has bolted," at which there was gay and sometime uncontrollable laughter, which, after it had died down, she continued:

"I mean it is one thing to try to stop oneself becoming pregnant which, after all, is a basically mechanical procedure, it is quite another to be able to make sure, for example, that one's children are three years apart or, how many children one wants to have."

"But you don't have to do it if you don't want a child," remarked Eliza.

"But sometimes you won't get the choice, yet another aspect of the rights a woman does not have, that is, a husband demanding what he calls his conjugal rights," said Honora, "something I've never experienced myself."

"What do you mean?" Emma asked.

"Well, Frederick and I decide together whether we are going to be intimate and we respect each other so much that sometimes one of us does not want to, so we don't. Neither of us demands anything."

"I am sure that is not a general rule," said Eliza. "I suspect that if a woman tells a husband they don't want it, she is frightened of him saying 'then, I'll go elsewhere.'"

"That certainly keeps whores in business," chimed in Nellie. "I had this fella once in Chatham that wanted it every week always with same story: 'My wife's too tired;' or, "my old lady's got a head-ache,' I tell you I soon lost count of the excuses, but clearly this old lady wasn't having any."

At which slightly embarrassed laughter rippled around the room and then rose to a crescendo that would have rattled the dovecots, had there been any.

"I don't get what's so funny, I thought he was rather sad, so I give it him once for free," at which the laughter was renewed.

"You see, darling Nellie," said Estella, "we laugh because none of us have talked to someone who has been on the streets before. So it is so new and so strange and you are so direct about it to us women who find talk about sex difficult. The laughter is partly nerves, isn't that right ladies, as right of the back of our minds, we wonder whether it could be our husbands. Am I right?"

There were murmurs of assent around the table.

"That is all so clear, Nellie," she continued, "and to be sure for those of you with husbands, it may perhaps be nerves, but I think there may be an element here of how women are not equal to their husbands. It is alright for them to go out and find a whore, but women can't do that, however much they might like to do so."

"Well, one hears of society women who take lovers," said Eliza, "not people like us," at which Estella and Mary exchanged a luke-warm smile.

"I suppose so," said Nellie, now warming to the subject, "but there's another fing about all this. I hope this won't shock you, but when I was about eleven, my father came on to me and used me as if I was his whore, and later my brother found out and he demanded it too."

No laughter this time, just a shocked silence.

"What I mean is," said Nellie quietly, "if a wife refuses 'cos she don't want to have another baby, then some men will turn to their daughters. Now if the daughters knew about birth control, that would be something."

"Oh, Nellie, my dear," said Honora, "that is so awful, I can hardly bear to think about it."

"Well," said Estella, "it's quite common actually. Harriet told me her father was on to her when she was eighteen, and she told her mother. Her mother went after him and dragged him into bed which I'd be sure she hated, but it protected Harriet."

"Two things occur to me from this discussion," said Mary: "First that this League of Free Women is so important. In a space of twenty minutes we have revealed a nest of very complex problems and that will, I am sure, occur with every topic. Second, we probably could not have got so far into these problems without Nellie's history and perspective, and that shows we must broaden our membership."

Again there were noises of agreement around the table. As the weekend went on, each of the topics brought out such a range of questions and problems that when Sunday morning came around, everyone was ready to relax a little. The weather was fine, and everyone was walking in the garden when a telegraph boy came up to the house with a wire for Estella.

She read it and went completely numb. She had to steel herself, summoning up every ounce of courage, the distress coursing through her body, and wishing so much that this was someone else's task. But it had to be done and done quickly.

She walked down the grass to where Honora and Mary were talking gaily. As she approached, the two women looked at her and knew something was wrong.

"I don't know how to tell you this, Honora, but I must."

"Oh, no is it Frederick?"

"No, my dear, It is Jude. He drowned yesterday swimming in an Italian lake, Lake Garda. Simon is on his way home with his brother's body. Frederick asks that you come home immediately."

XXIII

Before she returned to London two days after this shattering news, Estella spent only a little time with Nellie because Fletch was very ill.

"It's been coming on for a while now," said Nellie, "he's been having difficulty breathing. I mean, he still works too hard."

"It can't be that bad if he works, can it, darling?"

"It's his lungs, I fink. I hardly ever go near the Forge, you know, I have no need to, but I went the other day and there he was, stoking this fire of coal and the smoke was dreadful because the wind was blowing it in his face. I came away coughing. Horatio has started to cough a lot too now I came to fink of it."

"That seems to me quite dangerous. You don't want to lose him, of course, but if his breathing gets worse, well….."

"Oh, don't say that, lovey."

"I told him, see, why isn't there a chimbley like there is indoors? There used to be one, but it fell down. Then he gives me all sorts of reason why he couldn't have a chimbley, but he's started to make a metal one already."

"So then the smoke would not come in his face, you mean?

"Yes and a few days after he's got it, we'll see whether his chest gets any better: Same with Horatio."

"How did you enjoy the meeting?"

"Oh, it was so interesting to really talk with other women. Apart from you and me, I never talk with women, do I, stuck out there on the marshes. No, I don't mean that, 'cos I'm very lucky and very happy, thanks to you. But we do need more women like me if you know what I mean."

"I do, of course. But now you must tend to your Fletch and I must get to London and see what I can do for the Brandrams."

"Crikey, that is so terrible. Like with that steamer thing, I cannot imagine losing my Horatio. Poor woman, after all she's bin through."

Estella took her carriage over to Chelsea the next morning, very uncertain as to what she might do. She had been a major influence in the recovery of Honora's twins, so she felt close to them, especially as Honora was regularly consulting her about them. How does one bear the loss of a child, especially one who meant so much to her? A maid answered the door and she was shown into the living room where Honora and Simon were sitting in silence, neither of them looking as if they had had any sleep for days.

"I hope I am not disturbing you in your grief."

"Oh, not at all, Estella, you are the person we wanted to see as you have been so kind to us all."

"Thank you."

"I will go to my bedroom for a rest, I think," said Honora, "and then you can talk with Simon. I know he will tell you what happened as I cannot bear to hear it again. I will be down later."

Estella got up and put her arms around Honora, murmuring into her ear how dreadfully sorry she was. Honora hugged her tightly and left. Estella then went over to Simon sitting in the leather chair near the fire, and standing behind him, she put her arms around his neck, and he ran his hand along one of the encircling arms."

"May you tell me what happened, Simon?"

"Of course, I relive it in my mind constantly, so I don't find it difficult to speak it."

"But how come you were there? I did not know you were travelling."

"It is what those in the university call the long vacation and it was our first. We finished the term early in June and will not return until October. We decided we'd travel for a month or so, no real timetable. We particularly wanted to see the parts of Switzerland where our parents had been, the Jungfrau area. We did some walking there and then moved on to in the Dolomite mountains south of Innsbruck before making our way down through Austria to Lake Garda. We planned to go on to Verona and then to Venice. Frederick had given us plenty of money as a gift for our entry into Oxford and Cambridge."

"He is such a generous man, isn't he?"

"Yes indeed, but he is not well, you know. He gets these pains in his chest."

"Oh, dear, what a confounded nuisance at this time. I am sorry but go on."

"We stayed in a little village on the eastern shore of the Lake called Torri del Benaco. It was a charming place with a small harbor and an albergo which suited us well and our room had a magnificent view across the Lake. We took a boat across the Lake to Sirmione to wander around the Roman villa there. We spent a couple of days, going up into the mountains to walk, gazing at snow-capped mountains in Austria just roaming around. It was quite delightful. We were such good friends as well as being twin brothers.

"When we got back down to the albergo one evening, it was hot and the air was dense, and it was getting twilight. I suggested we go for a swim in the Lake before coming back for dinner. We had brought no swimming clothes, so we found a quiet spot, and stripped off to swim. No one was out walking as it was dinner time."

"Were you near the village?"

"Perhaps a quarter of a mile. So we were alone, and into the lovely warm water we went, splashing about, just as we had when we were children. The beach on the Lake was all stones, not like North Wales with its lovely sandy beaches. We had just got into the water, a man passing by shouted to us in Italian, but we didn't know what he was saying, though he was very agitated.

"But we started to swim out into the Lake. I thought my legs were getting cold, so I called to Jude just in front of me to say I was going back. He just went on swimming. I don't know whether he heard me.

"When I got back to the shore, I turned around to look for him. By now the moon was up but I could not see him, and although I was a bit concerned, I knew he was a strong swimmer and would soon return. You can imagine how concerned I was when he did not return, five minutes, ten minutes, half an hour, an hour before I had to confront the fact that he was not coming back.

"I dressed quickly and ran to the Albergo to raise the alarm. In a short while I was on a boat with lamps lit to the place in the Lake that I had last seen him. The two boatmen gabbled on in Italian, which I did not speak well, but they then took the boat well north of the spot where we were. Then a good half a mile from where I had last seen him, we saw him floating in the water."

"Oh, gracious me, how horrid for you."

"Yes, we pulled him into the boat, but he was obviously dead," said Simon, tears welling in his eyes.

"The boatmen could see we were brothers, of course. I tried to get some explanation from them which I eventually did the following morning. The owner of the Albergo told me that there were strong currents under the lake surface and that, at that distance Jude was from the shore, the water would be suddenly very cold. He also said that such deaths were quite common."

"So, were you not warned about the dangers?"

"There was a very small notice that we had missed because it was evening, saying that swimmers were *in periculo*. I saw it when I walked to the spot the following morning, early because I could not sleep. The Italian shouting at us was obviously warning us. I sent a wire to my mother which Frederick opened."

"Oh, my dear boy, what a terrible tragedy. When will the funeral be?"

"There has been some delay as the Italian authorities have to release the body, so we are not really sure when it will get back here. I saw no point in waiting for all that but I paid the albergo owner handsomely to ensure all was well for Jude to be brought home by train."

"Oh dear, oh dear, your poor mother and father. What about Jane your little sister?"

"She knows Jude is not coming back, but the sadder person is Margaret Culpepper. Jude and she were secretly engaged to be married. He was going to ask her father as soon as he got back. She is heart-broken."

Jude's funeral was a very somber occasion and to Estella the number of young men was quite surprising, friends from both Oxford and Cambridge who came to pay their respects, perhaps twenty of them in all. She did not go back to Cheyne Row for the reception, not simply because she was tired, but because it seemed inappropriate. Such a young man, full of promise in every way, a tragedy of unbelievable proportions whose effects would last.

Christmas at Numquam came four months later. Albert was now the man of the household. The Fletchers were there as usual as Victoria had come back to her parents' home earlier, and Harriet and the Macdonalds traveled up from London. Frederick and Honora came as well, and they had invited Margaret, with Estella's permission, to be with them.

Since Simon had told them of Jude's intentions, the Culpeppers thought it would be gracious to meet with him regularly which she much enjoyed, not least because she could reminisce with him about Jude. This year, Estella also invited Clarence and Emma whom she had come to love dearly for her innocence. Aubrey and Antonia were there too, but like the Smythes, they stayed nearby in the Blue Boar.

They all sat down to dinner on the first evening, and Frederick spoke immediately.

"We Brandrams know all too well that it is six months since we lost our dear Jude. But we know he would want everyone to have a lovely party, a very enjoyable Christmas, so we want everyone to think of him as here in spirit."

"So," said Simon, "can we begin with a toast to Jude and his memory. A fine loving brother, and a devoted son. We will miss him dreadfully."

"Amen," said Frederick quite loudly.

As usual, Estella was on the *qui vive* to see everyone was happy. She had seen the attachment between Albert and Victoria grow intensely over the months and they seemed ready to embark on a life together. Indeed, she had seen Albert talking with Fletch for some time in the Library, so she wondered whether a formal engagement might be on hand.

She spent some time chatting during the afternoon with Harriet who was tending to her baby Joseph, born couple of months ago. Relationships between the two women had cooled earlier but were happily restored.

"Why Joseph?" Asked Estella.

"After Pip's father in fact. I thought his name might send a signal."

"You are incorrigible, my dear."

"By the way," said Harriet changing the subject, "did I gather that Jude intended to ask for Margaret's hand?'

"Simon told me that was his intention."

"It is just that Simon and Margaret seem to be very close indeed. I passed them upstairs and was surprised by their attachment."

"That does not surprise me one bit. They share a love for Jude, so they are naturally drawn to each other. I'd be confident they will marry."

At dinner on Christmas Eve, Albert got up to speak just before the capons, turkeys and hams were brought in.

"I have an announcement to make. I am thrilled beyond measure that the lovely Victoria has agreed to be my wife. I had a long talk with Mr. Fletcher and he won't mind me saying he took a bit of persuading, not of course because he disapproved of me, but that the thought of his lovely Victoria not coming home made him very sad."

There were cheers and woops around the dining table with people getting up and kissing the bride to be and shaking hands with Albert. He then asked the maid to bring in champagne, which was of very high quality and very expensive, a nod to his time in France.

Nellie called for a toast in her inimitable fashion.

"Hey, everyone, this has become such a tradition and it is so good to see new faces. But I am so thrilled and excited by this news, I don't know where to put myself. Them two have both been born in the cottage where we live, did everyone know that? Anyway, here's to them: Victoria my darling daughter and Albert my son-in-law to be, and oh, crikey, I suppose I'll be a grandma soon! Cheers to them both!"

Estella added her love to them both and her excitement and how it would be a splendid wedding, though the date was not yet determined. Thereafter Christmas proceeded with the usual festivities. Clarence introduced them to a new form of charades. Emma was persuaded to sing. Missing was a pianist, but Simon knew enough to play some carols. When that was done and everyone was readying for bed, Simon decided to sing a song Jude loved to the words of a poem by Lord Tennyson:

'Sweet and low, sweet and low,
Wind of the western sea,
Low, low, breathe and blow,
Wind of the western sea!
Over the rolling waters go,
Come from the dying moon, and blow,
Blow him again to me;
While my little one, while my pretty one, sleeps.'

The mournful character of the music, like a lullaby, he sang without the piano. Margaret had to leave the room as she was so distressed. Honora was the picture of fortitude as she looked at her son with admiration for him and his love for his dead brother. Harriet and the other women wept, the men tried to stem the tears coming to their eyes, apart from Hamish who looked at Simon with a look of total astonishment on his face, as if in awe of how he was able to handle himself to do this.

The new 'chimbley' as Nellie called it, together with the fresh air from the sea had made a good impression on Fletch's lungs, so then, as usual, it was Fletch's turn with the other Fletchers to sing 'Drink to me only," with everyone who knew the words joining in. There was no dancing, it was too much of an ambiguous occasion with profound sorrow mingling with the joys of Christmas, and for some of the guests those joys included celebrating the birth of the Savior.

Simon found Margaret and took her out into garden, where snow had started to fall.

"Could you marry me?" he asked.

"I am perplexed," she replied, "I look at you and your resemblance to Jude is so strong, I find myself talking to you as if I was talking to him. But you are not the same person, are you? I don't know what it is that makes you different. When I heard you singing, it was as if he was there, singing that song, which he'd sung to me a number of times. I would have asked you not to sing it, if I had known you were going to."

"Yes, we are, sorry, we were different. Oh dear, I still cannot get used to his not being there. I do love you, you know, but there is something we have to recognize. If you love me as I love you, is that love really for each other, something that will wear badly once our grief at Jude's death begins to soften, as it must. We were studying the classics at Cambridge but there was this odd tutorial in modern poetry. I read some of Robert Browning, and there is a wonderful line in a marvelous poem called *A Toccata of Galuppi's* which read:

'What of soul was left, I wonder, when the kissing had to stop?'
I am concerned that it is grief that binds us."

"Oh, no, I don't think so. I like you very much indeed. I always have. I can see myself as your wife. In some ways, it was just an accident that Jude approached me seriously first. If it had been you, I would have responded. Oh, Simon, I am so perplexed by this world. Can we just go on being close and loving for a while and decide our future later. We don't need to be rushed into marriage just because of Albert and Victoria."

"All right, but I am not going anywhere."

"Now, that is a relief."

Estella was back in London in the New Year 1880 and had a message from Charlotte to say they were on their way back home. She had not seen Elizabeth for a long time either, but a week later she went off to a hotel in the Strand on Valentine's Day where Percy and Charlotte were staying before his presentation to the National Geographical Society about the work in Pompeii, a topic in which Estella had not the slightest interest, so she realized lunch might prove a trial.

It was not so. Charlotte was anxious to know about everyone in the Row and the lawyers. Estella rattled off things she could remember: The suicide of Philip Hardyman, the babies that had appeared; the departure of Pip and Susanna and family; Jude's death; Albert and Victoria; The League and Nellie, and much more.

"What happened to Elizabeth? We never see her."

"Now this is most interesting, Estella. Elizabeth was very attached to Timothy Egerton whom she met at the Embassy in Paris. He was posted to the Washington Embassy but she could not go with him as they were not married and I have an idea that this was a bone of contention but I think she was a little uncertain about him.

"She wrote to Lord Lyons before she left and asked for an introduction to the Embassy in Rome which he was delighted to give as Henry had been such a stalwart in Paris, and he asked her to visit the convent to see that his niece was well.

"So, she came out to see us in Italy and loved it. Like us, she found the Italians very crude in their talk and manners, but she decided to do a tour of Italy, concluding her peregrinations in Rome. She visited all the sights there for a few days, and then went to see Lord Lyons' niece, who was now at the mother convent in Rome.

"The niece, now called Sister Magdalena had heard from her uncle and welcomed her with open arms. She was invited to stay in the Convent which had a small set of rooms attached for special visitors.

"One thing led to another. She went regularly to their beautiful chapel and the next thing we heard was that she was taking instructions to become a novitiate. That's a sort of testing period before you take the vows, though I have an idea she has another testing period later. Of course, the order is not totally closed, so she won't disappear altogether."

Estella was open-mouthed as the story of Elizabeth unfolded.

"That is most extraordinary. I thought she was far too much a woman of the world to even contemplate such an existence. What do you make of this, Percy?"

"I am not at all sure that she will go through with it. We saw her on our way home, stopping in Rome for two nights. She said she was at perfect peace with the plan and she was being introduced to God and the Virgin Mary as if she had never heard of them before."

"What do you think? Will she take the vows?"

"I don't know. She did say that Timothy was very distressed indeed at this turn of events and has asked to visit her. She had not then decided whether to meet him or not. I said she owed it to him, and I think Charlotte agreed. If they meet, she will have the alternatives right before her. Apparently the nuns enjoy the music she plays, all religious of course."

"But Estella, tell me about you."

"Oh, me? I am getting old if healthy still. I am going to have to give up running the Board of the Trust, I think, and spend much more time at Numquam. If you are staying in London for a while, do please use New Queen Street. I have to be in Kent for a good while as Nellie and I are planning Albert and Victoria's wedding to which you must come. Please delay any plans to return to Italy until after that. It will be early June."

❧ ❧ ❧

Numquam House was in fine shape for the wedding reception, held in June 1880. Fletch and Nellie agreed that while it would be nice to have it at their home, they could not possible accommodate all the guests. Nevertheless, Estella insisted that they be the hosts.

All the Inns in the area were fully booked. On the church at All Hallows, the Reverend Windnortham, now a very elder and somewhat doddery cleric, was to take the service though Albert wished that Pip was on hand to do the honors. But at least the Vicar did not confuse a wedding with a funeral and he managed to struggle through the Service of Holy Matrimony and declare them man and wife together whom no man shall put asunder, and Albert kissed the bride.

The organ played *The Wedding March,* first played at the wedding of the Queen's daughter, the Princess Victoria, in 1858. Carriages travelled to and from Numquam House, though many of the Fletcher's guests were pleased to walk. Jonah Steppings was there, and the Friendly family. Various Pockets were invited though old ladies who had complained about Joe Gargery at Albert's mother's wedding to 'Old' Pip had long since been gathered to their fathers.

Estella was intrigued to meet Herbert and Celia Pocket who had been such friends of her husband Pip, indeed because all these Pockets were related, albeit at a great distance to Miss Havisham. Yet when they met, Herbert cried:

"Oh, Estella, you don't look a day older than you were at Beatrice's wedding."

"Thank you so much, Herbert. Tell me, how is Albert getting on, really. I mean he tells me everything is fine, but what do you hear?"

"Let me first say that we are delighted he is getting married. After all he was a wealthy young bachelor and had become a target for every socially climbing mother in the neighborhood with a daughter in need of a husband, and not merely those seeking wealth, but those who already had it.

"But he has already a very fine reputation in Hackney as a man of great honesty and integrity and who is very generous to his employees who adore him. He does not try to manage every bit of the business, but has given great responsibilities to his men, like that man Simplick over there who is his money person. It is very impressive."

"We love him coming to see us old people too. He looks a lot like Pip, don't you think?"

"Yes, I do. He has certain mannerisms which could come from nowhere else."

Simon was Albert's best man, though they did not know each other well but it was intended as an act of generosity to him in his time of sorrow. Yet Simon spoke brilliantly and with great humor about both bride and groom. Albert was brief and to the point, much as his father had been. Fletch managed a few words of congratulations and then burst into Victoria's favorite Robbie Burns song *A Red, Red Rose* that got all the birds within hearing distance chirping and singing as this powerful baritone voice delivered this beautiful love song.

The couple led off with a couple of country dances and soon the grass at Numquam was swirling with couples. One of the young Friendlys had more drink that he could hold. Estella was very cheerful, talking with all her friends. Fredrick Brandram had a very nasty turn and was taken into the house to recover. Victoria eclipsed everyone with her beauty and there was no prouder man than Albert.

As the evening wore on, Nellie and Estella sat together, hand in hand, on a garden bench near Molly's memorial. They were both very tired with their exertions to make this wedding the outstanding event it had been, a union of their two families.

They were silent, enjoying the sounds of music and gaiety beginning to diminish and guests left. Taking their leave of the hostess was not necessary as Fletch, proud as could be, stood at the door saying goodbye.

"Well, my dearest," said Estella, "isn't that wonderful?"

"Wonderful?" said Nellie, "it's a bleeding miracle, ain't it?"

EPILOGUE

One April morning in 1895, a group of lawyers were having a celebratory lunch at *The Cheshire Cheese*. Present were Mr. Hamish Macdonald, Q.C., Sir Clarence Fotheringaye-Smythe, Q.C., M.P., Mr. Sam Eustace, M.P. and Mr. Adam Masterson. The occasion was the thirtieth anniversary of the death of Nathaniel Jaggers, whose munificent legacy had endowed the Jaggers Trust for the Relief and Education of the Poor that was now regarded as one of the finest philanthropic entities in London, if not Great Britain.

Appropriate to the occasion was the meal of jugged hare, various root vegetables and claret that Mr. Jaggers used to enjoy, as the more elderly waiters reminded the party. The four men were enjoying their post-prandial cheese with brandy or port when a swarthy young man came up to them, his sunburnt skin indicating that he hailed from a foreign clime.

"I was told by your clerk that I would find you here."

"Wait, one moment, let me see," said Hamish, stroking his greying beard and getting out of his chair, "I don't believe it, you are Malcolm Gargery, Pip and Susanna's boy, are you not?"

"Indeed I am."

Lengthy introductions followed, an extra chair was brought up, a plate of jugged hare was provided and another glass for claret.

"Tell us more. What are you doing here? We have heard nothing of you except of your mother's untimely death."

"Yes, that was five year ago now, yellow fever I believe but I was in South Africa by then. I've been working with Cecil Rhodes in diamonds and, believe me, De Beers is the place to enrich oneself."

"And your father and sister?"

"My young sister Hannah went to school in Scotland and I will be going north to visit her as she has just completed a degree at the university in St. Andrews, a very old institution."

"But we never heard your parents' story."

"Really? I don't know why that was, though they scarcely found time for their children, let alone writing to friends.

"We started off in Tunis fourteen years ago now, but only for six months as we all found it quite unbearable, so we uprooted and traveled by boat to Capetown where my parents spent two years or less, establishing themselves with the Presbyterian Church there and making occasional visits to missions.

"I stayed in Capetown at school, as did my sister, and my parents went off into the bush of Barosteland to take over a mission from the previous pastor who had died. I went to see them once when I was eighteen, a terrible journey, but I was very glad to leave after a month. They seemed very happy in their work, though neither of them looked well and I failed to persuade them to recover for a year in England.

"Of course, then my mother died and I could not have gone to her funeral if I had wanted as in that climate she had to be buried quickly. My father got yellow fever too, but his constitution was stronger and he returned here to England for a few months to convalesce, but not in London. He was based at a Church house in Cheltenham. He made no contact with any of you at that time, am I right?

"I thought he would be lonely when he got back to Africa, and I owed it to my mother's memory to visit him at the Mission again. I was thunderstruck to find Harriet Middleham there with a child of her own. I was even more surprised when my father told me that they were married."

"Good gracious me," said Clarence, "I know Harriet disappeared to France or so it was thought."

"I gathered then that they had known each other before my parents were married and had kept in touch. My father is not getting any younger at sixty-three, and I think he could not see himself alone there. I gathered he had sent her a wire when my mother died, simply telling her the news.

"Then he contacted her from Cheltenham and she went there to meet him. They are planning to come home for a long spell, indeed they will have started the journey already. They will make it permanent, I think, as I was asked to retrieve the Cheyne Row House for them."

"Not needed, Malcolm," said Hamish, "we will be ready. You may not know this. Mary hummed and hawed about it, but finally we moved to the house where the murderer lived, but it seemed haunted to us, so when your parents' tenants left, we were pleased to pick up the lease."

"Yes, I have some good and some excruciating memories of our home."

"Now," said Hamish, "every two years when we have a lunch like this, we take a carriage to Highgate Cemetery to celebrate the lives of Pip and Estella Pirrip who are buried there, and we leave a wreath from the Trust on their grave. Would you care to accompany us?"

"Indeed, and you can tell me all about those other friends on the way."

As the carriage rumbled towards Highgate, Malcolm heard of the sudden death of Frederick Brandram and the swimming accident that killed Jude, and that Simon was busy working in the Foreign Office, married to Margaret Culpepper with their two children, Jude and Frederick. He had heard that Albert had married Victoria, the Fletcher's daughter, and that he has a successful timber company. He did not know they have three children, Beatrice, Pip and Ellen.

Then he was told of another young woman whom he perhaps knew slightly, one Elizabeth Fitzroy, the niece of Charlotte Mudge whom he did remember. Elizabeth had abandoned the idea of becoming a nun and had married Tim Egerton instead and they were now back in Paris at the Embassy after his tour in Washington.

Charlotte had married Percy Vere but they had both died in Italy a few years after a visit to London.

They reached the cemetery, and Hamish carried the wreath. They all fell silent walking among the graves and the ornate monuments.

But then, there they were. Clarence had not noticed on their previous visits that beside the Pirrip grave was that of Beatrice Pirrip and her daughter.

"Ten years since Estella died then?" said Malcolm, looking at the stone memorial and reading the epitaph: "'*tempore quo non extat memoria,*'what does that mean?"

"From time immemorial," said Hamish, "I was visiting her to discuss her will and she told me that was to be the epitaph as it was a phrase of Mr. Jaggers describing her relationship with Pip. She was at Numquam House, very cheerful and though she was eighty-one sharp as a pin.

She created a Trust with income, you know, which is administered by us. Her London house went to Albert with some money, though he didn't need it. She left Numquam House in Kent to Nellie Fletcher, then a widow who had become her live-in companion after Fletch, her husband died, and of course there was a good annual income for her too."

"She was certainly very generous, then?"

"Oh indeed, but a mere ten days after my visit, I had a wire from Nellie Fletcher saying Estella had died peacefully in her sleep."

"She really was the most remarkable woman I have ever met or am ever likely to meet," said Clarence, "I heard about her origins some long time after I joined the practice and I was in awe of her achievement and her generous, loving and compassionate personality."

"My father will be very sad indeed to know she is gone, though I suppose he would assume it," said Malcolm. "He told me once that Pip and Estella were the shining lights in his life."

"Yes, she was a shining light, a star that would not dim, and one more thing. She willed her portrait by Sargent to the National

Gallery, saying that no one would care that it was she in the portrait, as everyone would be admiring the painter's work and, of course, since then John Singer Sargent has become almost a household name in portraiture. I think visitors are in fact entranced by the personality that is there in the painting."

"I remember vaguely the two portraits in her house, but I was just a child. I will go to the Gallery to see her portrait once we leave here."

Hamish looked around at his colleagues quizzically and said:

"I've not been there in a while. Do you mind if we come too?"

END

Appendix A:
Primary Characters

Estella Pirrip:

b. 1804. m. Pip 1855. Molly's murder 1851. Widow 1870.
Member: Board of the Jaggers Trust, Living in Numquam House, Kent; Semper House, Soho, and 29 New Queen Street

Albert Pirrip:

b. 1853. son of (Old) Pip and Beatrice (nee Pockct). step-son to Estella.
1874 – 1877 with Elizabeth Fitzroy. 1878 legacy from Algernon Pocket.
Married 1879. Victoria Fletcher

Nellie Fletcher:

b. 1835 (?) Formerly Chatham whore, living in Gargery's Cottage.
Estella's lover and companion.

Horatio Fletcher:

b. 1835. Nellie's husband. 1868: Blacksmith at Gargery's Forge.
saved (Young) Pip's life at Balaklava 1854.

Philip Gargery:

b. 1837, m. 1865 (formerly Young Pip)

| | Former Preacher, son of Joe and Biddy Gargery, Manager of the Jaggers Trust. Lover of Harriet Middleham. Leave for Africa 1879 |

Susanna Gargery: b. 1843. 1865 m. Pip Gargery.
Children: Lachlan (b. 1867 d. 1876),
Malcolm (b. 1869), Hannah (1876)
Member: Board of the Jaggers Trust.
Family living in Cheyne Row,
Chelsea. Leave for Africa 1879.

Hamish Macdonald: b.1840. 1864. Lawyer in Jaggers practice. Senior Partner Courtisone and
Jaggers from 1873. Member: Board of
the Jaggers Trust

Mary Macdonald: b. 1838. (nee Hamilton). m 1871. Son:
James Irving b. 1872

Harriet Middleham: b. 1838. Former lover of Young Pip.
Member of the League of Women. 1878.
Reconciles with Susanna Gargery
1879. Son Joseph born.

Clarence Fortheringaye-
Smythe: b.1840. Lawyer at Courtisone and
Jaggers. From 1870.
m. *1878* Lady Emma Eustace.

Emma Eustace.   b. 1842, daughter of Lord Justice Eustace.

Elizabeth Fitzroy: b.1854. Daughter of Henry Fitzroy
(deceased), Niece of Charlotte Mudge.

Charlotte Mudge
  (nee Fitzroy).   b. 1814. Companion to Estella.
  1878. Moves to Pompeii to be with Percy St. John Vere.

Honora Brandram: b.1842 . 1861, raped in France. 1874. Recovers twins
  1876. Daughter, Jane Margaret

Frederick Brandram: b. 1820. Architect, husband of Honora, father of Jane Margaret.

Simon and Jude Jones,   b. 1860 Honora's twins. Brought from Orphanage 1872
  Jude Jones: d. 1879 (drowned). Engaged to Margaret Culpepper.

Adam Masterson   b.1847. Senior Clerk at Courtisone and Jaggers, then Lawyer
  m.1869 Anne Waters

Philip Hardyman: b. 1832. Lawyer, *Courtisone and Courtisone.*
  d. 1877 (suicide)
  m.1855 Jane Ellington

Jane Hardyman: b. 1830. Visit Estella in Paris after Philip's suicide. 1877

Mike Watson: b. 1868. Philip's rent-boy.

Countess Wassilko (formerly
  Mary-Lou Fitzroy   b. 1837. American wife of Henry.

Count Wassilko von Serecki

Nimrod Klein: Jeweler from Paris.

Robert Smith: b. 1850. Junior Clerk.

Nathaniel Courtisone.　　b. 1795 retires May 1878. Senior Lawyer

Minor Characters:

Randolph and Eliza Culpepper
　　　　　　　　Children: Timothy, Japheth and
　　　　　　　　Margaret

Aubrey and Antonia Penoyre

Timothy Egerton　　　　b. 1853 British Embassy, Suitor to
　　　　　　　　Elizabeth

Katherine Bradley, poet.

John Singer Sargent.

Monty Fortescue and Anna his wife.

Angharad Unworthy.　　Rich widow of Ezekiel Unworthy,
　　　　　　　　Estella's half-sister

Farmer Jones, Angharad's father, and Mrs. Jones

Jack Masham　　　　　b (unknown) Male Prostitute.

Algernon Pocket　　　　Grandfather of Albert Pirrip, Father of
　　　　　　　　Beatrice 'Old' Pip's first wife.

Herbert and Celia Pocket. Friends of 'Old' Pip. Distant relatives of
　　　　　　　　Albert Pirrip.

Sidney Street　　　　　Informer

Sir Charles Dilke, Bt. M.P.

Some other characters:

People in Paris

Lord Lyons	British Ambassador in Paris 1870-1872.
Sir Richard Harvey	Head of Chancery, Paris. 1877.
Charles-Emile Auguste Durand, painter	
Beth Morisot	
Dr. and Mrs. Sargent	
Monty Fortescue	Spy.
Agnes Street-Klindworth, International spy	
Edward, Prince of Wales	
Hortense Schneider,	diva.

The Building:

George Holditch;	Security in The Building (the home for prostitutes established by the Jaggers Trust.
Ethel Coldheart:	Prostitute, residents in The Building
Maud Armstrong:	do.
Emily Collins	do.
Mrs. Pottinger	Cook

Semper House:

Mr. and Mrs. Copperstone.
  Fanny and Clara, maids in the Building
  Male prostitutes
  Harry Myles
  Tommy Perkins
  Charlie Spence

Fanny Filby:	Maid, resident
Charlie Spence	Former resident

Others:

Alice,	Honora's maid.
Sir Bertram Bloviate	Member of Parliament for London North-East
Simona Rothschild	Albert's girl friend
Mrs. Pennyfeather,	Villain
Detective Johnstone.	
Superintendent Etherington	
Gareth Evans	Grocer, driver of cart in Covent Garden
Pocket and Pirrip	
Personnel:	Mr. Simplick, Finance Manager
Brian Woollhandler, foreman	
Mrs. Bird	Eliza Culpepper's cook.
Clive and Celia Enticott	Cheyne Row residents
Lady Dilke	
Angelo Bonacorsso.	Resident of Cheyne Row, murderer. Hanged, December 1876.
Tommy Perkins	

Appendix B:
Sources

Impressionism. Ingo F. Walther (ed.), Taschen, Koln.

We Are Michael Field. Emma Donaghue, Absolute Press. This book describes the life of the poets Katherine Bradley and Edith Cooper, aunt and niece, who were lesbian lovers.

The Princess Alice Disaster. Joan Lock. Crowood Press.

Mary Slessor: Forward into Calabar. Janet and Geoff Benge. YWAM Publishing.

Tales of Mean Streets, Arthur Morrison. Boni and Liveright. New York.

Franz Liszt and Agnes Street-Klindworth: A Correspondence 1854-1886, Pendragon Press.

Wikipedia provides an excellent source of information on many topics.

Leesburg 2021

www.Ingramcontent.com/pod-product-compliance
Lightning Source LLC
Chambersburg PA
CBHW051444260626
47162CB00001B/249